RELEASE DAY

RELEASE DAY SAGA
BY RYAN MATTHEWS

RELEASE DAY

KANO'S GRASP

ARJUN'S PATH

ZEPHYR'S HOPE

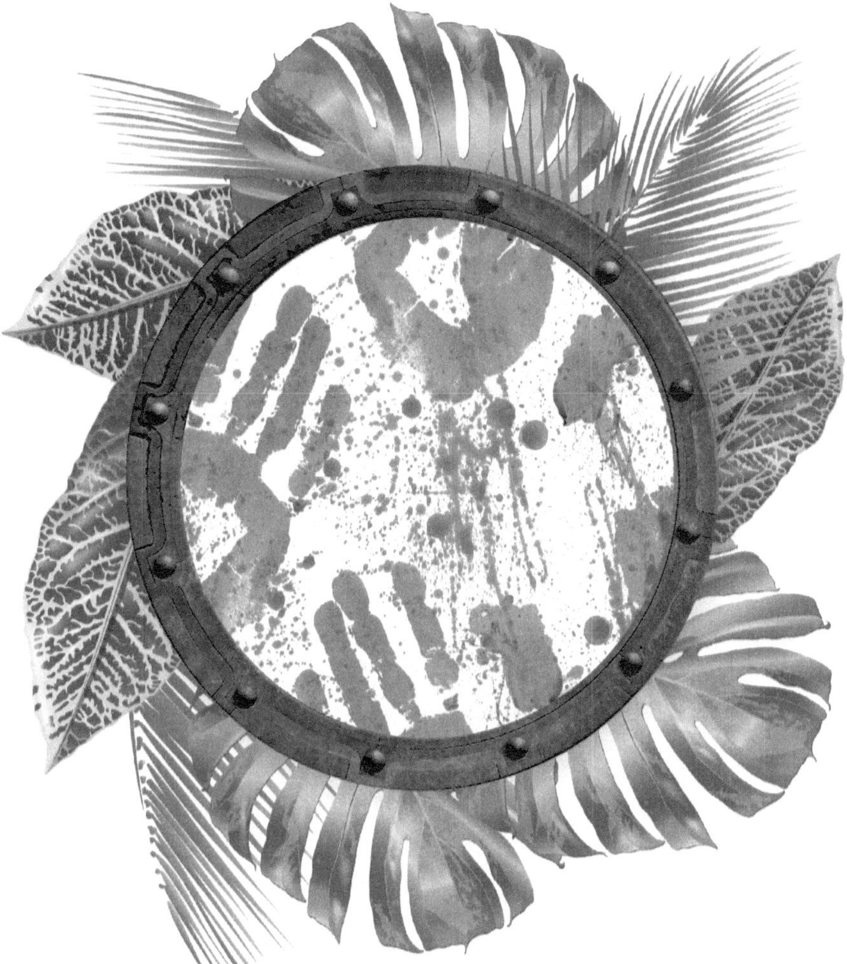

RELEASE DAY

RYAN MATTHEWS

Layout and cover design by Ryan Matthews
Images used under license from Shutterstock.com.

ISBN 979-8-9865388-0-8 (paperback)
ISBN 979-8-9865388-1-5 (hardcover)
ISBN 979-8-9865388-8-4 (ebook)

First Edition: April 2022

*For my mother, Melanie, who supported me in
every endeavor and would have undoubtedly
supported me in this one.*

PROLOGUE: PAK

I was running. Running like my life depended on it. In actuality, all of our lives depended on it. I had spent years training for this day. The day we permanently shut the gates to the city, sealing ourselves in indefinitely from the looming threat above. I pushed myself as hard as I could go, my injured leg doing everything it could to hold me back.

"Pak!" shouted Kiani, my friend and fellow access engineer, "For All!" he shouted, placing his fist over his chest.

Without slowing down, I shouted back over my shoulder, "For All!" I was hard-pressed to calm the twist of emotions inundating my mind.

I charged down the main access corridor leading to the ramp with the open armored double doors of the bridge, sweeping back the hair that kept falling into my face. After years of subterranean living, the usual metallic smells now felt more like home than the agoraphobia-inducing surface did. The clinking pipes, narrow corridors, and mesmerizing flashing lights were now more comforting to me than the tall evergreen trees and verdant mountains. I'd been underground most of my life, spending probably less than a month surface-side since I joined—still more than most. After surviving my attack, I wasn't in any hurry to return. My parents formed part of the Bandung team of First Builders when the extensive project began worldwide. The pod's construction was part of the most ambitious project ever undertaken by humanity and certainly the most ambitious in the Asian Territory.

A security guard stepped in front of me as I ran through the control room hatch, ducking to avoid the sharp lip inconveniently placed at forehead level. "Arok—" I said, catching my breath. "Citizen ID and code," he replied as he placed his hand on his auto rifle. Every day, we went through this. He lived on the same floor of the pod I did. Our wives were pregnant together and frequently shopped with each other in our level's market district. Hell, I think his wife still owed my wife a few ration points. Hurry or not, we observed strict security, and Arok wasn't one to slack on his duty. I took a slow cycle of breath, pulled out my identification, and thrust it into the reader, allowing the time for the pins to match with the holes while reciting my authorization code. The affirmative beep echoed from the device. Arok relaxed, and I ran onto the bridge.

The room reeked of stale smoke and burnt coffee, reminding me how much I missed nicotine and that I hadn't taken the time to savor my coffee this morning. After a sleepless night, I frantically jumped out of bed, scaring my wife, Susi, in the process. She was excited for me, too, just maybe not before she was completely awake. The rest of the bridge staff greeted me as I came in and quickly rattled off the night's briefing—nothing of note, just routine maintenance and supply checks. However, we had gained a few last-minute residents during the night. I sat in the access commander's chair, feeling the cheap foam compress under the weight of my body, and readied myself for the sealing of Pod Bandung.

The United Territories of Earth had begun construction of the pods in 2052. From the Arthropod Landing on October 23, ten years prior, it had taken humanity about a decade to realize it was a lost cause—at least for the moment. Damn inverts. They came to *our* planet and decided it was theirs. Initially, they landed in the Australian Territory, God knows why, but we were powerless to stop them. We were lucky to get ten of the eleven pods completed with the rate they spread. Since the ensuing loss of the radio frequencies, communication had become sporadic, arriving only hand-delivered by ground or sea-based transports. Save for Pod Wagga, which we believed destroyed, the pods of the world would be sealing their gates today until a solution could be found.

I ran through my routine morning checks, calling out the familiar list that now carried the weight of realism. "Ramps?" "Check," said an engineer from his station. "Hydraulics?" "Check." "Power?" "Check." "Guards?" "Check."

I continued to read down the list as I did every day, but today felt different. I was melancholic. Today was the day I completed the pinnacle moment of my career—and the day we simultaneously sentenced the billions left on the surface to an egregious death. According to the latest estimates, the Arthropods had reached all the corners of the globe, killing over half its population. The pods were built underground as enormous bunker cities to save humanity and give us time to formulate an offense. Now that we had completed them, it was time to close the doors against the invaders. Anyone who hadn't made it by today to one of the pods wasn't going to survive.

By the time my mind jerked back to the present, everyone in the room was staring at me. Even the tube monitors were buzzing with anticipation. Then the realization hit me that they were waiting for me to acknowledge the moment. It had never occurred to me to write a speech. I'm by no means an orator. "Mmm," I muttered out loud, improvising as I spoke. "Today is… Today is a historic day. Today we close the gates to survive. We face an uncertain future, but not a future we are relinquishing easily. A day of reckoning is coming, and we *will* return to the surface—with a vengeance." The engineers around the control room clapped nervously as a flashbulb went off in my face, momentarily blinding me. I took a deep breath to calm myself. As I was exhaling, the hardline rang.

"Bandung bridge, Access Commander Dasai speaking." I don't know why I said Bandung, nerves, I suppose. The hardline only communicated within Pod Bandung.

"Commander Dasai, this is Prime Minister Bolosan. Close the gates. For All." I heard the line click before I could respond with the obligatory response. Bolosan is a man of brevity and not very sociable, as demonstrated by his decision to remain in his personal office during the closure. My hands trembled as I replaced the receiver, the plastic sounding like chattering teeth as I sat it in the cradle.

"Bridge Access Control," I said, the shakiness of my voice apparent despite having uttered the phrase many times, "Close the gates."

Suddenly, a high pitch grinding and a low vibration ran through the entire city as the gates slid into place. While the main entrance was barely visible from the bridge's viewports, you could feel the thud the moment the gates completely closed. It was a feeling I imagined would linger in the memories of all the residents. I shivered, the room suddenly feeling colder.

"For All," I said, placing my fist over my heart.

"For All," responded the bridge crew.

Almost seven decades after the Arthropod Landing, we had willingly isolated ourselves from humanity's historic superficial habitat. Even guarded, we couldn't have kept the gates open much longer. The attacks were becoming more frequent and increasing in intensity. As I scanned across the monochrome monitors that observed the exterior perimeter of the city, I noticed movement. It was a group of families, maybe twenty, thirty people running out of the jungle. "Sir?" an engineer said, also catching the movement on the tube. I shook my head. It's easier not to feel the responsibility of the deaths caused by the gates' closure when you don't have faces to accompany them. Unfortunately, I no longer have that luxury. Forever I will see those mothers, babes clutched in their hands, screaming—pleading with us to let them in. The only reprieve I had from that moment was that the feeds were visual only. With great difficulty, I turned away.

With the task complete, I reduced the bridge staff to a minimal crew, giving everyone the afternoon to spend with their families on the inaugural holiday. I headed back to my district, but not before stopping to get a drink to relax my nerves. I went down a handful of levels into a seedy pub I frequented and got some potent local hooch. Everything was a blur. Here we were in an underground metropolis, crossing our fingers that we'd figure out a way to beat the Arthropods before we went extinct. Even though we could farm and recycle, I wondered, *Is this what humanity has come to?* With the gates open and the constant training, I had always been optimistic. With the gates shut, something had changed. I suddenly doubted if they'd ever open again. I stole a cigarette out of a dented pack lying on the adjacent table and smoked for the first time since I had quit.

CHAPTER 1: HUCK

God, *I want to go outside.* I sat in my bunk, surrounded by the worn, discolored pieces of paper I'd collected over a lifetime. I furiously drew the images that filled my dreams every night—impressions of the surface. I woke early, as was my habit, and scrambled for the nearest piece of scrap to sketch. Paper, even deteriorating scraps like these, were becoming increasingly rare. Despite Pod Horizonte's recycling facilities, fibrous items could only be reused so many times. Like the pods themselves, the base materials had to be approaching four hundred years old. Obtaining the compressed graphite wasn't a problem. Carbon was produced en masse by many of the city's processes. I would smuggle it out of our classroom sessions, which was far cheaper than purchasing it with ration points in our level's market. I looked down at my drawing and focused on the trees. Despite the monochromatic image, I could almost see the green on their boughs and smell the fragrance of their flowers. Our professors regularly showed pictures of Earth before the Arthropod Landing in our training. Unlike most of my cohort, I was excited by the prospect of Release Day. Not that I was looking forward to the imminent dangers the Arthropods promised, but rather the expansive freedom the surface offered.

My roommate, Zeke, stirred and prompted me to glance at the time display. I cursed silently and jumped out of bed, flinging the old dry papers everywhere. Fumbling as I collected them, I threw them back on my bed with one hand while running my fingers through my greasy black hair with the other. *A shower would have to wait.* By this time, Zeke was alert. He sat up with a grin, watching me amused, knowing I was late for training—again.

"How many laps do you think you'll have to run today, Huck?"

I shrugged as I smiled back at Zeke, crammed my arms through the sleeves of my jumpsuit, and disappeared out of the hatch. Zeke had already completed his training about six months prior and had extended his apprenticeship in the pod's energy production department, biding his time until our joint Release Day. Then, with his training in engineering, he was planning to join the residents of Pod Monterrey and design vehicles for the transporters. Typically, Release Day was twice a year. However, this year, the city's administration had decided to try something different and release double the candidates, hopefully increasing the odds of our survival.

I sprinted down the corridor, my nostrils filling with the smells of oxidized metal, stale body odor, and chemical vapor. They were omnipresent irritations, but part of life in the pod. My mind continued to dwell on the plants outside and how they must smell. *A heck of a lot better than this.* Under the daytime fluorescent lights, my light skin took on a green hue, like everything else. I was tired of this entire environment being a spectrum of dingy colors, interrupted with the occasional green, not the rich green of the outdoors, but a mucky, slimy green. After taking a dilapidated inter-district tram, I finally ran through the hatch of the training center.

"Nice of you to grace us with your presence, Candidate Huck," said Professor Leonor. "After the day's studies are over, report to Trainer Diogo for your tardiness."

I winced. Diogo was not known for his lackadaisical coaching technique. More so, he seemed to dislike me on a personal level. Training proceeded like any other day—survival this, history that. To me, all that mattered were the images. I had always been mesmerized by the slides from before the Arthropod Landing as our professor clicked through the carousel. Professor Leonor jolted me out of my thoughts with a sharp toot from her whistle. The rest of Cohort Delta and I stood at attention before following her out the hatch.

We walked down the familiar path to the sparring arena, littered with the detritus that seemed to collect everywhere in the pod. I was glad to be out of the classroom and heading for the arena. I preferred hands-on learning. My mind ceaselessly daydreamed about the surface during lectures. The threat of inevitable combat outside of the pod made survival and battle techniques feel more valuable than taking notes about ancient humanity. Once inside the arena, Trainer Diogo and Professor Leonor stepped into its sandy center. As always, the reek of sweat lingered in the humid air.

"Today, you will be demonstrating your prowess against the hook beetle," Leonor said. "As those of you who paid attention should recall, we studied their anatomy, strengths and weaknesses, and combat techniques in class. So consider this your final exam and be thankful it's not as intense as some of the other cohort leaders have chosen."

I tried to think back. That was the same day we talked about how the First Builders had constructed the pods in the areas of Earth with the highest population densities. When we had discussed the hook beetle, I recalled that humans named it for its giant hooked beak, capable of tearing its prey apart. *That would certainly be a strength. Weaknesses were...* I strained to remember. *...the sides!* The things had armored backs and tops, with plates in a scale formation but exposed sides. I wondered how many undiscovered

Arthropod species there were and how I could ever learn how to defeat them all.

"Who can tell me what happens if a hook gets its jaw on you?" said Trainer Diogo, pulling on a rusted chain hanging from the wall. From the chamber ceiling, a giant silly-looking mechanical hook beetle swung down.

Rachel stepped forward. "Sir, it rips you apart," she said, her stance giving away her excitement to battle.

"Exactly," Trainer Diogo said. "The hook has no mercy. None of the inverts do. They are killing machines. They have simple minds..."

"Like Trainer Diogo," Ana whispered, only loudly enough for the candidates around her to hear. I stifled a snicker.

"...They only think about sustenance, reproduction, and dominance," Diogo continued.

"I'm surprised he knows those words," Ana added.

I let a laugh slip. Before I knew it, Diogo was in my face. "What about this is humorous to you, Candidate Huck?" he yelled.

"Nothing, sir. They scare the hell out of me," I managed to say.

"Damn straight!" he barked. "Candidate Huck will be the first candidate to attempt to subdue the hook. Step forward."

Professor Leonor climbed to the elevated observation platform as I stepped forward, looking closely at the hook. It was a welded abomination. The intimidating part was a sharp metal beak attached to the front of the Arthropod, but the rest of it was a rather crude wire model covered in dry-rotted canvas spattered with the blood of unsuccessful past candidates. Diogo tossed me a spear.

"You'll find that a spear is one of the best weapons against most Arthropods," he said. "It allows you to be deadly at a distance that keeps you safe. The inverts aren't too smart, but they are lightning-fast and incredibly deadly."

Ade raised his hand, his ebony skin contrasting against the white sand of the arena.

"What is it, Ade?" Diogo asked.

"What about the smaller flying inverts?" asked Ade. "Wouldn't a spear be a poor choice against them."

"Alright, *Trainer* Ade, when you've spent your time outside, then you get to lecture me on weapon choice. Until that time, you will be training with the weapons of my choosing."

Despite the dressing down, Ade looked firm in his opinion.

"Proceed," Trainer Diogo shouted to me, sounding like a Roman emperor in the Coliseum.

The ridiculous but dangerous hook began to swing back and forth. I supposed it was too much to hope it would stay still and even more so to think it might drop candy like a piñata from Pod Monterrey. I smiled at the thought, crouching in a battle stance and waiting for the machination to advance toward me. Its movements were seemingly random, but I noticed a pattern after a while. I ignored the prompting to speed up from Diogo but relished in the excitement I felt from the cheers of support from my peers. Once I understood its flight path, I waited patiently for the right moment to strike, rolled, then popped up beside it just in time to thrust my spear into its side. Unfortunately, I misjudged the amount of effort the thrust took. Without any internal organs to slow the inertia of the spear, my follow-through led me to fall directly into the sharp spiny legs. The point gouged my upper arm, which began to spurt blood but fortunately didn't seem too deep. I heard someone behind me yell, "Medic!"

As our cohort's designated medical candidate bandaged my arm, I watched three more candidates successfully defeat the hook. The next attempt was a scrawny kid named Antonio. He was nice enough but tended to be a little cocky. He grabbed a spear and ran out to meet the Arthropod. Diogo brought it up to speed, and

Antonio froze. It was only for a split second, but it was long enough. The creature soared by; its namesake hook grabbed Antonio's arm below the shoulder, ripping it away. Professor Leonor was screaming, "Medic!" from the platform as Trainer Diogo struggled to arrest the machine's momentum. I watched as Antonio turned white, looking at the severity of his wound, the shards of skin hanging down, and an incessant stream of red draining to the floor. I heard the gut-wrenching sounds of vomiting behind me. The medic at my side sprinted off to give aid. Training or not, Antonio's incident reminded me how real the threat we faced was.

Horizonte wasn't a medically advanced pod. Since the Arthropod Landing, humanity's technological level had reverted back to the industrial age. Professor Leonor had told us some of the theories, but scientists still didn't completely understand them. The trained citizens in the medical district would stop Antonio's bleeding, prevent infection, and stitch him closed, but Antonio would never have another arm. Even simple prosthetic appendages were pretty useless in the field. Antonio would have two choices. He could continue on the standard path to Release Day without his arm, or he could choose to stay in Pod Horizonte, relegated to the work of a laborer. I'm betting he would favor Release Day.

Laborers worked in the lowest, harshest districts of the city, doing the undesirable support roles for the pod and earning minimum ration points, which were barely enough to live on. They lived in barrack-like housing, unlike the two-person candidate flats in the mid-levels of the city. Our cramped dorms only have space for our beds, desks, and a bathroom—our only place of privacy. Candidates had communal showers, cafeteria-style meals, and a meager monthly stipend of ration points. Educators like Trainer Diogo and Professor Leonor lived above us in the pod, but not at the top. The topmost level was exclusive to the military, political, and wealthy individuals. I even heard some top-level apartments had small portholes that allowed natural light into the space.

After Antonio's mishap, candidates cleaned and sanitized the area. Diogo and Leonor had the rest of the candidates finish the session without missing a beat. I hoped Antonio's injury might have brought me a reprieve from my laps, but that never crossed Diogo's mind. After completing my punishment, my legs burned, and my injury had soaked through its bandage. I was thankful; at least I had an arm. I swung by the Bambu Restaurant, not too far from my flat with Zeke. The dive was in a narrow alleyway that reeked of fish, but it was my favorite hangout. I spent a few ration points on a bowl of my go-to sustenance—egg drop soup.

After the light dinner, I headed back to my flat, stopping to peer high up the central shaft where I could see the faint natural light streaming from the viewports above the Nucleus. From my location midway down, I could hear the faint echo of the gate's movement. I gripped the peeling rail tighter as my excitement grew. No doubt it was the transporters stopping in for a bit to deliver critical information and supplies in our war against the Arthropods. I wondered if it was new seed strains from the scientists at Pod Pittsburgh or new Arthropod intel from researchers at Pod Baghdad. *How many visits does the pod get from the transporters every year?* As the world's center of energy production research and development, I was sure that we had plenty of information to share as well. I watched as men climbed into the cargo cranes and listened to their electric whine as they warmed up.

When I arrived back at our dorm, I slapped my keycard into the greasy panel and waited for the buzz heralding its opening. Zeke still wasn't back yet, so I laid down on my piles of drawings and daydreamed about the outside. I mentally counted down the days remaining until the next Release Day until I slipped off into unconsciousness.

CHAPTER 2: ARIADNE

I restlessly drummed the compressed graphite against the surface of my notebook, making mark after mark on the over recycled paper with each impact. I listened to Professor Lucas reiterate how to determine the best geographic route to a chosen destination pod. The nearer we came to Release Day, the more anxious I became. I tried my best to focus, but it was a losing battle. Class time was normally my favorite. I couldn't get enough information about the myriad plant species found on the surface. Maybe I would be able to focus better after training in my horticulture apprenticeship with Greenskeeper Chun. At least the day wouldn't be a total loss.

I still hadn't fully settled on which pod I'd like to select as my destination. My training specialized in medicine and food production based on my tested aptitudes. Most candidates trained in one area, but I had been adept at both. It would be a tough decision since both would play into my interest in plants. Though lately, I have been growing more fond of herbal medicine. Chun had even been kind enough to reserve me access to a pre-landing book on the topic. As a food engineer, I would have to make a lengthy trek north to Pod Pittsburg. However, my more substantial interest was in medicine, but the pod specializing in it was across the ocean! Candidates were free to choose any destination pod, but arriving at a pod with no need for your talents was a straight shot to an undesirable laborer position.

Every pod needed a plant specialist. Each pod had its specialization, but they all had to grow crops, though I never saw myself as a farmer. I was leaning towards Pod Munich, where I could work in medical engineering, but it seemed so far from Pod Horizonte. I couldn't fathom the notion of hitching a ride with transporters across a vast sea of Arthropod-infested waters, not to mention the extensive overland travel it would require. Candidates had made it to pods on the far side of the world. It was extraordinarily rare but possible. Aside from citizenship, the longer the journey, the more prestige it held. Transporters were a special breed unto themselves and also a faction a candidate could join. They were citizens not afraid of the extreme risks that accompanied living on the surface, devoting their lives to transporting goods and messages between pods. They'd also carry candidates if you caught them in a good mood. Their reputation was that of very short, but essential, lifespans.

"Ariadne?" Professor Lucas asked, his arched eyebrow disappearing under his shaggy hair, indicating it wasn't the first time he'd asked me.

"I'm sorry, Professor Lucas. Could you repeat the question?"

He smiled and shook his head jokingly. "Of course. What type of Arthropods would you likely run across in dry, rocky terrain? Would you fight or flee? And how would you adapt your course?"

I thought for a moment, pushing the thoughts of pod selection out of my head. It wouldn't do much good choosing a pod if I didn't know how to get there safely. Transporters could help me in my quest, but they wouldn't hold my hand from gate to gate. Release Day was fast approaching for my cohort and others. I needed to be paying attention.

"Professor, in that terrain, you'd most likely find multipedes and bone arachnids. Because multipedes—"

"They're called *pedes*." interrupted Omar, an arrogant scowl across his brutish face.

Professor Lucas gave him a disapproving look. "As you were saying...."

"Because multipedes, *pedes*, have a durable exoskeleton that runs the length of their body and almost completely surrounds their circumference, you must roll them over to give the opportunity of attack. This maneuver is nearly impossible given its length and the poison-tipped barbs along its body. Bone arachnids, *eights*, hide in their burrows, almost invisible until prey comes. It's best to avoid them as well. Therefore, I would adjust my course to avoid traveling through the given terrain. A detour would have a higher likelihood of survival and possibly provide more resources than the arid terrain of the example."

"Well done!" said Lucas, "But remember, sometimes these paths are unavoidable. You need to be prepared to face your problems. You can't always circumnavigate them."

The chimes concluding another training day sounded. Without lingering to socialize, I took off for the district's nearest physical training center to burn off my excess energy. Omar caught up with me before I was halfway there.

"Ariadne?" I spun around to his mischievous smile, which almost made me forget how stunningly limited his intellect seemed.

"What do you need?" I said, sighing.

"Sorry about back there. Want to hang out with us tonight? We're getting some banger hooch and hanging out in the central forum. It should be abandoned."

"As alluring as that is, I'll pass. We are too close to Release Day to be getting buzzed and risking time in the brig."

"Come on! What are they going to do? Banish us? We need

to find some way to blow off steam. *Especially* the closer we get to Release Day."

"Not interested," I said.

"Whatever." Omar turned on his heels and walked away irritably.

I knew Omar since our selection for the same cohort, before he shaved his head to look like every other muscle-bound grunt. Trainers would monitor the candidates from the moment their parents handed them over after weaning. I avoided using "abandoned" like others, but it's not like the term was incorrect. Parents were little more than genetic contributors to the pod's candidate pool. They relinquished control of their children just months after birth. Matriarchs raised infant recruits until they reach walking age, at which point a selection committee assembles the cohorts. The trainers based cohorts on researched ratios of body types and intellects, which candidates typically demonstrated by the aforementioned benchmark. Infants that were physically or intellectually inferior, the unabled, remained with the matriarchs until they reach their Release Day. Then, the pod's administration unceremoniously and unforgivingly released them from the pod with the rest of the fully prepared candidates. The matriarchs tried to prepare them for survival, but it was a futile gesture. It was one of many things not spoken, though we all know none of them would survive. "It's the way of things," Prime Minister Carvalho would say. *Well, it's a crappy way.* "For All," my ass. *"For Most" is what we should say.*

Once I arrived at the training center, I walked to the locker room with its familiar odors of pasta and rubber and changed into my workout jumpsuit. I was lucky to have the space to myself. As I shuffled past the mirror, I allowed myself a moment to appreciate my reflection. Usually, I put little effort into my appearance, but today, I liked what I saw. My brunette hair wasn't frizzing out of my ponytail, my face was clear, and my abs looked terrific. I left the locker room with a grin of satisfaction on my face and began my routine. While I was working on my arm strength, I overheard two of my cohort members discussing how a candidate from Delta had lost an arm in the arena. While sparring tended to have injuries and even sometimes death, I was immediately thankful that Cohort Gamma didn't train with Diogo, where those things seemed to occur with more frequency. After finishing my workout, I headed back to my dorm for another night of restless sleep as my mind continued to ramp up for Release Day.

I arrived as instructed at Pod Horizonte's central forum the following day. The space was the largest communal area in all of the city. It was directly under the Nucleus, and almost entirely spanned the central shaft into the surrounding districts. The mold and lichen were overtaking its worn structure millimeters at a time, just like everywhere else in the pod. I tried to imagine what the city had looked like when it was new, as the First Builders walked the halls and admired their work. How long had they expected us to be down here? How long were these cities designed to last? Will we *ever* reclaim our planet from the Arthropods?

I formed up with my roommate Krista, keeping an eye out for my boyfriend Nikos, who I had yet to see. I risked a glance over at Omar, who was looking a little ill this morning, and was thankful I had passed on his offer. We were all lined up in our once white canvas training jumpsuits, which simply bore our name and merits. Ranks were not part of training. Prime Minister Carvalho, also the Senior Training Commander, believed that leadership arose naturally and wasn't something given. I stood with my back erect for ages as my patience dwindled, waiting for Carvalho's address. Finally, he strutted onto the upper platform suspended from the Nucleus, notably avoiding the lower stage closer to our level.

"Candidates: Years ago, I addressed you when you began your candidacy in earnest. Now I address you on the cusp of your journey into citizenship. As you are aware, your destination pods will award citizenship immediately upon your arrival." He scanned the room in a contrived gesture. "You will face numerous challenges on your journey, some more difficult and dangerous than others. Statistically, only one out of five of you will make it to your destination.

"Once you are released, your journey is entirely up to you. Those of you who have chosen your destination—proceed to it. Those of you that wish to return to Pod Horizonte must serve a year with the transporters. You have but one task—survive. By doing so, you have permission to reproduce, and more importantly, to aid in the fight for our survival against the Arthropods.

"Since overpopulation first began causing problems within the pods, candidates have been trained by each pod for the Path to Citizenship. You are the outcome of this process. You and your peers around the globe will be the 90th heat of candidates. As you are aware, in honor of the 300th anniversary of the Arthropod Closing of the Gates, Pod Horizonte will be releasing not the standard three but six cohorts. Your instructors tell me that you are six of the best cohorts they have ever seen. I stand here to tell you the pride I feel when I look at you. I wish you and the other cohorts all the best of luck on your Release Day. For All."

"For All," we replied, saluting.

"One out of five," Krista said to me as we filed out from the densely packed forum space. "Is that going to be you or me? Well, probably me. You know everything there is to know about everything."

I shook my head, saying, "Written knowledge is a far cry from hands-on experience. If I'm attacked by a desert borer, explaining how I could drown it won't make much of a difference when its rotary teeth tear through my abdomen."

Krista tilted her head back and laughed. Her laughter warmed my heart. Krista had been my closest friend for as long as I could remember. Looking across at her, I admired her dark complexion and her beautiful hair. Even under the fluorescent bulbs and sweating through a crappy old jumpsuit, she was unfazed and happy as always. We made our way through the humid claustrophobic corridors to the cafeteria and met up with the rest of our cohort for lunch.

CHAPTER 3: HEMANT

I laid on the weight bench staring up at the concrete ceiling through its flaking paint as I pushed up on the weights. It had been a struggle to find motivation the last few weeks, with the physical and psychological training becoming so repetitively mundane in the face of Release Day. It had transitioned from being some distant nebulous concept to an immediate reality. I pushed the bar up one last time as I felt my endurance finally running out.

"You can do it, Hemant!" shouted Akhil, who was working out in the row behind me.

My brother Arjun never looked up from his work.

I pushed through, letting it drop back on the supports. I was at my peak fitness level and restless with all of the waiting. I was worried most about my twin brother, the little genius. He might be far more intelligent than I am, but physically he was pretty weak. With the dangers the inverts posed, I was concerned that his intelligence wouldn't be enough to protect him, so that responsibility inevitably fell on my shoulders.

Our training had decreased in intensity over the last few weeks. I guess our trainers realized that if we didn't have the techniques and knowledge down by now, we weren't going to. So whether it meant more training, studying, praying—or even partying—the last few days in the pod were our own. They didn't need to keep reminding us of the dismal chances of survival. I sat up, lingering on the edge of the bench as I watched Arjun scratch notes from a book into his journal.

"Arjun, give it a break."

"Need I remind you that we won't have any resources on the surface? We need to take along as many details as possible."

"Have you at least been practicing with your razor net?" I asked.

"Hemant, I'll be fine. If anyone needs more practice, it's you."

"What? I train all the time!"

"You're forgetting something," said Arjun, tapping his finger on his temple.

"Oh, well… That's what I have you for."

"I may not always be around to bail you out of trouble."

"Bail *me* out? Look at me." I gestured towards my muscular physique. "There's *no way* I'm letting some damn invert lay their filthy appendages on you, okay?"

"Then it's settled. We both have to survive," said Arjun.

"If only it were that easy," I said, laughing. "I don't suppose all that reading has built up your appetite."

"I'm not opposed to eating."

We walked to the market district to get something to eat, circling the platform that looked out onto the central shaft. Fruit was difficult to come by and expensive, but I was willing to spend the extra points. It's not like I was going to need them once I was outside. I might as well enjoy the best cuisine I can afford until our departure. I caught myself wondering what the pod's exterior would look like when we ran out onto it. The main gate was parallel to the surface, so I assumed the top was flat, but aside from that, I really didn't know what to expect. We pushed through the crowd of morning shoppers before ducking through the ornate fabric entrance of a produce stall.

"Morning," I greeted the fruit monger. "Got any bananas?"

"Hah! No," the vendor said. "All I have left are blueberries and strawberries," she said. "And no samples."

"Dang!" I said to Arjun. "You okay with blueberries? The strawberries look moldy."

"The strawberries are fine!" the monger said, defensive.

"Neither is 'fine,' but we'll take a mark of them."

After arguing over the price of the slightly shriveled fruits, we paid the points and walked around the pod, munching on them by the handful. Lately, every time I had eaten the rare treat, they seemed to have less flavor. If we survived long enough, soon we could have all the fresh fruit we wanted from the surface. There had been a swarm of rumors in recent months that the inverts had figured out when Release Day was scheduled and would be patiently awaiting our exit. *God, I hoped not.* The damn aerials were always watching the skies, so I supposed it was only a matter of time before they picked up on the pattern. There would be no immediate return to the pod after the massive main gate's closure. If the inverts swamped us, we were screwed. Our only hope was to get our bearings and make for cover. My priority was always Arjun. I have loyalty to the rest of Cohort Epsilon, but my brother comes first.

Arjun and I were two of a handful of candidates whose parents made Pod Horizonte their destination pod. Aside from our relationship, the only thing the matriarchs had been able to tell us about them was that they had come from Pod Bhopal. Bhopal and Wuhan were the two most populated pods and suffered many more detrimental effects from overcrowding. Their candidate cohorts were supposedly multiple times larger than Horizonte's and they included broader age ranges. Whoever's dumb idea it was to send kids out as a method of population control should have the feet gnawed off by a cave grub. Surely there was something more sensible than this nonsense. Here we were in a war with an invading species, and we were fruitlessly wasting human lives. We stopped about halfway back to our dorm, having eaten the entire mark of fruit, and sat on one of the benches still in decent repair.

"If we could volunteer for Release Day, would you leave?" I asked.

"Of course. My duty is to humanity," said Arjun. "The work they are doing at Pod Baghdad is where I would be the most beneficial. Why?"

"I was just thinking about how that would affect my decision."

"It wouldn't. I know you too well."

"That's the same conclusion I came to, but I'd want you to stay."

"Then I'm glad that we don't have to have that discussion. It's quite convenient," said Arjun, always speaking with sharp honesty.

I wanted to return to the pod of my ancestry. Not just for that reason, but because I was desperate to fight these monsters. The best way to accomplish that was training as part of the Bhopali Special Forces. They studied more than survival. They study offensive strategies, advanced combat, specialized weaponry, and group tactics. With zillions of inverts covering the planet, we needed front-line fighters to support the egg heads in the R&D departments of the pods. Arjun wanted to study the inverts. For years, he had known that he wanted to be an exo-entomologist, which had become the most advanced word in my vocabulary thanks to his annoying repetition. His aptitude tests had shown he was smart enough to do anything he wanted. Mine noted, well, that I'd make a good special forces grunt.

We stayed on the bench for a while, enjoying the comfortable breeze propelled by the ubiquitous circulation fans. The air here was far less stale than the barely ventilated dorms. Looking past the Nucleus' umbilical, I watched the residents on the shaft's far side as they milled through the districts. I wondered what their stories were. If they weren't candidates, they had most likely been through Release Day, either here or at another pod. I wondered what they had experienced and how many people they had known who died. It was a shame the subject was a cultural taboo.

"I'm not sure how much longer overpopulation will be an issue," I said.

"Just now realizing that?" Arjun replied.

"Yeah, it takes me a minute longer than you, smarty pants."

"In what respect were you thinking?"

"As the invert population explodes, won't it get harder to survive out there, meaning fewer citizens and fewer births?" I responded.

"Yes, that's correct," said Arjun.

"Are there more respects?"

"Yes, several."

"Like…?"

"Food quality, for one. I'm sure even you have noticed the decline, being very familiar with caloric intake."

I couldn't tell if that was a dig at me or not, so I let it slide.

"Resource limitations. The First Builders didn't mean for this pod to last forever, only until we could find a method to eliminate the Arthropods. Unfortunately, unless humanity becomes more proactive, I anticipate our extinction within the next two hundred years."

"That's depressing," I said, not knowing what else to say.

Arjun nodded.

Extinction. That's a heavy thought. One thing Arjun knew was statistics, so if he thought that to be a likelihood, it's a good bet it would come to pass. So it was all the more critical for us to make it. I hated to say it, but he was right. He needed to be at Baghdad. Getting to Pod Bhopal will be tricky, with it being such a vast distance away from Pod Horizonte. At least I can accompany Arjun to Pod Baghdad on the way. I would drop him off on the doorstep. Guaranteed citizenship right there for him. I expected to qualify for entry into the special forces. Pod Bhopal was so far from Horizonte; I think the journey would speak for my abilities. If not, I'd be happy to show them my capabilities. Hell, maybe from there I could shoot my way from there to the proposed Hive deep in the Australian Territory, taking the Queens with me. That's a fun thought.

The theory was that the inverts overran Pod Wagga before the First Builders could even complete it. No one could make contact with anyone there, so it was considered dead. Professor Graça said that the Arthropod Landing occurred deep in the middle of the Australian Territory. In their arrogance, the pre-landing governments assumed that the Arthropods weren't intelligent. Treating them initially as only a mild threat is part of the reason the Earth was so quickly overrun. When the UTE finally decided on an attack strategy, the Arthropod reproduction rate had skyrocketed exponentially. Once the statisticians and astrobiologists fully realized the threat level of the Arthropods, the UTE commissioned the pods, focusing all of Earth's population on their completion.

If Professor Graça and Trainer Marcia had taught us anything, it was that the inverts might be innumerable, but they had vulnerabilities and were defeatable. Well, that and they were good at killing and eating everything that moved. Graça said that, unlike native insects, the alien Arthropods were exclusively carnivorous, being both predators and scavengers. Much of our training had centered around surface survival and available resources. The most disgusting lesson was when we learned that the researchers at Baghdad had discovered that humans could safely eat thoroughly cooked inverts, provided we stay away from their toxic blood analog. *Gross.* Arjun can keep Pod Baghdad all to himself if that's what's on the menu. I'll take the nutritionally deprived hash of Horizonte over whatever resides inside an invert's exoskeleton.

I rose and started walking back to the dorm. I got riled up thinking again about the position the administration was putting us into, and more importantly, what Arjun was going to endure. We took a shortcut through the horticulture district, knowing most of the caretakers had gone home for the evening. As we walked down the tight corridors approaching our barracks, we saw Prime Minister Carvalho ahead in a junction, his hair slicked back as usual. We backed into the shadows, knowing it was highly unusual for him to be on a candidate level, especially at this time of night. Normally, I wouldn't dream of spying on the minister, but my curiosity got the better of me. A muscular candidate came out from one of the corridors, immediately rewarding my patience.

"Omar," Carvalho said, closing the distance, "I trust you're ready?"

"Of course I'm ready! What do you think? I'm down here sitting on my ass or hiding in my dorm, crying like the rest of these cowards?"

"That's not what I was asking and you know it. You'd better be ready. Release Day will be here whether you like it or not. You *will* survive. That's not optimism. That's an order."

"Yes, sir," Omar responded, giving a mock salute.

Who can show that type of insubordination to the Prime Minister?

"You have a duty to your pod and your family. And you *will* uphold it." With that, the minister turned on his heels and briskly marched off.

Omar slapped his palm forcefully against the wall and mumbled something inaudible before angrily strutting away.

We slowly pulled ourselves away from the wall we had attempted to blend into and headed to the dorm.

"That was bizarre," Arjun said.

I nodded in agreement as my mind replayed the interaction.

I had so many questions running around my head. Of course,

we all had a duty to humanity. It was why we spent our entire lives training. *Family though?* No one had a family. Our parents were responsible for our existence, but being removed from their possession at such an early age, the closest semblance we had to family was our cohorts. By the time we arrived back home, I still had no further understanding of the situation. I rested my mind for what seemed like ages under the communal shower head, letting the water wash away the tension and concern. Hot water was so underrated, but it was one thing we had plenty of. That and excess heat. We had perfected water recycling. It was a shame that less lossy methods of recycling other things had eluded us. I realized at that moment that I should enjoy hot showers as long as I could. Once I left this pod, it would be a very long time before I got to experience one again.

CHAPTER 4: GUILHERME

It had been a year since Aline left. I stood staring forlornly at her empty side of the closet, having just donned my crisp, but tattered, grand major's uniform. Clothing in immaculate condition was a rarity, if it existed, in Pod Horizonte. Even decorated officers like myself wore well-kempt, but aged, uniforms. Upon closer inspection, you could easily find its restitched seams, and despite the attempts to match the fabric, the patches were frequent and conspicuous. I sighed as I stared at the cluster of naked hangers. I had come home that day to catch my wife in the midst of throwing her few belongings in our tattered old duffel bag.

"What are you doing?" I asked, feeling stupid for asking such an obvious question.

"What do you think?" she said, throwing a few more items in the bag. "I'm leaving. I've requested a mid-level cohab. Maybe with a housing partner, I won't feel so alone. I didn't even bother with the compatibility checks; I took the first place I could find."

Her cool delivery was like a dagger through my heart.

"I didn't realize we were having problems," I mumbled.

"That *is* the problem," she said as tears welled up in her eyes.

She zipped the sides of the bag and threw it on a narrow, scuffed cart I didn't recognize. So often, I had seen the same bag packed for short trips to the relaxation parlor or the small waterpark. Then I realized that those happy memories were more than a decade old. I turned to reply as the door snapped closed behind her. At that moment, I realized she was right, and I was alone.

It was easy to make excuses. I was bound to my job. It was considered a disgrace to abandon your post or shirk your duties. A feeling that was amplified when the wellbeing of the pod was dependent on my work. Failure to perform was an immediate referral to an undesirable laborer position, at which point the Tribunal Council stripped you of your privileges, rights, and honors. Because the pod needed every capable body, there was no confined punishment. Instead, you were labeled a laborer and relegated to the city's most challenging and unpleasant jobs. In severe cases of criminal behavior, you were banished from the pod weaponless, meaning almost certain death by Arthropods.

I tugged at my uniform's sleeves one last time. I checked my overall appearance, adjusting the alignment of my beret in the mirror as I slid the closet door shut. The routine had become a daily reminder of my abandoned relationship. I couldn't help that the prime minister required the regents to be on duty for so many hours a day. Initially, I had demonstrated aptitude in engineering, and after becoming a citizen, I excelled in my work to the point of being recognized by the minister. Eventually, Pod Horizonte's citizens elected me to be one of the regents. Maybe I had chosen poorly prioritizing my career over my relationship. It seemed a little late to be dwelling on that now. To think I had also demonstrated aptitude as a professor. At the time, the prospect conjured images of me sitting in a humid, cramped office preparing lessons from moldy old resources. The ironic reality was I worked in a humid, cramped office, often looking through moldy old resources. Maybe if I had been a professor, I'd still be with Aline.

I walked into the apartment's cramped kitchen, prepared a cup of green tea, and patiently waited for the water to steam. Officially, I was attempting to improve the quality of life for the citizens of the pod. Unofficially, and more importantly, the prime minister had tasked me with figuring out how to stretch the pod's resources as long as possible. Regardless of my duties' nature, the secret had already gotten out. Rumors of the pod's decline swirled among the residents, and the administration was doing little to fight them. I had chosen my duties over my wife. I hoped one day she would understand I had done it for her more than anyone else.

I poured the hot water into the cup and let it steep, mesmerized by the leaves slowly drifting to the bottom of the cup. I sat on the small futon in the living room, absent-mindedly running my hand across the pilling fabric. The sofa, like everything, was gradually succumbing to overuse. The springs were all overstretched and groaned with each sitting as though they were going to give out.

Pod life had become quite monotonous and embedded in my daily routine, I failed to notice the little changes. Upon closer inspection, I could always find evidence of repeated repairs and patches extending the life of the essential workings of the city far beyond their intended lifespan. With each recycling, the original material further degraded. The quality of nutrition and materials was waning, despite the research and development from Pods Pittsburgh and Bogota. The First Builders started constructing the pod cities back in '52 to house humanity temporarily. I doubt anyone expected them to be used this long. As it stood, we were only marginally closer to exterminating the Arthropod threat than when we began. Their reproduction and infestation rate, combined with our severe lack of information, had led me to the conclusion that they would most likely eradicate us before we did them.

Even more troubling, we wouldn't be learning anything new from Pod Bogota's material recycling department. The last communication we had from them was more than a year old. It wasn't much of a surprise when six months ago, the local transporter team brought the news of Pod Bogota's destruction with some newly developed high-producing food strains. That day I had returned to my apartment and wept profusely. I had been able to keep my optimism for many years, but at that moment, I became acutely aware of the decline of humanity. An entire city, hundreds of thousands of people, roughly a tenth of the world's population—dead.

I sipped my tea, savoring the delicate flavor made even more subtle by the depleted substrate the plant had been grown in. The transporters had informed us that something had destroyed the pod from the outside. We were alarmed. We were unfamiliar with any Arthropod technology capable of penetrating our defenses. I had thought it would be a production-related failure in our pod that brought about our demise, but it would appear that our enemies had found a weakness of our "impenetrable" cities. We immediately dispatched a long-distance message envoy to Pod Baghdad. Hopefully, their Arthropod R&D department would investigate the incident and find some defense against the new unforeseen threat.

In another week, we would dispatch another six cohorts of candidates to pursue the Path to Citizenship. Initially, I thought the process to be inhumane. Over the years, the routine had forced me to become calloused to the inevitable loss of life, which I justified as an essential step towards our continued survival. The hypocrisy wasn't lost on me, having been one of the few homegrown candidates. Those who qualified and desired available positions in Pod Horizonte had a more straightforward, comparably safer task. On our Release Day, our mission was to survive a year serving with the local transporters, which I had done in one of their pump houses. It was supremely dull, but by comparison, significantly safer. I had used the isolation wisely and designed several new systems for the pod, a contributing factor in my election to regent. Back then, the only ones who had perished after the initial Release Day had done something foolhardy. I had enjoyed the experience outdoors during the rare and short-lived moments of safety. It rustled a feeling of longing for the outdoors in my chest.

Placing my empty cup of tea in the sink, I pocketed a berry flavored ration bar from the cabinet with the wonky door. As I ducked out of the apartment's hatch, I thought, *"How can I help us survive another day?"* I hoped with the tiniest spark of optimism that we would have a breakthrough soon before it was too late "for all."

CHAPTER 5: HUCK

With so few days left until our release, what little sleep I had was tainted by terrors. When I gave up on sleep, the scratchy sheets were adhered to my skin with sweat. I quietly dressed so as not to disturb Zeke and snuck out of the dorm. I took the elevator down to Level 90, the last stop before the laborer levels. As long as I stayed out of the overworked laborers' way, they didn't seem bothered by my presence. I walked along the catwalk above the deepest levels of the district, a bluish light from the reactor mixing with the orange of the sodium lamps bathing the incomprehensibly large room in a purplish glow. I let my mind wander, my boots scuffing on the metal grates as commands were shouted below. In a matter of days, I would be focused exclusively on survival. As excited as I was about finally getting to observe the planet's natural beauty, a small part of me would miss the innate comfort of the surrounding metal and concrete I'd grown up in. Pod Horizonte was home and I was going to try and soak as much of it in as possible before I left. Diogo snuck up behind me while my mind was preoccupied, taking in the inorganic smells and discordant sounds.

"Hey Huck," he whispered to avoid spooking me.

I wasn't familiar with the gruff trainer's friendly side. "Hey," I said, unsure of how to respond to his informal approach.

"I come down here when I can't sleep." He leaned on the rail, appearing lost in thought. "We leaders of the cohorts have one of the most difficult tasks. Not because training you numbskulls to wield a spear is that particularly difficult, but it takes a toll on us." He took a deep breath before continuing. "We know most of you won't survive. I think we've all stopped attending the observation ceremonies, even when it's our cohorts. I honestly can't understand why anyone watches the release." In the pulsing light, I swear I saw moisture in the eyes set deep within his hardened face. "That's what it's about, though, survival of the fittest. You're ready, you know. You'll be one of the ones that make it."

With a pat on my back, he walked away with no further acknowledgment of our conversation. I remained on the suspended platform for a few moments longer before heading back to my dorm. *Survival of the fittest.* All around the world, people can reproduce as they see fit, giving birth to as many children as they like before giving them over as wards of the city. Releasing all of humanity's offspring would undoubtedly eliminate the "weak," but at what cost? Maybe any species that sacrifices its own isn't the fittest. What if the fittest were the Arthropods we were trying to fight? Maybe we were just postponing our inevitable end. Despite being surrounded by the ambient heat of the nuclear furnaces, that thought made an icy shiver run down my spine.

As I entered the confined dorm, I found Zeke sobbing and shaking in his bed, deep in the throes of a panic attack. I rushed to his side, sitting on the scratchy wool, and put my arm around him. In addition to our survival and career training, every candidate had core training in citizenship, which included psychological intervention. But when it came down to it, I simply followed my gut as I helped my friend regain his composure. I held his icy hands as I cradled him in my arms. His sobs briefly became louder before eventually settling down into a light whimper.

"I'm terrified," he finally confessed to me through a deluge of tears.

I honestly hadn't been as fearful as I would've expected. I'd run through a gamut of emotions, but fear hadn't been the strongest. Anger, maybe, at those who would force us into almost certain death. I wasn't overconfident, nor was I fearless. I had apprehension and concerns, but ultimately I was filled with optimism and excitement about being outside of the city for the first time. Arthropods were just an obstacle whose existence felt almost theoretical, having never seen one face to face like some other candidates.

To console Zeke, I responded truthfully, "We all are."

Once Zeke had calmed down, I managed to doze off for a few hours. When I woke up, he was already gone. Since there weren't any required classes or training sessions today, I presumed he had left for his apprenticeship. After grabbing a quick breakfast in the cafeteria, I made my way down to the recycling department to help with any available tasks. Even though I had technically completed my apprenticeship, I still enjoyed the energetic environment and voluntary contribution. Upon my arrival, I realized frantic would have been a better description. Everyone was running from desk to desk, and the tension in the air was palpable. I grabbed Technician Heitor as he ran by me.

"What's going on?" I asked.

"We've just used the last of the raw materials in the pod," Heitor said, catching his breath. "Took us several hundred years, but we did it."

"We've known this was coming. Surely there was a plan in place," I said.

"There is. We told Grand Major Leal, and he ordered everyone in the department to track down as many unrecycled non-metallic materials as possible and attempt to get the owners to part with them. We still have plenty of waste coming in, but without any fresh materials to combine them with, anything the laborers produce will be junk."

"And he thinks people are going to hand over their belongings?"

"He said that if we can't get enough donated, then we'll have to start confiscating materials."

"Jesus. Confiscation isn't what I signed up for."

"Welcome to the club, Huck. Now, if you are here to help, grab a list of addresses and start knocking on doors."

•••••••••

I was assigned with nine others to the apartments of one of the upper floors. The residents of the upper levels were a snobbish, self-centered bunch, and we were about to ask them to give away their possessions with nothing in return. *This isn't going to go smoothly.* Even with the group of us divided up, visiting this large number of apartments was no small feat.

After splitting off from the others, I chose my first corridor. There was no visible litter, burned-out bulbs, or graffiti compared to the passages below. Instead, the walls looked freshly painted, and though there was visibly cracking like every other floor, the residents had made more effort to repair and conceal it. The lights were a brighter, more natural color than the lamps below, making my complexion appear healthier in comparison to the sickly hues of our levels. As I approached the first apartment, I wondered where *they* obtained their replacement materials. I knocked, and as the hatch silently opened, I detected the floral scents lingering on the air escaping the residence.

"Can I help you?" a well-groomed man asked, eyeing me up and down.

"Yes, sir," I said, struggling to remember the dialogue I had come up with in the elevator. "We've depleted our raw materials, and we are collecting source materials that residents are willing to donate for processing."

"You need what?" he asked.

"The pod needs some of your things, anything that's not metal, so that we can recycle it."

"Why?"

"So that we can mix the recycled waste with new materials for durability."

"I think I understand. You want to take my hard-earned possessions so some braindead greaser can have a new end table. Go banish yourself," he said, slamming the hatch, which made more of a soft thump than the angry clank he intended.

My door-to-door visits had gotten off to a great start. I spent the day getting similar responses ranging from simple noes to furious obscenities. Almost every conversation ended with a "thumped" door, which became humorous after a while. I managed to set foot in a few apartments before they realized my purpose, but the inhabitants promptly shooed me out.

The people up here lived differently than the people below. I had never had any reason to visit the apartments, only occasionally coming to the upper floors for the aptitude tests given in the Nucleus. Even then, it was usually a direct trip up and back. Here each apartment had numerous furnishings, function-specific rooms, and space. Lots of space. I struggled to reconcile the overcrowding on the lower levels with the open spaces that existed up here. I found it ironic that the people who had the most were the least willing to share, even for the benefit of all. I suppose our city's slogan didn't apply to them.

My training and experience in recycling had taught me that our resources were finite and becoming ever more so. I had heard rumors that other parts of the infrastructure were crumbling as well. If there were any truth to the gossip, soon everyone would be in trouble. Not just the laborers, not just Pod Horizonte, but humanity. I only hoped to survive from the upcoming Release Day to Pod Bogota, where I had to believe that I could make a difference. Humanity needed more time to counter the Arthropod threat. Though at our current rate, the more significant threat was coming from within.

CHAPTER 6: ARIADNE

Krista and I stepped into the sprawling arena for our final training session, kicking up dust as we walked and feeling the sticky heat permeating our bodies. I couldn't put my finger on it, but something was different. Trainer Lourenço was standing alone under the direct light of the arena; a sinister shadow playing out under his facial features. Everyone in the cohort felt the same sense of apprehension as we filed in, huddling together for the illusion of protection it offered. Once inside, the heavy gates closed behind us with a loud boom that made my heart skip a beat. Lourenço cleared his throat.

"Welcome candidates of Cohort Gamma. After much deliberation, we've decided to add a new, unexpected element to your training. We feel it comes at great risk but is worth the experience it offers you. Of course, the sacrifice of some of you will be greater than others."

I felt my skin prickle into goosebumps at his last utterance. Training was already quite dangerous. It was common for candidates to break bones, get bruises, and even lose appendages. However, our trainers deemed the exercises an "acceptable risk" because they approximated the challenges we would face on our journey. The idea that training was about to become more dangerous could only mean deadly. Either our trainers thought it was of the utmost importance to survival or took a twisted pleasure in our suffering. I sincerely hoped for the former.

Lourenço continued, "We know three out of five of you will die on Release Day. We have tried year after year to improve that statistic...."

I cringed at being a "statistic."

"...Each year, the Arthropods grow in number, intelligence, and coordination. They reconnoiter our cities, watching for patterns and sharing knowledge through their antenna bug network. So after discussing it, we thought some real-world application might improve the odds of your success."

Some of the things our trainer said sounded eerily familiar to the justifications of pre-landing dictators we had studied in history. It made me wonder if our trainers had our genuine interest at heart. I asked myself if Lourenço observed Release Day, would he cheer us on or take a sadistic satisfaction in our violent deaths?

"Without further ado, I present to you your final training exam," said Lourenço.

No sooner had he finished speaking, Professor Lucas, who I hadn't even realized was present, walked over to the wall and pulled on a rust-clad lever, which finally budged on the third attempt. He sprinted to the wall-mounted ladder, ascending to the observation booth far above the sandy floor to join Lourenço. With the tug of the lever, a loud clanking resonated from far above our heads. As if choreographed, we tilted our heads up to ascertain the source of the sound. From an aperture opening in the ceiling, a riveted metal container began its descent. Over the clinking of the chain wench, I could hear a second sound, a higher-pitched whine. My stomach dropped as I realized it was not a mechanical sound but a feral screech. At that terrifying moment, I had the realization that they were going to pit us against a live Arthropod. My body tingled from my head to my toes as my brain played roulette with the fight, flight, or freeze responses. Gradually my training took over my body's primitive response, and I began to assess the situation.

Scanning the arena, I saw a rack with our usual assortment of weapons leaning against one of the looming red walls. Despite the consensus of a spear being the ideal weapon against Arthropods, I had devoted my specialization to the recurve to supplement the standard-issue secondary weapon—a dagger. I was not particularly strong, but I was quick and quiet. In close-quarters combat, I would be deadly. When I saw the worn, familiar grip of my favorite bow, I felt a surge of enthusiasm. I tugged on Krista's shoulder and took off in a sprint to the rack, and snagged my bow and blade before the container had reached the sand. Though we were trained as a cohort, it would be every candidate for themselves outside of the pod.

Snapping out of their daze, the rest of the candidates followed suit, gearing up while Krista and I were taking our defensive postures. Out of the corner of my eye, I noticed that Krista had selected the katanas she preferred for their swept blades, perfect against the vulnerable sides of the fleshier Arthropods. Once prepared, I evaluated the threat. As the container loomed just above the ground, the screech emanating from inside became more frantic. The durable iron-based metal, already rusting around the edges, shook as its occupant became increasingly agitated. The haphazardly assembled exterior had barred air vents on the top of each side caked with dark green sludge. Judging by the disturbing sounds and the container's volume, I mentally ran through the list of possible creatures that could be inside. The size was right for a spring tongue, but they made a gurgling sound. The screeching could identify a wake strider, but even with its legs bent, they would be far too long for the box, nor were they aggressive. Other Arthropods we also ruled out before it hit me—a bone arachnid! It felt as though all the oxygen had disappeared from the room.

I forced myself to recall my lessons from Professor Lucas. Bone arachnids preferred dryer climates but could be found almost everywhere on the planet. Their name originated from their ultra-hard exoskeleton that resembled sun-bleached bone. In their foreign way, they bore some resemblance to Earth's native spiders. Lucas had said they were lightning-fast and deceptively sneaky. Humans or animals shelter in burrows might find themselves face to face with the multi-eyed fiend. "Likely the last thing you'll ever lay eyes upon," I remembered him saying. I struggled to recall any of the monster's weaknesses in vain, but I couldn't panic. Ahead, something was happening.

With a loud clunk and hiss, each latch around the top of the box flung out in sequence. The antiquated iron chain that had lowered the container to the sandy arena floor retracted, taking the lid with it. I hoped we might get advice on engaging the threat, but no such luck. I looked up at the observation platform to see Lucas and Lourenço pointing to us and nodding their heads. I got a look of approval from Lourenço, I assumed in response to being the first to obtain a weapon. As the lid disappeared, I saw the distinct pale crab-like leg begin to emerge from the box, immediately followed by a second on the opposite side. Our modern brains may override our primitive thoughts, but I was unbelievably terrified. I had to force my body to begin moving in a responsive stance. *Aware. Mobile. Alive.* I vaguely perceived Krista at my side saying a mantra to herself.

The bone arachnid had fully emerged from the container in all its terrifying glory. Despite fitting snugly into the three-square-meter container, the spider had a nine-meter circumference and a five-meter height when fully expanded. Its multiple eyes gave it a 270-degree view, with its only blind spot being directly behind. Below its banks of eyes were humongous, needle-sharp fangs glistening with fresh venom. Running down each leg were spines, adapted to rip through a chitinous exoskeleton, and easily capable of mangling the soft flesh of a human. Like many Arthropod species, it didn't discriminate between local fauna and their own species—dead or alive.

Spear-armed candidates began taunting the creature from around the arena. The first wave of attackers were the candidates possessing dominant personalities with more brawn than brains. The spider was becoming increasingly annoyed, benefitting those of us who chose stealthier approaches hidden by their distraction. Then, across the arena, Foster found out just how quick the eight was. As he lunged forward in a taunting motion, with his spear extended in front of him, the spider retaliated, darting forward in the blink of an eye. Before anyone could process what had happened, the creature had pinned him against the battle-scarred wall, its giant fangs sunken completely into his chest. His black-haired head hung down sullenly, limp like the rest of his corpse. Even distantly acquainted, I could feel my cheeks flush in anger as I watched his uniform gradually change from dirty white to dark red. I fought to hold my breakfast down.

I heard another candidate scream, "Kill the eight!" charging towards its rear in a fury. I noticed the eight's head had subtly rotated and could see him coming, but it was too late for a warning. If I had thought this Arthropod was weaker outside of its burrow, I was wrong. With awe-inspiring lethality, it dropped Foster to the sand and spun around, centrifugal force encouraging its momentum. Like a saw blade, the legs spiraled through the yelling candidate and time momentarily stopped. He looked up and around with disbelief as a line of red appeared above his waist. His torso and legs slid into two distinct heaps with a greasy thud as they fell to the ground. This time I couldn't help it. I retched into the sand, quickly wiping my mouth with the back of my hand before returning to an offensive posture.

Using the filthy container for cover, I ran to it, sliding and pivoting my back against the cold metal. I could hear the fabric of my jumpsuit brushing against its oxidized surface over the screeching and hissing coming from the container's far side. The eight's rank lingering odors wafted from inside. I gathered my composure and caught my breath.

"Think! Think!" I whispered to myself.

Krista, next to me against the box, turned to me. "Don't *you* know how to kill these things? I know you're not sitting around reading romance novels!"

She was right. I sat around reading reference books for Pete's sake. *"What have I learned?"* I asked myself. Then it hit me. I knew they couldn't see behind, but only if they were preoccupied enough to keep them from swiveling their head to their posterior. I still couldn't remember reading what their weak spot was. According to the research from Baghdad, surviving observers reported that they always found them facing forward in their burrows. Therefore, their weak spot must be on their abdomen. I spun out from behind the container and stole a glance. The spider was busying itself with three candidates, and I noticed a velvety patch on the underside of its abdomen. Maybe for waste, reproduction, or another unknown function. Making the approach even more difficult was the fang-like spine on the tip of the abdomen. *"No worries,"* I thought, rolling my eyes. I turned to Krista and shared my plan. I had noticed that the eight lifted its abdomen as it lunged forward. I saw the shock in her eyes as I gestured. She nodded, knowing that we had few other choices. It didn't appear that this blood sport would end until our cohort had successfully defeated the spider.

As we slowly approached the spider from the rear, I locked

eyes with Omar and his buddies taunting it with the spears. Understanding passed between us. He nodded to continue our advance, shouting something indiscernible to the others with him. In moments, we were within meters of the Arthropod's rear. As predicted, the spider lunged towards Omar's group. With fluidity and grace, Krista sprung forward, slicing the spike from the end of the abdomen as I simultaneously dropped to my knees and launched an arrow deep into the creature's velvety patch. A hot, sticky black substance drained down from the arachnid's injuries. The creature let out an ear-piercing screech as we retreated, flailing in uncoordinated convulsions before collapsing into the steaming hemolymph-soaked sand. Omar jumped onto the eight's back and drove the blade of his naginata down through its armored head, rendering it lifeless.

Dueling claps echoed down from the observation deck from our trainers.

"Great job, everyone," said Trainer Lourenço, his voice echoing from his perch above. "Especially you, Omar, well done."

My jaw hit the floor. I looked up at Professor Lucas questioningly, but instead of urging Lourenço to make a correction, he just shrugged. I had passed my "exam," but it was a hollow victory given the losses. And I was seething.

CHAPTER 7: HEMANT

Drenched in sweat, reeking to high heaven, and with dried viscera clung to our jumpsuits, Arjun and I looked as through we had just stepped off a battlefield. Which was in actuality, not too far from the truth. I was pissed that our trainers had the gall to throw a live invert at us as a surprise ending to our training. *Why couldn't we have gotten the mechanical one like everyone else?* The vast arena had been inundated with Epsilon candidates, the lot of us barely filling a sixth of the sheet metal clad space. Graça and Marcia dropped a bone arachnid into the already blood-saturated sand as if it was no big deal. No one had even bothered to clean up the aftermath of the previous cohort's horrific experience. I wondered how many of them had needlessly died.

As I fought, I watched in dismay as our one-hundred strong cohort fell to ninety-two. I had prepared for the catastrophic death toll on Release Day, but it was heart-wrenching to see my comrades fall to their death before having left the pod. After a grueling half-hour battle, Arjun had finally noticed the vulnerable area on the underside of the eight's abdomen. Thank the universe! I spread the word to several others, and we made our advance. Brandishing my war hammer, I was able to distract the eight. Its desire to pounce was almost palpable, but it knew that with a misjudged lunge, the bludgeoning weapon could easily crush its skull. It felt like an eternity of playing cat and mouse, but before I knew it, the others had flanked him and managed to inflict enough lethal damage through the creature's Achilles' heel to put it out of commission.

Arjun was disgusting, his face covered in sand adhered to his skin by sweat, but unhurt. Unfortunately, I hadn't made it away unscathed. I was as much of a mess as Arjun but had taken a swipe from one of the creature's blade-like legs during the stand-off. The laceration had been in an unarmored area and I was extraordinarily fortunate that it was just a graze, but it had still opened a shallow gap in my side. Nothing a medic couldn't fix, but the dried blood from the initial wound had drenched the fabric of my jumpsuit, ruining it. I was relieved we had survived but furious at what our trainers thought necessary to put us through.

After a quick stop at our dorm to grab fresh jumpsuits, we visited the communal showers. I cleaned myself up and I sutured my laceration—a skill I was becoming more adept at doing. After we left, we strode past several restaurants in our district, the various cultural odors invading our nostrils. I laughed aloud, thinking about how each ethnic tradition offered the same limited base foods the pod offered, changing only the spices. I hadn't expected to have an appetite after the day's trials, but the smells awakened my stomach. Upon eye contact with Arjun, I realized he was thinking the same thing. He pointed at the Bambu restaurant, a Wuhan-influenced diner, and we ducked inside.

The tight space was reasonably crowded, forcing me to protect my injury from the bumps of careless elbows. We ordered our food from a wispily-mustached host who could've cared less that we were spending our ration points in his establishment.

"Want to carry it back to the dorm?" I asked Arjun.

Before he could answer, two candidates at a half-empty booth waved us over. One was light-skinned with short, curly black hair and athletically fit. The other was dark-skinned with close-cropped hair and a wiry, muscular build. We had caught them in the middle of a laugh, both grinning from ear to ear, and we welcomed the relief from our dismal day. As we each sat, they introduced themselves. The curly-haired one introduced himself as Huck and the wiry one as Zeke.

"What cohort are you guys from?" asked Huck. "I'm from Delta, and Zeke is my roommate, from Beta. We're both in the next Release Day heat."

"We're from Epsilon. I'm Hemant. This is my twin brother Arjun. He's the smart one. We're in the same heat."

"Judging by all those fresh bandages, I'm guessing you guys got the live invert final. Is that right?"

"Yeah. It was… something else," I said.

"It's pretty convenient to meet you two then," said Huck.

I glanced at Arjun, making sure he was comfortable with the invitation. Cohort cohesion was drilled into us from day one. We were encouraged to bond with our cohort above all others, but this close to Release Day, I didn't see any harm in making a few friends within the same heat. Friends could wind up being more beneficial than any weapon outside the pod. Since we'd been young, Arjun had always been unbelievably shy, often coming across as uninterested. He was more interested in studying than socializing, but that didn't mean he wasn't interested in establishing deep relationships with others. It's one of the many facets of my brother that made me care for him so much and the reason for my surprise when he excitedly spoke up.

"I agree. Have your cohorts begun pairing off by destination or into survival groups? Have you made plans for how long said groups wish to remain together? Have you mapped out and studied the terrain which you wish to cross? Have you studied the Arthropods you may encounter—"

"Arjun!" I interrupted, shaking my head and laughing. Arjun looked chagrined. "Give them a second to answer one question before you fire off another, okay?" He looked at me sheepishly before Zeke responded.

"It's fine," he said as he chuckled. "I love his enthusiasm." He turned towards Arjun, leaning his runner's frame across the table. "Some of us in Beta have begun grouping, but there are still a fair number of candidates who are unprepared—which alarms me."

"Delta too," Huck interjected.

The waitress brought over our food. She was an older woman with the chestnut complexion typical of descendants from the pod's founding inhabitants. The food she sat down on our table was anything but exciting. It had the same recognizable forms and colors of all the local fare. Everything was grown from modified seeds in recycled substrates or aquaponically with little variation. Only those on the uppermost levels received anything other than the nutritionally-lacking slop everyone ate. Getting full wasn't typically an issue, whereas feeling satisfied and revitalized was. We ate when we were hungry, but I rarely had any substantial cravings. None of the food was that interesting. It was nourishment and little more.

Zeke continued, "Both of our cohorts finished the program doing only a simulated Arthropod battle. As nuts as it is, it puts you guys in a position to understand just how real the threats we face are. If we go out unprepared and too individualized, we will take an insane number of casualties."

"We each have cohort members with various strengths," I said. "I think the smart option would be to divide up into small diverse attack groups."

"On the surface, that seems like a good idea, but if each cohort of a hundred splits off into groups of ten, that's sixty small groups running around. It would be unproductive chaos," said Arjun.

"What the hell are we supposed to do?" Huck asked. "Wouldn't larger groups be equally unproductive?"

"Maybe, but without being able to review the mag tapes of previous Release Days, I can't evaluate the most effective strategies," said Arjun. "I suppose I could run mental simulations based on my studies of Arthropod behaviors."

"Mental simulations? As in, you'll lay in your bunk and think about it?" I asked, leaning back against the tattered cushions of the booth. "Could we find a way to watch the tapes?"

"Even if we could screen them, the footage would be traumatizing," said Zeke. "That's the reason the tapes are confidential. Though it would be the same carnage we will experience firsthand. Ironic, isn't it?"

"Where do they keep the tapes?" Huck asked, his eyes glinting with mischief. "Do you think we could just borrow them for a bit? It's not like anyone would notice, right?"

"Hardly," Arjun said. "All recorded logs are kept in the Nucleus vault."

The Nucleus was only accessible with permission, usually only given to candidates for aptitude testing or disciplinary hearings. Aptitude reevaluation appointments were possible to obtain but rarely accepted, booked far in advance, and frequently canceled without reason. While the common space was reasonably accessible to the public, getting through the guard checkpoints to the secure levels where the vault was located would be next to impossible.

"How badly do you need those tapes, Arjun?" Huck asked.

I looked at Huck, unable to hide my surprise. "Are you nuts? How would you possibly get those tapes? Do you know what the punishment is for crimes like that?"

"Banishment," Huck replied, unfazed. "And how is that

different from Release Day? I'm alone instead of with a big group drawing attention."

"And unarmed, man," I said. "Not to mention you can't ever enter another pod."

"I think if I helped the cohorts survive on Release Day, one less recycling technician at Pod Bogota wouldn't affect humanity too much."

"You're nuts," I repeated, shaking my head. "but maybe we need nuts to survive."

CHAPTER 8: GUILHERME

The sound of my heels clicking against the concrete floor bounced back from the far wall, playing on my mind like an invisible pursuer. I intentionally took the more circuitous route to my office every day to pass the top-side viewports. While the ports' angles limited visibility, the natural light and moving clouds did wonders for my aching soul. The only pod location with a better vantage point over the surrounding landscape was the bridge, which even I only had access to upon invitation. The bridge, located on the topmost level of the Nucleus, was the control hub for the entire city. It was not a place I could simply visit to admire the local scenery. For now, the ports would have to suffice. Once I had taken in as much of the world's natural beauty as time permitted, I headed for my office.

With each passing day, my work became increasingly futile, making me less optimistic about extending our resources. It was simple. The nutrition level of our foods was falling close to the danger level, and the recycled goods were weakening to the point we wouldn't be able to create new products without fresh material. You can't fight entropy, especially with finite resources. Humanity needed to resume its dominant place on the surface, or soon, we would die below it. *We're already buried. It's convenient, really.* I pushed the defeatist humor out of my mind before continuing on.

Those of us fortunate enough to live and work on the higher levels had better access to resources, but soon enough, the shortfalls would affect everyone. Even indirectly, once the workforce started to suffer, it would put all the pod's residents at a significant disadvantage. It's not as if the people of the upper echelon of society have the training to farm crops or animals, operate plasma recyclers, or repair nuclear reactors. Nor could we rely on advanced technology like those before us. We all had essential roles in society, though the notion often escaped the upper-level residents.

Before the Arthropod Landing, computer and robot technology ran most of the world's daily monotonous operations. Large swathes of humanity lived off basic income, and work had become optional for much of the global population. History had taught us that with this "advance," motivation and creativity had dwindled. Any aspirations to expand into the universe were lost, and humanity stagnated. Shortly after the arrival of the Arthropods in '42, anything that used a microprocessor or wireless communication ceased to function. The completion of the Arthropods' aerial network didn't thrust us back to the Stone Age, like the adage, but it did push us back to the Industrial Age. Almost overnight, humanity had returned to the few remaining traditional books, wired communication, and physical labor. The setback made the organization and construction of the pods that much more difficult for the United Territories of Earth. There were anecdotes that the First Builders accomplished the pods with little more than slide rules and telegraph keys. *Humanity seemed to be its most creative when it was the most limited.*

I sat down at my battered desk, going over the same numbers that had been discouraging me for weeks, viewing the same downward trends. I had read and reread through my office's library, looking for any potential information that could be of use. Over a year ago, I had dispatched a message envoy, desperately seeking information from Pod Bogota about furthering our recycling methods. The lack of response to this envoy was the first hint something was amiss in the former Latin Territory.

I reclined in the chair to the music of its overstretched springs and stared at the mottled green ceiling. Over the centuries, various objects had rubbed off the paint, allowing the underlying material to oxidize. Then, as my mind began to wonder, I had an epiphany. The only hope for the future of humanity was to leave the pods once and for all. There was no way around it. Only one minor hurdle—we had to eradicate the Arthropods.

I snuffed at the thought. We only had to accomplish what humanity had been trying to achieve for the last four hundred years. But then something else occurred to me. For years, I had kept in touch with a distant friend who I'd met through my research. Over a year ago, Dieter had excitedly contacted me about a collaboration with Pod Baghdad. They had jointly developed a portable hybrid chemo-nuclear bomb at Pod Kano that held promise. I had immediately informed Prime Minister Carvalho of the development expecting the same enthusiasm, but he was surprisingly unenthused.

In hindsight, it had seemed to me that Carvalho and the other regents were uninterested in changing the status quo. As long as their lifestyles didn't change negatively in any noticeable way, what happened elsewhere in the pod was of no great concern. I would always present my disconcerting annotated reports, to which I would receive little response. They were aware of the issues but uninterested in pursuing lasting solutions. The morning would come when they would turn on the tap to find no water. They would eat breakfast to feel no benefit. They would wake from their slumber to nothing but darkness. They would take a deep breath to taste no oxygen. Only then would they register our dire situation.

I responded in a dispatch to Dieter, congratulating him and the other developers on their achievement. Only recently had he replied that the device would be minimally effective against the Arthropods on the surface. The weapon would be most advantageous if placed inside the Hive, where it could destroy the Arthropod Queens and cease their inexhaustible reinforcements. Dieter had already dispatched several reconnaissance teams to the Hive with no success, but maybe he had been approaching it the wrong way. Maybe what we needed was a small group of elite candidates. And the best candidates came from Pod Horizonte.

•••••••••

I left my office feeling lighter on my feet, having established a new intention in my mind. I was the best I felt since losing Aline. I decided to dedicate all of my energy to getting humanity safely back surface-side to begin rebuilding our once-great civilization. I just had to figure out how a grand major with minimal clearance could secretly do it. If I presented my proposal to the regents and Prime Minister Carvalho, they would laugh me out of the room. *This is from a group that doesn't even smile.*

I needed to think, having no idea where to begin with my objective. I needed a frothy steaming cup of matcha. When my wife and I were dating, one of our favorite places was a crappy dive called Bambu. It was a hole in the wall, but before I had my posting, it was a place that had been very special to us. It dawned on me that I hadn't been there in decades. She and I had gone there after living on the upper-level diet for a few months. The food was virtually unpalatable by comparison. How we had ever loved the mediocre Wuhan-inspired food left us gobsmacked. How fortunate we had felt for what we had then, but still not without the guilt for those eating the less than desirable food downstairs.

I went back to my apartment and changed out of my uniform. There was nothing inherently wrong with visiting the lower levels while wearing it. Most people were kind enough, except the few who would inevitably yell commentaries about privilege and corruption. *Not that they were usually wrong.* Being in the circles I was in; I saw more than a few examples supporting their disdain.

As I approached the district where I remembered the restaurant was, the walls glimmered with the excess moisture in the air. The heat was suppressing, and the melange of smells from the diverse establishments were familiar, intriguing, and stomach-turning. Without too much difficulty, I found the place I was looking for and stepped in. The place hadn't changed in the slightest over the decades. The noise level was mind-numbing, but I found my way to a back table and cozied up in the corner of the booth. Somehow the regular din was almost meditative between the boisterous voices, clattering dishware, and shuffling bodies. A skinny, acne-scarred waiter took my order before scurrying off. Before long, he was back with my tea. It tasted as uninspired as I expected. It was grainy and fishy, but I could detect the hints of matcha flavor lingering somewhere within and considered the trip a win. As I relaxed in the steam of the gaiwan, I serendipitously heard an interesting conversation from the adjacent table.

CHAPTER 9: HUCK

I sat across the table from Hemant and Arjun, my mind spinning. Our barely touched food had long since gone cold. Realistically, I had nothing to lose by stealing the tapes. Being banished alone didn't seem that bad compared to being released with a larger group. If I survived, which I believed I could, maybe I would live independently. Maybe I could find a nice little cave to hole up in. However, it'd probably be a safer bet to live with the survivors that supposedly dwelt on the surface. The pod was filled with rumors perpetuated by the transporter teams who claimed to have seen them. Many residents assumed that the stories were flights of fancy like the old sailor myths of mermaids and krakens. Either way, I knew if there was anything I could do to help the cohorts survive Release Day, I would do it. I never considered myself a hero, but I understood duty and obligation when I saw them.

As far as the task of breaking into the vault, I had no earthly idea. Over the years, I had developed a few friends spread throughout the various trades. Maybe one of them could use their knowledge to help me with my felonious mission. It might cost me my entire savings of ration points, but maybe I could call in some favors. It wasn't as if the Arthropods would accept the points. My thoughts were interrupted by Zeke's bony elbow digging into my ribs. I looked his way and then to what had caught his nervous eyes. In front of our table stood a lean, older gentleman. Dressed in casual clothes, his authoritative demeanor and rigid stance screamed high-ranking military. We had been caught openly discussing illegal activities, which alone would be cause for life-long demotion to laborer status.

"May I join you?" the man asked, his tightly cropped salt and pepper hair dissipating any doubts about his occupation.

The eyes of my companions simultaneously turned to me. Somehow in that instance, I became our little posse's leader.

"Sure," I said, unsuccessfully attempting to hide the quakiness in my voice.

"I couldn't help but overhear the nature of your *conversation*," the man said as he pulled a vacant chair from the table behind him. The people barely stirred at the chair's departure.

The blood in my veins turned to ice. Seeing the faces of my tablemates, I wasn't alone. However, something about this man's delivery kept me from outright panic.

"I would advise you to guard your thoughts more carefully," he began. "You never know who's listening. I'm sure you are aware that the administration rewards reports of illicit behavior. For enough points, some people would report their own partners. I would encourage you all to conduct yourselves properly according to the candidate guidelines you are already familiar with."

We all nodded sheepishly.

He rose and, taking care of our bill, disappeared into the crowd without saying more.

"That was… awkward," I said, feeling my heightened pulse.

"And strange," Arjun said, still brimming with anxiety. "He of all people knows that it is an offense to ignore credible criminal threats."

I looked over at Zeke, who was staring down at the table, consciously breathing in an attempt to calm his adrenal response.

"That assumes we're credible," Hemant said, chuckling nervously in an attempt to lighten the mood. "What's that? I thought he took the bill."

I looked down and saw where the bill had been; there was a napkin with raised indentations indicating writing on the opposite side. I hurriedly flipped it over to find a note saying, "You'll need help. 75th Floor. Recreation District. 1900."

I looked at Arjun. "He's not ignoring us at all."

•••••••••

In an attempt to keep the meeting discreet, I decided to meet with our military friend alone. After sharing the note's contents with the others, we argued whether we should trust a stranger who conveniently appeared in our moment of need. It was all a little suspicious, but I was willing to consider it fortuitous. It was that opinion that landed me the job of liaison. With the simple act of asking those two worn-out companions to join us for dinner, our lives had all taken an exciting detour. Living is all about taking risks. Even though the others were a little circumspect of the encounter, I was willing to meet with the stranger. I had left the others together in my apartment anticipating my return.

I stood leaning against an aquaponic planter in the recreation district, waiting for the mystery rendezvous at the time and location that the note had stipulated. Despite the willingness to take the risk, my palms were clammy with perspiration. I watched several young candidates playing on the swings in the local park. A matriarch sat watching them giggle and play under the sun-spectrum lamps, the once red playground equipment now almost pink from the fading caused by the artificial light. It brought back a feeling of nostalgia from my youth when I played on my own district's recreational equipment. As I took in the surroundings waiting for my newest acquaintance, I saw residents of the nearby apartments watching the children and feeling a similar sentiment.

Still sporting the same attire and poise, the older man approached from around the corner, budging me from my thoughts. He seemed unconcerned about being seen, having picked a relatively trafficked public space. As he approached, he motioned with his hand to an old-fashioned park bench nearby, placed next to the decorative koi pond providing the nutrients for the nearby vegetation. We sat for several long, awkward moments before he spoke.

"My name is Guilherme Leal, but please call me Memo. I'm a grand major and regent of Horizonte. You probably haven't heard of me, even though I'm an elected official. I tend to exist behind the scenes." He paused. Then making eye contact, he said, "We have a common interest and are in a position to help each other."

"I'm Huck," I said, still feeling trepidatious. "I think I know how you can help me, but how can I help you? Why did you decide to help us?"

"In my position, I oversee the recycling and nutritional processes. My job is to increase their efficiency and quality, which is constantly dropping."

"My aptitude is in recycling!" I said, my timidness disappearing. "I've been helping track down new materials, but I'm in the next Release Day heat, so I don't know how long I will be able to help you here."

"That's great, but that's not why I brought you here. The pod is dying, Huck. We need to make the surface habitable again. The administration of the pod sees our plight as a lost cause. They're just going through the motions, unconcerned with anything but how their lives are affected. We've lost the fighting spirit that humanity has displayed throughout history. It's as if we've already given up."

"That seems like more than I can change. How do you expect me to help?" I asked.

"I only recently snapped out of my daze. We must be more proactive in annihilating the Arthropods at their source—the Hive. They're burrowed deep into the Australian desert, where they first landed. I have a plan, but I need people I can trust on the outside."

"Why isn't this coming from Prime Minister Carvalho?" I asked.

"I don't suppose there is any point in keeping secrets. By discussing this, I'm writing my banishment sentence," the major said, taking a long steady breath. "The reason it isn't coming from Carvalho is that he's part of the problem."

"What do you mean?"

"Carvalho is only interested in what benefits him. The lower the pod's population, the more resources are available for those left."

The implication of what he was suggesting began to hit me. Carvalho wasn't interested in releasing us to win the war. He was releasing us to lower the demand on resources.

"Whoa," I said, filled with righteous anger.

"I know," the major said.

"What do you need me to do?"

"I need you and your friends to survive. I'll get you the tapes since I agree that they will help you. In return, I want you to pick up a weapon from Pod Kano, carry it to the Hive, and shove it up the inverts' collective ass."

"Wait. What?!" I asked, perplexed. "To be clear, you smuggle the tapes out of a secure library, and the four of us parade down into *the Arthropod Hive* with some bomb offering it and ourselves like a housewarming gift?"

"I don't appreciate insincerity, Huck. If we are going to help each other, I need you to take this seriously."

"I'm sorry, Major, but this is insane! How can we do what ten pods and countless highly-trained people couldn't do over the last *four hundred years?*"

"Nine pods. I'm afraid we lost Bogota. And Memo, please. Trust me, I believe your small group has what we need. I'm offering you a chance to change the world. Now, I can't answer all your questions tonight. I need to get back up top. Think about it, okay? I'll be in touch."

Memo stood and walked away. Despite being seated, the dizziness I felt was so intense that I had to grip the bench's armrest tightly. Not only did I just find out the pod was on its deathbed, but my destination pod no longer existed. *What had happened? Were there survivors?* Memo had given me a new destination, but it was a suicide mission that would take me half way around the globe. I had so many things to tell the others, but I felt so lightheaded I thought I would pass out.

I nearly jumped out of my skin as a hand touched my shoulder.

"Spare some points?" I turned to see a failed one, who had tapped my shoulder with his only hand and noticed he was also missing a leg. His odor was worse than the exhaust from the farms, and his ragged clothes looked as rough as they smelled. I handed him a few points, knowing he needed them far more than me. He nodded thanks and headed off to beg other residents.

I had an epiphany as I watched him walk away. The status quo needed to change. The pod couldn't hang on indefinitely like a failed one, weakened and scrounging around as we dwindled to nothing. In merely a day, the major had dashed my future to pieces, but I decided I had a new future in mind—a future that had me ultimately traveling to the deadliest place on the planet—the Australian Territory.

CHAPTER 10: ARIADNE

I jolted awake to Krista screaming in her sleep. I sprung to her side, trying to calm her unconscious thrashing. I was briefly thankful that weapons weren't allowed in our rooms. I couldn't make out what she was saying, but I was pretty sure she was having the same recurring nightmares that plagued everyone. I cradled her body, speaking to her soothingly until I felt her tension dissipate. I sat there for a few minutes before I looked down, realizing her deep brown eyes were open and staring up at me. "Thanks," she said. I smiled back and felt a motherly tenderness run through me. I brushed some hair out of her face, noticing it was damp with sweat. I stole a glance at the clock. It was early but going back to sleep didn't seem like an option.

"Want to grab a shower?" I asked. "It'll refresh you. I could use one myself."

Krista wordlessly agreed.

I was right. After the shower, she felt significantly better. Because it was earlier in the morning than usual, the facilities were unoccupied, and I enjoyed the water's saturating warmth and rare privacy. On the way back to the dorm, we disrupted Omar and his companion in the dark corner of a communal area, her tongue down his throat and his hand up her shirt. Krista and I looked at each other, shaking our heads. We were all in our hormonally-heightened teenage years, feeling the ever-present tugs of attraction. There were times with Nikos, when I had to reluctantly part ways and give our aroused bodies time to calm. Despite the sometimes overwhelming pull of sexuality, we had been taught and conditioned to avoid it.

It was forbidden to have children unless you were a citizen. There were methods of protection, but it wasn't worth the risk. The punishment for a poorly-timed pregnancy was automatic demotion to laborer for the father and mother and immediate termination of the pregnancy, discouraging any potential parents from considering the backchannels of reproduction. There will always be rule breakers. Some would-be parents could even hide pregnancies for long periods before being inevitably caught. With a prying glance in the shops, you could find contraband concealed by shelves and blankets. Powdered milk and cloth diapers were hot commodities for the few women who delivered in secret. But no one escapes Release Day. Upon discovery, the administration transferred unauthorized infants to the matriarchs and banned the infants from being trained. Once of age, they could choose between labor or release, the latter meaning almost certain death.

Back in our dorm, Krista stared through our warped wall mirror, brushing out her hair as her reflection duplicated her motions, her mind still haunted by the nightmare.

"You want to talk about it?" I asked, watching her take a second to pull her thoughts to the present.

"We leave home in days," Krista said. "This is all we've ever known. *If* we manage to survive, we have to trek across the planet. You've seen the way some of the failed ones look—the ones with the Shock. They spend their entire lives in a daze. Even the citizens never seem to escape the trauma. I wonder if it would be better to die than live like them."

"Please don't say that," I said, slipping my hand into hers. "We have each other. We'll watch each other's backs—and minds. Whenever you go to a dark place, I'll be there to guide you out. You'd do it for me."

"Thanks, Ariadne. I couldn't bear to lose you. I love you."

"I love you too, Krista." I smiled and watched as her trademark smile began to reappear. "We are going to march out triumphantly on Release Day. We are going to stand arm in arm with the rest of Gamma. And we are going to kick invert ass!"

"Yeah! And then march to Pod Pittsburgh with entrails clinging to our blades."

We laughed hysterically, helping melt away the tension and anxiety of Release Day that haunted us. How six hundred people were going to coordinate in battle was beyond me. I began to see the flaws in our training with so much dependence on individuals. Our education in group tactics was sorely lacking, presumably because our trainers knew most of us wouldn't survive, leaving many of us on our own.

"Ariadne?"

"What?"

"You were lost on the surface again."

"Sorry. I was wondering why we didn't spend more of our training on team tactics."

"You are overthinking it. We work together in the arena all the time."

"We learned how, but it wasn't something they expressly taught us. And what about the other cohorts? Are we all going to be doing our own things? As much as I love Cohort Gamma, isn't this about everyone's survival?"

Krista just stared at me. "Maybe they have a bigger picture in mind. They've been doing this for years, so I assume they know better than we do."

"Maybe," I said, "But whose bigger picture?"

•••••••••

I spent the afternoon tending to the plants in the horticulture district, something that had always put me at ease. There was something meditative about pruning the various plant species, each requiring differing techniques. I strode through the aisles, examining each plant for signs of withering or disease that needed removal. I felt my face flush as my mind flashed back to the anger I had experienced in the arena. I wasn't specifically directing my ire at anyone, but I desperately wanted to be treated as a competent member of my cohort. No matter what I accomplished, what marks I received, or how much I trained, it always seemed only to be adequate.

In my distraction, I had accidentally clipped a healthy fruiting limb off of one of the vines. Greenskeeper Chun appeared and placed her calloused hand over my trembling one, which was still gripping the shears tightly. Guiding my hand with experienced deftness, she helped me prune the remainder of the vine before gently taking the shears, placing them on the workbench, and grabbed my hand.

"You have a sharp mind, Ariadne," said Chun, patting my hand. "Remember that without focus, a sharp mind is just like the shears, easily damaging something perfectly healthy."

"I'm sorry. I'm distracted and upset about something that happened yesterday. Not to mention, I'm worried about Krista and Release Day," My eyes began to blur from the tears. "Sometimes, I wish I could prune off my emotions."

"No, *háizi*, your emotions make you who you are," she said. "Though you make an interesting point. Don't completely prune off your emotions, but you can prune them, encouraging the positive growth and removing the negative."

"I'm not sure I understand."

"Feel your emotions. Control them. Let go of the parts that cloud your judgement."

I took a moment, absorbing the profundity of her words like the plants around me absorbing their nutrients. I watched as she stood and returned to her delicate pruning, demonstrating a level of patience only obtained from years of mindful practice. After a few moments, I rose to leave and heard her voice behind me.

"There is one other thing," she said. "If you are willing to suffer a little more plant wisdom. There's nothing wrong with a little herbal remedy now and again."

She took my hand and placed a dried, wormlike root into my hand before closing my fingers around it.

"Valerian. Grind it for a tisane. It will help you and Krista find some peace. It's that pink flower over there." She said, pointing, then whispered, "Get it as often as you like."

Chun winked and smiled, filling my chest with much-needed warmth as I left to find Krista for our upcoming tea time.

CHAPTER 11: HEMANT

I stood in the corridor, tapping my foot impatiently with the same rhythm of the flickering light above me. After returning from his meeting, Huck had shared the shocking news of Bogota and the major's extreme proposition. Huck made it clear that Major Leal wasn't requiring any of us to join his mission saying that we were all free to make our own choices. I told Huck to banish himself. Of course, I would do it. Despite it being slightly suicidal, it was a chance to make a real difference for the future of humanity—or die heroically trying.

In the brief time we had gotten to know each other, Huck and I had developed a ludicrously strong bond. Arjun was already willing to follow this candidate we had previously known only in passing to the ends of the Earth—literally. Naturally, if Arjun was on board, so was I. I had never seen Arjun like this. Before, heading to Pod Baghdad to study the inverts was his singular focus. Now all he could talk about was how applied field research was more advantageous than academic lab studies. We would be committing ourselves to a much longer journey with something far more dangerous on the other end. *What the hell had we done?* The major had some master plan involving planting a destructive device deep within the terror-inducing Hive, but how our little band would accomplish it was beyond me. Huck and the major would hold another discreet meeting to discuss the theft of the tapes.

Huck had awoken me in the early morning to accompany him to the second meeting with Leal. Unfortunately, his procrastination had meant I didn't have time for my one notable vice—coffee. As it was, I found myself waiting around in a poorly-lit corridor reeking strongly of moldy cheese. My annoyance at our newfound leader was rising the longer he forced me to wait without the comfort of caffeine. The major had relayed his most-recent message through a failed one instructing Huck to meet him in this sparsely populated, run-down district on one of the lower floors.

Huck should've already been back, turning my annoyance into concern. We were already several levels below my comfort zone. I sincerely hoped that we could trust the failed one's discretion. I stared at a rat across the passageway from me, suspecting that if my paranoia caused me to keel over, the vermin wouldn't hesitate to drag me off for breakfast—a striking similarity to invert behavior if you ask me. Despite the warm, humid air currents blowing through the district, my fingertips felt like ice. I glanced down at my hand, realizing my palms were sweating. I've never been the nervous type, but I'd also never done anything illegal. I didn't wholly trust the major. I was pretty sure if it came down to it, he'd throw us under a tram and continue gallivanting around the Nucleus. I thanked the universe that Arjun wasn't here. He'd be drawing more unnecessary attention to us with frantic pacing and possibly hyperventilating. Then again, he might be doing that back in our dorm anyway. I quickly pushed that thought out of my head, knowing my worry would do nothing to help him. I flooded with relief when I saw Huck quickly round the corner ahead of me.

"Hey," Huck said, catching his breath.

"Hey yourself," I said. "One, what did you find out? Two, can we talk about it on the elevator out of here?"

"Sure," Huck said, stepping onto the nearby lift. "So I met with Memo—"

I snorted. "I can't get over you being on a nickname basis with a grand major. Sorry. Keep going."

"I met with *Major Leal,* and he's got a plan to get us the tapes. He's doing all the hard parts for us. There's no way we could get through vault security to help him out, so he will assume the majority of the risk and smuggle the tapes out."

"What's the catch? There's always a catch," I said.

"The catch is that because he's a regent, he can't leave the Nucleus with the materials because he's too closely watched by security. So he needs us to sneak into the Nucleus to smuggle out the tapes."

"You just said there was no way for us to get through security."

"This is the part you're not going to love."

"Huck, I haven't *loved* any of this from the moment it began. I planned to survive Release Day, drop off Arjun at Baghdad, and get my ass to Bhopal. It wasn't exactly kicking back in the upper levels and drinking the good stuff, but it didn't involve life or death sentences. So now, regardless of how I feel, what do we need to do?"

"Since Memo's job is optimization, he has access to much of the pod's architectural drawings. He was able to sketch out the service tunnel layouts. We'll have to crawl through a maintenance hatch." Huck hesitated. "We have to look the part. We have to dress as laborers."

"Holy Hell." I took a few moments to take this in. Then, taking a deep breath, I agreed.

•••••••••

That evening, Huck and I stood side by side in the maintenance elevator on the way down to the deepest reaches of the pod. Usually, we would take a standard one down, but they stopped at Level 90. Since only laborers lived below that, only the freight elevators ran below that. They were larger, slower, and more utilitarian but ran the whole gamut of floors. The one we were in now stank of stale bodies and refined petroleum. Unlike the enclosed cars of the elevators above, this one consisted of little more than a framed platform of diamond plating surrounded by waist-high bars to prevent passengers from rubbing against the concrete walls. The platform descended slowly enough to enjoy the extensive graffiti that was so prevalent that it blended into a shaft-length mural. The obligatory distasteful sexual comments were scattered throughout, but most of the message centered on feelings of oppression and hatred towards the higher levels. A certain amount of aggression was aimed at candidates, adding to our discomfort. We made eye contact, coming to the same conclusion. Not wishing to go any deeper, Huck reached out for the dangling controls that told the lift to stop on the next floor.

As the car stopped with a lurch, we stepped off onto the deepest floor either of us had ever occupied. We had dressed for the occasion in our grungiest clothes to avoid unnecessary attention. I had gone as far as to smear universe knows what from the elevator's support bars onto my sleeve for added effect. A splash of dark fluid covered the spot on the wall that would typically indicate the floor number. I wasn't concerned about the level number enough to linger long enough to decipher it. These overcrowded floors had a rough reputation, and we had no desire to experience it firsthand. Thanks to their differing layouts, there were more places to hide but more ways to get lost.

I put aside my discomfort and disgust and remembered why we were here—to obtain the maintenance suits. Huck gestured with his head towards the wall, and I followed suit. I relied on him to get us to the barracks using Memo's rudimentary map. Our likelihood of scoring two maintenance suits would be highest from the supply district, always located next to barracks. The biggest obstacle would be the increase in the concentration of laborers as we got closer to our destination. I felt a strange sensation as I followed along our path, knowing that I spent my entire life in this pod, but this portion of it felt unknown and undiscovered. We silently continued our journey, staying in the shadows afforded to us by the poor lighting.

The wider corridors seemed to stretch on endlessly, feeling more extensive due to their capacity for transporting larger machinery. Suddenly when rounding a corner, we ran into several laborers, whether coming to or from work, we didn't know. We tried to conduct ourselves like we figured everyday laborers might. The group initially nodded in greeting, but on closer inspection, confronted us.

"We don't recognize you guys," one said, using the rough dialect of the depths.

"We're from the lows," Huck responded, mimicking their lingo.

"That's funny. You don't sound like you're from the lows," the laborer said. "We can hardly understand them."

"We're recent demotes," said Huck. "We're on an errand for the big boss."

I could tell Huck was getting more uncomfortable with the conversation. I was afraid he was already saying too much, digging deeper into a hole we couldn't escape.

"Where are you guys headed? If you're lost, we'll help you."

"No need, guys. We know the way," I said, beginning to walk away. Huck followed suit.

"Damn lowers," one muttered. "They're so strange."

"Yeah," I heard another agree as their conversation receded into the distance.

Once we were out of sight, I heard Huck let out an audible sigh of relief. "That was close. I don't know what we would've done if they had found us out," he said, mocking their accent.

I laughed. I'd never get used to the unusual accent of the lower levels. "Based on what they said, I hope we never have to speak with anyone from further down."

"Agreed."

After what seemed like hours of tense travel and thankfully no more conversation, we saw our target in the distance—the barracks. Huck turned to me and grinned. I took a moment to look around the vaguely familiar layout and saw what looked like their supply district, positioned where on another floor might be the market. Even though the ass-end of the pod has a remarkably different layout, the number of similarities was striking. I tapped Huck on the shoulder and gestured to the entry to the center. He nodded, showing his understanding. The present issue was that our destination was across the wide district square, the one well-lit place on the entire level. Aside from the litter blowing in the air currents, the area was fairly empty between shifts. If someone caught us with the suits, we might could play it off as two young off-duty laborers heading to a shift. But if they saw us stealing, our nefarious intent would be obvious, whether our identities were revealed or not. We had to do this right. Laborers were not known for an organized system of justice. They typically dealt out punishments in-house and on the spot, something I'd very much like to avoid.

Huck turned to me and whispered, "Can you run fast for a big guy?"

"Do I look fat to you?" I said as I rolled my eyes.

"I didn't know if you spent all your time on deadlifts."

"I can run fast enough. Maybe not as fast as you, but don't you worry about that."

"Okay. If we're caught, we're screwed. Let's walk over there as nonchalantly as possible. It looks from here like there's no one inside. I guess it's not near any shift changes. We act like we're gearing up early for a shift. Then we walk out like we know what we're doing."

"Sounds good. Anything else," I asked.

"Let's avoid talking this time," said Huck.

"Agreed."

We each took off across the plaza, careful to avoid tripping on all the broken debris. *Jesus.* Just because the Council relegated laborers to the lower levels didn't mean they couldn't take care of where they lived. Candidates are messy too, but I can't relate to the laborers. The work they do for the pod is honorable, but the conditions that led to them here, frequently not so much. The irony of the situation was the heist I was currently participating in was one of several activities in my immediate future that could very well result in my demotion. I reminded myself to give Huck another tongue lashing if we escaped unscathed. Finally, we arrived outside the entry hatch of the uniform supply center. I looked at Huck, who gave the go-ahead and entered the building between the racks of foul-smelling work suits.

As I stifled a gag, my first thought was, *Instead of an outfitter, we found a damn laundromat!* No wonder the roll-up door was open. I nearly jumped when I saw a man looking at me from behind the counter. Behind the desk was a broad-shouldered, bearded laborer looking right at me. For the briefest moment, I couldn't move a muscle. I nodded in greeting and quickly turned my attention back to the task at hand, thankful he didn't seem to care enough to respond. Who in their right mind would steal this crap? I started grabbing the gear I needed. The shop kept the suits in no discernable order, nor did they have any markings to identify the size.

I risked another glance at the man and noticed his eyes seemed to be boring a hole through me. My extremities turned to ice, and my mind spooled up with possible reactions to the scenario. *He knows we're candidates.* I noticed Huck had his back to the man but stared at me with great concern. He was trying to size up the situation without knowing what was happening. My first instinct was to run, but I knew we needed this gear. The thought crossed my mind to knock him unconscious, but any misjudgment would bring down all kinds of hell upon us from the nearby barracks, likely with us ending up as pig food. Before I could decide how to proceed, it occurred to me that he hadn't so much as twitched since he saw me. As I risked eye contact once more, I began to look carefully, realizing that I saw no signs of life at all. I tested the theory by rocking slowly from side to side and saw no pupil movement. I could see Huck mouthing to me, "What are you doing?" I pushed my way through the racks to the checkout station, again noticing no movement from the clerk. I peered over the desk and surmised what had transpired, seeing an empty bottle on the floor.

"Tainted hooch," I said out loud to Huck.

Huck turned around and was startled, only seeing the clerk for the first time. "Whoa!"

"He's dead. Died with his eyes open. Let's get what we need and get the hell out of here before they hang this on us."

"Yeah," said Huck, struggling to look away from the man's corpse.

We grabbed the suits that looked like our size, then headed to the rack of helmets, boots, and gloves and selected those as well. The odor and thickness of the air were still off-putting, but my thoughts were of concern for the dead clerk. I wondered under what conditions for his demotion were. Was his drinking a result of his situation or the cause? Did he have family or friends that would miss him? I wished I could do something but could think of nothing that wouldn't make our theft appear even more suspicious. Huck and I grabbed tool belts and, after a glance to see if the coast was clear, headed out the hatch and had an uneventful trip back to the elevator. We carried the gear through the dorms in recycling bags to disguise their appearance and limit suspicions of their smell.

We reached my dorm first, Arjun busting out the hatch to embrace me. Huck soberly waved goodbye, feeling the same heaviness that I was, and we parted ways until the next stage of our mission. For people who would become so familiar with death, we sure were uncomfortable with it.

CHAPTER 12: GUILHERME

Three Days. That's how long Huck and his friends had to discover something helpful from the magnetic tapes before their release. Even with all of the planning, I still found every aspect of the heist disconcerting. I justified my actions knowing the tapes were the key to increasing their odds of survival and my mission's success. None of the regents associated with candidates, just like the citizens avoided the laborers. We each had our social castes and stuck to our circles within them. My apathy had kept me detached from the candidates, easily allowing their cohorts to head off to their Release Day demise without much of a thought. But Huck and his companions were growing on me.

Since losing Aline, I had all but ceased social activities. The senior staff didn't seem to notice or care. I found the interactions with Huck refreshing after the social dormancy. With newfound optimism, I felt more energetic and vivacious, a feeling that would last provided they didn't catch me stealing the tapes from the vault.

The prime minister's duty was to heavily scrutinize officers, holding them to a higher ethical standard than the average citizen. It was a practice that had clearly fallen to the wayside, but would undoubtedly be employed should they catch me. For us, there was no demotion to laborers. The punishment for almost every conceivable crime was banishment. Unlike citizens or candidates, we were given one item they weren't—a pill. If we chose, we had the option to bring our lives to an abrupt end. There was some redemptive dignity in this, akin to the archaic traditions of the samurai *seppuku*. Death being the great equalizer, our essence would be returned to the pod in the form of recycled nutrition, as were all residents. Admittedly, I had no desire to be banished or recycled. I wanted to see humanity permanently eradicate the inverts and return to our rightful place on the surface.

I headed to the Nucleus across one of the numerous retractable catwalks, taking me from the surrounding districts to the hub looming above. I stopped midway across and took in the lengthy view down. Regardless of how decrepit and confining the pod could feel at times, the sheer magnitude of its construction was still awe-inspiring when I took the time to appreciate it. It still amazed me that the First Builders had managed to create such marvels of engineering on a global scale while enduring attacking Arthropods. Standing here, I felt a wave of vertigo as I took in the 500-meter view down the central shaft, where a faint purplish glow barely illuminated the bottom. Taking my time to lean back from the rail, I continued the rest of the way across to the security station. The guard casually checked my likeness before depositing my punch card into the reader. He waved me on before I had the chance to recite my authorization code. I felt a flutter of momentary optimism. If security were this lackadaisical on the way out, this would be a walk in the recreation district.

It was always stifling and humid in the Pod Horizonte. I never knew how much was due to the nature of the pod or the climate of the region. Regardless, I was sweating profusely and silently hoped none of the senior staff would attribute the perspiration to anything other than the oppressive heat. I continued to round the corridors of the Nucleus until I arrived at the entrance to the vault. My presence among the pod's records was nothing suspicious. In addition to the catalog of mag tapes dating back to the earliest days of the pod, the restricted vault also included the architectural illustrations of the entire facility. I frequently referenced the diagrams and specifications when I proposed improvements to the systems. Unlike the tapes, I could check out the drafts and other materials. Inside the vault was a magnetic reader with an audiovisual tube that could be used to view the tapes. Upon leaving the vault, the circulation clerk would pat down each person as a matter of procedure. Despite having thought about it all night, I didn't have a plan in place for smuggling the tapes past him. Every conceivable idea had a slew of potential weak points. I was going to have to improvise.

As I neared the vault, the circulation clerk saluted me without standing. "Welcome, Major." Clifton and I had grown casual with each other over the years. But, like all clerks, his attention to detail and regulations was nearly infallible. Honestly, it was a trait I admired in him. He was one of the many candidates born in Pod Horizonte who had elected to return to the pod as a citizen years before my return. Being such a soft-spoken, calm-mannered man, I wondered how he had managed to stay alive during his pump house experience. I'm sure it involved his evident ingenuity and extensive research. He had always gone out of his way to be helpful and kind, but now I was plagued with guilt knowing I was about to deceive him and take advantage of our relationship.

After some small talk, I headed into the vault, which happily was just out of the visual range of his seat. The vault was around the exact center of the pod. It was one of the few circular rooms in the entire city. Between the meticulous nature of the clerk and the library's restricted access, it was one of the cleanest rooms in the city.

I paced around the exterior wall looking at all the mag tapes from the pod's three centuries of existence. I questioned whether the oldest ones would even hold up to viewing. The initial inhabitants created many of the smaller objects within the pod after the sealing of the gates. I wasn't sure if longevity was the highest priority in creating the archival storage, seeing as we had already surpassed the expected life cycle of the pod's construction. I ran my hands over the spines of the plastic clamshell cases, wondering what other hands had touched these over the years. I had a new appreciation for all the data stored within each of these rectangular prisms. After a few more minutes of strolling, I heard Clifton calling, "Let me know if you need anything," before presumably going back to a novel or ledger. Releasing the urgency of my situation, I quickly pulled myself out of the nostalgia and focused on my task. I identified the section I was searching for and selected the Release Day tapes from the last two years, four tapes in total. I removed them from their cases and spread them out in my tattered uniform's various pockets to limit any noticeable bulk before returning the empty clamshells to the dustless shelves. I grabbed a blueprint of the recycling center's decomposition housing to avoid suspicion before ducking through the hatch to the check-out desk.

I laid down the draft as the wizened clerk began the check-out procedure, silently praying that the thickness of the uniform would prevent him from feeling the tapes during the pat-down. Desperate for ideas, I noticed he had precariously perched his tea on his desk. After handing my back the tube containing the drawing, I clumsily swung it around, knocking the drink into his lap. The scalding beverage must have burned intensely, judging by the surprising speed with which his aged frame moved. What I hadn't accounted for was in his haste to end his discomfort, he barreled through me. Unprepared for his desperate advance, he knocked me to the ground. I watched in horror as the tape from my right breast pocket skipped out across the floor, incriminating me. I froze. Seemingly oblivious to pain, Clifton reached down and picked up the tape. I slowly pushed myself up off of the floor to face him with what little dignity I had remaining. We made eye contact over his half-moon glasses, and in my peripheral vision, I could see him rhythmically tapping the cassette on his palm. He reached over and silently tucked the tape back into my pocket, buttoning it and patting it for good measure.

"I trust you'll have it back before anyone misses it."

I nodded, my mouth too dry to voice a response. Clifton smiled and waved me on. I was out through the hatch before I felt as though I could breathe again. He had me, and we both knew it. There was no way I could've known it beforehand, but he had trusted me. He understood why I had intentionally soaked him in scalding tea, but I regretted that I hadn't had the presence of mind to apologize. I booked it towards the outer perimeter of the Nucleus to hand off the tapes to Huck and Hemant, who should be arriving soon. I could count on a thorough security sweep upon leaving the Nucleus. If they caught me with any contraband, my choice would be the quick pill or a long walk. There was no point in expecting any of the leniency I had received from the vault clerk.

Struggling to keep my pace regular, I guided myself towards the level's maintenance hatches where Huck and I had agreed to rendezvous. While it was unheard of for laborers to socialize with officers, it wasn't unusual to find a member of the senior staff dressing down a laborer for the slightest misstep. I saw the slatted ovular hatches ahead and pondered how to look inconspicuous while I waited for the handoff when I saw a conveniently located snack kiosk. I sat down and ordered some *pão de queijo* and attempted to return my respiration and heart rate to their normal levels. The *pão* arrived, and like everything else, it tasted overly recycled. Though at the moment, blandness was precisely what I was craving most.

As it turned out, my appetite hadn't been what I expected. I couldn't even make it through the first bun. Maybe it was nerves. It didn't help that the boys were late. Really late. I wasn't completely aware of what security measures were present in an active tunnel, but all I could hope was that they could handle it. Maybe I put too much responsibility on them. I needed their help and trusted that I had chosen them wisely, but it was challenging to avoid fearing the worst. If something happened to them, not only would the plan unravel, but I wouldn't forgive myself for bringing about their punishment. I would face any consequences honorably, for they would be just.

CHAPTER 13: HUCK

Zeke and I returned to our dorm after a delectable dinner from one of the higher-level eateries. With pockets full of ration points and three days until Release Day, we had been determined not to eat the standard fare again. In a matter of hours, it was highly likely we would be dead. Why spend our last meals eating gruel? Craving Bhopali food, we had spent liberally on endless helpings of garlic *naan* and *murgh makhani*. We were fully aware that the cooks made the food from the same rudimentary components as almost every other dish in the pod, but that didn't negatively affect the satisfaction radiating from our content distended bellies. During the trip back to the dorm, I had sought out every failed one hidden away in the dark corners of the district. I handed each a handful of points, hoping they'd be more likely to spend it on food as opposed to hooch or worse—Dust. Mentally healthy or not, I had chosen to ignore the impending danger as long as possible, choosing instead to enjoy my last days in the pod to the fullest. Arjun had no appetite due to anxiety, but my body had the opposite reaction. They would need to roll me up the incline on Release Day at this rate.

We paused at the railing circumferencing the central shaft, staring up at the specs of natural light raining down from the near infinitesimal viewports surrounding the Nucleus so many levels above. Part of me couldn't wait to experience the outdoors with every sense I had. Sure, the Arthropods were up there, but so was freedom and nature that encompassed our forefathers. Zeke leaned back against the barrier next to me, his thin frame not posing any threat to its durability but making me uncomfortable nonetheless, considering the length of the fall should it fail.

"You thinking about the surface again?" Zeke asked.

"Of course. I can't help but be optimistic about what's out there. We weren't meant to live underground. The more I think about it; I'm glad I'm not heading to Bogota. It felt like I was supposed to do, but not what I wanted to do. We have a real mission, a chance to make a real difference, and I'm thrilled about it, which isn't something I could say for Bogota." I looked Zeke in the face. "Did the matriarchs ever tell you the story of *The Nine Companions?*"

"No, but I've heard of it. I'm not a fan of fantasy. I don't like the idea that some people have special abilities when others don't."

"And how is that different from here?" I said, gesturing towards the Nucleus towering above.

"Fair point," said Zeke. "What's it about?"

"These small, simple folk have this insane mission traveling across the land to destroy a powerful ring. Yet, despite all the enemies and odds stacked against them, they do it, saving everyone in the process."

"So you're comparing us to these *little people?*"

"Yeah, but we stand a better chance. We're bigger. And better trained."

We laughed loudly, bringing some stares.

"Come on," said Zeke. "Speaking of missions, you and Hemant have a little something you guys have to do."

"Yeah. It's about that time."

We walked the remaining stretch to the dorm. No sooner than Zeke closed the hatch, I pulled out the bag containing the maintenance suit from under my bed.

"Man, I wish there was somewhere else you could keep those things," Zeke said, holding his nose.

"I know," I said. "It'll be out of here in a second."

A knock made both of us jump. I knew it was just Hemant, but I covered the incriminating bag with my laundry to be safe.

Zeke casually smacked the controls as a candidate taller than Hemant, sporting a similar build and a shaved head, barged in.

"Who the hell are you?"

Without answering, he picked up several of the drawings I had laid out. "Garbage," he said and flicked the top sketch onto the floor. "Garbage," he repeated the action and continued until he had carelessly thrown all my work onto the ground. Then, he scanned the room as if looking for more of my things to trash.

"Here's the deal," he said, staring us down. "If you numskulls get in my way on Release Day, I'll kill you myself. So there. You've been warned."

"What the hell, man?" Zeke objected. "We don't even know you."

He pushed his sturdy finger into Zeke's chest, forcing him into the wall—hard.

"It doesn't matter to you, *larva*. Just stay the hell out of my way. Clear?"

Zeke nodded. He turned to me, and after a brief staredown, I nodded as well. *Asshole*. I wouldn't mind if two dusters flew off with him the second he left the pod.

"Good," he said, sniffing. "It stinks in here." He turned and walked out before I could say anything else.

"What in the world was that about?!" Zeke asked.

"I have no idea!" I replied as Hemant walked in with his bag over his shoulder.

"Are all Beta guys on a power trip like that? I asked.

"Beta, I figured he was from Delta," Zeke said.

"He's actually from Gamma, and his name's Omar. Something sketchy about that dude," Hemant said, just seeing the mess on my floor. "Everything okay?"

"I suppose so. That was strange." I uncovered my bag and hoisted it onto my shoulder. "I'll explain on the way."

"I'll get your stuff cleaned up, Huck," said Zeke.

"Thanks, man," I said. I nodded to Zeke, and we headed off toward the lower access points for the Nucleus' maintenance hatches.

•••••••••

Hemant and I dropped the foul-smelling bags onto the concrete floor, having just arrived on the maintenance subfloor below the central forum. From here, we would ascend the network of maintenance tunnels to the Nucleus, which allowed the laborers to work out of sight of those who didn't wish to interact with them. Considering the laborers' amount of time in the vents, I doubted that they ever needed a map. We weren't so fortunate. I slipped my hand into my pocket, satisfying my paranoia that Memo's diagram was still there. The tunnels were foreign to me, and I had no idea what obstacles might lay in wait for us. Under normal circumstances, Memo had said that master control would shut down the tunnels for maintenance. However, because this was an unsanctioned excursion, we would be working within active shafts. My mind had drifted more than once to the thought of a spinning ventilation fan turning me into a fine mist, but with effort, I pushed the negative thought out of my head.

The access area below the forum was low ceilinged and, thankfully, deserted. We pulled the gear from the bags, again stifling our gag reflexes as we hunched over to avoid banging our heads on the conduits above. When this was over, I would take a long, cleansing shower. Once we had the suits, boots, and helmets laid out, we stashed the bags behind the nearest tube. I wasn't looking forward to donning the helmet and breathing through a filter, undoubtedly far past its service period. The suits were bulky, and it was apparent that dexterity hadn't been a consideration in their design. The suits creator's needed general-use apparel, so whether you were unloading spent fuel rods or changing out a light fixture, this was what laborers wore. We found out the hard way that suiting up was not a one-person job. Getting into the mounds of fabric that composed the suit was the easiest part. Hemant helped me stand and get my suit sealed up. I stepped into my boots, only lacking the helmet, which I was putting off until the last possible second.

"Now the hard part," I said, turning to Hemant.

Hemant had already wriggled into his suit and was struggling to stand, the tug of gravity pulling him down towards the earth. I reached out to help him up.

"Hold still," I said, fumbling with the zipper. "You'd think they'd make these pull tabs larger."

Once I finally grabbed hold of the tab, I slowly and steadily pulled it up, determined not to lose it from my grasp. Without fail, the zipper slipped from my fingers several times in a cloud of curses before I finally managed to get it to the top. *I hope we aren't in a hurry when it comes time to remove them.* Hemant put on his boots, and we carefully reached over to grab our helmets in the top-heavy suits, silently cursing ourselves for not having placed them on a higher surface. I put the helmet over my head and wasn't disappointed by the odor. After a few deep breaths, I forced myself to tune it out and focus on the mission ahead.

"You ready?" Hemant's voice rang loudly through the garbled static. The suits were equipped with ultra short-range transmitters and receivers; though the signal quality was so poor even at this distance, we may have been better off using hand signals.

"I suppose," I replied, nudging the push-to-talk lever inside the helmet with my chin. "You are really loud, by the way." I saw Hemant smile.

Hemant leaned over and flipped out the latches on the nearest maintenance hatch. "After you," he said after hinging the panel down to the floor.

I leaned down and stuck my head into the pitch-black shaft. "How do you turn the helmet lights on?"

"Hold on. I see a switch on the back of your helmet." I felt a little pressure and watched as Hemant cycled through the red, then blue options before settling on the white beams.

I backed out of the tunnel to return the favor, temporarily blinding Hemant in the process before climbing into the tunnel.

The tunnel's long, smooth, vertical walls were sporadically interrupted by tight seams, access panels, and side tunnels. The tube appeared to ascend infinitely. The Nucleus was there, somewhere far above us, hidden within the labyrinth of tunnels. I pulled out Memo's diagram and committed the next few intersections to memory before placing it back into the sealed breast pocket of my suit, and we began our ascent. After several floors, my helmet had already started to fog with the condensation from my increased breathing and profuse sweating. The vapor was staying out of my field of vision but had made it difficult to view the periphery. Hemant and I limited our conversation, checking in with each other as little as possible due to fear of detection.

At the first intersection, I felt a sudden and powerful change in airflow, and Memo's comment about active tunnels resurfaced in my mind. Fortunately, the draft was coming from behind, making our climb thankfully easier. As the hot, stagnant air dissipated, we noticed the vapor within our helmets subsiding. The positive change refreshed us, quickening our pace. Hemant and I stopped at a well-placed landing at the halfway point.

"Dude, I'm starving," Hemant said, breaking our stint of radio silence.

"Same," I said. "But even if I could eat in this helmet, I don't want to."

"Agreed. How much do we have left to go?"

I pulled out Memo's diagram and referenced it once more. "It looks like we're about five floors away from the vault. According to this, we will encounter some security measures soon. Memo said he wasn't even privy to the exact measures but assured me that he had confidence that Hemant and I could bypass them based on other systems he knew. Unlike Zeke, I had never been particularly adept at hands-on work, but with the plethora of tools at my belt, I was hoping we could figure something out with our combined knowledge.

After catching our breath, we continued our journey up. The draft vanished, and again we felt the excessive weight of our apparel and the encroaching vapor across our lenses. Long before we arrived at our destination, we heard the first security measure of our trip. We treaded slowly until we could see the threat. An aperture-style hatch sat about two meters above us, opening and shutting in quick alternating intervals. *One, one thousand; two, one thousand.* I said in my head before the blades shut again. Two seconds. Not long enough to move our entire suited bodies through the opening. I wasn't sure how much protection the suit would provide, but I was positive that the blades of the iris wouldn't slow down as they sliced my body into two distinct halves. I looked down the ladder at Hemant through my legs.

"What do you propose?" I asked. We couldn't hang here forever. My arms were already burning from the climb, as I'm sure were Hemant's.

"Maybe that panel to your right? If that doesn't work, we can try jamming a screwdriver in and hope it doesn't trigger an alarm."

That's a fun thought. Racing through a blade of death, hoping a centimeter-wide shaft of metal lasts long enough to keep us in one piece. I clipped the safety carabiner to the ladder and leaned over. The bolts of the panel had years of crust from oxidation. I hoped to get them off without shearing their heads, a difficult task even with good tools. I fished in my belt for the ratchet, which was easy enough to find, then dug out heads until I managed to match up the right size for the bolts and began to work. The rectangular panel was only held in place by six bolts. The first three came out quickly and went straight into my pocket. Corrosion froze the fourth one in place, so I removed the last of the bolts before coming back to it. After several minutes, I wrenched the head clean off the shaft. I returned the tool to my belt and started prying the plate with my hands. Despite being recessed into the wall, the panel flexed enough to wedge my gloved fingers under it and use the leverage to remove it. I passed it down to Hemant, who reached out to grab it with his bulky gloves and lost his grip. The panel fell onto his knee before sliding off and bouncing violently and noisily down the shaft.

"Are you okay?!" I yelled. The panel had weighed six or seven kilos and seemed to have hit him directly in the knee.

"*Arrrgh.* Don't know. Someone probably heard that." He pulled his free hand back from his leg. Blood was already pooling into the fibers of his suit.

"I'm not worried about who heard! Get your first aid pouch, left pocket!" I watched as he struggled to get out the gauze before deftly wrapping it around his leg. *I'll give it to Hemant; he knows field medicine.* "What do you need?"

"To get this over with!" he said.

"Can you go on?" I asked, receiving a scowl in return. "Okay. On it."

I refocused on the panel and found the electrical controls to the aperture above. At that moment, I was eternally grateful for the minimal core training I had received in electric circuitry. Without a better solution, I cut the wire and held my breath. The aperture had just begun to close and froze in place, the blades only centimeters out from their recesses.

"I'm assuming you timed that, Huck."

I shrugged in response, sensing some anger from Hemant. I shrugged it off and continued the never-ending climb. We found another outcropping at the next intersection, and while smaller than the previous landing, it provided us with a much-needed opportunity for Hemant to properly dress his wound. He had already soaked through the first bandage, so I gave him the gauze from my kit, hoping to avoid additional injuries.

"We can't go back this way," I finally admitted.

"I know,' he said. "How are we supposed to get past Nucleus security?"

"I don't know. I'll think of something. Let's just get to the damn handoff."

"These tapes better be worth it," Hemant said.

"I have to believe they are," I said. "Can you move?"

Hemant nodded. We reluctantly climbed back onto the ladder and, with the breeze again urging us onward, climbed until we reached the floor below our destination.

"According to the diagram, we are just on the other side of the vents from Memo. We are almost 45 minutes late. He's going to be pissed."

"He's not the one crawling through hot-as-hell ductwork and slice-happy hatches. Can we please get this over with?"

I pointed up at the impregnable security hatch and the pin-card authorization slot. "Any bright ideas?"

CHAPTER 14: ARIADNE

I flew up the flight of stairs to Nikos' dorm, hearing the distinct buzz of the lights in the background as they bathed the stairwell in their greenish hue. It felt like forever since I had seen him, and I couldn't wait to wrap my arms around the warmth of his body. The stairs helped burn off the pent-up energy I had from anticipating the upcoming release, not to mention, taking the elevator up one floor seemed silly. I arrived early to our arranged rendezvous, hoping to surprise him. As the stairs doubled back, I heard his voice saying my name. I slowed my pace thinking I would catch him saying something sweet but his words froze me in place.

"...she'd die before she'd let an invert take me. That'd save me the trouble. Why bother breaking it off when she probably won't survive anyway. At least her friend Krista put out. If there's a chance I'm not going to survive, I want to try *everything* life has to offer."

Krista? I asked myself as I felt my heart shatter. My best friend. My roommate. My confidant. I had seen them hanging out together but never imagined the two people I cared about most tearing me apart. My heart was broken, but my face burned. Surging forth instead of tears was anger. Raw, unbridled anger. I stormed up the stairs to confront him and found him talking to Omar and his cadre. I could feel Omar and his friends drooling excitedly over the drama that was about to ensue. I didn't want to give them the pleasure of a performance, but I was far past the point of caring. Fueled by passion, I slammed Nikos hard against the wall, something under different circumstances I might have enjoyed. I knew it had the desired painful effect when I heard the breath whoosh out from his lungs.

"Ariadne —," he wheezed.

"Don't speak to me. Ever again."

I had always been more committed to my training than Nikos ever was. He could stand his own ground, but I had always been the better fighter—a fact he was about to understand thoroughly. I swung as hard as I could, connecting with his face and feeling his jaw snap beneath my knuckles. After that, all I saw was red.

·········

When I returned to my senses, I was sitting in the Resolution Chamber with Professor Lucas speaking calmly to me. I felt as though I was emerging from a coma.

"Ariadne, what happened to you?"

"What happened?" I asked, unsure what exactly had transpired.

"You nearly killed him. You injured Nikos so badly that they are delaying his Release Day until the next heat. That's extremely rare," Lucas said, pushing his chair back from the stainless steel table. "Jesus, Ariadne."

"What happened?" I repeated.

"You really don't remember, do you?" He breathed out slowly, running his fingers through his damp curly hair. "Okay, where do I start? *Hmm.* A candidate ran up to me, gasping for breath and begging for me to follow her. I could tell it was an emergency, so I followed her. When I arrived, I found you pummeling the piss out of the one which I presumed was your boyfriend. With Omar's help, we pulled you off of him. Ariadne, when I saw Nikos, I *barely* recognized him."

The tears that had evaded me early found me. They were pouring down my face in a deluge that could submerge the lower levels. I had lost control and snapped. Something that had never happened to me. Never. The memories of Nikos and Krista suddenly flooded back in a frenzy, and again, my anger began to seethe.

"Ariadne—"

"Stop saying my name like that! It's patronizing!"

"I'm sorry. This is just a side of you I've never seen before. I don't know what led to this, but you *will* be held accountable for your actions. You have to face the Tribunal Council. I can help you through the process, and maybe we keep the punishment minor with Release Day days away, but I have to know what happened."

So I told him. I told him everything, including how I felt at fault for adhering so strictly to the candidate guidelines. After teaching me my entire life, Professor Lucas had become like the parents that I wasn't allowed to have. Because I trusted him, I couldn't stop hemorrhaging information. Probably far more than he cared to know. Before it was over, he had come around the table and was embracing me from the side. He brushed the hair out of my face that was clung to my cheeks with tears.

"I'm sorry about all of that. It doesn't excuse your response, but I'm sorry you had to deal with that situation." He hugged me again. "We'll talk about the tribunal in the morning when you've had a chance to get some rest and compose yourself, okay?" He stepped out, leaving the door open. A pod security guard came in and told me they were honoring Lucas' request to release me on my own recognizance until the council summoned me. I expected a long, lonely walk back to the dorm, but Krista caught me off guard when I found her waiting in the drab lobby of the chamber. She had been bawling as much as I had. Any other time, I would've run to comfort her, but not this time. Not ever again.

"Ariadne, I —"

"Don't! Don't you ever come near me or speak to me again. I don't care where you sleep tonight, but it sure as hell better not be our dorm." She began sobbing into her hands. I didn't care. I pushed past her, bumping my shoulder into hers, and headed out the chamber's hatch.

I started down the corridor from the Nucleus where the chamber was, trying to wipe the tears from my face and look somewhat normal in the throngs of citizens going about their business. I still received a few strange looks, but I pushed myself on. I had barely reached the end of the Nucleus' catwalk when I was slammed into the railing by what felt like a freight train. I lost my balance and found myself face down on the floor grating. I peeled myself up in time to see a candidate in a bulky orange maintenance suit sprinting as fast as the cumbersome apparel would allow.

"What the hell?" I said to myself, knowing he was too far ahead to hear.

I felt an arm around my bicep, quickly jerking me up. It was another candidate, this one in the same stupid suit. Even through the helmet's foggy shield, I could see his rugged, wheatish complexion, though not quite as dark as Krista. Krista. I felt the heat returning.

"You okay?"

I nodded.

"Sorry. I, uh, have to go." Then he took off after the other one, his speed noticeably slowed by a limp.

I stood up, leaning against the barrier, wondering what the ordeal was about when again, someone slammed me to the side. This time I managed to keep my balance, stifling a yell as I reeled from the pain in my side. This time it was a security guard who had thrown me into the railing, giving pursuit to the two candidates in work gear. Again, I struggled to wrap my mind around what was going on. I had just experienced one of the most emotionally painful days of my life, and oddly I found myself in another unusual situation.

I didn't black out again, but I didn't remember the rest of the walk back to the dorm. I went straight to bed, turning out the lights on the way. My mind wandered to the tribunal. I had no idea what to expect as a sentence this close to Release Day. I pushed the concerns out of my head and tried to relax. I just wanted to sleep. Even with only the faint night illumination on, I could still make out the dark images on the wall that composed more than a decade of memories with my former best friend. I pulled the rough spun blanket over my head and cried myself to sleep.

CHAPTER 15: HEMANT

It took significant effort to ignore the intense pain in my leg and move near my full velocity. I was quick for a stocky guy, even with a full loadout. The problem is now I was running in a baggy twenty-kilo suit with a deep laceration on one leg. It wasn't remotely optimal for running from untold numbers of highly-trained security guards. The last time I bothered to look, I had only seen one. Thankfully, we knew the district layouts well, and we were doing everything in our power to slow the guards' progress by slinging down plastic food crates, metal clothing racks, and anything within our grasp. There were closed-circuit camera boxes throughout the pod, but Huck (who I could no longer see) and I hadn't taken off our helmets. We must have been quite a sight.

When we'd been back in the tunnel, we had been blocked just outside the maintenance area where we were supposed to meet the major. Huck was as perplexed as I was at how we would bypass the secured access hatch. We had just started to toss back and forth ideas when the hatch opened before us and the major extended his hand to help us up. As much as I appreciated the help, he almost pulled my shoulder from its socket, yanking me from the tube. I hadn't realized just how strong he must have been under his uniform. For the next few minutes, I enjoyed prolific pain in my leg and shoulder.

"What the hell were you doing down there?! You're lucky the entire security platoon didn't hear all that commotion! I knew it was you two amateurs immediately! What the hell was I thinking?! You'd better be bloody ecstatic you're both so late that everyone just happened to have gone to lunch!"

I knew it was part of the plan to be dressed down while he slipped us the tapes, but this felt more authentic than I had anticipated.

"What are you talking about?!" I asked, "We've committed as many risks as you! We stole these stupid, stinking suits and climbed up who knows how many floors to fetch these tapes! I know we aren't perfect, but what exactly have you done?"

"I betrayed a friend, for starters," said the major.

He walked away in a forlorn huff and plopped down on a stool at a nearby kiosk in front of some half-eaten bread. Huck walked over to him.

"Major?" Huck asked.

"What?" replied the major.

"Um, the tapes," Huck whispered.

A light seemed to have turned on, and his tension slightly dissipated.

"I'm sorry, guys," he said, keeping his voice low. "Look, we've both made sacrifices. Let's try this again."

He rebounded quickly and began berating us again, this time with finger-wagging. Thankfully, this time it seemed more scripted and less personal. I felt terrible that we hadn't been as successful as we hoped so far in our mission, but it appeared everything was still, for the most part, going to plan, aside from my injury. He concluded his performance with rifling through Huck's bag, within which he deposited four tapes.

Even with the pain, annoyance, and exhaustion, the optimistic feeling I had seeing those tapes in our possession made my heart leap. On those tapes was hope. The moment was short-lived, as people began filtering back into the space, sporadically coming off of their lunch breaks. The major subtly gestured for us to get lost back down the vents. He immediately saw our hesitation, looked at my leg, and put two and two together. He nodded and headed back to his bread, looking fed up with us.

Huck kneeled and replaced the tunnel cover before we headed out of the space, trying our best not to make eye contact with anyone. Maintenance workers were a reasonably common sight throughout the pod, but they usually remained out of sight. Attempting to walk out of the Nucleus from one of the primary entryways was a little ballsy, but we didn't have much choice. We were going to play the injured-worker sympathy card. Huck led the way down the stairs as we headed towards what seemed to be the most crowded entry/exit ramp, hoping to hide among the numerous people.

Good thinking. I would've told Huck, but we were maintaining complete radio silence. We had no idea who might be listening. I would've headed for the least populated thoroughfare had I been on my own, but that might attract more attention if I couldn't blend in with any crowds.

We stepped out onto the landing of the Nucleus' primary civilian floor. Civilians were allowed into the Nucleus for a handful of reasons, with most of them being legal related. Today was a somewhat busy day, judging by the large numbers of people filing through the depressing space painted with the icky green hues the First Builders found so attractive. The area reminded me of the pre-landing pictures of the bustling megacity metros, complete with the ticket kiosks, which were, in this case, pod security checking for entry clearance. Fortunately for us, the exiting traffic didn't appear to be going through any type of checks. We merged into that queue and bided our time, praying that everyone would assume we were just two on-duty laborers. We were minutes from being home-free. Unfortunately, right when we were about to step out through the double-doored hatch, our luck ran out.

"You two! Stop for a moment," a clerk of some sort yelled at us.

We slowly stopped and turned, glancing at each other as we did. A nasally-voiced runt of a man was hailing us. My initial thought was, "*This* is the guy that's going to bring us down?"

"I have no scheduled maintenance in this area today," he said, looking through the crumpled papers on his clipboard. "Take off your helmets and show me your identification and work order."

Huck stepped forward. Huck had a way with words and a winning personality, but I didn't know how he would get us out of this one. "My partner's hurt. We need to get him to a medic immediately."

"He's sufficiently bandaged," the balding clerk said. "You have enough time to provide me with the requested documents. Now remove your helmets, lest I shall have to summon a guard."

What an ass. I confess I hadn't lost much sleep thinking about the burdens of the laborers, but here I was, seriously hurt, and this clerk on a power trip was refusing to allow me adequate treatment because of my social caste. I made a mental note to be kinder to laborers in the future.

Huck raised his arms to take off his helmet, then tugged my arm, and we sprinted out of the large hatch and down the catwalk through the throngs of people.

"Stupid, stupid, stupid," I muttered within the confines of my helmet. I knew we were in trouble standing there but running? Had Huck seen my leg? The pain was throbbing, and I tried my best to ignore it, hoping I wasn't bleeding out into the fabric of the heavy suit. I knew I could rest when we were safe, so I pushed on, hoping it wouldn't be detrimental to my health. Behind me, I heard the half-pint man frantically summoning security and listened to the scuffle and grunts of displeasure behind me, indicating that others were pushing their way through the crowds. Ahead of me, I saw Huck barrel through a female candidate roughly our age with the green armband of Gamma. She was struggling to rise, and I saw the crowd of people on the relatively narrow catwalk was getting perilously close to trampling her. As quickly as I could, I reached down to help her up, and after making sure she was alright, I sprinted off again. *God, the pain.*

Running through the floor's market district, I noticed that the wares here were substantially higher quality than those displayed on our levels. I didn't exactly have time to stop and examine the prices, but I was pretty sure they matched the quality. *Not that it matters,* I thought as I slung another table into the pursuing guard's way. I heard the shopkeeper screaming obscenities disputing my heritage. I suppressed the guilt I felt for the damage I was causing to the vendors' products. I ran past stall after stall, weaving back and forth, trying to lose the guards. I finally rounded a large bend and ducked into the shadows. As long as they weren't searching by smell, I felt safe for the moment. Sure enough, I watched through the mesh walls of the nearest stalls as three confused guards kicked over some fruit crates in frustration at losing their prey. I allowed myself a sigh of relief and was once again reminded just how much I wanted to be free from this suit.

Realizing that I was in a blind zone of the cameras, I went ahead and fumbled at the helmet's latches around my neck. Getting them open with the swollen fingers of the gloves was a daunting task, but after some struggling, I accomplished it. *Jesus, fresh air tasted good!* I flung off my boots and realized with an alarm; I had left my standard-issue boots at the base of the access tunnels. I silently cursed myself when I realized I would be walking back barefoot. I slapped at my back, desperately trying to reach the zipper tab for the body of the suit, reminding me of Memo's callous yank on my shoulder. I finally grabbed the strap that functioned as the zipper pull and yanked it down. I clamored out of the suit as though it was on fire. Slowly cooling sweat saturated my jumpsuit, but man, it felt good to be free. The moment was short-lived when I felt the stream of wetness on my thigh. I looked down, realizing that I had bandaged my wound over my suit. The same suit I had just removed. The clothier at the nearest stall was helping the adjacent stall owner straighten up the damage done by the guard. Adding theft to my growing list of infractions, I stole a red natural-fiber scarf to use as a tourniquet for my dripping leg and grabbed a pair of feminine slippers to give me at least some protection from the harsh grating of the city's floors.

Stashing the suit into the nearest maintenance closet, I headed home along the least populated route I could conceive. Finally, after over an hour of sneaking around and many strange looks, I made it back to my dorm, where a much-relieved Arjun greeted me.

"Brother! I'm so glad you are back!" he said, embracing me. I felt a trembling in his thin frame and knew my absence had affected him more than he let on. "Since Huck arrived, we've been growing more and more concerned that they caught you. He looked me up and down, checking for injuries. Vishnu, help us! You need a medic!" He looked at Huck.

"On it!" Huck said, flying to the door. "I know someone we can trust."

"I helped him get his suit off. We threw it in the bin of one of the younger cohorts.

"You should've hidden it in Omar's recycling," I said, smirking. "He terrorizes all the candidates. The least we could do is return the favor."

Arjun laughed. "Do you have the tapes?"

"Yeah. Here they are," I said, handing him my bag.

"I'll sneak into the Epsilon lab tonight. There's a multi-head cassette reader there."

"Please hurry," I said. "Release Day is only three days away."

"I haven't forgotten. I'll have something for you tomorrow."

Huck returned with Jerome, one of Delta's medics. Jerome's eyes widened when he saw my wound. He made me sit up and quickly got to work. Twenty minutes later, I was stitched and patched up and given meds to keep any infection at bay.

"You're lucky it didn't hit bone," Jerome said. "I don't know that you would've had a chance come Release Day given that. If you guys don't need anything else, I'm heading out. Please try not to get hurt again between now and then, okay?"

I nodded. "Thank you, Jerome. For this and your discretion," I said, handing him a cluster of ration points.

"Sure thing," he said, smiling as he ducked out the hatch.

Huck turned to me. "Man, I'm glad you're okay! I didn't mean to abandon you. I turned around and realized I'd lost you. I knew we'd be headed to the same place and hoped you'd make your way back safely. Although I didn't expect you to arrive in those," he said, gesturing at my slippers.

"It's all good, man," I said, laughing. "Or at least it should be once Arjun plows through these tapes."

CHAPTER 16: GUILHERME

After the handoff, I made my way back to my office, though concentrating on my work had become an impossible task. Instead, my mind dwelt on whether or not the boys had reached safety. Knowing that Pod Horizonte was on its last leg only added to my distraction. I leaned back in my chair and stared up at the ceiling, exasperated. Still adhered to its surface was the handmade sign Aline had hung years ago that said: "Miss you!" I couldn't bring myself to remove it. I still deeply loved her, feeling the ache in my chest when I over thought about her absence. I hoped she had found happiness, though I was also a little jealous it hadn't been with me. I had only myself to blame, having spent all my time trying to prevent the pod from falling apart, only to have my marriage collapse, just like the pod would inevitably do. I questioned whether I had wasted my life, knowing full well I hadn't but allowing myself the moment of self-loathing. I hoped that what I was doing now would contribute more than my previously futile work ever had. I doubt anyone will ever see me as a hero, but I hoped Aline would.

I stood and walked to my little antique bar cart, taking a moment to appreciate the patinated brass and glass handicraft that was now so rare in the pod. After the day's events thus far, I desperately wanted a drink. I poured myself an upper-floor whisky, self-aggrandizingly called "Tier One." I planned to mix in some soda but decided to hell with it and drank it neat.

"Major Leal?" my intercom screamed, scaring the mess out of me.

"Y-Yes?" I stammered, waiting for my heartbeat to return to its normal rhythm.

"Prime Minister Carvalho would like to see you in his office. Now, if possible."

"That would be fine. I'll be there shortly."

But the intercom was already dead. Carvalho's assistant was not particularly chatty.

I rubbed the bridge of my nose, trying to think through the buzz that was already forming. If there was any reason the minister was meeting with me, I had forgotten it. I tried to remember if there was anything I needed to bring, but after not coming up with anything, I embarked empty-handed on the journey upward through the Nucleus. I took the stairs, having already spent too much of my life on automatic pilot. When I arrived at the prime minister's office, his assistant waved me in with a flick of his hand, never bothering to look up from his work.

A 360-year-old pod can only look so grandiose, but Carvalho's office was nothing if not posh. I understood that the most powerful person in the city needed to keep up appearances. Still, considering the working conditions of literally everyone else in the Nucleus, it seemed out of touch. Even the other regents' upscale offices looked dismal by comparison. Admittedly, I had opted for a less desirable space, but that was because I found that I could get significantly more work done without the frequent interruptions that were commonplace closer to the bridge. He frequently called in the regents to discuss developmental progress, allocate resources, or deal with judicial matters that ascended past the Tribunal Council. I wasn't a stranger to the space, but I had never felt comfortable there.

"Ah, Memo, a pleasure as always," said Carvalho, looking up from the slew of papers on his desk.

I never cared for the minister's insincerity. Or anyone's for that matter.

"How's Aline?"

"She left me," I said, putting my beret on the hat rack.

"Oh, so sorry about that. Drink?"

I declined with a wave of my hand, still trying to hide my already swimmy state from the whiskey I had just finished.

"I called you in because there was a security breach within the Nucleus. Two men, we believe either laborers or disguised as laborers, broke through a Nucleus checkpoint after being questioned by an official," Carvalho said, taking a sip of his drink. "There was no record of a maintenance request for that part of the Nucleus. On reviewing the footage, we found something interesting. When we tracked them back to where they got in, we found to my surprise—you—letting them in. Considering our decades of work together, I wanted to give you a chance to explain what transpired before I draw any conclusions."

"Understandably so. I admit it looks suspicious given the situation." The air in Carvalho's office was pleasantly cool, but I felt perspiration begin underneath my uniform. "I was getting something to eat when I heard a commotion within the access tunnel. I couldn't speak to any maintenance requests, but I decided to check it out. Ultimately, I determined that it was two intoxicated laborers. I tried to find evidence of their drinking in their toolbag but quickly gave up. I told them to get lost and finish their job when they were sober."

"See, I never doubted you for a second. I just needed the

clarification. You're dismissed. And sorry about Aline, old chap. There *are* others who love a man in uniform," said Carvalho, waggling his eyebrows.

Reigning in my disgust, I managed a salute and left. He couldn't seem to fathom that love could be a factor in a relationship. To him, a partner was like food, something to be consumed before moving on to the next dish. I suppose he had gotten too used to the idea of recycling. Yet, ironically, he was not immune from material degradation himself.

Walking out through Carvalho's office doors, I passed a down-on-his-luck man waiting for an audience with the prime minister. I was initially surprised that Carvalho would see someone of low social rank. Dismissing the thought, I took a step to continue when he glanced up, and I felt a spark of recognition. *The failed one!* It was the same one I used to send my message to Huck. *Damn sellout.* I quickened my pace and retreated to my office as fast as possible without raising suspicion.

Once to my little sanctuary, I collapsed into the worn cushions of the guest chair in front of my desk and began to hyperventilate. Running my fingers through my hair, I questioned what I had done. I struggled under the rising panic to see reason in the decisions that had led up to this point. I stumbled back to my cart and shakily poured another few fingers of whiskey into my glass before gulping it down. I sat back against the wall and waited for the depressant to have its desired effect. After some time had passed, my breathing began to slow, and my pulse returned to its normal level. Standing slowly, I walked behind my desk and stared at the schematics lying there. My eye drifted to the picture of Aline next to my drafting graphite. Despite no longer being together, she was still my inspiration for ceaselessly helping humanity. That same inspiration had spurred me to lay the groundwork for the Hive mission. Aline's likeness comforted me, and I knew I had made the right decision and would stand by it. I only hoped that none of the blowback would affect Huck and his friends.

I pulled myself together and tried to think clearly. I realized that Carvalho only knew circumstantial information. He would know I sent a message to a candidate, and I think it was safe to assume that he knew that message's content, but he couldn't have known what went on in that meeting. By the time I had restored my composure, it was the end of standard office hours. I walked to the hanger on the back of the door and realized I had left my beret in Carvalho's office. I cursed myself for the oversight and begrudgingly began the trek back up to his office, praying he had already left for dinner or another romantic interlude.

Thankfully, his assistant had already left when I arrived, leading me to believe he had as well, but as I approached the ajar door, I heard his voice.

"—don't care," said the minister.

"But someone will notice!" cried a young, gruff voice.

"Don't worry about that. I don't want this *Huck* and his friends, whoever they are, to survive Release Day. That's final. I'm not clear on what Leal is up to, but it's only going to cause problems for us down the line."

"Problems for *us*, or problems for *you?*" the young voice asked.

I heard the distinct sound of a hard slap against skin.

"I don't care what your relationship is to me," Carvalho said. "You don't get to speak to me with disrespect! Make sure this guy and his chums don't leave the vicinity of Pod Horizonte alive, or consider yourself banished. I'll make damn sure no pod *ever* lets you in."

"Yes, sir."

"You know what to do and where to conceal yourself. Make. It. Happen."

I heard shuffling and realized they were getting up to leave. I darted over to the assistant's desk, which thankfully had a modesty panel that ran to the floor and hid underneath its work surface. The curiosity to see who he had been talking to was overwhelming, but I knew if Carvalho saw me, he would make sure I had a surface-side sightseeing tour before day's end. So I waited for what seemed like ages after they'd left before feeling safe enough to climb out and fetch my beret.

There was no longer much point in being meticulous in my deception, but it was still unproductive to be blatantly obvious. The minister knew about my alignment with Huck, but it was to my advantage that he didn't know that I knew. Technically, I was only diverting a few candidates on a Hail Mary attempt to solve our Arthropod problem, so I couldn't understand why there was any reason to prevent the mission aside from it not being sanctioned. It only added to my suspicions about something being amiss in the leadership of the pod. A problem which I suspected wasn't limited to Horizonte.

After swinging by my apartment to change into civvies, I made a beeline for Huck's place. I was dying to know if Arjun had figured anything out.

CHAPTER 17: HUCK

I was dying to meet up with Zeke and update him on all that had happened. When I had finally gotten back to the room, I found a message on our chalkboard saying he had gone for a run, so I changed out of my nasty jumpsuit and headed to the track to see if I could squeeze in a few laps with him. As much as I'd love to watch over Arjun's shoulder as he deciphered the accumulated information from the tapes, I knew the distraction would drive him nuts.

The walk back to my dorm had been surreal. It was as if every candidate in the upcoming heat was out, filling the corridors with raucous sounds and vibrant energy. With training complete and restlessness coming to a head, everyone had it in their mind to cut loose for the last few days of safety we had. I pushed through candidates slapping playfully, fondling intensely, and drinking profusely. At one point, a candidate thrust a bottle into my hands. I never was much for drinking, but I went ahead and took a swig. *Eh, what the hell.* Whatever the intense liquor was, I felt it warm my insides from my mouth to my stomach. I handed it back to the girl, thanking her, but she had already turned to offer it to someone else.

I continued to push through and made it to the market district, which for once was less crowded than usual. I continued toward the fitness area but was stopped by a hand grabbing my wrist. I looked down to see a wizened female shop vendor still sitting on her floor cushion, her gray hair curling out from under her embroidered shawl.

"Here. Take," the shopkeep said, tucking a small purple vial into my hand.

"I'm sorry. I'm not here to buy anything," I said as I tried to return the item to her.

"Not for buy. For take." She closed my fingers around it. It felt cool to the touch.

"What is it?"

"For to stop venom. Save you."

"Thank you," I said, confused. "Why are you giving me this?"

She struggled for words. "Feel promise," she said, touching my chest, "in you."

I graciously accepted the gift and pulled away gently. As I walked away, I turned to glance back and saw the woman smiling, her eyes glimmering in the dim light of the stall. I didn't understand why a woman of such simple means gave me something she clearly valued. It made the gift all the more meaningful. I tucked it into my upper jumpsuit pocket where it would stay safe. I knew there would be plenty of need for it come Release Day, and I wanted to have it handy.

I arrived at the track and saw Zeke plowing around it at his usual pace, far quicker than the average candidate. When he rounded the bend, I waved to him and mimed myself running. He motioned me to come on, so I jumped onto the track with him without bothering to change. Candidate jumpsuits were multifunctional, though like the laborer suits, were not perfect for any given task. It's the sacrifice you make for such adaptability. I pulled alongside Zeke, who had graciously slowed to an average human stride so that I could maintain the pace. Zeke was the fastest runner in the cohort, possibly in the pod, but was also modest enough not to show off.

"How'd it go?" he asked.

I filled him in on all that had happened—getting the tapes, Hemant's injury, the revelry in the corridors, the strange shopkeeper. He listened intently as I breathlessly relayed the information.

"That's great news about the tapes. After this, we should go check in with Arjun and see if he feels like there's anything useful. We can check in on Hemant too."

"Sounds like a plan," I said.

"I agree about the vial being helpful. That was kind of her to give it to you, Mr. Promise."

"Please don't make that a thing," I laughed.

"Whatever you say, Mr. Promise."

I punched him in the arm. "Can we shower first, though?"

"Sure. I'm pretty sure Arjun doesn't want us loitering around him smelling like this."

•••••••••

We met Hemant at his dorm, who guided us to the Epsilon lab. Considering all the festivities in the passages, we doubted that academics would be crowding the lab. Typically, candidates weren't permitted in the facilities of the other cohorts unless they were communal spaces like the arena. Thankfully, there wasn't a soul around to care. Hemant hobbled over to the access panel and punched in the code, each button making a satisfying click when depressed into the panel.

The hatch's hydraulics hissed as it swung open, and we proceeded in. Arjun was sitting with his back towards us on the far side of the room where the cassette reader was.

"Arjun," Hemant whispered, motioning for us not to make too much noise.

"Arjun," Hemant again whispered, but with more emphasis.

"Arjun," Hemant finally said in a normal voice.

We saw Arjun startle, nearly falling out of his chair. He spun around to face us, his face a deathly pale. We could see his hands trembling. His breath seemed to come in gasps.

"Arjun, what's wrong? Talk to me," I said, placing my hands on his forearms. "We didn't mean to scare you like that."

It was evident that the jump scare wasn't the only thing to blame on his near-catatonic state. He began speaking so softly we had to strain to hear.

"They're all massacres. Complete massacres. Everyone dies." He said, making eye contact with me. "Everyone!"

He began screaming and flailing. Hemant had to restrain him, but not before he had broken some glass flasks next to the station. Hemant finally was able to pin him to the floor, wrapping his arms around Arjun's shoulders. Thankful Arjun was the one panicking and not the other way around. I don't know how any of us could've restrained Hemant. I noticed Hemant's leg was bleeding again through his bandage, but he shrugged it off. I knew it was mostly an inconvenience for him, but I still felt a twinge of guilt every time I saw the injury. Once Arjun was calm, Hemant gradually let him up. In the meantime, Zeke had fished an electrolyte pouch from the lab's first aid kit and was administering it to Arjun. Arjun regained his composure and slowly began to speak again.

"I'm sorry. I don't know what came over me." The tears were streaming down his cheeks. "I began watching the first tape. The furthest one back chronologically. There's a lot of footage of the empty surface with no action. There is dialogue present over the footage, the audio feed from the bridge. There are different angles of the surface present on the tape, but I can't see any views from inside the pod. I sped through the footage until I began seeing candidates emerge. The Arthropods come. They just keep coming!"

Hemant jumped up and consoled Arjun, who then began to relax again.

"I'm sorry," said Arjun. "It's just I've never seen carnage like this. It's more violent than I ever could have imagined. It's hopeless."

"How is it hopeless?" I finally asked.

"The Arthropods come, the candidates fight, then the candidates die." Arjun paused. "I finished the first tape, and I didn't see any survivors. Not two in five, like the minister says. I saw none. None!"

We all sat there horrified.

"What about the other tapes?" Zeke asked. "There's got to be survivors from other Release Days. Surely that one was a fluke."

Arjun shook his head. "I scanned through all four tapes. I didn't see any survivors on any of them. The Arthropods are intelligent, coordinated, and relentless. It's an extermination, and the officials know it!"

We sat in stunned silence for ages.

Eventually, I broke the silence. "Did Memo know about this?"

"Not that I know of. I never heard his voice on the recordings. I need to scour the tapes, but it's hours of footage and audio, not including the various angles."

"Are you sure you are up to it?" Hemant asked his brother, obviously concerned.

"Yeah. Yes," said Arjun. "I have to be." He took a deep breath. "If we want any chance of survival, I have to find a way."

"People need to know about this," said Zeke. "They are sending us in waves of three hundred—"

"Six hundred," I interrupted.

Zeke continued, "They are sending us in waves of six hundred to our deaths. If everyone knew, there would be a revolt! We have to share this information!"

"I agree, but we should do it right," said Arjun. "I have an idea."

●●●●●●●●

Zeke and I left Arjun to his work. Hemant had elected to stay as emotional support for his brother, but not before swearing to stay out of Arjun's way. When I had left, it looked like he was falling asleep on the lab's couch, his fresh bandage free from the blemishes of new blood. I felt as though I was trapped in a time-dilating haze as I pushed through the inevitable crowds of boisterous candidates. Previously, Release Day had filled me with mixed emotions, knowing many of my companions wouldn't survive the week, but now I was overwhelmed knowing that everyone I was beholding would likely be dead in a matter of hours. What reason would the pod's administration possibly have for sending us all to our deaths? How far down did the corruption go? *Memo had to know, he's a regent for chrissake.*

I didn't have to wait long to confront him. As we approached our housing district, coming directly towards us was the major, looking all grins and dressed in what he thought passed for casual on our floor. The upper levels had distinct stylistic nuances and didn't exactly blend in with the middle levels.

"I'm so glad I found you," he said. "Can we go somewhere more private to speak?"

Neither of us was pleased to see him or in the mood for banter. Finally, I managed to eke out, "Yeah, we need to talk. Follow us."

I led the way down the side passage away from the enthusiastic celebrants and pulled the major into an abandoned common room. I checked the hall once more before locking the hatch. The room had portholes out to the corridor. Still, I felt as though the privacy would be more than sufficient, especially given that everyone seemed more interested in the camaraderie at the moment.

I turned on the major the second I felt comfortable doing so. "Why the *hell* didn't you tell us everyone dies?!"

I suppressed the desire to throw the man against the nearest bulkhead. I was pretty strong, but I'm pretty sure under his pressed pants and high-collared knit top, he would be stronger. Not to mention assaulting a senior officer carried with it a considerable sentence, not that it would be worse than our upcoming death sentence.

His smile vanished. "What do you mean *everyone dies?*"

"Everyone. Dies," I repeated. "Arjun has already seen enough of the videos to tell us there are no survivors from any of the last four releases."

"I-I-I-I had no idea." The major stuttered as he collapsed onto the nearby bench. "I knew the odds of survival were low, but that's why I wanted you to review the tapes. I wanted to ensure that you four survived to complete this mission. I promise I didn't know."

"You honestly had no idea? None?" asked Zeke, getting into the major's face.

"None whatsoever." Memo seemed visibly shaken. I believed him.

"How does a regent not know what has been happening every Release Day, for who knows how many years?" I asked.

"I haven't gone to the viewings in a long time, Huck," Leal said. "I'm invited, but I don't. I never wanted to witness the violence. I've always chosen to exist outside of the administrative atmosphere and lifestyle. I prefer to keep my head down and do my duty. As a result, I'm left out of many conversations. You have to believe me."

"I do," I said. "You've given me no reason not to." I sat down next to him as tears began to form in his eyes.

"If what you say is true, then your survival is even more of paramount importance," Memo said. "That's why I wanted to talk with you. I've plotted your route to the Hive."

CHAPTER 18: ARIADNE

I didn't sleep well. No surprise there. I didn't feel like facing the intense crowds of candidates down at the restaurants, eating like there was no tomorrow. Instead, I opted for breakfast takeout from the cafeteria. Without a doubt, I would be the only one. I put my hair back into a tight ponytail, slipped on my jumpsuit, and started in the direction of the cafeteria. I saw several candidates in the corridors, many hungover and under-rested. I hoped they would take a bit more precaution tonight. Tomorrow, a fuzzy head and a slight delay in reflexes could spell death. My mind wandered back to all the affection I had seen the night before, hoping they had all protected themselves. Not that it was any of my concern. Hiking across the globe under constant threat of attack was daunting enough without the side effects of pregnancy. Not to mention, I wasn't sure what other pod's policies were in regards to admitting infant-toting candidates.

I was surprised to see another candidate eating in the cafeteria. I'd recognize her distinct hairstyle anywhere. Krista. Of course, she would come here, though I was surprised that she wasn't eating breakfast with Nikos in his room in the infirmary—the little traitor. I kept my eyes directly focused on the food line. Fortunately for me, the cafeteria staff had given up on serving, and takeaway boxes were set out for easy grab and go. I picked one up, making a beeline for the door. Out of the corner of my eye, I caught Krista looking at me while fiddling with what appeared to be potatoes in some form. By the looks of things, she didn't have much appetite. It served her right.

Back at my dorm, my appetite eluded me as well. I knew I needed my strength, so I forced myself to eat as much as I could stomach before sitting back on my bunk. I shut my eyes and meditated, trying to bring some peace to my chaotic mind. After which, I ran through a tai chi routine, adapting for the cramped space so that I didn't have to leave the isolation the dorm provided. I was on the next to last pose when I heard a knock at the door.

"That better not be you, Krista. You can get whatever you need this afternoon when the council is trying me for nearly killing your lover."

"Ariadne, it's me, Professor Lucas."

I opened the hatch and saw Lucas leaning against the jamb.

"Glad to see you're up. We need to talk about the tribunal. I'm going to represent you."

"Um. Thank you."

"Don't thank me yet. I can't promise you anything but a fair hearing. You are guilty of the accusations they leveled against you. I will be called as a witness against you as well. I hope that we can avoid anything that amounts to a death sentence."

"Where do we start?"

"Let's head to one of the group study rooms, and I'll coach you through the process as well as explain how to conduct yourself during the trial. The thing to remember is what you don't say is just as important as what you do."

•••••••••

"The Tribunal Council of Pod Horizonte calls Candidate Ariadne of Cohort Gamma to justice," said one of the three council members. "I'm Grand Major Mota, next to me is Grand Major Leal, and lastly is Grand Major Ferreira."

At Professor Lucas' behest, we rose. "I'm Lucas Macedo, professor of Cohort Gamma, representing Candidate Ariadne."

"Professor Macedo, are you aware that according to the docket, you will be representing Candidate Ariadne and testifying both for and against her?" asked Major Mota.

"I am, your honor," said Lucas.

It was strange to hear Professor Lucas referred to by his last name. Most of the cohort leadership insisted that we call them by their title and first name, preferring the informality it carried with it. I was pleased to have a familiar face here with me, but it didn't reduce my nausea. Though the trial was open to all candidates and citizens, there had been no one in the spectator seating when I had come in. I had never been inside the council's chambers before. The space was spartan, the fluorescent lighting giving everyone an inhuman appearance. The council sat in an elevated position compared to our table, with the seating behind us. Tribunal cases had a reputation for being dealt with quickly, simply, and firmly. There was no appeal process.

The proceedings went on with the council listing my accusations, announcing that I had no prior disciplinary record and was in excellent standing within the cohort. If it weren't for the fact I was sitting in on my trial, I would have blushed from the praise. The only person admitted for the examination process was Professor Lucas. The council seemed to have no interest in dragging the case out.

"State your name again for the record," said Major Ferreira, who was leading the examination.

"My name is Professor Lucas Macedo."

"Let the record show once again that this is the same professor that is representing the candidate in question," said Major Ferreira. "Professor, did you witness the candidate physically attacking Candidate Nikos of Cohort Gamma?"

"Yes."

"Was she coming to a stop of her own accord?"

"No."

"Would she have stopped before she killed him?"

"Objection. Conjecture," said Major Leal.

Major Ferreira showed his palms to indicate he was backing off the line of questioning.

"Did you have to remove her from him forcefully?"

"Yes."

"And what is Candidate Nikos' current condition?"

"He's alive and expected to pull through."

"How close was he to death, Professor?"

"Objection. The professor isn't a medically-trained citizen," said Leal.

"Major Ferreira...," said Major Mota.

"In your opinion as a seasoned professor, did you believe his life was in danger?" Major Ferreira asked, looking at Leal for an objection that didn't come.

"Yes, I did."

"Thank you. Let the record show that the council will postpone Candidate Nikos' Release Day due to extenuating medical circumstances. That's all for me." Major Ferreira said, returning to his elevated seat as Major Leal stepped down to begin his line of questioning.

"Professor Lucas, as previously stated, I'm Grand Major Leal. I just have a few questions for you." Immediately, I noticed that Leal's persona was warmer and friendlier than Ferreira's, though I wasn't sure if that was because he had the more positive task.

"Does Candidate Ariadne generally get along with her peers?"

"Yes, she's an exemplary candidate."

"Objection. We've already addressed the candidate's standing as a trainee, and I would very much like to close this case before lunch," said Major Ferreira, slightly reclining in his chair.

"Major Ferreira, refrain from including your personal opinions in the record," corrected Major Mota.

He nodded in response but looked no less annoyed.

"Does the candidate have any unreported history of violence or violent tendencies?"

"No, she does not."

"In your professional opinion, do you believe Candidate Ariadne is a continued threat to any candidates, including Candidate Nikos?" continued Major Leal.

"No, I do not."

"That's all I have."

"The council will take a brief recess to discuss the hearing. We will reconvene when we've reached a decision."

We all rose and left the chambers. On my way out, I spotted Krista, who had snuck in the back, watching my conviction for the assault. I avoided looking at her, but she placed her hand on my arm.

"Don't touch me!" I blurted, thankful the councilors had already vacated the chambers and didn't see the sudden outburst. Krista jerked her arm back as her eyes welled up, but she didn't break my gaze.

"I'm sorry, Ariadne. I'm so sorry."

I marched out of the courtroom, suddenly feeling guilty at the resentment I held. I suppressed the undesired guilt just as Krista had when she screwed my boyfriend. We had barely sat down in the lobby of the Resolution Chamber when an aide told us the council had already reached a decision and were waiting in the chambers. My heart was beating in my throat as we filed back in to hear the verdict. After being seated, Major Mota rose to read the decision.

"The guilt of Candidate Ariadne is undeniable in the action against her fellow candidate, Nikos," said Major Mota. "The council finds that despite the crime being a momentary lapse in reason, it still placed a fellow candidate in mortal danger."

Knowing it was coming didn't make it any easier to hear. I felt as though I would vomit.

Mota continued, "For this reason, we sentence Ariadne to banishment. She will participate in Release Day—unarmed and unarmored—placing her in the same fatal danger as her victim."

All the air vanished from my lungs. They might as well have pushed me down the central shaft of the pod, for I was as good as dead.

Professor Lucas stood and yelled, "That's not equivalent at all! Release Day already has abysmal odds. At least give her the armor or the weapons!"

"Our sentence stands," replied Major Mota. "And may I remind you to keep order."

"Wait!" I heard someone scream.

"What?!" Major Ferreira said, obviously miffed that the back and forth was holding up his lunch.

"I volunteer for her sentence," the voice said as I realized whose it was.

"Are you aware of the consequences, Candidate?" asked Major Leal.

"I am," said Krista.

"Then the council approves the sentence migration to Candidate…."

"Krista of Cohort Gamma."

"Then the council approves the sentence migration to Candidate Krista of Cohort Gamma. Dismissed," said Major Mota, cementing the trial's closure with a wrap of his gavel.

I stood there in the chambers in shock at what had transpired.

Lucas grabbed me by the shoulders, looked me in the eyes, and nodded. Then he gave me a gentle hug before stepping out into the lobby, leaving me alone with Krista.

"You didn't have to do that. That was a stupid thing to do!" I wanted to add a barbed comment about her and Nikos, but I held my tongue.

"I did. It was my fault, and this is my apology. I'd never be able to live with myself if one of us died tomorrow, still mad at the other. If nothing else, I wanted you to know how truly sorry I am. I love you, Ariadne! You're my sister!"

Damn. It's hard to stay angry with someone when you have a history as we did. I felt the anger dissipating from my chest and knew I wanted to forgive Krista instead of desperately clinging to my resentment. Krista had made a mistake and was anxious to prove to me that she was sorry for the damage it had caused.

"I love you too." I wiped my eyes, which had started flooding my face. "I have to know, how could you sleep with him?"

"I know it doesn't make it okay, but it was just the once. Nikos came one evening looking for you when you had gone to the gym. I let him wait inside, which was the first mistake. He had come to try and seduce you, and I made an easy target." Krista looked down at her shoes. "It was actually terrible. I tried to make him stop, but…." Krista looked at me, her eyes pleading for understanding.

"Oh, Krista! Why didn't you tell me?" I said, feeling the last of my animosity towards Krista drift from my body. "He was a real douchebag. You know, part of the reason I attacked him was that he said if I died, it would save him the trouble of breaking up with me."

"That despicable ass. I wish Nikos were in on this Release Day. I would tie him up like a roast for the inverts."

"That would serve him right," I said, knowing that no one deserved to die at the appendages of an Arthropod.

We held hands and walked out of the courtroom, where I left all my hostility towards Krista. It was good to have my friend back. "You know I'll sneak you a weapon, right?" I said.

"I was kind of counting on it."

CHAPTER 19: HEMANT

I was shaken awake with Arjun's slender face staring back at me. I nearly fell off the sofa I had dozed off on.

"Get up! Get the others! I've found something! And get us breakfast too. I'm starving."

I hesitated for a split second, letting the grogginess dissipate, but Arjun was having none of it in his excited state.

"Why are you just sitting there? Go! And bring tea!"

I groaned and stood. Looking down, I realized I was still wearing my boots. Man, I must have been tired. I left to do all that was expected of me but not before changing my bandage again. That couldn't wait.

An hour later, I had breakfast for myself and Arjun and had brought back a well-rested Huck and Zeke. Huck was excited to relay all that the major had shared with him, but Arjun was desperate to go first.

"So, I told you everyone dies. That's still true. Maybe a few candidates escaped, but I couldn't find any on the tapes. Without a doubt, it's a massacre," he said, shoving his breakfast into a bun, making an impromptu breakfast sandwich.

"Our imminent deaths haven't hurt his appetite," said Zeke.

Shoving a bite of his breakfast in his mouth, Arjun continued. "It looks like the majority of the Arthropods that attack on Release Day are hook beetles and bone arachnids. There are some others, but they compose ninety percent of the attacking force."

"I suppose that's good since we've fought one of the two of those," I said.

"Yes, but keep in mind that there are going to be hundreds of them tomorrow," said Arjun.

"Would it kill you to tell us something optimistic, man?" asked Zeke.

"There's not a lot in that category, I'm afraid," said Arjun. "Each time, the candidates come up the incline and out of the pod. Then, as if summoned, the hook beetles appear, hovering over the mountains to the southeast. They close the distance in minutes, and about the time they arrive, so do the ground-based bone arachnids."

"You said there were others?" I asked.

"Yes, pill bugs. They present less of a threat. Though killing them is dangerous if not done correctly. They tend to scavenge on the carnage left by the predatory Arthropods. I believe they are low on the food chain. They like to eat before the larger ones finish killing and begin their grazing.

"Dude, you're talking about *us*, not meat! Show some respect," said Zeke.

"But that's what we are to them. It's no different from the pigs we slaughter for food within the pod. We are all part of the food chain. In this case, Earth's new food chain."

"It's *still* messed up," Zeke said. "How do we dominate the food chain again?"

"What about the pod artillery?" I interrupted. "Aren't there projectile weapons up there?"

"They take down some, but the Arthropods are fast, and human operators have their limitations, especially without the aid of pre-landing computer targeting systems," Arjun answered. "Candidates also surround the targets on the ground, so friendly fire is a real threat."

"Then what do we do?" I asked.

"We hide, don't we?" Huck spoke up after being awfully quiet.

"'He that fights and runs away, may turn and fight another day, but he that is in battle slain, will never rise to fight again.' Tacitus, I believe. Sound logic," said Arjun.

"But run and cower while the inverts kill our friends?" asked Zeke.

"If that's what it takes to survive and bring an end to the larger threat," said Arjun.

The room got quiet. I looked around, seeing everyone coming to terms with what we'd have to do. It was a hard pill to swallow, hiding instead of battling as they trained us to do. But dying wouldn't serve anyone. If we survived, I promised myself I'd make up for it, taking a handful of inverts with me for every candidate they slew.

"Okay, where do we hide?" Huck asked.

"I think there is a body of water to our north," Arjun continued. "There is an area in the footage where the trees break. The Arthropods seem to avoid it, but it's about a kilometer away, which is a long distance when a swarm is pursuing you. The research from Baghdad seems to indicate most Arthropod species dislike bodies of water. I think we can hide underwater there until the swarm leaves."

"I'm sorry, did you say underwater?" I asked. I didn't want the group to know, but I had an irrational fear of water. I hadn't even told Arjun. I could suppress the fear to survive, but only if my life depended on it.

"Yes, but we will need weights to hold us down and something to breathe through," answered Arjun. "Those will have to be prepared before our departure in the morning."

"I'll take care of that," said Zeke. "I know my way around the machine shop where I intern."

"Is everyone clear on the plan?" asked Arjun.

We all nodded. "I think so, now about what the major said—" began Huck.

"Not so fast. There's more," Arjun interjected.

Huck gestured for Arjun to go ahead and waited patiently.

"There is an audio track on the mag tapes, not from the outside, but the bridge," said Arjun. "No one on the bridge seems surprised or concerned at anything happening. Instead, they play through the protocol as though they are reading a script. It's difficult to hear through all the various conversations, but it seems there are some on the bridge amused by the battle."

"All the chatter?" asked Huck. "I thought the bridge was only for the minister and the regents."

"It is, but I assure you, there are more people on the bridge than just the pod administration," said Arjun. "That brings me to my next idea, how to share what we know."

I sat upright as my newfound anger turned to intense curiosity.

"We live-stream the Release Day feed to the entire population of Pod Horizonte."

•••••••••

After taking a break to eat our last lunch in the pod, we met back in the vacant Epsilon lab. In my transition to survival mode, I was barely interested in acknowledging the upcoming milestone. The festivities outside were getting louder and wilder as the candidates continued to celebrate as if there would be no tomorrow, appropriate as that might be. I knew I needed to make sure the last of my gear was ready, but Huck had yet to share Memo's plan with us. I'd been itching to find out.

"I spoke with Major Leal—" Huck began.

"Are we trusting him?!" I asked. "You heard what Arjun said. They were enjoying it. How could he not be involved?"

"He's not, Hemant. Zeke and I had a long chat with him. I trust him."

"Okay," I said, still having reservations. At this point, it was a little late to come up with an alternate plan, so I kept my opinion to myself and let Huck continue.

"Leal has plotted our journey to the Hive. If we can survive Release Day, we have a route."

"I'm sorry. I still don't understand how we are going to do this. I'm all about smashing the entire invert population into paste, but how can the four of us make it to the Hive, much less conquer it?"

"Humanity has thrown everything we have at the inverts. Memo is under the impression that they've all just given up. He thinks a small team like us stands a better chance than a large force. If we can somehow plant this device, the theory is that the entire reproduction and command system will break down. We'd still have innumerable Arthropods to eradicate worldwide, but there would be an eventual end to the fighting."

"There's logic to it," Arjun stated. "What does the journey entail?"

"It's going to be an incredible undertaking, but on our way to the Hive, we are going to swing by several pods and enlist their help. For the major's plan to work, our team has to remain relatively small, but we can pick up the device and resupply."

"So we're going to the Australian Territory. Um, How?" I asked. "That's on the other side of the planet and across oceans. I wasn't the biggest fan of geography, but I remember that much. Candidates train their entire lives to trek to their destination pods. A mission of this caliber would be far more difficult than any single pod-to-pod trek. What's to say we all even get to the Hive?"

"There are no guarantees, but Memo has given me some ideas. We hook up with some transporters for one."

"Transporters are a rough bunch. Supposedly they don't appreciate candidates piggy-backing either," said Zeke. "Once we cross the Andes and get to the west coast, how are we going to avoid attacks and whatever else on that much open water?"

"We're going the other way, Hemant. Through the territories. We have to pick up the device from Pod Kano in the Saharan Territory. I know we'll encounter far more Arthropods on land, but the less time we can spend on open water, the better. There we are sitting ducks."

"I don't like it. I think this is the stupidest—" I began.

"This *is* the plan. No one is making you—" Huck interrupted.

"*But,* I think that's all we got. I won't speak for Arjun, but I'm in. It sounds challenging, and I am dying to decimate some inverts," I said.

Huck smiled.

"I'm in," said Zeke. "You know I'd go wherever you need me to, Huck."

We all turned to Arjun, who was silently pondering with his head down.

"You okay?" Huck asked.

"Yes, of course. I was thinking about how I needed to adjust my packing strategy," said Arjun.

We all continued waiting.

"So, are you in?" Huck asked.

"Yes, I think my knowledge would be helpful to the mission."

We cheered, happy we finally had something to be excited about again.

I hid the tapes in the lab, which the major had warned us against returning, then headed out to do one final check of my gear. After that, it was on to the Grand Feast—a last extravagant dinner traditionally thrown in honor of all the candidates, which would be twice the size this season. After which, the bacchanalia that had begun in the hallways would undoubtedly reach its climax. Before heading in for the meal, we briefly reunited outside of the Forum.

"I forgot to mention something you guys should know," Huck added. "Major Leal said someone will be trying to kill us tomorrow."

CHAPTER 20: GUILHERME

I woke up in the early hours of the morning, unable to return to sleep. I lingered in bed, fruitlessly waiting for slumber to consume me once again. I finally gave up the pursuit and took the elevator down to the Bambu restaurant for another cup of their mediocre matcha. The restaurant was just raising its roll-up door, the decrepit gears and rusting chain protesting at their early awakening. After placing my order, I took my chipped little white and blue gaiwan and sat at one of the small bistro tables the host had dragged outside the door. The few candidates I saw were milling around nervously, biding their time until the release, now only hours away. The rest I optimistically assumed were completing the last steps of their preparation instead of sleeping off the night's bender. Mostly, I thought of Huck and his companions. I prayed they would survive the day to go on and carry the considerable yoke I had laid upon their shoulders.

I wanted so badly to go to wish them off. Despite Carvalho's knowledge of my plan, I had to keep up the appearance that I was unaware of it. I finished the mildly fishy tea, taking time to revel in the warmth emanating from the open kitchen behind me.

I was nervous, especially after being blindsided by the fact that no candidates had been surviving Release Day for years. It had plagued me all evening how the administration that I was technically a part of had continued with the charade as though the candidates had any chance of survival. The leadership of this city had degraded, just like the pod around us. I knew that the administrations of the various pods had stagnated, but I hoped that the disease we faced hadn't become contagious. The intake clerks provided me with overall numbers of new citizens because it pertained to my work, but they didn't give me demographic information for the recent arrivals. It would be intriguing to know if there were any pods from which we had received no recruits. I had seen a noticeable decline in the numbers but had attributed it to the rise in predation by the increasing population of Arthropods.

I flipped an extra ration point onto the wobbly table and took the lift back to my apartment to don my dress uniform. Release Day was a city-wide holiday, with only the most essential workers punching the clock. Almost the entire population would be wishing the candidates well as they strode past for the final time. The incline would be shoulder-to-shoulder with the parents unknown to candidates, who would cram themselves in as close to the ramp as possible to watch their children file out and wish them luck. Couples could easily calculate when their children's Release Day was despite being separated from their offspring. They would all be there shoving and sweating, trying to figure out who belonged to whom. Once I dressed for the ceremony, I headed for the incline, hoping my uniform would convince a generous citizen to relinquish their prime viewing spot. I preferred being alongside my constituents on such an important and emotional day. I arrived shortly at the already overburdened catwalks, watching them ever so perceptibly bend and sway under the excessive strain of the traffic when a bridge aide found me.

"Major Leal, you've been invited to participate in the ceremony on the bridge."

"I would prefer to stay down here, please relay that to—"

"It was the prime minister, sir," stated the aide. "I don't believe he meant the invitation to be optional."

"I take your point."

"If you will follow me, please," he said before turning back.

The aide led me to a less populated catwalk further away from the action of the incline, and we entered the Nucleus without further issue. We took the tight spiraling aides' staircase, quickly ascending through the Nucleus, the aged white paint of the banister flaking off onto my hand as it glided along the railing. Security at the bridge's entrance seemed more relaxed than usual, which I thought was strange, but I didn't dwell on it. Even more bizarre was the number of civilians stepping into the bridge. Even at my high position, invitations to the control center were rare, and I enjoyed being there even less. Today upper-level civilians filled the space, dressed in their finest formal attire, and welcomed into the normally restricted area.

"What's going on?" I asked the aide.

"The visitors? They are guests of the minister and the regents."

"When did they start inviting guests?"

"It's been this way for the last several years. It's been a while since you've been here sir."

The sharp realization was like a slap in my face. The increased mortality of candidates was no coincidence. Still in a daze, I was ushered in as a guard announced me. I was flabbergasted at the surrounding environment. Release Day has always been a big, multifaceted event. It was a time for candidates to prove their valor, a method to diminish the Arthropods' population, and it was a barbaric way to control the population. It wasn't always somber, but it wasn't celebrated—not like this.

I panned across the bridge, taking a moment to assimilate what I was seeing. *This is a damn social banquet.* Clustered between the pod's worn and dated control panels were wealthy civilians dressed in their evening best to watch the violence like a spectator sport. Placed down in front of the electrical grid display was a white linen-covered buffet table with more gourmet food than even my regent's salary could cover. The mood was anything but respectful for the supremely high cost the candidates were about to pay. And the entire gathering was accompanied by pleasant, orchestral music.

I dry swallowed, coming to terms with the leadership's reduction of Release Day to entertainment. *What had we come to? How were we ever going to retake Earth, sending candidates to their deaths for our own twisted enjoyment?* A pit formed in my stomach. I wanted to collapse to my knees and retch all over the deck. I had felt the symptoms of corruption but never imagined the size of the tumor.

"Major Leal, good to have you with us!" the Prime Minister said over the ambient music.

I spun around slowly, attempting to refrain from spewing my stomach's contents onto the minister. "This is not what I anticipated," I managed to say.

"What? Do you mean when we used to watch Release Day like a funeral? No more of that. Now we celebrate the event as the Romans did in the Coliseum. This isn't a day for sadness. Quite the contrary. This is a day for rejoicing! Our candidates will perish valiantly, taking many of the Arthropods with them. Who could want a more honorable ending than that?"

"It doesn't seem appropriate, sir."

"Appropriate? Major, you spend far too much time locked up in that closet of yours you call an office. Allow me to show you the full enjoyment that one can have on Release Day." He raised his hand and gestured at an aide with what appeared to be sparkling wine.

"Try this. It's a fantastic local vintage, specially made only a few floors away. Not like that solvent they drink lower down. They tell me this takes about three thousand grapes per bottle. In my opinion, completely worth it. Grapes aren't what they once were. As you are no doubt aware."

"Three thousand grapes could feed a lot of people, sir."

"Or they could get a few beautiful ladies drunk. Why waste it on those who can't appreciate it? Don't live in the past, Major. Our future is bleak. Humanity has had a good run. We might as well make the most of the time we have left."

"I'm not giving up! Those kids that die today could be our future!" The bridge was a large room, but not so large that a mid-level officer yelling wouldn't get everyone's attention, but I could no longer restrain myself.

With a gentle wave of his hand, Prime Minister Carvalho signaled to everyone that all was well and they could return to their revelry. He condescendingly put his hand on my shoulder. "Major—Memo, you wouldn't be in your position had I not wanted you there. You have potential, and frankly, we need your abilities to keep the pod functioning. But you're missing out on the obvious solution. We simply need to reduce the demand for resources. And that is where this comes in." He motioned to an engineer, who toggled a switch on his panel. "Don't act like an honor scout. We can all live in harmony and watch each other die from starvation—or—fewer of us can live exceptionally well until we die from natural causes. I know my preference. Now, don't think I don't know what you and your friends have been doing. I've set up something to take care of that. You need to think about where your allegiances lie before tomorrow morning. Until then, try and enjoy yourself."

Before I could say more, his attention vanished into the cleavages of several ornately dressed women who'd joined him.

"Davi," one whined, "Why did you make us wait a whole year this time?"

"Because, my dear, I prefer to give you double the... *stimulation*," he said, stroking her arm gently. Again, I felt my gag reflex reappearing. "I wanted to do something special for the tricentennial anniversary of the Closing of the Gates."

They giggled at his pandering wit before hooking their arms in his and spiriting him away. I wanted no part of this. I had warned Huck of the impending threat, though I could not identify who it was, at least he was aware. I couldn't imagine the challenge of surviving the Release Day on its own, much less with the additional threat of assassination. I could only hope that the would-be assassin would fall before he could follow through on his assignment. While I was one of the least restrained people in the city, I ironically felt like a prisoner. I panned the various regents in the room. They all looked as though they had taken the minister up on his offer of the luxurious lifestyle. I thought I was alone until I felt a hand pushing into mine. I turned to find my estranged wife Aline in a sparkling red dress, looking as incredibly beautiful as ever. My heart instantly transitioned from the pit of my stomach to the back of my throat.

"Aline? It's you," I said, perplexed.

"Yes. It is," she said, sweeping her hair behind her ear.

"What are you doing?"

"With my hand or *here*?"

"Both, I guess."

"I'm here because Carvalho invited me. He keeps referring to me as a 'beautiful lady.' As far as what I am doing with my hand, I wanted to let you know I'm here for you. I heard part of your conversation—as did everyone else—and realized that you've rediscovered the man I married. I missed that passion of yours."

CHAPTER 21: HUCK

For the candidates with any sense, they had devoted our last afternoon exclusively to gear preparation. The administration had ordered the candidates to disperse from their revelry in the corridors, encouraging them to prepare for the most important day of their lives. Some candidates had groaned and whined, but most knew how foolish it would be to skip the critical step. Each of us had trained our entire lives for our release and journey, and it would be a shame to meet our demise due to ill preparation.

Zeke and I took our bags to the various supply areas, in which all the items had been made freely available to all candidates. I tried to strike a balance between my needs and equipment weight, not forgetting to account for the extra weight of Zeke's overnight handiwork. As it was, I had already exceeded my estimate of fifteen kilos spread among survival items, light armor, dry rations, a concealment bivvy, and my sketchbook. Adding yet another degree of difficulty was the need for gear and apparel that could survive our underwater stint while remaining functional and light. I pushed out through the throng of candidates blocking the entrance once I finally had everything. Weapons weren't allowed to be carried in the pod by non-security personnel, but there would be allotted time in the morning to make our selections before forming up on the incline.

Once packed, Zeke and I dropped our packs and armor in our dorm and left for the Grand Feast, set up on cohort-length tables in the central forum. Carvalho had addressed all six cohorts before we began eating. Maybe I had imagined it, but he had seemed too excited about Release Day. The extensive meal was the best food any of us remembered eating. Despite the mouth-watering spread, I didn't have enough appetite for the number of courses presented. The lengthy tables were arranged by cohorts, but even surrounded by my lifelong peers, I felt somewhat isolated without my roommate and newfound friends that I was split off from. The air had been thick with energy, filling the ordinarily dismal chamber with life. At least the amoral administration had the decency to feed us well before knowingly dispatching us to our deaths, a fact that tore me apart to keep secret. I wanted nothing more than to climb onto the center table between the ornate settings and warn everyone of the deceitful ploy, but I knew the only result would be mass chaos. As it stood, the corrupt administration was currently hiding their misdeeds, but once we exposed them, they would likely abandon the facade and rule the pod with an iron fist. I hoped that somehow we could increase the survivability of as many future candidates as possible.

After dinner, before everyone became too intoxicated—by chemicals or hormones—security marched everyone through a temporary medical tent set up in the back of the communal space. Multiple medics were administering the obligatory tattoos for our upcoming journeys. The permanent brand served as an indicator of our eligibility for citizenship. Upon arrival to our destination pods, the tattoos would be completed, thus marking us as newly minted citizens—a mark that myself, Zeke, Hemant, and Arjun were unlikely ever to get. It was one of the many costs of our mission. Surely if I helped save the world, they would give me an honorary mark of citizenship. I snickered out loud at the humor of my predicament. The tattoo was relatively painless, feeling more like a burn than a needle rapidly entering and exiting my skin. The mark was the simple letters "HZ" representing my source pod. Once we had achieved citizenship, an artisan would enclose the tattoo with the gear-shaped symbol of the pods.

Zeke, Hemant, Arjun, and I met up afterward to compare tattoos and verify our Release Day plan yet another time. Once we felt as prepared as we could be, we split up in an attempt to get the much-needed sleep for the terrifying morning we faced. After refusing my help numerous times, Zeke headed to the Beta machine shop to fabricate our breathing apparatuses and weights. I headed back to the room for the last time to what would be the most frustrating, disjointed, and nightmare-plagued sleep of my life.

●●●●●●●●●

It was morning. *The* morning. Release Day. The culmination of all of our training. I was preparing to form up in the central forum, which had been converted to the staging area for the release. The tables were gone, replaced by nervous candidates and loaded weapon racks. There was no turning back. My excitement for the surface's freedom I longed for was hampered by anxiety filling every crevice of my body. I could see others experiencing every conceivable emotion—excitement, agitation, anger, horror, despair, panic. Several recruits were getting physically ill in the face of the inevitable battle. Zeke grabbed the three of us and parceled out his creations, sluggish from his late night. I wouldn't forgive myself if he lost his life, saving ours. He had crafted weight belts from lead radiation insulators for each of us. I had to remind myself that their considerable weight could make the difference between life and death. He then handed us the L-shaped pipes to provide the much-needed air to survive our long duration underwater. I noticed far more equipment in his bag than we needed.

"What's with all the pipes? Why didn't you let me help you?"

"I wanted to do it this way, so only one of us is sleep deprived. I had enough materials for about twelve more. It's not much, but every set I made is another potential life. I'm going to hand them out to a few others and spread the plan."

Initially, I didn't love the idea, fearing it might attract unwanted attention to our hiding spot from the others and Arthropods, but then felt a twinge of guilt at the thought. Almost six hundred people were going to die today. Every person I could help today would be a win against our nefarious administration.

"Awesome idea, Zeke. Let me know if you need any help, okay?"

Zeke nodded and ran off.

"Hey, Arjun," I said. 'How long do you think we will have to be underwater?"

"I don't know. Hours. Hopefully, not days. There can be some nasty side effects of being underwater for days. Also, the water quality is unknown. It could contain toxins that could leach through our skin, so it's in our best interest to surface as soon as possible."

"Arjun, please try not to share facts that aren't helpful," said Hemant.

"It's okay. I'm getting used to the oversharing," I said. "You guys ready?"

"Yeah. As ready as I can be, I suppose. I helped Arjun pack last night, which mostly meant limiting the reading material he could take, then I packed myself. All that remained were weapons—a war hammer for me, a razor net for Arjun, and daggers for each of us. Arjun snagged some rigging for traps last night too. His devious little mind comes up with some nasty tricks."

"Good. I need to get a crossbow and a dagger myself as soon as they let us. I figured you for a projectile-weapon man."

"Nah. Well, maybe. Arjun has a knack for pointing out all the flaws in my ideas. He went on and on about the attraction risks and ammunition limitation. He said killing one invert might attract three more that you wouldn't have enough ammunition for."

"A hydra of sorts," added Arjun. "Pod Kano is getting increasingly better at crafting stealth projectile weapons, but they can't overcome thermodynamics."

"I'm not completely sure what either one of those is, Arjun, but since your mind is your primary weapon, I'll defer to your advice," said Hemant.

"Speaking of weapons…." I nodded towards where several pod security guards used large rings full of jangling brass keys to unlock the multiple weapon racks.

"Hell, yeah!" Hemant said.

All the candidates simultaneously flooded the inventory. There were more weapons than I had ever seen at once. There were even several utterly new to me. There were ranged weapons like firearms and my crossbow; long weapons like spears and Zeke's halberd; short weapons like daggers and swords; bladed weapons like axes and naginatas; blunt weapons like maces and Hemant's preferred war hammers; thrown weapons like shuriken and knives; and trapping weapons like snares and Arjun's razor net. It looked like the smelters down in the lower levels had been slaving. They might be social outcasts, but they made damn fine weapons. I walked over to where the crossbows were and picked up one. It didn't matter which, seeing as they were all identical, but this one was speaking to me. I ran my hand along the black composite body, thinking, *This will do quite nicely.* I picked up as many bolts as space allowed, their weight being negligible, and turned to return to my cohort for the march out.

On the way, I was busy admiring the craftsmanship of the crossbow and ran directly into a female candidate from Gamma picking out a recurve bow.

"Oof," she stammered.

"I'm sorry," I said.

"It's okay," she replied, rubbing her arm.

She looked familiar, but I couldn't place her. I saw a breathing tube sticking out from her survival pack.

"You're headed to the lake too?" I asked, gesturing to the pipe.

"Yeah, the guy who gave it to me seemed to think it would be the only safe hiding place. It certainly couldn't hurt."

"No, it couldn't. Good luck today."

She looked at me quizzically before smiling. "Thanks. You too." Then she turned and walked back to her cohort for the parade.

I stood there dazed for a moment, unsure if the warmth in my face was due to the emotional flood of anticipation or attraction. Finally forcing myself back to the present, I walked to where my cohort was slowly beginning to form rank and joined them. I ran through my mental checklist, making sure I was completely prepared. I had gone over the list a hundred times last night but did it again for good measure. My light armor was on, and I packed my bag, making sure the lake gear was easily accessible. I wrapped my jittery hands so tightly around my crossbow that my knuckles turned white. I was as ready as I could be, but my heart felt like it was going to explode as an announcement rang out from the ceiling.

"Candidates: This is Prime Minister Carvalho. *This* is your day. *This* is why you trained. Go out today, the 300th anniversary of the Closing of the Gates, and valiantly battle for humanity. I wish you all good fortune in your destinies. For All!"

As the massive doors to the incline out of the pod began to creak open, in one emphatic voice, the entire heat of candidates yelled their response, "For All!"

CHAPTER 22: ARIADNE

earing so many people united chorally was awe-inspiring regardless of my pessimism. It was akin to the battle cries of the raging warlike clans that filled humanity's early history. Then, ahead of the sea of candidates, the pod's main gate began parting with an initial jolt, startling everyone. The sea of candidates stood at attention, facing the incline which would carry us out to the surface. I looked over at Krista and smiled, glad to have her back by my side. I still felt the slight tugs of anger towards Nikos if I dwelled on the past. Best to put that to rest for good.

"Here we go!" I mouthed to her over the din.

"I know!" she mouthed back.

Everyone buzzed with a combination of excitement and fear. I had no idea what to expect. Up until now, the only thing I knew was there would be countless Arthropods and few survivors. I imagined that everyone thought they would be one of the survivors, but the reality was that was impossible. My goal was to survive or take as many inverts with me as possible. Despite being unarmed and unarmored, I sincerely hoped that Krista would survive with me too. Our plan to hike to Pittsburg together had been dashed apart by her banishment. Where I had a "HZ" tattooed on my hand, she had the Greek letter theta. The letter had its archaic roots tied in death and therefore was only used as a mark to identify the Banished. The somber stamp reminded me of her willing sacrifice for our friendship. Unbeknownst to Krista, I had also made a sacrifice. Though it had taken a considerable portion of my carrying weight allotment, I had an extra light armor suit with me for her. If there were going to be sacrifices for our friendship, it would be a burden we both carried. I hadn't been able to sneak two katanas into my pack, but I did have a spare dagger for her once we were out of the pod.

As the cohorts began marching out, the reality of the situation hit me. I heard a cacophony of yells, whoops, screams, cries, retching, and even laughter. I listened to a few screaming their refusals but knew it was futile. Pod security would relentlessly force them out. My stomach had been in knots, but Greenskeeper Chun had brought some more valerian root to me from the aquaponic gardens late last night, and it seemed to be helping a little. As I started making out the trees and mountains in the distance, my emotions began taking hold, both urging me forward and willing me back simultaneously. Lined up the incline as far as the eye could see, on both sides were what felt like the entire population of the pod cheering us on and wishing us well. Tears welled up in my eyes. The residents seemed to want the best for us. I wondered if my parents were up there, not that we would recognize each other, but curiosity filled my mind as I panned the faces of onlookers. The intensity of the moment filled me with a strength I couldn't describe, a strength I was sure I would need.

The city's gates continued to rumble apart, disappearing into the surface of the pod, revealing the sky above. Fresh air blew in on the currents of the wind and filled my nostrils with smells unlike I had ever breathed. On the one hand, we were walking out into the open world, where humanity had lived in relative safety for ages. But, on the other hand, we would be entering into a battle with carnage the likes of which we couldn't imagine. Any remaining traces of the valerian root's effects vanished as the first candidates stepped out onto the surface—Earth's surface. Shivers began to run down my spine as I did what so many candidates had done before me.

It was finally our turn. Krista and I stepped out of the gate and crossed the remaining paces across the surface of the pod until our feet touched the bare soil. *I'm standing on the surface!* I was tempted to freeze and take in the surroundings but knew others were waiting behind me. As we dispersed out, I realized there were no visible Arthropods. It was deafeningly quiet aside from the trampling footfalls of the candidates. My ears began to ring in the eerie silence. All the candidates fanned out, standing at the ready, knowing something was coming but not when or from where. I panned the skies like those around me. Laying between me and the mountains in the distance were strange geometric shapes covered in vegetation. From the pre-landing images we had seen in class, I knew they were the derelict evidence of humanity before the Arthropods' arrival. Between the trees and under all the brush lie the vacant shells of buildings, vehicles, and homes, all rotting away with time.

In the distance, someone yelled, "There!"

Then another, "Here they come! Over the Mountains!"

And another, and another. Nervous cries began to erupt as some candidates formed up in defense and others scrambled in panic. All the training in the world couldn't truly prepare some for reality. Sadly, they would be the first to go. They were the reason our trainers had been so hard on us, the wrinkles that they couldn't thoroughly iron out. I scanned for what the others had seen and finally spotted them. Coming over the distant mountains were dots. Hundreds and hundreds of dots. Each speck represented an Arthropod, poised to devour every candidate present. *Not this candidate. Not today.* I grabbed Krista's arm and ran toward the nearest brush-covered area.

Krista and I had been standing in the central forum when a Beta candidate offered us some heavy, haphazardly created items, telling us his crazy theory about hiding underwater. Undeterred by the weight, Krista was enthusiastic about the idea, especially considering her unarmored body. I had committed myself to fight—if necessary to the death—alongside my fellow candidates, but when I had seen just how many of those tiny black specks were coming, the water seemed like a far more intelligent plan than hand-to-hand combat. Hiding felt cowardly, but survival seemed wise. I hoped others would realize the desperation of the situation and hide too. It was becoming evident that this battle would be a slaughter. I slung my pack onto the ground and pulled out the armor.

"You didn't!" Krista exclaimed. "Man, Ariadne, I'm glad you're so stupid!"

I smiled and threw the armor to her, which she frantically donned. Next, I handed her the sheathed dagger, weight belt, and homemade snorkel.

"Let's go swimming!" I yelled, and we started running multiple kilometers northwest to our potential refuge.

A lot of chaos began unfolding in the clearing. The inverts were getting closer, but I dared not look. As we ran, we started hearing ear-drum shattering screeching and mind-jarring cracking. The entire forest was exploding. Krista tripped over a piece of metal sticking out of the ground. As I spun around to help her, I saw what was happening. The sky darkened with thousands of hook beetles, now less than a kilometer away. Where numerous trees had reached the heavens before was now a trampled wasteland of splinters, stampeded by the plethora of bone arachnids emerging from the former treeline.

"Holy Hell!"

Krista looked up from the ground, speechless.

I jerked her up, and we began sprinting. Our actions weren't cowardice. They were self-preservation! Behind me, the first screams reached our ears, standing every hair of my body on end. Some candidates were already falling victim to the inverts. Candidates we had lived with, laughed with, and eaten with—dead or dying. We ran hard; our intensity further emboldened with every violent sound in our wake.

After running over a kilometer, we saw the most welcome sight ahead of us. Still another kilometer or so away, a vast lake lay extended to the trees in the distance, providing ample protection for the numerous candidates that had joined us. Behind me, I heard the inevitable advance of the Arthropods. I risked turning and saw that the inverts had caught up with us. I had no idea how to close the remaining span to the waterfront.

"Krista! We have to fight, or we'll never make it!"

Krista, who had run a little ahead, wheeled around and faced southeast with me, her hands flying to her mouth as she witnessed the wide-spread carnage. Scattered in our path already lay the bodies of hundreds. Even with my adrenaline surging, I felt my blood freeze in my veins. Extending to the treeline were dead, mutilated candidates, some of whom I recognized, their appendages and viscera dispersed across the blood and hemolymph-soaked terrain. The damn inverts had mercilessly ripped them apart, having no regard for human life. I swallowed the bile and harnessed my anger as I took my bow off my back and an arrow from my quiver. It seemed like a futile effort, but I was going to stand my ground.

"Krista, run!"

"Like hell, I will!" She ran over to the body of Asa, a fallen member of our cohort, and picked up her katanas before quickly rolling out of the way of one of the attacking hooks.

When she stood at my side, she said, "We'll cry for them later."

Several other candidates gathered around us, coming to the same conclusion we had. We barely had a chance to ready our weapons before the creatures were upon us. The fight was a never-ending blur of eights and hooks. Barbed legs and razor-sharp beaks thrust into our midst from the sides and above, grabbing candidates by the arms before dragging them out of our cluster to be torn apart by the additional waves of inverts. There was no refuge to be found. Despite our slashing, stabbing, and piercing, we made no headway. We were being forced back to our goal, only to die within sight of it. My face was hot with tears, blood, and offal as I fought endlessly, watching candidates disappear or be ripped apart around me. Thankfully, Krista was still battling by my side, but for how long? I didn't understand how the pod's leadership could frivolously sacrifice all of our lives and training. And to accomplish what? An infinitesimal dent into the Arthropod population.

As my final shard of hope drifted away, I saw a pill bug out of the corner of my eye gnawing on what used to be Onveer, who had been such a kind and energetic soul. I nocked one of my few remaining arrows and shot the polie through the eye, feeling the slightest bit of vengeance fly with it as it completed its arc. I couldn't bear the sight of a freaking invert eating one of my peers. The stupid little bug violently exploded, catching all of us off guard and maiming two of the attacking eights. I looked around, momentarily deafened by the shock and pelted by chitinous debris.

"Of course! The pill bugs! Hit the pill bugs! They are little bombs!" exclaimed a thin Epsilon member armed with a razor net.

"This is our chance! Run!" yelled a bulky, hammer-wielding candidate.

With renewed vigor, those of us with ranged weapons began to target the pill bugs, which had previously not been on our radar because of their passive nature. Between the helpful distraction and considerable damage inflicted by the polies, we made slow but noticeable progress back towards the lake. I laughed and cried in relief, thinking the reaction was an abnormal response given the situation. Yet, I felt optimistic for the first time since I had turned to help Krista up off the ground. That was until Zeke, the candidate who had provided us with the pipes, yelled, "Behind!"

CHAPTER 23: HEMANT

Battle sucks. It sucks in the most incomprehensible way you can possibly imagine, yet you can't imagine it if you haven't experienced it. I felt every single emotion in my arsenal during the ferocity that is war. In the forefront of my mind was one thing—Arjun. All my strength, endurance, willpower, and motivation resulted from his existence. As long as he was with me, I was unstoppable. My hammer dealt out the justice of the righteous anger overflowing from my soul with the sight of each maimed and eviscerated human.

The plan for the lake had been a good one, but the number of foes we were up against was insurmountable. Arjun had been right. Everybody would die given anything short of a miracle. All we had was the plan, so that's what we did. For a split-second, I had stood frozen in fear as the inverts first crested the mountains. As they approached, it spurred me into action. Once I realized the sheer number of opponents, Arjun and I called for others to follow and we took off towards the lake, driven by primal fear and subconscious instinct. Only a handful of candidates followed, primarily those to which Zeke had given his machine-shop creations. The rest stood in formation, either from fear paralysis or ignorant courage. The handful of us sprinted towards the lake as the cracking, tearing, and screaming first reached our ears. My skin was crawling with pinpricks at the loathing I had for the pod's administration. I hated them all for putting us in this situation. It was as if the inverts knew precisely when we were coming. Was it because we were stupid slaves to the tradition of anniversaries? *I don't know.*

We caught up with two female candidates just as we saw the first glimpses of the lake, but our optimism was short-lived. The inverts, which were much faster than us, caught up as though we were standing still.

"Stay behind me, Arjun!" I yelled.

"We'll never make it!" he responded.

At least behind me, I could protect him. The hooks and eights charged our front and flanked us. We fought while being pushed back towards the lake we were determined to reach, but so unlikely to. The fight was growing more and more desperate. My comrades were disappearing all around me, being pulled out by the legs and mandibles of our enemies, only to have humanity's demotion on the food chain brutally illustrated before our eyes. The situation felt so bleak. With every swing of my war hammer, every explosion of chitin and viscera, I felt more and more fatigued. Even with the powerful love of a brother—I was failing. My eyes began to tear up, knowing that I didn't know how long I could protect Arjun despite my best efforts.

Suddenly, one of the girls next to me fired an arrow at a target I couldn't see, and a powerful explosion threw me onto the ground next to my brother. I slapped him conscious, suppressing the rising panic in my throat. Thankfully, he woke immediately. I didn't know what had happened, but we had to take advantage of the situation. I pulled him up as he turned to determine the cause of the explosion.

"Of course, the pill bugs! Hit the pill bugs. They are little bombs!" Arjun yelled.

Immediately, everyone who had a weapon to aim started shooting the polies. The battlefield became a minefield as explosions all around began quaking the earth.

"Run!" I screamed.

We took off once again towards the lake but almost immediately found ourselves face to mouthparts with what looked like a giant fuzzy ant.

"Behind!" Zeke yelled.

"Whoa! Damn!" I said, turning.

"Avoid its head!" Arjun screamed. "Don't go into the water! Don't go into the water!"

Immediately, we found out why Arjun had been so quick to abandon his plan. Suddenly, a frog-like tongue projected out of the invert's mouth and snared the candidate next to me by the chest. I stood in horror as he was sucked back into the creature's mouth, the impact folding him in half backward, snapping his spine as he vanished into the creature's maw."

"Jesus Christ! What the hell is that thing?!" I screamed.

A number of the panicking candidates ran towards the water, precisely what Arjun had instructed us not to do.

"No!" Arjun screamed at the top of his lungs. "They're water dwellers!"

As the candidates approached the shore, more of the ant-like creatures climbed out of the water onto the beach, unleashing their tongues and further reducing our number.

"Here! Everyone here!" Omar yelled frantically. He pulled back some of the underbrush near the lake and pointed to a small cavern's opening. All the remaining candidates of the group sprinted towards the cavity, giving little thought to what might lurk inside. Anything was better than the abysmal odds up here. I was thrilled to not spend time underwater. One after another, each candidate jumped down to the ground a few meters below the opening. I stood back to back with an unfamiliar well-built candidate, and we barricaded the entrance, warding off the attacking hooks with ineffective thrusting blows until everyone had vanished within the cave. Sadly, the eights were more interested in feasting on the corpses strewn across the expanse. I wanted to be sick, but not until we were safe. At last, I turned to jump in, my fellow soldier gesturing for me to go first. I leaped down, feeling the impact on the damp rocks in my knees.

"Come on!" I yelled.

He jumped in but suddenly froze in mid-air, a look of profound surprise on his face. I looked at his chest and saw an eights' legs poking through his abdomen. Before I could react, he vanished up through the hole.

That was all I could take. I leaned over and vomited onto the ground all the bile contained in my stomach before walking further into the cramped cavern to join the others. I wrapped my arms around my brother and cried like a baby, realizing I'd never again be the person I was yesterday.

We all stood around in various stages of the Shock for what felt like hours, listening to the horrendous sounds of consumption from above echoing down into the cavernous space. Looking around, only twelve of us remained in the cramped, subterranean den. I wasn't aware how many, if any, had survived the beasts' attack, but at the moment, I was grateful that I had my brother.

"Something attracted them," Arjun said, breaking the silence.

"Yeah, us," said Zeke.

"No, I mean something drew them to us. I've studied Arthropod behavior long enough to know that it was unnatural."

"Who cares?! All our friends are dead!" said a blond girl from Beta that I didn't recognize, collapsing into sobs.

"What do you mean *unnatural?*" asked Huck.

"I don't know," said Arjun. "Certain energy patterns attract them. What if someone in the pod intentionally did so?"

"If that's the case, it's sickening," Huck said.

"It's jacked up! That's what it is! Are you saying that we died for what? Just to reduce the population?" I asked.

"I'm not sure, but that would be a logical assumption," said Arjun.

"God, no," I said, shaking my head. "If that's the case, we should have dragged the minister and his damn regents out here with us. What were those things that came from the lake? Did you know we were going to be underwater with those things?"

"I'm sorry. The creatures were spring tongues. I was aware of their existence, but Pod Baghdad didn't believe their habitat extended this far south of the equator." answered Arjun. "I never would have put us in harm's way."

"What are you guys talking about?" asked a Wuhanian girl wearing the green armband of Gamma. "What plan?"

"We had a crazy idea to hide underwater until the inverts left. It didn't pan out, but we're alive, so we've got that." Huck said. "Speaking of which, whoever Memo warned us about didn't survive. No one ever raised a weapon to me aside from the inverts."

"What the hell are you talking about? Someone trying to kill you? During this?!" the Wuhanian asked, angrily gesturing to the opening.

"Don't worry about it. It's nothing now," said Huck.

I looked up to see Omar walking into the next room of the cave, presumably seeking some alone time to process what we had experienced.

We all suddenly jumped as a crack of thunder jolted us into the present.

"Great. Rain," said a male candidate. "And we're in a freaking hole."

As if a divine answer to his comment, rain began coming down, slow at first but before long in sheets. Thankfully, our hole had drainage from the water flow that formed the space over centuries. We all had a lot to talk about, but everyone was in desperate need of rest.

"There is one saving grace to this day," said Arjun.

"What's that?" Huck asked.

"Last night, I snuck up to the signal relays of the pod and spliced the exterior cameras and bridge audio feeds with the public service channel. When the bridge activated the feed to see what they couldn't from the viewports, it displayed on every linked monitor in the city.

Huck, Zeke, Arjun, and I all grinned as the others looked on, perplexed.

"It's a small win, but I'll freaking take it," I said.

CHAPTER 24: GUILHERME

I had never witnessed Release Day. I had been invited to view the event but had never accepted the offer. Afterward, I fully understood why. It was the most egregiously violent, stomach-turning display I had ever observed. Judging by the disturbed look on my wife's face, she felt the same way. I couldn't figure out what had been more distressing, the annihilation of the children or the exhilaration by the spectators. Aline and I had watched in horror as the Arthropods laid waste to the next generation as politicians and civilians looked on in astonishment, often criticizing the candidates' actions as if it was a performance.

Grand General Nakamura sat in the back of the control room, his excessive weight bulging over the sides of his overburdened chair. He spouted off traits of attacking Arthropods and noteworthy candidates like sports statistics while harassing the young aides who tended to him. Debauchery of the worst sort filled the bridge, sickening me. Several guests, presumably new to the experience, could be seen turning shades of green at the sight unfolding before them. We all turned away, repulsed as the Arthropods scoured the battleground, consuming the remains of the courageous candidates and cannibalizing the carcasses of their fallen.

The Arthropods mercilessly overwhelmed the emerging candidates. As a trained military officer, I immediately realized the desperation of the situation. I silently cheered for every candidate that successfully fled into the surrounding jungle and undergrowth. After what felt like an eternity of exposure to the gruesome scene, I realized across the entire battlefield, not a candidate stirred. There wasn't a single visible living candidate. Arjun had been right when he had said that no one survives. I had to hold out hope that some, especially my group, had survived despite the minister's threat. *I have a pretty good idea what to tell him about my allegiances.* I looked down and realized my hands were white, locked in a death grip around the polished handrail and my wife's hands. I slowly unfolded them, gently massaging them, encouraging the circulation to return. Aline seemed almost unaware, lost in a trance of emotions.

"We need to leave—*now*. Maybe we can slip out of here before anyone notices," I said, looking into Aline's eyes and seeing her awareness return. "Are you with me?"

"Yes," she said, nodding emphatically.

I grabbed her again by the hand, and we made our way to the door. Security was too interested in the free food and attractive guests to bother with protecting the exits. You can always depend on the distraction of bored guards. We heard the minister's voice echo over the entire bridge as we approached the passageway.

"What?!" he screamed.

An instant and complete silence descended over the bridge in response to his angry outburst.

"The exterior feeds and bridge audio seemed, um, they seemed to have been played over the public feeds, sir," an engineer repeated, stuttering in fear from his station.

"How the *hell* did this happen?!" Carvalho yelled.

"Arjun," I whispered to myself as I felt a wash of relief and delight that I no longer carried the burden of this information alone.

"That's not all, sir," the engineer said, cringing. "The interior feeds are showing the people starting to revolt. They are gathering outside the districts, sir."

"What?" Carvalho yelled.

"The people, sir. They're revolting," the engineer repeated.

"We have to get out of here, right now!" Aline pleaded, tugging at my sleeve.

We immediately pushed towards the exit, but not before my eyes crossed with the minister's. At that moment, he had my answer.

"Seal off the Nucleus. And get these damn freeloaders out of here," Carvalho said, to the dismay of the civilians who had overestimated their importance to the pod's leadership.

Such is the allure of power. Aline and I sped out of the Nucleus shoulder to shoulder with security, but on separate missions. Upon reaching the public foyer, I saw the front lines of the mob composed of angry residents, thirsty for the blood of their corrupt, and I redirected us to the aides' stairway. While it may not have security protecting it, I knew it would be safe because of its less prominent nature. We descended to the base of the Nucleus without difficulty and crossed a minimally-used service catwalk to safety.

"We have to get out of these formal clothes, or that mob will tear us apart."

We ducked into an abandoned market stall, the owner presumably with the rest of the mob, and grabbed some civilian clothes before sneaking into a cramped storage closet. I realized gratefully that few knew what I looked like, being a much lesser-known politician.

Standing among the market's inventory of chemical cleaners, I watched as my wife disrobed from her alluring attire, momentarily mesmerized by her attractive figure. I saw her looking back at me with a smile before quickly donning the rest of her stolen outfit as I did the same. We walked past the stall on the way back to the center, and I left a few ration points under a stack of garments, compensating the owner for what we had taken. As we approached the city center, we could hear chanting and yelling, calling for the minister's head. We walked to the central shaft's railing and saw where the Nucleus' occupants had withdrawn the catwalks, sealing it off from the rest of the pod. I felt a shiver in my spine, knowing the battle outside would only be the first in a series of conflicts.

"We have to go into hiding," I said. "My—our apartment address is public record. We weren't a part of this, but the protestors won't see it that way. I don't know that Carvalho won't send someone after us either, which would exclude your apartment in the mid-levels too."

"That's okay. I have everything I need," Aline said with a grin.

After the day we'd experienced, I was amazed that either of us could manage a smile, but here we were.

"Good, because I think where we are going is going to be pretty spartan."

"I trust you," she said.

•••••••••

That evening, we had secured ourselves one of the nicest apartments in the lower levels. That's to say that we had a cramped private flat with a bathroom and shower. Most of the lower levels had barrack-style housing. A few traditional apartments were set aside for management, albeit they were dingy, heavily oxidized, and roach-infested. Looking around, we had two things: each other and safety. No one was going to bother looking for us down here.

I was happy I had a friend down here. Years ago, I had been part of a hearing for a young man named Fabrice, to whom we handed down the sentence of life as a laborer. I supported his innocence, but the two other justices of the Tribunal Council overruled me. While we hadn't kept in touch after the hearing, our mutual respect had endured. When we arrived at the front hatch of his apartment, he hadn't hesitated to help us out generously. Being a prolific inventor and excellent logistical manager had earned him the highest position of the laborers and one of the few private apartments, which he loaned us without question. Being single, Fabrice had been more than happy to have an excuse to pass the time in the male barracks. We sat across from each other, content despite the significant lifestyle reversal.

"Is this okay?" I asked.

"Of course it is. Luxuries are superfluous. Remember, my father raised me with grime under his fingernails."

"I just... I don't know how long we'll be here. I think Carvalho wants my head on a pike."

"It's okay, really." She reached out and took my hand. "Tomorrow, we can talk about what's next."

"What about tonight?"

She rose and took the step across the room to me, straddling me as she sat on the bed and kissed me on the lips.

"We make up for lost time," she said, turning off the room's illumination.

CHAPTER 25: HUCK

My first night outside the pod was miserably long and sleepless. Like the other survivors, I rested against the wall of the cavern chamber with insufficient space to do little more than crouch. Anything was better than the alternative above. Once the chilly rain started pouring in, the situation became nearly unbearable, filling the space with several inches of discolored, murky water tinged with the fluids washing down from the battleground above. I understood that combat would be gruesome, but I was wholly unprepared for the reality. Everything I had experienced blurred in my mind, making it near impossible to focus on the present. Sleep eluded all of us, but I tried to rest and recuperate however I could.

Eventually, the sun began shining into the humid grotto, bringing with it a notion of clarity and optimism. The water had receded, but the rain had drenched our clothes with dampness that extended into our bones. Arjun was the first to stand, his apparel sagging under the excess weight of the moisture. He walked under the opening, closing his eyes as he reveled in the drying warmth.

"It should be relatively safe to go up now," he finally said. "Arthropods tend to gorge themselves before returning to their primary habitats. There's still plenty of danger, but the swarm should be gone."

"Provided the attractant you mentioned is no longer active," I said.

"You guys seem to know a lot of things we don't," said the girl I recalled from the bow rack. "Since we're probably the only survivors, do you think you could share it with us?"

"Of course. Sorry. I'm Huck. Why don't we start with names?"

"Ariadne," she said, looking at the candidate to her left.

"Krista," the girl said, unsuccessfully attempting to hide her mark of Banishment.

"Arjun."

"Zeke."

"Hemant. I'm Arjun's brother."

"Omar," said the jerk who had trashed my room.

Of all the people to survive. Wait. Don't be stupid, Huck. At this point, every single life has value.

The blond girl who naturally would've been next turned her head away, not ready to speak.

"Ade," said the only other survivor from my cohort, Delta.

"Mei," said the girl who I had seen furiously throwing knives in battle.

"Ciro," said a young boy with a smaller stature.

"Akhil," said a curly-haired boy with the fuzzy beginnings of a mustache.

"There'll be plenty of time to get to know each other on the road," I said, "but I suppose I owe you guys an explanation."

I briefly summarized the experiences that had led us to this point. I told them about Major Leal and his mission, our discoveries from the tapes, and the implications of Arjun's live broadcast. They all listened intently, only asking the occasional question for clarification.

"Wow. So it *was* you and Hemant who ran into me that day on the catwalk. I knew it!" said Ariadne when I had finished.

"Yeah, sorry about that, Ariadne. We were in a pretty big hurry," I said, rubbing the back of my neck.

"You guys saved our lives, you and Omar," said Mei. "Thank you."

"I'm glad," said Zeke, his voice cracking. "I just wish we could've saved more."

"I doubt we could've fit more than two or three others in here. We only survived because we were so few," said Omar.

"He's got a valid point," said Arjun.

"Those were our friends you're talking about! They're dead! They're all dead. We are cowards!" screamed the withdrawn blond.

"I know," I said softly. "We all lost people up there. I know a few of you, but most of you are relatively new faces to me, which means I've lost almost everyone I know. We will mourn, but right now, we have to move."

"You don't have to ask me twice! I'm not spending another night in this damn cave," said Hemant.

"Agreed. What's the plan, Huck?" asked Ade.

"I'm glad you asked," I said.

I went over and picked up my soggy pack. The irony humored me. The bag wasn't nearly as saturated as it would've been if we had executed the original plan. I pulled out a bagged map covered in annotations.

"I mentioned the major when I was filling you in. He is largely responsible for this plan," I said.

"You mean the one that involves trekking halfway across the world to the literal most dangerous place on the planet? That plan?" Akhil asked.

"Yes, Akhil, that plan," I said. "You're free to head off on your own to your direction, but Zeke, Hemant, Arjun, and I are going.

Of course, I'm not forcing the rest of you to do anything, but you are welcome to join us."

Akhil sat silent, debating his options, as did the others. I pulled out the map and motioned to Hemant to help me hold it, being short of a flat, dry surface.

"This is a transporter map facsimile of the southeast Latin Territory. For those of you rusty on geography, Pod Horizonte is here," I said, pointing to where someone had marked our pod on the map. "The major recommended that we head southwest on an old roadbed to the Dead River, a route the transporters frequently use. From there, we hitch a ride with them northeast up the Dead and Strider Rivers to the town of Wet Church. After that, we will proceed to Tank Town by land, the port where Memo said the transporters had a method for carrying us across the ocean to the Saharan Territory, where Pod Kano is located."

"Jesus, is that all?" Omar asked.

"Again, you don't have to join us," I responded, growing increasingly annoyed.

"Why don't we just head up the coast?" Ariadne asked. "It would be a straighter shot. Easier to navigate too."

"It is shorter, but the transporters don't run that route for some reason. Which also means it would be on foot," I said.

"The transporters have a worrisome reputation," said Mei. "What makes you think they will help us?"

"The major said if we told them he sent us, they would help," I said.

"That's good enough for me," said Mei. "Not sure what else I would do anyway. All the people I was going with are probably dead. Saving the world sounds like a hell of a challenge."

Ariadne looked at Krista as if to confirm their decision.

"Krista and I are in, though for the record, I think the coast would be a better idea," said Ariadne.

"I've trusted Ariadne as long as I've known her, so I'm in. And how can you be misled by someone who uses a bow?" said Ciro, smiling at Ariadne, his bow visible behind his green armband.

I panned the remaining three male candidates, who each nodded in turn. I noted the slightest perceptible hesitation from Omar.

"It looks like that's everybody," I said.

"Not everybody," said Zeke, nodding towards the blond, now sitting furthest away. He gestured to give him a moment before walking over and crouching down next to her.

"Leni, are you okay?" Zeke asked.

I realized she was sporting the Beta color, Zeke's cohort. She looked up at him, red-eyed and with a look of equal parts contempt and anguish.

"What the hell do you think?"

"I know how you feel. Deep down, we're all feeling it, but we have to move. Will you come with us?"

She stared with barely contained rage.

"I'll go with you and your stupid friends, but only because everyone I knew is dead! And you all are walking around like it's no big deal. Screw you all!"

Zeke looked back at me with his subtlest shrug.

"Let's get moving," I said. "Any idea how to check the clearing?"

"What makes you think you're the leader?" Omar asked.

I got sheepish for a second. I hadn't thought I was being bossy.

"Because he is, *Omar*," said Hemant. "Major Leal chose him for this responsibility, not to mention, I didn't see you taking charge. So, if you're done bickering…, yes, Huck, I have an idea."

Hemant took a knee and motioned for Arjun to hop up. When he was straddling his neck, Hemant rose.

"Wow, bud, you're heavier than the last time I did this."

I heard a few snickers and was glad he could lighten the mood. Arjun was thankfully very light, despite Hemant's jest. He walked over to the hole where we had entered as Arjun ducked. Arjun was eye level with the edge when they stood under the hole.

"Can you see anything?"

"Not really. I need just a few more centimeters in height."

"I can't stand on my tiptoes with the extra weight. Can you pull up on the edge at all?"

"Maybe. Let me try."

Arjun pulled up on the rocky outcropping, relieving the weight from Hemant's shoulders ever so slightly.

"I can see up the hill. I don't see any Arthropods," he said, letting his weight collapse back onto Hemant's shoulders. "Can you turn me towards the lake?"

Hemant obliged, and Arjun repeated the process.

"Clear this way too."

There seemed to be a noticeable sigh of relief among the group.

"Let's get out of here," I said.

• • • • • • • • •

We stood in the center of what had been the battlefield, conscious not to let down our guard. I had piggybacked up and out of the hole, ultimately pulling Hemant, the heaviest of us, out by his arms. It took me, Ade, and Omar all together to do it. He was cumbersome, but I was glad we had his muscles on the team. We panned the former scene of combat and carnage. The inverts were nothing if not tidy, picking the place clean of the fallen candidates and dead Arthropods. The only signs of the battle that remained were the damaged surrounding area, the weapon-littered ground, and the stained earth.

Several collapsed to the ground, overwrought with the raw emotions of the moment. Others stood feeling the anger bristle in our fingertips. I heard what I assumed was Leni getting sick behind me. I hated the inverts then more than I ever had. I turned towards the pod. I knew that they couldn't hear me, but I yelled anyway.

"Are you happy?!" I said, pointing to the center of the battle. "They're all dead because of you! You assholes!"

I heard a few others agree.

"Shut up, you're going to attract the inverts!" said Krista.

"No, they can't hear, *per se*," said Arjun. "They feel vibrations, but I believe his yelling will dissipate before it carries far enough to make a difference."

Krista seemed notably nervous but held her tongue.

"Let's go before I start getting sick like Leni," said Ariadne.

We began to march, staring at the distant elevated portion of the pod we all knew was the bridge. Even though it was visible, it was still too distant to make out anything through the viewports. There was no telling how many people inside the pod watched us through the exterior feeds. The first survivors in untold years. *Screw Carvalho and his agenda.* I hoped that the rerouted feed had enlightened the residents of the pod to his corruption. Hopefully, we had set it on a path to improvement.

"We did the right thing," Hemant said, coming up next to me. "I'm thinking about it too."

"I know. I'm just hoping the transition isn't too rough on the innocent."

"That's out of our control," he said.

I nodded, continuing through the dense brush. As we neared the southern part of the combat zone, the brush was becoming noticeably thicker.

"Where are we headed?" asked Ariadne, catching up to us.

"Once we are south of the pod, there is supposed to be some old major roadbed heading southwest."

"Assuming it's still there, assuming we can find it, assuming it is navigable...," she said.

"Yeah, yeah," I said. "Look. If all else fails, we head due west, and we will hit the river. So, as long as we are moving westward, that's all that matters."

"That makes me feel better. Are you using the sun for direction?"

I hadn't known this girl long, but the peppiness of her personality revitalized me a little. I appreciated having her on the journey.

"Not exactly," I said, grinning. "I'm cheating. I saw a road sign back there."

I reached into the chest pocket of my jumpsuit and pulled out my small sketch of the map I had made for quick reference, my hand brushing against the vial of antivenin sharing the same compartment. Ariadne saw a large open cut on my forearm, to which I hadn't even given much thought.

"Oh, Huck! We have to take care of that," she said.

She grabbed my arm forcefully, jerking me down to my knees to examine it. She reached into her pack and pulled out a small jar of something green before opening it and slathering it onto my arm.

"It's a salve I made from plants in the pod. It should keep infection at bay while the laceration heals."

Now I was even more appreciative that we had her with us. It hadn't occurred to me that none of us had more than the core medical training for the journey. She stood after she'd finished and addressed the rest of the group.

"If any of you have any cuts, scrapes, or bruises—let me know immediately. I can try to take care of them. Don't try to tough out any injuries, rashes, or bites. The stuff topside can be pretty brutal."

Ade, Ciro, and Mei all stepped forward to see our newly-minted medic.

"Too bad you can't do anything for the others, gesturing with a sweeping motion towards the blood-soaked landscape," said Leni.

I made eye contact with Ariadne, who shrugged it off. Once

we were all patched up, we paused and took one last look at the clearing of the pod. No one said anything, but we all felt it. I was sad to leave my home, grieving for the dead, fearful of the enemy, nervous about the unknown, but hopeful for the future. I paused to appreciate my first view of the rising sun, feeling its heat on my face and relishing in the freedom of the surface. I turned and crossed into the shaded tree line of the jungle in search of my destiny.

CHAPTER 26: ARIADNE

I had spent the last few years devoting countless hours to developing my plan for Release Day, then the last few months analyzing it—honing it. Then, in a matter of minutes, it evaporated into the thick surface air. I held onto my map only on the off chance it would somehow prove useful. But, to be honest with myself, once Krista had been banished in my place, I knew our joint destination of Pod Pittsburg was off the table. It had taken me some time, but I had come to terms with it, instead trying to embrace the freedom of improvisation, though relinquishing control was not my forte. Krista and I were forging our path together. We'd leave the memory of Nikos behind in our trail of dust. Now, we had new plans and new friends.

"Quite the crew, huh?" Krista said, sneaking up next to me.

"Yeah. Not what I expected, but they seem like good people," I replied.

"Plus, Zeke is kind of cute, don't you think?"

"He is, but that's not what's on my mind at the moment."

"You saw what happened back there. We don't know how long we have—especially out here. If I want something, I'm going to go after it. Starting with that one," Krista laughed and pointed at Zeke. "You and Ciro would be cute together, you know."

"I don't think he's my type," I said, but Krista seemed oblivious, already thinking about something else.

"Do you think they'll give you guys citizenship at Kano? You're not staying, but technically, you will have made it there. Isn't the accomplishment itself in the spirit of citizenship?" Krista stumbled over a root but caught herself. "Damn humidity. It makes everything so slick."

"I don't know. Nothing about this is traditional," I said.

"We're putting a lot of trust in Huck and his general friend," said Krista.

"Major. Not general, but I agree. I'm warming to the idea of a long-distance adventure to save the world. It reminds me of a story I read once."

"Everything reminds you of a story you read once, Ariadne."

"True," I said, laughing. "Man, it's hot out here. I miss the pod's climate control."

"But do you *really* want to go back, knowing what we know now?" Krista asked.

"Absolutely not. Add 'end corruption' to our to-do list," I remarked, laughing.

Mei caught up with us, trudging through the thick brush.

"I'd be nice if we could find a trail through this mess," Krista said.

"I don't think you want that," said Mei.

" Why not? It would make walking a heck of a lot easier," said Krista.

"Only if there's a trail wide enough for us, it's probably an invert trail. I'd prefer not to be part of a buffet," said Mei.

I struggled to read the subtle emotions through her unfamiliar Wuhanian features but came up empty-handed.

"Relax, it was a joke," she said with a laugh. "We should be on the roadbed soon enough. Even without centuries of maintenance, there should be some paved surface left that will improve our pace."

"Right," I said, thinking to myself that this was going to be a long trip if I didn't learn to read her better. Cohorts bond tightly through training, but cliques were inevitable even with the efforts to avoid it. Mei had always run with the more adrenaline-starved candidates of Gamma, a personality trait that made her a fearsome warrior and a welcome addition to our team.

We continued walking in silence for a bit, hearing only the crunch of the vines and detritus under our feet.

"Ow! Dammit!" Leni yelled from a few people back.

Being the unofficial medic, I wheeled around to offer aid. This hadn't been what I'd pictured in my journey abroad. I had demonstrated aptitude in botany, so I had studied food production, hoping to become a research scientist at Pod Pittsburgh. During those studies, I developed an interest in herbal medicine, which had already shown itself to be far more effective on the surface than the proper fertilization of root vegetables. Shoving my bow out of the way, I kneeled next to Leni, who was holding her shin and restraining a scream.

"What's wrong? What happened?"

"Can't you tell? I'm grabbing my freaking leg. It's the part that's bleeding everywhere," she said, gritting her teeth.

"Don't be an ass. Ariadne's trying to help," said Mei.

I carefully took off her shin armor plate and rolled up her jumpsuit. Right above where the armor protected, Leni had a long, horizontal laceration directly under her knee. It looked like a clean-cut, at least.

"Someone give me a first aid kit," I said.

Next to me, the guys had come up, Huck rummaging through

his rucksack before handing me his kit. I pulled out the roll of gauze and antiseptic wash.

"What kind of medic are you, not having a first aid kit?" Leni asked.

"The type who, one, isn't a trained medic, but still healing your ungrateful ass. And two, the type who was too busy stuffing a spare layer of armor for her friend into her pack to have room for a kit," Krista retorted.

Leni fumed but said nothing. I had lost too many people to let anything happen to the ones left. Regardless of how she felt about me, Leni was my patient, and I would treat her. I hoped, though, that she'd get over whatever mood she was in and join the living. Once I fixed her up, I began looking around for what had caused the injury. All I could get out of Leni was her pointing to where it had happened.

"I think I found it," said Akhil next to me.

I leaned in to examine it. It was the barely legible remains of an aluminum road sign. It must have caught Leni's leg at just the right angle and sliced open her skin.

"Hey guys, we have to be careful. A lot of the crumbled civilization remains under the vegetation. We can't see it, but it's got a lot of sharp edges," I announced.

"Not to mention pitfalls," added Hemant. "Tread lightly."

We had all turned to continue our journey south, but Huck had lingered to pull the sign out from the vines.

"Hey guys, we're here. This is the right roadbed!" he said, with a grin on his face.

"I'm thrilled our navigator knows where we are," Omar said, meandering away.

I watched Huck's grin of accomplishment droop slightly. I walked over and gave his shoulder a rub of confidence.

"He's a jerk," I said. "We need a pit stop. It's mid-morning, and at this pace, we need to eat and drink frequently."

"Sure thing. Eating frequently may be an issue, though. I don't know how much food everyone brought, but I have an idea."

Huck stopped to address the group.

"Hey guys, Ariadne says we need to take a rest and food break," he said. "Since she's our medic, I'm following her advice. I also think we should pool our food and ration it out."

"Screw that," said Omar.

"Man, I brought food for me, not everyone else," said Ade.

"Hell no," said Akhil. "Not that anyone would like what I brought anyway. No one has good taste."

"Okay then. Let's just eat and get moving," said Huck, then adding in a whisper, "That went over like a lead balloon."

"I could've told you that last part was a bad idea," I said.

"It made sense to me."

"I'm not saying it didn't make sense. I'm just saying I knew it wouldn't go over well. We're dealing with survival here. Most of these candidates put the self in self-preservation. They'll help the fallen but don't count on many sacrifices for the common good. Don't beat yourself up, you're doing well."

"I never thought of myself as a leader. It just… happened. I'm doing the best I can," said Huck.

"I know you are. Now quit moping and eat. We need to find shelter for the night," I said.

After a brief rest and refuel, we rose to continue our journey southwest. Mei, Krista, and I stayed together, feeling some camaraderie among each other as the only girls. Leni followed at a distance, hopefully taking the time to allow her toxicity to dissipate. I tried to identify familiar plant types in their native setting as we walked along. Recognizing species from illustrations in a book or specimens in a horticulture lab was remarkably different from the field. Nevertheless, I appreciated the beauty and intensity of the biological diversity that had swallowed up the remaining traces of humanity.

"Hey, Ariadne," said Ciro, matching my pace. "Since we both have bows, we could do some hunting when we stop for the night, saving our dry rations."

"I have to admit, that sounds fun," I said. "Hunting and foraging will keep our skills sharp."

"I can't hunt, but I'm plenty stealthy," said Mei. "I'll cover you two while you two gallivant through the woods."

"If it's the same to you guys, I'll stay at our campsite," said Krista. "I'm not great with nature. That's half the reason I was going with Ariadne to Pittsburgh."

We all laughed.

"Hey, Arjun!" Ciro yelled. "Is it safe to hunt out here?"

Arjun slowed down, letting us catch up.

"Of course. That is if you can find any prey. The Arthropods have hunted most of the larger animal species to extinction, nearly including humans. I would imagine you would be most successful with rodents and reptiles, the small creatures that might have escaped the interest of the larger Arthropods."

"Yum, rodents," said Krista.

"The other issue is cooking and cleaning. For example, if you cook meat over a traditional campfire, you risk attracting Arthropods from kilometers around. Additionally, any internal organs you discard would attract them as well."

"So, what are you saying? We can hunt, but we have to eat it raw?" Mei asked.

"Not necessarily. There are underground cooking methods popularized in the Asian Territory that may suffice. There's also fish, which can be eaten raw, but again there's the issue of—"

"Everyone stop," Omar commanded.

We all froze.

"What is it?" Hemant whispered.

"Look around," said Omar.

We all began looking. Buried within our conversations, we had unknowingly walked into the center of a strange circular formation grown over with ivy.

"Is it part of an old structure?" Ade asked.

Arjun walked closer to one of the ovular crenellations and pulled back the vines obscuring it.

"Oh, crap," Arjun said.

"What is it, Arjun?" Hemant asked.

"Wait. Arjun is freaked out? Should we be panicking?" whispered Zeke.

"We should leave now," said Arjun. "We are already halfway through. Let's push on to the other side as quickly as possible. Keep your voices down and tread lightly."

"I thought you said voices don't matter," Akhil whispered.

"Generally, they don't. At least not from a distance," Arjun whispered, holding his finger in front of his mouth for emphasis.

I took several careful steps forward before something in the undergrowth caught my leg, and I went down, scraping my hands in the process, but not before knocking down one of the oblong forms. I watched as it rolled and time froze. I saw that it was not remnants of an artificial structure but instead had all the characteristics of a meter-long cocoon. For a split second, I thought everything was going to be okay except for my scraped hands and bruised ego, but then an ear-piercing whine came from the cocoon I had toppled. All the cocoons began to echo the high-pitched whine, vibrating the air around us.

"Run!" yelled Arjun.

This time, no one stopped to ask questions.

CHAPTER 27: HEMANT

We ran through the trembling eggs as they oscillated in harmony, unaware of the severity of the danger they presented. I could recognize Arjun's steady breathing behind me as I ran, so I directed all of my attention on following the rest of the group running through the underbrush ahead of me. As we darted between the concentric rows of eggs, I felt as though I was running across a king's head between the spires of his crown. Then, suddenly, we heard a deep, rhythmic fluttering coming from the distance.

"Don't stop running!" Arjun screamed. "If the air gets hazy, hold your breath!"

If something clouded the air, it didn't sound like anything I wanted to breathe, but I would do exactly what Arjun suggested and continued running. Sure enough, as the fluttering got closer, we began to notice the air discoloring, and I realized that the whining had ceased. The sound of silence was far more terrifying than that of noise. I held my breath as best as I could, but we'd been running our asses off for several minutes. My lungs and eyes started to burn, but I kept my pace as the air turned opaque around me. I could no longer track Arjun through his breathing, so I had to trust that we were together. Just when I thought my lungs were going to explode, we ran down a slight incline, reaching clear air at the bottom. I breathed in huge gasps, collapsing to the ground, as did those around me. I almost gagged at the horrific smell and desiccating taste on my tongue, but it was oxygen—pure, delicious oxygen.

"What the heck... was that?" Krista asked between breaths.

I looked around as Leni tumbled last down the slope and realized we were all accounted for.

"You okay?" I asked.

"Do I look okay?" Leni replied, a handful of minor scapes visible on her face and arms.

"It was a... powder moth," answered Arjun, taking deep droughts of air. "They exude dust... to deter predators... toxic to humans…. My guess is... it has… a calming effect... on the young... in their cocoons."

"You mean the eggs?" I asked, finally regaining my breath.

"Not eggs... but have similarities," Arjun corrected, finally catching up on his oxygen. "A cocoon is the pod that retains the immature form... of a creature until it matures."

"Well, I learned something new today. That and the next time I see those shapes, I'm going to run like hell."

"Will it come after us or eat us?" Leni asked.

"I don't think so," Arjun said. "I think it's mostly interested in protecting its offspring. As for their diet, they drink rotting carrion."

"Gross," said Omar, "That's grosser than Ahkil's food."

"Shut up, man! Go eat your fine dining, you upper-crust ape," said Akhil, shoving Omar in the chest. "Don't think I didn't notice. You have upper class written all over you."

Omar thrust Akhil back, and they interlocked.

"Stop it!" screamed Leni.

Huck tried to jump between them but was thrown to the ground, covering his back in detritus from the forest floor. He quickly sprung back up and repeated his attempt to restrain Akhil. I stepped over to the altercation and put Omar in a headlock.

"What the hell are you doing, man?" I yelled as Huck successfully restricted Akhil's movements. "We're on the same side!"

The two calmed down, and we slowly released our grips. Omar walked off into the surrounding woods in a huff. While it didn't seem wise to be alone on the surface, I let him go, knowing he could handle himself. Akhil angrily straightened his armor and jumpsuit before squatting on a downed tree at the edge of the small clearing.

"Well, that was fun," said Huck. "How can a candidate have upper-level mannerisms? I mean, did you notice, Hemant?"

"There have always been rumors of elite parents who keep tabs on their kids. I noticed a few strange quirks, but I honestly didn't think much about it," I said.

"I wonder who his parents are?" Huck asked.

"You can't tell?" Akhil smirked, chiming in from his self-induced timeout. "Look at his face. *Recognize anyone?* Candidates can have privileges if they come from privilege."

"I don't see it," Huck said.

"Idiots," said Akhil, turning away again. "I should've gone on alone."

Ariadne approached us, interrupting the discussion. "We need to get moving if we're going to find somewhere safe to set up camp for the night."

"You're right. We're rested. Let's eat on the move," said Huck. "Someone get Omar."

"I got him," said Mei, before disappearing into the woods.

We all began to move out just as Mei brought Omar into the clearing.

"Guys, you need to take a look at this," she said, turning Omar around.

Attached to Omar's back was a half-meter-long black creature.

"What is it?" asked Omar, with a slight tremor in his voice. "She won't tell me."

Arjun ran over.

"Be careful, Arjun," I said.

"What is it?" Omar asked, his concern becoming more noticeable.

"It's not serious, Omar," said Arjun calmly. "Akhil, I need your khopesh, please."

"I'm not helping that upper-crust trash," said Akhil.

"Akhil!" exclaimed about half of the group in unison.

"Alright!" he said, walking over and handing it to Arjun hilt first.

"Thank you," Arjun said, looking Akhil in the face.

Arjun took the hooked blade by its hilt and deftly swept up with surgical neatness, severing the blood-sucking proboscis' connection between Omar and the bug. The writhing, squealing thing fell to the ground, where Mei quickly dispatched it with a knife thrown directly into its head. Arjun pulled the remaining proboscis from Omar's back, still convulsing in his hands.

"You're okay, Omar. Ariadne is going to need to treat that, though," said Arjun.

Omar turned, and when he saw what was on the ground, he gave a little shriek.

Akhil erupted into laughter. "Not used to bugs up there, are you?"

Omar looked at Akhil with hatred and, surprising us all, held back his hostility and thanked Akhil for the use of his sword.

Akhil laughed for another minute but, realizing he was alone, let it fade off, still mumbling to himself, "Scared by an invert."

Ariadne made her way to Omar as everyone looked at Arjun, now expecting an explanation from the de facto expert.

"It was a blood midge," he said. "They're quiet, they're

everywhere, and while not particularly deadly—they can drain enough blood to send you into hemorrhagic shock."

"That sounds bad," understated Krista.

"Yes. The symptoms progress through dizziness, confusion, and eventually death," said Arjun. "But they are obvious to others even if we don't feel their bite. So we need to make a habit of checking each other."

Ariadne lowered Omar's shirt over his freshly-applied bandage.

"You're good as new, minus a little blood," she said. "We're good to go, Huck."

"Alright, let's get moving," he said.

·········

The afternoon travel down the overgrown roadbed was a relatively unexciting one. The remnants of ages past littered the path, stitched together by the vines consuming it. Travel wasn't too troublesome, even with the growth disguising the road's cracked surface and the trees growing through the pavement. Despite being reclaimed by nature, the land's man-made formations were still apparent in every direction. The humps of disintegrating vehicles dotted the dilapidated highway, no longer speeding down its fresh tarmac. Collapsing signposts, cracked overpasses, and concrete barricades regularly marked the former motorway. As I walked through the former city, I could identify what were once the buildings, storefronts, and homes that served the almost eight million people that lived in the former municipality of Belo Horizonte. A pit formed in my stomach, knowing that only a tiny fraction of the population of the Latin Territory had made it to one of the region's two pods. I loathed the inverts. They had no place on our planet. I was glad I was part of the mission to help take it back, regardless of the odds we faced. At least I was doing something. I was going to get my hands dirty, and it was going to feel good.

We walked for hours, mostly silent, first southwest before directly south. I think we were all mentally parsing through the last 36 hours. I knew our goal was west, and I trusted Huck and his map to get us there. It began to rain heavily around mid-afternoon. We took cover under a graffitied overpass, one of the few still standing, and waited for the weather to let up. Sitting next to Arjun, I ran my hands along with the faded colors on the concrete that were still visible, knowing it had been painted by an artist hundreds of years ago. I felt a connection with them. Humanity hasn't changed much. If anything, we've just regressed. The First Builders meant the pods to be places of safety and growth, but they had become prisons, suppressing humanity's progress instead of encouraging it. Yet, even with the perils of the surface, I felt a certain freedom here. I took down my hand and noticed Huck had joined us.

"Crazy, isn't it?" Huck said. "Knowing someone completely ignorant of a world free of Arthropods stood here and painted that."

"Yeah," I replied. "And here we're standing, imagining a future free of Arthropods. So in that sense, we're the same."

"I wish we had some paint," said Huck. "I have my pencils, but nothing that wouldn't wash away."

"I can help with that," said Ariadne. "I knew it wasn't smart to waste precious pack space on these, but I couldn't bring myself to leave without them. It's not enough for a mural, but we could do something."

Ariadne held out her hand. Within it were several partially used tubes of paint and a brush. She sat her pack against the column and began to contemplate the space next to the graffiti.

"I know," said Huck.

He took one of the tubes and began painting, using his hand as a palette. The others, who had been resting and snacking on the slope of the underpass, gathered around to watch. Even Omar and Leni were interested. Once the shape started to form, Ariadne realized what Huck was doing and joined him. Once they had finished, they stepped back to appreciate their work.

"We should all sign it," said Mei.

Everyone took a turn painting their name underneath the artwork.

"It's perfect," said Krista.

The rain had stopped. We all donned our packs and continued our journey south, leaving a beautiful, albeit small, sunrise to greet future travelers.

•••••••••

As the sun began to set, we arrived at what appeared to have been a major intersection. The first stars began to twinkle in the sky, wowing each of us. Keeping my focus on the road ahead became difficult as Arjun and I watched the awesomeness unfold above our heads. I couldn't help but think it was the same sky humans had stared at for ages. It was hard to believe that at one point, humans had remote colonies on other planetary bodies and yet now could barely survive on our own.

"This is where we head southwest again," Huck said, interrupting my thoughts as he looked down at his map for reference. "It looks like a few kilometers ahead might be some building that we can rest in for the night."

There was a noticeable groan from the others, having been walking for hours. We were hungry, tired, and irritable, but we pressed on. None of us wanted to keep hiking across the city, nor did we want to camp out in the open. We continued walking until we began to see an incremental change in scenery. The city's ruins transitioned into much larger buildings, and the road was lined with crumbling concrete walls, slowly succumbing to the creeping vegetation.

"Where are we?" I asked Huck.

"It's labeled on the map as 'Industrial Zone.' I suppose this is where all the factories were. This was where they made everything," Huck answered.

The prospect of a possible historic manufacturing facilities tour seemed to excite Zeke.

"Do you think this is where the engineers worked?" he asked.

"I'm sure they did," Huck answered.

"Do you think we could stop at a few places? Just stick our heads in, you know?"

"I don't know, man. Every place we 'stick our heads in' could expose us to more risks. Let's just find a place to bed down, okay. Do you see that building up to the right?" Huck said, addressing the group. "It seems to be intact. Let's see what's inside. If it's clear, that's where we'll camp."

Zeke was disappointed, but no one else was in the mood to argue. I had extensively trained and exercised in the pods. Still, I was running on little to no sleep, dealing with sweltering environmental conditions unknown to us and trudging through grueling terrain. I was exhausted. I climbed the barricade and walked to the bay door of the building.

"Is it too much to hope that it just opens?" asked Ade.

"Ready yourselves," said Omar, reaching down to open the door.

Everyone stood in a battle stance with their weapons up as Omar pulled and pulled, making a significant amount of noise but not budging the door.

"Let's find another entrance," said Huck.

"You think?" said Omar.

Huck let the sarcasm slide but was obviously annoyed. I walked around to the side to a standard door with a bar lock. I took my war hammer and, in a single swing, had the rusted lock broken off.

"Get ready," I said.

Everyone prepared again as I opened the door. Inside, it was quite dark. Kudzu had covered the skylights, allowing traces of the setting sun's light to filter into the space. However, once our eyes adjusted, we saw that the place was mostly vacant and free of threats.

"I think we're good," I said.

We filed in. Several people already had their lights out and were shining them around. It was a vast space, partially filled with antique assembly machines and dead computer interfaces. A significant portion of the dilapidated building looked dedicated to shipping, with multiple bay doors and haphazardly-thrown pallets.

"This is amazing—a real computer. I wonder what it was like using one of these?" Zeke said, tapping on the gunky keys excitedly.

"Play with it all you like. I'm going to get some rest," said Akhil, pushing past me to an area clear of pallets, already pulling out his bivvy.

"We need food," said Ariadne. "Mei, Ciro, and I can go hunting. We can be back within the hour, hopefully with something to eat."

"Are you sure that's a good idea?" Huck asked.

"We don't have enough rations to last us much further," said Ariadne. "We have to start hunting and gathering. Ciro and I can teach the others, but right now, it'd be faster if we just did it."

"If we must," said Huck. "Get back before it gets too dark out there, okay?"

"Trust me. I'm not trying to stay out there at night, even if the stars are insane," she said.

I made my way to the shipping area and set up Arjun's bivvy before setting up mine. The bivvies weren't protective in any way, but in addition to being a thermal layer, they would conceal our heat and odor from the Arthropods. I sat down on a stack of intact pallets to remove my boots. I removed my socks and found just what I had suspected, a crap-ton of blisters. I put ointment on them and bandaged them as best as I could. I wasn't going to sleep in boots, but I sure as hell wasn't removing my armor. I figured I would lay down until Ariadne, and the others returned with dinner, but I had barely crawled into my bivvy before I was fast asleep.

CHAPTER 28: GUILHERME

I woke up next to Aline and laid there staring at her peaceful, sleeping face until she woke and looked at me.

"You are so much more beautiful in person than my memory," I said.

Aline bashfully shoved her face into the pillow as she smiled. I ran my finger down her exposed back, watching her flinch as the caress tickled.

"Now what?" she asked, turning to face me.

"We can stay in bed all day."

"I'm sure you'd like that,' she said with a grin that melted my heart. "That might be fine for today, but I meant the bigger picture. We can't hide down here forever."

I sat up slightly, leaning against the coarse surface of the wall with its untold layers of paint. Last night, after our little reunion, I had told her everything about the dire situation of the pod and the mission I had sent Huck and the others on. I didn't know if they were still alive, which had caused me endless grief. She had kissed me lovingly, telling me how grateful she was to have married such an honorable man. I blushed again, thinking about the compliment.

Our time apart forced me to realize how important our relationship was to me. I'd been so stupid. I had been viewing our separation as a necessary sacrifice when in reality, it was laziness on my part. Focusing on my personal life made saving the pod become my driving force. I was grateful that when Aline had seen my response to Carvalho on the bridge, she had decided I was still worth the effort. It was a moment I'd subconsciously longed for since the hatch to our apartment closed behind her.

"I know," I answered. "I honestly haven't thought that far ahead. I suspect a coup is inevitable, and it'd be best to be as far from the pod as possible when that happens. Before you came back into my life, I was thinking about finding Huck and joining his team."

"So you would run away, right when the pod needs you most?" She asked, sitting up next to me, the pilly sheets falling distractingly low. "Do you remember what I said to you about being an honorable man?"

"Yes," I said.

"You are a passionate and honorable leader. You have forgotten how to be that person, slaving away in your office, focused on the minutiae of your work. The people elected you, and you haven't stopped representing them like the other regents have. You need to get out in front of the residents and assume your place of leadership."

"Wow," I said, pausing. "I'm not the only one who's passionate. You're absolutely right." I held her hand in mine. "I'm going to need your help."

"Every step of the way. But first, we *could* linger in here just a little longer," she said, pulling me close, no longer covered by the threadbare sheet.

•••••••••

We went to the laborer mess hall for breakfast, expecting pretty dismal fare, and it lived up to our low expectations. There was a significant disparity between the food of each of the pod's primary divisions. None of the other residents lost any sleep over the quality of the food served below them. To the rest of the pod, laborers were criminals, miscreants, or invalids. No one cared about them as people, much less about what they ate. Our breakfast consisted of a soggy starchy mush that could hold my bent metal spoon upright, an indiscernible meat hash that varied in texture and shades of beige, root vegetables mostly too fibrous to eat, and rubbery eggs with an off-putting odor. We were worried about dropping nutrition density among the food groups in the upper levels, but the food was still relatively enjoyable. Despite the chefs' attempts to spice and flavor, the cast-off ingredients meant the food was minimally edible. If you could stomach it, filling was just about the only positive attribute it had. We did our best to choke it down as the other diners stared in curiosity.

It wasn't every day the lower levels had guests, much less from the upper levels, at least not without a security entourage that frequently left laborers bloody and battered in their wake. That's not to say there weren't convicted criminals from the higher floors, just that most of them had methods of avoiding punishment—usually through nepotism, bribery, or blackmail. The upper crust certainly wasn't without their less-than-legal vices and methods.

Despite our efforts to be inconspicuous, word had quickly spread of our arrival and our stature. We were under the respected protection of Fabrice, but we could sense the uncertainty and animosity directed towards us. It was something I needed to address—fast. I feared for our safety if I didn't. The laborers weren't all violent convicts; most of those the Council had banished. That's not to say there weren't any with an aggressive tendency and a chip on their shoulder. Being a member of the

Tribunal Council that had demoted many of them only made the situation more tenuous.

We left the mess hall quietly, trying to avoid eye contact, and went to find Fabrice. After talking to a few seemingly trustable laborers, we found him in the machine shop control room divvying out tasks to the various supervisors.

"How'd you guys sleep last night?" he yelled over the mechanized din of the factory floor below.

"Great!" I said, maybe a little too emphatically.

He arched his eyebrows but didn't pursue his evident curiosity.

"What can I do for you?" he asked.

"I want to address all the laborers publicly," I said.

"You want to undress all the laborers publicly? How exciting!"

"No! I want to talk to all the laborers at once!" I yelled louder.

"Relax, I heard you the first time. I just wanted to give you a hard time," Fabrice said, grinning. "Let's go into the office. It has a sound dampener."

"Okay," I yelled back, my voice already feeling stressed from the interaction. I wasn't sure how these guys communicated all day without going hoarse.

Once we were in the room, Fabrice shut the door, reducing the decibel level significantly.

"That's better. Now we don't have to yell at each other," said Fabrice. "Why on earth do you want to talk to all *these* grease monkeys?"

"I want to assure them I'm not part of the corruption in the Nucleus," I looked at my wife, who nodded supportively. "I want to lead a coup, and I think it should start down here."

Fabrice just stood there for a moment before dropping with a thud into his beaten-up chair, which was far past its service life.

"Okay," he finally said. "Could you be ready first thing in the morning? We could do it between the third and first shifts in the auditorium. It's already wired with a local-only feeds. Not that the rest of the pod would watch our plays anyway."

Aline and I looked at each other, smiling. It was a quicker start than we had imagined, but we would be ready.

"Sounds great!" I said. "Wait, you guys put on plays?"

"Of course. We need entertainment too. It helps pass the time and relieve tension. What's better than watching a hundred-kilo wrench wench with a lower-level drawl play Juliet?"

Aline and I laughed ourselves breathless. "I'll have to see that someday," I said. "So you guys are still pulling regular shifts during the revolt?"

"The need for maintenance doesn't take a break, regardless of the stupid crap admin pulls. If this ship sinks, it won't be because we weren't bailing. Not on my watch."

"I see why they made you their leader," I said.

"I didn't realize the depth of your dedication to the job," said Aline. "I'm sorry I underestimated you all."

"No worries. Everyone above Level 90 does," said Fabrice.

"That's something we are going to do—making sure everyone truly knows how important you are. That's how we can take over the Nucleus."

·········

Fabrice was a man of his word. The following day, his assistant brought us to the auditorium which doubled as their theatre. Fabrice had told the laborers that attendance was optional, but viewing was mandatory. Since he sandwiched the broadcast between shifts, we expected a small audience in the auditorium. However, even entering backstage behind the tattered curtain, I could hear the murmuring of a much larger crowd. As I peered through the folds, ignoring the reek of the mildewed fabric, my heart fluttered.

I saw that laborers filled every seat and lined the aisles, sitting and squatting on the dingy floor, desperate to hear what I had to say. I knew from my demographic studies that the entire population of the depths couldn't fit into the ample space, but they were giving it their best effort.

I turned to Aline, my face as white as a sheet, feeling that the remarks I had prepared were grossly inadequate.

"You'll be great," she said, adjusting my collar. "You are already one of their leaders. You're just volunteering for the rest of the role."

"Yeah, but I'm responsible for why quite a few of these people are here."

"Unless you unfairly judged them, they did the crimes you convicted them for. They can't hold the consequences of their actions against you."

"Tell them that," I said, forcing a chuckle.

"Be yourself," she said, doing one last visual check of my uniform.

I had removed as much of the flair from my uniform as possible, feeling that it increased the perceived separation between our two existences. I wanted to address them as a fellow resident and elected representative, not an authoritarian leader. I took a deep breath and ambled out onto the bare concrete floor of the stage. The ambient noise disappeared, the only sound being the grit of the surface rubbing under my feet. I was thankful for the intense lights shining in my eyes, limiting my awareness of the audience beyond. I could only see the first few rows but was grateful for the facial feedback.

"My fellow residents," I began. "My name is Guilherme Leal, officer and regent of Pod Horizonte. As you have undoubtedly heard, the pod's central administration has sequestered themselves within the Nucleus after the pod-wide broadcast of the release. I don't have to remind you of what you heard and saw. You witnessed the corruption of our government firsthand—a government in which I was supposed to be a leader. I come before you today to apologize not for their actions but for my apathy as the evil grew. Though I wasn't a part of it, I willfully ignored the signs. That ends today! I want to start by rebuilding our trust, camaraderie, and democracy within the pod. Let's build an actual future for ourselves. One where the divide between the levels is only a figment of the past. One where our children aren't subject to the depravity of Release Day. We need to heal, but we need to exorcize the infection before we can. Today, I call on you to take the first step of rebellion with me as we turn off the electrical supply to the Nucleus of Pod Horizonte!"

There was the briefest hesitation during which my heart completely stopped beating, followed by thunderous applause, cheers, yells, and obscenities directed at the Nucleus. My pulse gradually resumed as I let out an enormous sigh. I had won over the laborers—and was now the leader of a coup.

CHAPTER 29: HUCK

Last night I slept like crap, and yet it had been a vast improvement in comfort over my previous night in the cavern. Ariadne, Ciro, and Mei had come back with edible greens, berries, and mushrooms. Unfortunately, they had been unable to find meat of any sort—not that we would've known how to prepare it safely. The berries were quickly devoured between those of us still awake. No one was interested in the greens, but Ciro and Ariadne were happy to have the mushrooms all to themselves.

I woke up for the umpteenth time, the morning sun shining through the busted skylight on the eve of the building and straight into my bivvy. I slithered out of the narrow tent and collapsed it, packing it tightly into my bag. After wandering to the other side of the building to relieve myself, I returned to find Omar and Ade sitting together. I surreptitiously stole a lingering glance at Omar, searching for the recognition Akhil had suggested but didn't see it. Then again, I had never been great with faces. I noticed that without the protection of Ade's darker pigmentation, Omar was beginning to blister from the sun across the top of his forehead, his closely shaved hair not offering much protection. I walked over and sat down across from them, watching Ade as he twirled his machete on the ground.

"You should see if Ariadne can do anything for that," I said to Omar, gesturing to his head.

"Thanks, Matron," Omar said, "If I need help. I'll ask Ade."

"What is your problem?" I asked calmly but not hiding my annoyance.

Omar stood. "My problem? My problem is a snively runt like you ordering me around when *I* was the one who saved *your* ass, or did you already forget about that?"

"I'm not ordering you around," I said, confused by the outburst. "And I appreciate all that you've done for us. I'm just trying to follow the major's wishes."

"Well, the major didn't have me around to ask, or I'm pretty sure he would've offered the task to me," Omar said.

I noticed several others were looking out of their tents at the commotion that had awakened them. I felt belittled but decided that if I was going to lead, I needed to act like it. So I stood and walked closer to Omar.

"You weren't. The major trusted me to lead this mission. You will too," I said, then stupidly added, "or you can walk your ass back to Horizonte."

I saw stars before I realized what had happened and they weren't the ones in the sky. I was instantly on the ground, my shoulders throbbing, with Omar's naginata shaft across my neck, pinning me down.

"I was supposed to kill you, but I couldn't! I should've let you die when I had the chance! I could've been a regent!" he yelled, his spittle spraying my face.

The next thing I knew, Hemant and Ade had grabbed him from behind and were pulling him back to the wall, arms locked through his. I got up slowly, testing the weight of my torso on my arms before standing. I swallowed painfully where my Adam's apple had been pressed into my trachea by Omar's weapon. I felt the numbness of my face already subsiding, waiting for the pain to take its place. I walked over to where they had restrained Omar.

"I think you need to give him some time," said Hemant, struggling to keep Omar pinned chest-first against the wall.

"No," I said. "Turn him around."

Hemant looked at me questioningly but obliged. Then, no sooner than Omar had spun around, he spit into my face.

"Filho da puta," Omar swore.

I returned his gaze, summoning all the confidence I could muster. Then, in his anger, I realized who he resembled—Prime Minister Carvalho. The realization hit me like a second punch, this time to the gut. That's why he had the idiosyncrasies of the upper levels.

"What did you mean, you were supposed to kill me?" I asked.

Omar continued his struggle against the arms restraining him, breathing heavily and sweating as the day's temperature rose.

"Who are you?" I asked. "Carvalho's nephew? Cousin? Younger brother?"

"His son," said Omar, dropping his head in shame.

From behind me, I heard more than one gasp and watched as Hemant and Ade almost released him in surprise.

"His son?" I asked.

"Yeah."

"So why were you supposed to kill me?" I asked.

Omar initially resisted but swiftly calmed as he realized the desperation of his plight without our support.

"He didn't want you to succeed," Omar eventually said. "He said if I ensured that you four died, I could have Leal's place after his banishment."

"It was *you* Leal warned me about," I said.

Omar nodded. Unbeknownst to me, I had foiled his fast track to regent.

"He must have heard some of our conversations," said Omar.

"You guys weren't great at hiding them," said Hemant, surprising both of us. "I saw the two of you talking one day, but without any context, I just thought it was strange."

"He thinks he's untouchable," said Omar. "I'm coming to the conclusion that I was expendable. He hasn't exactly sent out the bandwagon to rescue me."

"Look..." I said, rubbing at the dull ache forming in my neck. "You didn't kill us, nor do I want you to leave, but I need you to respect my role as leader. Do that, and you'll always have a place with us."

"Let me go," Omar said calmly to Hemant, who, after looking at Ade for confirmation, let him loose.

"Deal," Omar said, extending his hand. "I doubt I have a place to return to anyway."

"And also don't kill any of us. Enough inverts are trying to do that," I said, shaking his hand.

Behind me, a few others yelled their support. I sighed with the full volume of my lungs, having suppressed my fear and nervousness through the entire event. Despite my budding leadership abilities, I was thrilled that the confrontation had ended well. However, if our mission was going to be a success, we had to be open with each other. I hoped to avoid any more unpleasant surprises within the group.

We all sat down and had a reasonably quiet breakfast from our rations, everyone already having had enough interaction for the morning. Once we broke down our camp, we gathered around the map.

"Here we are in the Industrial Zone," I said, making sure to include everyone in the plan. "From here, we head almost due west until the road directs us southwest again. I propose we stop there for the night. The trip would be about the same distance we covered today. The Dead River would be less than a day from there."

"How are we going to travel the river if the transporters aren't there?" asked Akhil.

"Making boats is out of the question. The best thing would be to find a safe building and camp until they return," I said, seeing a few others nodding in agreement.

"That could be months, though," said Ariadne.

"We could hike upriver," Arjun proposed. "It would be dangerous, but we'd run into them eventually."

"I know we'd be backtracking, but we should go up the coast. There would be ample food and high visibility," said Ariadne, as the ones who hadn't agreed with me nodded.

"We're going to trust the major," I said, taking charge. "Let's head to the river. If the transporters aren't there, then we can reconvene."

The reactions were mixed, but everyone followed my lead. Ariadne did as well, a bitter look on her face as she withheld her dissent. We pulled the pallet away from where we had wedged it against the door and left the factory. Once back on the street, we continued our western journey to the river, our pace slightly higher than the day prior.

"Seems like we are getting our jungle legs," Zeke said from my side.

"You had jungle legs before you left the pod with all your track time," I said.

"Running and hiking are different, Huck. Not to mention, the track was for all the candidates. It's not like you didn't know what we'd be doing out here," he said. "Anyway, I think the river is a good idea. You made the right call. Well, maybe not as far as getting smart with Omar."

"Yeah. That wasn't a great idea," I said, rubbing my jaw as the comment drew attention to the fresh injury.

We walked ahead in silence for a bit before Zeke caught back up with Arjun, who was more interested in talking than I was. We continued east, the scenery appearing similar to the day before, with Hemant and Omar taking point and Ade and Akhil bringing up the rear. We saw a plethora of graffiti, resisting the urge to add our own to each ancient human expression. Ariadne's paint was low after our small mural, and I was sure she wanted to save the rest. I had been too tired to draw in my sketchbook last night, but I found the natural landscape around me awe-inspiring. I desperately wanted to share my art with Ariadne, but it would have to wait until her temper dissipated.

"Hey," Krista said to Zeke, intentionally having passed me.

"Hey," Zeke responded.

I rolled my eyes.

"Where were you headed? I mean before all this." Krista asked, gesturing to the group with her hands.

"Monterrey," said Zeke. "I'm an engineer. I wanted to build vehicles for the transporters and the special forces stationed at Bhopal. What about you?

"Building things, that's cool," Krista said. "Ariadne and I were going to Pittsburgh. She's really good with plants."

"What about you? What are you good at?" Zeke asked.

"I don't really know," said Krista. "I can hold my own in a fight, but I wasn't strong with any particular aptitude. I guess I just haven't figured out what I'm good at yet."

"I kind of like that you don't fit in a mold. It makes you different," said Zeke.

"Different good or different bad?" asked Krista.

"Different good, definitely," Zeke said, smiling at her.

Krista wrapped her hand around Zeke's bicep as they continued walking together, conversing. I was happy for Zeke. Krista seemed like a cool person. In all the years I had known him, he'd never had a romantic interest. After all that we'd been through, we could all use something else to occupy our minds. Behind me, I heard Ciro and Arjun geeking out together about the various mushroom species they had encountered. *Nerds.* I laughed. Thinking about the friendships already forming, I worried that the odds were still stacked against us all surviving. Heartbreak would undoubtedly play a part in our journey, but I tried to distance my mind from the idea and focus on the positives—I was alive, for one.

We stopped for lunch at a scenic overlook north of the roadbed. It didn't appear to have any evidence of human construction. I wondered in years past if it had been a preserve of some sort. After nibbling all I could stomach of yet another ration bar, I pulled out my homemade sketchbook and began to outline the hills I was facing. As I was penciling in the wispy clouds, I noticed dark spots that seemed to hang in the air statically. They hauntingly reminded me of the approaching Arthropods on Release Day.

"Arjun," I called. "Do you have a second?"

"Sure," he said, getting up from next to Ciro.

Arjun came over and stood next to me.

"That's a nice drawing. I like your cross-hatching," he said.

"Thanks, man. While I was drawing, I saw those specks on the horizon," I said, pointing. "Are those Arthropods?"

Arjun looked, shielding his eyes from the glaring sun.

"I believe so, but let me check something. I don't think they pose any danger."

Arjun walked over to Hemant, who took something from his pack and handed it to him. He returned to me and pulled what looked like a bizarre old set of binoculars.

"They are survey binoculars. They're all I could find in the supply station."

I leaned over to deposit the bottle into my bag, I looked up to see Ariadne further downriver, her damp undergarments clinging revealingly to her body. We made eye contact, and my face flushed with embarrassment as I quickly diverted my eyes.

Akhil returned from over the guardrail and deposited something into his bag. A souvenir, I suppose. Back in the pod, I had seen citizens with Arthropod talismans, presumably collected during their time abroad or watched as eager buyers argued in the markets over some pre-landing human artifact. I sat there for a moment longer, giving everyone the much-needed time to get sufficiently hydrated and rested before hitting the road to cover the last remaining kilometers.

"We need a name," I said as we walked along.

"A name?" asked Hemant.

"A name. All the great platoons of history had badass names."

"What about Invert Slayers?" said Akhil.

"Hive Harassers," said Mei, laughing.

"Maniacs," said Leni, with no hint of sarcasm.

"Alright, maybe that was a stupid idea," I said.

"No, It's good," said Ciro. "Having a name would benefit us."

"The Uninvited," said Omar. "We are unwanted by the pod and unwelcomed by the inverts."

"And grossly underestimated by both parties," I said.

"I like that name," said Krista.

"Me too," said Ariadne.

"Well, that's it then. We're the Uninvited," I said.

After a few more hours of traveling, we arrived exhausted at another cluster of shipping facilities and eventually found one still intact. Once we had cleared away the centuries of plant growth, we found the door and quickly gained entry without relying on Hemant's hammer. Everyone threw out their bivvies and crawled in. No one seemed to have the energy for hunting tonight. Before falling asleep, my last thought was that we would be in trouble if we didn't get real food soon.

CHAPTER 30: ARIADNE

G_reat._ I woke up to my stomach cramping. Cross-country trekking was challenging enough on its own without the added discomfort of a period. I was aggravated by the hot and muggy climate, by the cumbersome extra fabric I had to wear, and by Huck's choice to make ourselves an invert smorgasbord by the river as we waited for the transporters. If I saw an invert today, I might just rip it apart with my bare hands. I wasn't the only one who was groggy and sluggish this morning. The coffee might have been crappy in the pod, but at least we had it. Today was the third day without caffeine, and I wasn't happy about it, adding the cherry on top of my heaping pile of negativity.

"Hey," Huck said, sitting down.

Please don't make me have a conversation right now.

"Everyone is getting hungry for some real food. Arjun explained how he thinks we can cook safely. Could you guys hunt for something while we dig a cooking pit? Arjun said banana leaves would be helpful if you can find them close by."

"Whatever you need, Huck," I said. "Anything else you guys need while we're out? Fresh ground coffee? Slab of smoked bacon?"

Huck looked at me confused as I left him with his mouth agape. I felt guilty, but I was annoyed. I picked up my pack, left my bivvy erect, and went to track down Ciro and Mei. Once I had roused them from their slumber, we left out the side door to find food. In all honesty, I was starving and ready for a real meal, too. Something that consisted of more than a standard-issue rations.

We made our way through the buildings and headed for a nearby clearing, hoping to find edible wildlife. We pushed our way through the jungle, climbing over toppled trees and through the thick vegetation, making sure to mark the path for our return trip. I took in the surrounding picturesque scenery, letting it revive my senses and dissipate my irritation. There was something special about nature's capabilities when human intervention didn't hamper it. When we had passed through the wooded area, a pink-tinged sunrise peering over a beautiful tall grass meadow greeted us.

"I could linger here for a while," I said, appreciating the early morning's cooler temperatures.

"It's beautiful," added Ciro. "I wish Arjun could see this."

I smiled. I looked at Mei, who was oblivious to the changing colors in the sky. Instead, she focused on something in the distance. My mind immediately changed gears as I readied myself for a less relaxing situation.

"What is it?" I whispered, feeling my muscles tighten.

Mei slowly pointed. I followed her finger, expecting to see some violent threat the three of us would have to face alone. I was pleasantly surprised by a fluffle of rabbits about thirty meters away. I slowly stepped forward as stealthily as possible, nocking an arrow onto my string as Ciro did the same. Working in synchronization, Ciro and I pulled the strings back to our faces and let our arrows fly. Mei let out a little squeal of delight, possibly the most emotion I had heard from her since we met. We had successfully shot two rabbits.

"That was amazing," Ciro said. "It was like we practiced that."

"It's an archer thing," I said, smiling.

Mei rolled her eyes. "Let's go get them before some invert shows up and ruins our fun."

"Agreed," said Ciro.

We walked over and picked up our prey.

"Hiratake!" yelled Ciro happily, pointing at some mushrooms on a tree. "They aren't native. They must have been cultivated and naturalized themselves."

"I'd say this has been a successful mission then," I said. "Maybe if we cook the mushrooms this time, the others will appreciate them."

"If not, more for me," said Ciro, grinning.

"See any banana trees?" I asked Mei.

"No, but let's head back. We can spread out a little and see if we can find one," she answered.

I nodded, and we began walking back, rabbits and mushrooms in tow. When we arrived at the edge of the trees, we spread apart as far as possible while staying in sight of each other. Then, about halfway back, Ciro spotted some.

"Over here!" he yelled.

We walked over to join him, now close enough to our camp, we could leave the path without fear. There was a cluster of banana trees, and even better, there were ripe bananas. Ciro was about to climb the tree when Mei pulled out her dagger and chopped the tree down.

"Well, that works," said Ciro, giddy at the prospect of fresh bananas.

When the tree was down, Ciro grabbed a banana and screamed. Then, he began flinging his hand, crying.

"Ciro, what's happening?!" I yelled to no avail.

Mei grabbed Ciro's hand and looked at it. Ciro had stopped screaming but was tearing up quickly.

"It's a bite," said Mei. "Doesn't look like more than just a pinprick."

"That was stupid. That was so stupid," said Ciro, sobbing. "It was a banana spider. I knew they existed, but I was so excited, I didn't think to check them."

"Is it venomous?" I asked, being more familiar with plants than animals.

"Deadly," Ciro answered, whimpering. "The good news is they don't always inject venom."

"Well, did it?" prompted Mei.

"I don't know," he answered, regaining his composure. "We'll know in about an hour."

There was nothing more we could do for Ciro except wait. We carefully inspected and collected the leaves and fruit before heading back to camp. As soon as we were in the building, the group swarmed the bananas. Uninterested in the bananas, Arjun took Ciro back to his bivvy, comforting him. We gave the rabbits and mushrooms to Huck before I walked off to check on Ciro, leaving Mei to help with the food preparation.

"It's been a half-hour," said Ciro as I sat. "It hurts like hell, and my finger is swollen, but I'm clear-headed and breathing fine. I think I'm in the clear."

I squeezed his unhurt hand. "You scared me back there."

"I'm sorry about that," said Ciro. "I freaked out."

"No worries. As far as everyone here is concerned, we're heroes," I said. "They're wrapping the rabbits in the leaves and are going to cook them underground. It'll take a while, but Arjun says it'll minimize the odor."

"It's not perfect, but it should do the trick," added Arjun. "I think it's best if we leave immediately after eating."

"I agree," I said. "Speaking of which, let's go get something before our muscle-bound friends eat it all."

·········

Unlike the previous days, we started our trek with full bellies. Between the rabbits, mushrooms, and bananas, there had been enough for everyone to have a decent breakfast. I felt more invigorated from the tiny amount of food than anything I'd eaten in the pod.

Today was the day we would reach the river, though we didn't know exactly what to expect when we got there. Hopefully, a staffed pump house where we could get some information. We hadn't seen any recent evidence of the transporters' passage, so I assumed they must take a different route from the Dead River to Pod Horizonte. I was just happy that Ciro was fine. The idea that I could've lost him so quickly to a stupid little spider didn't sit right with me. I had a deep love for nature, predominantly plants, but nature can be a cruel thing the second you don't respect it. That was something we'd all do well to remember.

Because of the time lost cooking breakfast, we opted to eat lunch en route. Between the fresh food and excitement to reach the river, we made good time. We would easily reach the river long before dusk. I continued walking for a while, lost in my thoughts.

"You okay?" asked Krista.

"Yeah," I replied. "Today has kind of sucked."

"What are you talking about? You guys fed us all breakfast."

"Yeah, but we almost lost Ciro, and to top it all off, I started this morning."

"Geez. Sorry about that," said Krista. "I'm sure I'll have to deal with that soon enough."

"What about you?" I asked. "Now that I think about it, you don't look so hot yourself."

"Breakfast isn't sitting right. I think suddenly going from bars and packs to a full meal has been a rough transition for my gut."

"I could see that being an issue. How are things with Zeke? I see you guys talking all the time."

"There are no *things* yet, but I like him. He's neat."

"I haven't heard more than a few words from him, so I'll have to trust you on that. He seems—Wait. What is that?"

Several others had stopped walking and were listening too. There was a repetitive banging of what sounded like metal. And voices! We heard voices!

"Maybe it's the transporters!" Huck said.

"Or maybe it's a group of disgruntled Banished," I said. "We have to be careful and make sure first."

"Good point," said Huck. "Ade, Akhil, Check it out and let us know."

They silently ran off ahead while the rest of us took a moment to rest. Finally, after about ten minutes, Ade returned alone.

"Where's Akhil?" Huck asked.

"With the transporters," said Ade. "When we realized who they were, I wanted to greet them. Akhil mumbled something about them being the enemy and advanced to spy on them. The idiot wasn't acting right when they caught him. They are questioning him, but we need to talk to them. Now."

"You did the right thing, Ade," said Huck. "Let's go, but just me at first. I don't want them on the offensive."

"You can't go alone," I said. "Let me and Hemant go with you."

"Fine," said Huck, still feeling our tension.

We walked together, approaching in the open so that the transporters would not perceive us as a threat. When we came around the rubble that had disguised our approach, the transporters immediately noticed our presence.

"There's more of them!" one shouted.

A bald transporter sporting a handlebar mustache stepped out from behind a large armored truck.

"And who might you be?" he asked as the group surrounded the three of us.

"I'm Huck. This is Ariadne and Hemant. We're candidates from Pod Horizonte. There are twelve of us, counting the one of us in your possession. The rest are holding back," Huck said, attempting to hide the nervousness in his voice.

"Nice to meet you, Huck," said the burly man. "We don't see many of you guys from Horizonte anymore. I'm Boss Mueller. These guys around you are the Misfits. Now Huck, do you care to tell me why your man was spying on us? Your honesty is very important to me."

"I apologize," said Huck. "We wanted to make sure you weren't a hostile group of Banished."

"Well, we certainly aren't that!" Mueller said, laughing. "You can have your boy back, but make sure he knows we don't appreciate being spied on."

"Thank you, sir," said Huck.

"Don't *sir* me. I'm certainly not an officer," said Mueller. "Call me Mueller or Boss, I'll answer to both. Now, it looks like you guys have been on the road for a while. Why don't you call your friends so we can share a bite? I promise my men will leave your lady folks alone—mostly. Then you guys can be on your way."

Mueller turned and began talking to his men. They were a rough-looking crew as we expected but seemed kind enough. By the looks of things, the racket we had heard was them collecting scrap metal from what appeared to be an old smelting facility. The materials, while oxidized beyond recognition, seemed to be mostly intact. Mueller approached Huck, holding Akhil by the collar.

"Here's your boy. He sure seems a little road weary," said Mueller, arching an eyebrow.

Akhil seemed oblivious to the predicament he'd put us in and walked back to join rank with Hemant. When Mueller saw me leering at the metals, he responded to what I had been thinking.

"Aluminum ingots. We load up as many as we can and haul them to Pod Monterrey up in the American Territory, now that Bogota's gone," added Mueller. "Monterrey will make whatever we need, provided we keep the materials coming. Now, go and get your friends. I'll have the guys double the stew."

We began walking back to the others. I was excited to find the transporters, but we still had to convince them to take us upriver. I also couldn't keep my eyes off Akhil, who was acting quite strangely.

"Are you sure we can trust him and his men?" I asked. "I don't particularly like this guy, Mueller."

"They seem okay," Huck said. "We kind of have to."

I hoped Huck wasn't so desperate to follow Memo's plan that he neglected to evaluate our colleagues properly. I wasn't pleased with Huck's river gamble, but it had worked out, so I decided to let it go.

"And what about him," I said, gesturing to Akhil.

Huck shrugged. I focused my attention back on the road, annoyed that Huck didn't seem to be taking Akhil's strange behavior seriously. When we got back to the others, Huck mentioned the dinner invitation, and they needed no further convincing. The prospect of real food even energized Leni.

I watched Akhil out of the corner of my eye, taking in his jerky movements and apparent paranoia. Were his strange actions early symptoms of the Shock that plagued so many of the failed ones back in the pod? If we weren't careful, I was afraid that his actions could irreparably damage our relationship with the Misfits, and therefore—our entire plan.

CHAPTER 31: HEMANT

Arjun and I walked back to the transporters' temporary camp. They had hung olive-drab canvas from the sides of their vehicles, which they arranged in a circular pattern around their work area, reminiscent of old wagon trains. Their vehicles were matte beige and armored, with various openings and armaments. "I doubt an invert could get through one of those," I said to Arjun. The fleet consisted of several different types of vehicles. By the looks of things, there was one for people, one for cargo, one for fuel, a box truck, and a flatbed with several small buggies. I must have been gawking because a member of their convoy approached me.

"You like what you see, huh?" he asked.

"Very much," I said, impressed. "With enough of those, everyone could live on the surface again."

"Not quite, boyo. Name's Otto. Chief Engineer of the Misfits," he said, momentarily standing proud and erect, before returning to his usual posture. "There are still a few inverts who can get their mitts inside this bucket of bolts, but not many."

"I'm Hemant. This is my brother Arjun. And the guy excitedly bounding over here is Zeke, our engineer."

"A pleasure. Yeah, this thing will resist all the small inverts, but the hook can get its damn beak inside and pry it open like a tin can. We don't have the means to have a contained atmosphere, but we can seal it up from the likes of a duster when they fly over powdering us like crops. The biggest danger we've come across is the damn polies. The flipping inverts are not as dumb as we think. The dusters can pick 'em up, then drop 'em like a bomb. You take a direct hit from one of those, and you won't have to worry about choking on the powder."

"They drop the pill bugs like bombs?!" asked Arjun.

"Absolutely," said Otto. "We couldn't wrap our heads around how they destroyed Pod Bogota until we watched 'em do it to one of our supply vehicles. Lost two good men, God rest their souls."

"Jesus!" I said.

"These things are incredible," said Zeke upon his arrival, running his hand along the truck's side. "What armaments do they have?"

Zeke seemed thrilled to finally have another mechanical engineer to engage in conversation.

"Everything you can imagine, and maybe some things you can't," said Otto, winking. "They have smoke screens, harpoons, mortars, and good old-fashioned lead slingers."

"Cool," Zeke said, mesmerized.

I had to admit; I appreciated the equipment and load-outs myself.

"The issue with the louder weaponry is it attracts more, so we have to use it wisely. My favorite is my newest project. There's a big invert, one we've never seen. We've only found evidence of where it's been. So Kurt, our invert expert, took samples of its excretion smears, and we've been testing it out as an aerosolized deterrent. It seems to drive most of the bugs away but stinks like hell."

"There's something bigger than a cave grub?" asked Arjun.

"Far bigger than one of 'em fatties," said Otto. "I'm talking about scores of trees down—dead inverts spread all over its wake."

"I have studied the Arthropods to a great extent, but I've never heard of one of those."

"You wouldn't. The academics in Baghdad don't value the opinions of us average citizens with dirty hands. We could tell 'em exactly how to defeat the inverts for good, and they'd say, 'We'll take that into consideration,'" said Otto, imitating a snooty accent. "I can tell you what to look for if you're out on your own. Watch for the inverts behaving weirdly. They don't even seem to care about us when one of 'em's around. I can't say I'm disappointed that we haven't run into one."

"Grub time!" yelled Boss Mueller.

"Yeah!" said Otto. "There's nary a cook in this hemisphere that can hold up to the likes of Kurt."

Arjun and I gathered with the others under the canvas of the supply truck. A sizable cast-iron pot was hanging from a tripod above a gas burner running from under the truck. The smell escaping from the vessel was limited by the lid but smelled so rich I thought that I could chew the air.

"Gather up," said Kurt. "Visitors first, Otto."

Otto hung his head and stepped back.

Kurt handed us each a battered aluminum bowl and equally used spork.

"Rules are: one, no one eats until we say grace; two, everyone cleans their dishes; and three, scarf it down, so you don't attract inverts—or Otto," said Mueller.

No sooner than everyone had their food, Mueller asked everyone to bow their heads. I didn't know what religious convictions to expect from this eccentric group.

"We are grateful for our living. We are grateful for our dead. We are grateful for our food and a place to rest our head," prayed Mueller.

"Amen!" said the Misfits in unison.

Afterward, everyone, standing or sitting, devoured their food. It was the best food I had ever eaten. Ever. In all my sixteen years of life in the pod, I had never tasted anything this good. Judging by the smiles on the other's faces, we were all thinking the same thing. The idea of traveling with these guys was growing more appealing by the moment.

Ariadne was the first to speak up. "That was incredible! I specialized in food in the pod, and I never knew food could taste like this!"

"That's the problem with the pods. No truly fresh ingredients. Fresh off the vine from down there is a far cry from fresh off the vine up here," Kurt said. "Thankfully, the inverts don't seem to care about our vegetation. Otherwise, we wouldn't have a chance."

"It's not just fresh ingredients," said Mueller. "Kurt was one of the best cooks in Pod Munich before Release Day. Since we journeyed down here to become transporters, he's honed his craft with the local ingredients. He could take my leg off and make me want to eat it."

The transporters all laughed like a group that had been together for a long time. For the first time in a while, I felt safe and comfortable.

"I'm not in any hurry to eat anything from you, Mueller," Kurt said, which only made them laugh harder. "I'd rather eat an invert."

"I bet you'd make it taste good," said Otto.

"You'd eat anything, though," said Kurt to a shrugging Otto.

By now, we were laughing with them. If nothing else, this group was entertaining. After dinner, we cleaned our dishes from a spigot on the truck, letting the wastewater run into a nearby ditch.

"How do you guys get around?" Krista asked. "I mean, you need fuel, right?"

"You've heard of the pump houses?" asked Mueller.

"Yeah," said Krista. "They were a Path to Citizenship option, but to be honest, I don't remember much about them."

"Correct, but maybe not citizenship for you, young one. That mark on your hand didn't escape me," Mueller said as Krista tugged her sleeve down over her hand in embarrassment. "Don't fret. All that matters to me up here is your character. You're either brave—or a coward. These inverts will be happy to show me which one you are. But I digress. The First Builders created the pump houses to give us two necessary things—water and fuel—both of which they extract from the ground. We use natural gas to run everything."

"And you can carry a lot of it because it compresses, correct?" asked Zeke.

"Smart boy, that one," said Mueller, pointing to Zeke with his spork. "The pump houses require little maintenance but need someone around to keep an eye on things. That's where the local candidates come in. They need their little merit badge, and we need someone to take care of the place. So it's a win-win."

"What do they do for food?" asked Krista.

"Well, we can provide them with some each time we pass by, which isn't very often, but most of them grow food underground aquaponically. At least enough to subsist on. The attendants can eat the plants or the fish, as long as they don't overeat either one," Mueller said, laughing. "They can't exactly farm. These inverts recognize behavioral patterns. We have to vary up our routines for the same reasons. Now, if that's all your questions, we best get to sleep. The Misfits have a long day tomorrow, and I'm sure you need to get a move on as well."

"We were hoping you guys could take us upriver," said Huck.

"I'm sorry, boyo," said Mueller. "We don't just pick up candidates at their leisure. We have enough mouths to feed as it is."

"Major Guilherme Leal sent us. He said you'd help us."

"Memo!" Mueller said, instantly recognizing the name. "What

a good guy. He served with us for a while. I miss the bastard! How is he?"

"He's good, I guess," said Huck. "He sent us on a mission of sorts and said you would help take us north."

"I'm sorry lad, but he's mistaken," said Mueller regretfully. "Memo is a great guy, but we still don't have room to spare for you all."

"He sent us on a mission to infiltrate and destroy the Hive," interrupted Ariadne. "The pods are dying, and humanity's time is more limited than we thought. He's put a plan in place, but we have to get to Kano."

"Well, that's all out in the open now," I mumbled to Arjun.

"The Hive, huh?" Mueller said, playing with the ends of his garish mustache. "That sounds like one of his damn-fool ideas. I'm anxious to hear more about this plan. Alright, you've convinced me, but I have a few conditions. For all of you."

"We're willing to do whatever it takes," I said, speaking up.

"You don't have a choice. The accommodations are rough and cramped, even more so with you all. There's virtually no privacy," Mueller said, looking primarily at the girls. "The hours are long, and I *every* damn one of you will pull your weight and follow my orders, or I'll throw you out of the convoy faster than Otto inhales food, understood?"

Mueller looked at each of us in turn as we nodded, accepting his terms.

"One more thing. If through cowardice your actions cause someone to get maimed or killed, I'll dispatch you myself. Now, who wants a nightcap?" Mueller asked, his mood suddenly brightening.

The transporters all passed around a large flask. Everyone except Omar and Ade was a little too wary taking a swig after Mueller's little speech. The transporters slept in their vehicles, but without the extra space, the rest of us camped next to the convoy in our bivvies. I was looking forward to getting a move on tomorrow, though I still wasn't too excited about being on the water.

•••••••••

I woke up to the sounds of chaotic movement and wormed my way out of my bivvy. My limbs felt strange as the blood flow returned to them. Sleeping in an insulated bag wearing armor was getting old fast. Even though the armor was meant to be light, malleable, and comfortable—it wasn't. I stood, seeing for the first time the commotion buzzing around me. The Misfits were breaking down their camp with the practiced precision of repetition. Huck and the rest of us were waking up to the same realization, immediately joining the hustle, first packing our packs, then helping the transporters load up. Kurt handed each of us a breakfast wrap.

"We don't take our time in the morning," said Kurt. "Unless you get up at dawn, you miss the coffee, breakfast, and the slow rise. So shove this in your stomachs. There may be some tepid coffee in that pot over there."

"Coffee? Did he say coffee?" asked Ariadne.

"I think so," I responded. "If we don't tell the others, that's more for us."

I ran over to the pot, resisting the urge to pour it directly from the pot and into my mouth. Instead, I flipped over two drying metal cups and drank deeply, struggling not to gulp it down. Kurt was right, it was lukewarm, but I didn't care. I had missed coffee more than I realized. Once Ariadne and I were happily fueled up and buzzing on caffeine, we went back to join the others, who were getting placement assignments from Mueller. I saw Ariadne wrap her arm around Krista's shoulder, who then suddenly threw up on the cracked pavement.

"Nerves got the best of ya?" asked Mueller.

"Maybe," Krista said, wiping her mouth. "I only ate a few bites of breakfast. I didn't have much of an appetite."

"Not a problem, provided you don't get motion sickness," said Mueller. "These trucks will drive over a mountain, but it won't be comfortable."

"Great," said Krista to Ariadne, low enough that Mueller didn't hear.

"Can I ride with Krista, Boss?" asked Ariadne.

"Sure, you guys take the personnel carrier. There's enough room in the floorboards for a puke bucket. Kurt will set you up. The rest of you have your seating assignments. Everyone take a piss before we're off. No one wants to stop this convoy because someone didn't drain the lizard," said Mueller, then hesitated. "Damn. My apologies, ladies. I'm not used to having refined companions in our company."

"We're not 'refined companions.'" I heard Ariadne mutter.

Within minutes, we were in the vehicles, ready for departure. Unfortunately, I couldn't get a seat with Arjun. Instead, I was sandwiched between Otto and Kurt in the supply truck. The bench was wide enough, but the gear shift was between my knees, promising to make it a fun ride. I was looking forward to finally making more significant progress than we had been on foot.

As the vehicles started up, I expected loud rumbles and giant plumes of exhaust emanating from the monstrous machines. Instead, I only heard a low whine accompanied by vibration through the chassis.

"Not what you were expecting?" asked Otto, noticing my face as we pulled out. "The eggheads in Monterrey have found ways of making these beasts run almost silently. We only really attract the inverts when we're doing a lot of ground-pounding."

It was impressive. Progress was slow in the vehicles. They were narrow and had suspensions that could cross many obstacles, but nothing they did was fast. Still, I was sure it was faster than we could walk. And we were certainly more protected. On the other hand, it was hot, even with the windows down. We were sweating so much I imagined it pooling in the floorboards. The mosquitos kept flying in and biting us, but Kurt handed me a funny-shaped leaf.

"Rub it all over your exposed skin," he said. "It keeps the little buggers away."

I nodded in appreciation and rubbed away. I don't know that they stayed completely away, but it seemed to help. After only a few hours of riding, the river appeared in front of us. It was browner than I had expected, but it still represented a milestone. I had imagined it would be blue like the images of water we'd seen in class from before the invert landing. Nature never ceases to amaze me. The smells, sights, and sounds were new and overwhelmed my senses. I could live the rest of my life up here, never getting bored of the scenery. The surface was where humans belonged. I was glad I could play a part in our return to it. The vehicles all pulled to a stop on a concrete pad next to a strange-looking building, and everyone began to hop out.

"This is a pump house," Mueller said, pointing, as we gathered around him.

The building was a tall trapezoidal prism on a circular base with an open hatch, out of which was coming a tall, slender woman with ebony skin.

"And this is Grace, our barge pilot," said Mueller.

"Freeloaders, Mueller? Really?" asked Grace.

"Their friends of Memo," answered Mueller. "What they are doing is important."

"Sure. Hitchhikers are always doing something *important*," Grace said, making air quotes. "Especially if they can pinch a ride off us. Let's get you guys topped off and onboard. Gretel is ready and waiting."

"Gretel?" Ade asked.

"Gretel's the barge," answered Mueller. "And you respect her, or Grace will have you underwater scraping barnacles and dodging spring tongues."

"Any of you guys want to stay and run the pump house?" asked Grace, gesturing to us with the wrench in her hand. "When we got here, there were no signs of the guy we left. It needs a new operator. It'll earn you citizenship."

She said the last part in a sing-song voice and let it linger like a dangling carrot. Then, when no one took her up on it, she shrugged and moved on. After loading the vehicles with gas and water, the Misfits began rolling them onto the double-platformed barge. Grace gave the all-call and readied to get underway. Everyone piled on board, and we slowly pulled away from the makeshift dock.

And so it begins.

CHAPTER 32: GUILHERME

The day I spoke to the laborers went by in a blur. Despite having been the arbiter of their sentences, most were quick to embrace me as their once and future leader. I had meant every word I said. It was time for the caste system of the pod to fade into obscurity. I didn't know how much longer humanity would need to live in the pods, but we sure as hell couldn't continue our divided way of life.

Surrounded by a crowd of inquisitive laborers, Fabrice, Aline, and I made our way down to the Master Control Station. As we walked down the dimly lit corridor, we came upon freshly-painted graffiti, the headache-inducing chemical smell still lingering in the air. The painting depicted me ascending to the Nucleus, climbing up a pyramid of dead laborers.

"I'm sorry about that," Fabrice said. "I'll have it taken care of immediately."

"There's no need to apologize, Fab," I said. "There's going to be a lot of people still angry. They see me as just another corrupted leader who's coming to take advantage of them. Only time will show them who I truly am. I just hope that none of their resentment turns to violence."

"I'll have some of my trusted people keep an eye on you. They'll stay out of your way but keep you both safe."

I couldn't help but be concerned about the pockets of laborers that opposed my leadership, but I couldn't dwell on them. We stayed just long enough for Fabrice to order the artwork's clean-up before we continued to the station. While the bridge had complete control of the pod's systems, the Master Control Station had local cut-offs for the systems supplying the bridge, giving us the advantage. With the bridge removed from the loop, the station could manually allocate the production output to the rest of the pod. Usually, the threat of pod security kept the laborers from ever attempting a political overthrow like this. They would undoubtedly find themselves convicted and labeled as banished the following morning if security didn't execute them on the spot. Fortunately, the Nucleus had imprisoned itself when it had retracted the catwalks. The hatches could open without power, but the catwalks had no manual controls, trapping the administration and the bulk of their security force inside. What few remaining guards roamed the pod outside of the protection of the Nucleus were most likely attempting to hide from the aggressive mobs of protesters.

Once we were safely in the station, our impromptu security team escorted the non-essential personnel from the orange-tinted room. Fabrice explained the plan to the engineers sitting at their rudimentary blinking control panels, but word had traveled faster than we had, and they had already prepared. Several laborers positioned themselves against a wall covered in conduits, resting their hands on several giant red levers, waiting for the signal to begin the shutdown procedures. Fabrice took a deep breath.

"Shut off Main Power Feed to Nucleus," commanded Fabrice.

"Nucleus Main Power Feed off," came the response.

"Shut off Backup Power Feed to Nucleus," commanded Fabrice.

"Backup Nucleus Power Feed off," came the response.

Even over the din of the reactors, generators, and pumps radiating through the insulated observation windows looking out on the level below, we could hear the city-wide shouting from the residents, alarmed at the power's absence and anxious for its return.

"Reroute Main Power Feed to Primary Pod Power Grid," commanded Fabrice.

"Main Power Feed rerouted," came the response.

"Reroute Backup Power Feed to Secondary Pod Power Grid," commanded Fabrice.

"Backup feed rerouted," came the response.

I was amazed at the skill and professionalism demonstrated by the laborers thus far. They had a reputation in the upper levels for being unlawful, coarse, and incompetent, but what I saw was a well-organized machine. At that moment, I speculated that it was something that the Nucleus' occupants realized as well.

"It's done. I'm sure we have their full attention," said Fabrice, turning towards me. "Right now, they're frantically trying to see if they can override us, but I assure you it's futile. Just as with the pod, they only had the illusion of control. The real power lies with the people."

"Thank you, Fabrice," I said, clamping my hands on his shoulders. "I couldn't have done this without you."

"Oh yes, you could have," he responded. "You are far too modest. It's something I like about you. If you ever grow tired of him again, Aline, make sure you send him my way," Fabrice said, jesting.

Aline giggled, wrapping her arm through mine. "Thanks, but I think I'll hang on to him for a while."

"There's going to be a lot of scared and confused people up there," I said, changing the subject. "Do we have a way of addressing them through the public channel?"

"Absolutely," said Fabrice. "We have an old studio down here, but no one has used it since before I was sentenced. I'm not even sure what for. I can dredge up the guy who used to run it. But, it might take a few days to get it up and running."

"Could we do it by tomorrow morning?" I asked.

Fabrice thought for a few moments. "For you, yes. We'll work around the clock to make it happen."

"Thank you," said Aline, kissing him on the cheek.

"*Avec plaisir,*" said Fabrice, grinning.

•••••••••

True to his word, I was in the studio in front of a large, boxy camera with multiple lenses the next morning. Behind the obsolete device were Fabrice, Aline, and the older men and women who previously formed the studio's production department. They all had bags under their eyes, having spent all night replacing cables, repairing components, and training the younger generation how to operate the antiquated equipment.

The studio had been in considerable disrepair. Sitting unused, it had become a nesting place for rats and other vermin. It still smelled odd, but it looked clean and presentable for the pod-wide address. (At least in front of the camera.) Fabrice assured me that I could talk freely without fear of the bridge eavesdropping. I was nervous, knowing the hard-wired feed would reach every resident. I wanted to convey the same message I had in my speech directed at the laborers, yet I didn't want to sound repetitive to the untold numbers of laborers who would also be tuning in. I took a deep breath and nodded at Fabrice, who cued the production staff. An amber light appeared on the massive camera, and Fabrice mouthed, "Go."

"Greetings," I said, taking a deep breath. "I am Guilherme Leal, a Grand Major of Pod Horizonte and one of your elected regents. In light of Release Day, it has come to our collective attention that the administration of our pod has become malignant. With that new understanding, I have joined forces with the laborers, the backbone of our pod.

"I come before you to apologize to you for my apathy leading up to this tragedy. It was a mistake that I've already begun to remedy. Going forth, our pod will be governed with democracy, transparency, and unity. But first, we must rid ourselves of the cancer filling the Nucleus.

"As you undoubtedly noticed yesterday evening, we took the first step and cut off the blood flow to this tumor. We will immediately exorcize this cancer, calling for the complete surrender of Prime Minister Carvalho and the regents to the new Tribunal Council. There, they will receive a fair and just hearing, answering to the atrocities we've endured. Today, we create a new, united pod, free from the horrors of the past—a pod that will remain strong until we return to the surface once again!"

I looked urgingly at Fabrice, who waved at the production booth. The yellow light faded.

"How was it?" I asked, not having the crowd's response to gauge my success.

"It was great!" said Aline, her remark permitting a break in the silence. I heard whoops, cheers, and applause from around the studio.

"That was fantastic," echoed Fabrice.

"After that, I'm either going to be elected Prime Minister or be targeted for assassination," I said to Aline and Fabrice.

"You wouldn't be doing it right if you didn't ruffle some feathers," Fabrice said.

"How long do you think we'll have before surrender starts looking like a viable option to the bridge?" I asked.

"I don't know that it will," said Fabrice. "The non-administrative personnel are the only ones likely to surrender. Carvalho and the regents know that their outlook is grim even with a fair trial. They no longer have the control over the council they used to. Surrender almost certainly means death, so they'll fight tooth and nail before they give up or let anyone else do so."

"I hope it doesn't come to that," I said.

"Unfortunately, I think we can count on it," said Fabrice. "We're going to have to invade the Nucleus. We need an invasion force."

"I don't want to establish a democracy based on violence," I said.

"We don't have a choice," said Aline. "The revolts are already turning violent. Residents beat a guard to death yesterday. This democracy needs to be set up by those who plan to participate. Why not construct this invasion force from the residents of all levels? Direct their anger in a more productive way."

"That's a good idea," I said. "Before we ask the people to put themselves in harm's way, we need to gauge their reaction to the idea of this coup."

"Absolutely," said Fabrice. "If the people aren't on board, this will be a very short insurrection."

•••••••••

We started our pod-wide tour on the 90th floor, the first floor above the lower levels. We took the elevator to the 91st floor before climbing the remaining stairs. No sooner had we set foot on the landing of the 90th floor, an endless crowd met us with applause and cheers. I looked at Aline, aghast and thrilled.

"My speech must have hit home," I said.

"This is exactly the response we needed," she responded, elated. "We can do this."

A sense of pride filled my bosom. Anyone could purport to be a leader, but only a real one had followers. I allowed myself a moment to feel the flood of emotions and recognize the responsibilities of my newfound post. We didn't have the time to parade through the pod, kissing babies and shaking hands like the politicians of old, but it was good to feel the energy of the people and their excitement for change.

We did a brief stop every few levels, each crowd getting progressively larger as word of our tour spread. Something felt different when we stepped out of the elevator on the 55th floor. People were cheering, but something unknown was causing my skin to prickle. I looked at Aline, who was feeling the same sensations. We interacted with the crowd of supporters briefly and had turned to make an early return to the lift when we heard shouting. I spun on my heels in time to see three citizens sprinting towards us with lit Molotov cocktails, screaming, "Kill them all!" Fabrice's guard detail quickly took down the two men, safely exploding their containers away from the assembly, but the woman escaped their barrage. Just before she came within throwing distance, one of our supporters tripped her, causing her to stumble to the concrete floor, busting her glass canister as she did so. She was immediately engulfed in flames, writhing and screeching in agony as the crowd distanced themselves from the spectacle. Aline buried her face in my chest. Some men had run to get water, but with no source nearby, everyone was forced to listen to her screams until her life vanished amidst the plumes of greasy smoke.

"Can we go back now?" asked Aline, tears filling her eyes.

"I have to see this through. No one wants to rally behind a coward," I replied. "Why don't you head back? I'll have a guard accompany you."

"No. If you're going to stay, I will too."

I became more impressed by the inner strength Aline revealed to me with each passing day. We continued the journey up but with much less enthusiasm than when we had begun. By the time we reached the first of the upper levels, the volume of supporters had noticeably diminished. I surmised that it was due to either fear of retribution for involvement in the corruption or perhaps concern over the idea of forced equality among the pod's residents—both of which were unfounded.

We worked our way to the top floor, where we were met by the least amount of residents thus far. Only those with the most money or clout dwelled on the top floor, essentially, those who had the most to lose in a power transition. Of those present, a few were trying to schmooze the potential future leader, but for the most part, it was genuine interest in the cause. Working among the top floors had an eeriness to it that was unexpected. The dark Nucleus was ever-present, silently looming over us from the central shaft as we toured. I could imagine the eyes inside, peering out at us from a distance. After their Release Day fiasco, they had heard the mobs and responded by isolating themselves. Now they listened to the cheers and knew it wasn't for them. I knew inside they were preparing for the imminent invasion. The security force inside had the most advanced weaponry and training in the pod. If I weren't careful, I would be responsible for a significant loss of life. Fabrice was right. We had to take the Nucleus, but we had to weigh the cost carefully.

With our tour finally completed and us on the verge of collapse, Aline and I took the elevator back down to the 90th floor, making sure to ignore every call on the way down. As we took the stairs down to the 91st floor to resume our journey, part of me wished we had simply taken the freight elevator, but Fabrice had thought it unbecoming.

"The first thing we have to change is this damn elevator arrangement," I said, exhausted. "Physical barriers only add to social ones. Increasing the ease of access within the entire pod is one of the first steps towards unity."

"You are starting to sound like a politician," Aline said, squeezing me tightly.

•••••••••

The following day we set up for the second time in the broadcast studio. Again, the same crew gathered around. This time the trainees were taking the reins of the process, as the older generation graciously stood observing from behind at the ready. I was pleased to feel the optimism of change throughout the pod. As I waited for the signal to begin, my eyes wandered to the collapsing cosmetic ceiling above me as I smelled the distinct odor of overheating electronics. I was hungry for change, too. A change that would eventually lead us back to the surface.

Following the same procedure as from the day before, Fabrice initiated the broadcast. After making several speeches, I was beginning to feel more at home in front of an audience, whether in-person or remote. I had never been much of an extrovert, always preferring driving from the backseat, but Aline was right. There was a desperate need for new leadership. As the only elected, capable, and honest official, it was my duty to fill it.

"Residents of Pod Horizonte." I said, "It was heart-warming and awe-inspiring to feel your overwhelming support yesterday. I am honored that you would allow me to lead you as we stand against immorality. Initially, I asked you to join me in spirit as we incapacitated the Nucleus, but now I must ask you for something more—participation. True democracy doesn't begin overnight, nor does it begin alone. For this reason, I ask that every able-bodied person join us in the central laborer hall at 0600 sharp tomorrow morning. Many of you trained for years, even decades, to pass the challenges facing you on the Path to Citizenship. I will ask you to draw on that knowledge and experience, however painful it may be. Tomorrow we will begin a campaign—a campaign that will go down in our pod's history as the day we stood against corruption and came out victorious! Today, we'll stand for our pod, and soon— for our world!"

I watched as the camera's light went dim. Fabrice came out clapping.

"That was amazing!" he said, grinning from ear to ear.

"And exactly what we needed," said Aline.

CHAPTER 33: HUCK

Two days. The two blissfully uneventful days traveling up the Dead River was precisely what we all needed. It was revitalizing to spend my spare time drawing and admiring the passing scenery instead of worrying about the deadly Arthropods. Mueller had said that the Arthropods weren't as bad on this river. Something about the toadies, what the Misfits called the spring tongues, not liking the shallow water. We had continuing concerns for the airborne Arthropods but had only seen the aerials in the distance so far. Mueller gave us numerous tasks to earn our keep, but with a full crew, it was mostly either busy work or the less desirable tasks pawned off by unwilling crew members. While I'd typically pal around with Zeke, he was more interested in spending time with Krista. I could usually find them sitting next to each other, leaning against the tires of the cargo hauler, jerking apart when anyone came around the corner.

Mueller exaggerated when he said there was no privacy on board. It wasn't a large barge at all, barely fitting on the tiny river, but there was a little space around the vehicles in which we could walk, pee, or in Zeke's case—make out. The double-platformed barge barely held the length of the five large vehicles of the Misfits. Most of us passed the time wherever the shade was or shelter in case of rain, though Grace rarely left the pilothouse, only allowing Mueller to take the helm in her absence. All the vehicles had their doors and canvas panels strapped open for ventilation, but I still sweated profusely.

Finally, we stopped at night, sleeping on the banks before quickly moving on the following morning. Last night we had camped in a bit of clearing just to the side of where Grace had docked the barge. After setting up a perimeter, myself and a few others went on a jog to maintain our physique and burn off some energy. Krista had wanted to run with Zeke, but her lack of endurance cut the run shorter than we would've liked. By the time we returned, Kurt had dinner almost finished. We ate and washed quickly, a vital habit we adapted to well. About half of us slept in bivvies, the rest in the vehicles. The mosquitos were particularly annoying, but we preferred them to the Arthropods.

After getting underway, Otto sat down with me and helped me better understand the map Memo had given me. He said we would reach the large Red Sands Reservoir around lunchtime, where we would likely run into more water-dwelling Arthropods. I was on edge but comforted by the experience and weaponry of the Misfits transporting us. We continued north on the Dead River, making good time on the straights but slowing down frequently for the river's tight bends and shallow sandbars. I had spent the morning sitting in the shade underneath the flatbed sketching Arjun and Ciro. They were together on the back of the barge, examining the carcass of a blood midge that Ade had discovered on himself after breakfast.

Lunch would be fresh sashimi. Kurt had been excitedly talking up this meal since we came aboard. Unfortunately, living up to its name, the Dead River's fish population was too low for a decent meal until we entered the waters closer to the reservoir. So I sat continuing my sketch, the base of my hands turning gray with the excess dust from the graphite. I was eventually interrupted by a faint swishing sound, signaling someone's approach. I looked up to see a pair of legs halted in front of me, the owner's foot tapping impatiently. Ariadne leaned over and spied me camped out under the vehicle.

"For it being such a small boat, you can be a hard person to find," she said.

"I like it under here," I responded. "It's as close as I can get to somewhere cool."

"*That,* I understand. What are you drawing?"

I hesitated nervously for a moment before thinking better of it and then slid my sketchbook over to her.

"It's beautiful. How often do you draw?"

"As much as I can, at least when I can find the paper. It took me several weeks to scrounge up enough paper to make this book. I bound it myself," I said, flipping it over and showing Ariadne the irregular binding stitched by my inexperienced hand. "Back in the pod, I spent all my time drawing what I imagined the outside to be."

"How does it measure up?"

"It's a thousand times better. Though it was significantly less dangerous in my daydreams."

She laughed. "We're not fighting for our lives every second like our trainers led us to believe, but it's certainly no cakewalk. I feel like our journey might be possible, though getting all the way to the Australian Territory… I'm trying not to think about that yet. 'Focus on the next step, Ariadne.' I keep telling myself."

"That's good advice. I have two goals: to live."

"Um, that's one goal, Huck. Trust me. I'm good at math," Ariadne said, smiling.

"No, it's two. Live, as in stay alive, and live, as in enjoy life. I'm trying to stay positive about the mission, but I know the reality of the situation. If my time on the surface is short, I want to take in as much of it as I can. The one thing the Arthropods can't take from me is my experiences."

"That's a nice sentiment, but don't over-romanticize our journey. You still have a big responsibility as our leader. We need your head on Earth, not in the clouds, okay?"

I nodded to her, wondering which of us was the actual leader. I found her unusual green eyes distracting, then felt my face flush as I remembered my glimpse of her that day downriver.

"That's exactly what I mean! You are already thinking about something else." She shook her head, annoyed. "Now, the real reason I'm here: Kurt needs our help catching lunch. He's going to show us how to clean them too."

"I remember that from our survival training," I said.

"Where they explained with an illustration? Something tells me the real thing is different," said Ariadne, climbing out from under the truck.

"I guess you're right," I said, but she was already out of earshot.

I followed Ariadne to the lead platform, where Kurt already had Omar, Ade, and Leni casting lines off into the water. As I walked up, Kurt handed me a rod.

"You won't have to wait long. There are plenty of fish. Just throw your line in, wait for a bite, tug it back, and reel it in. There's a bucket over there in the shade of the truck you can throw your catch. We'll go over cleaning when—Would you look at that?"

We all swiveled our heads, following Kurt's gaze. Getting closer and closer to us was a giant, spider-like Arthropod unlike any I had ever seen. It had an elongated blue-gray body, a funny face, and extraordinarily long limbs.

"What the hell is that?! Ade, my naginata," said Omar.

"No," Kurt said, motioning with his hand to back down. "It's friendly." Then addressing everyone, "Guys! Strider up ahead! Starboard side! Don't engage!"

Everyone who wasn't attempting to fish arrived quickly. As per usual, Arjun was the first with the questions, his shyness vanishing among his curiosity.

"Wake strider! Are there a lot on this part of the river?" he asked.

"Yes. Even more, when we arrive at the reservoir. If Grace slows when we come alongside it, we can touch it. They're harmless."

"You go right ahead. I'm not touching a damn invert!" said Hemant. "It's lucky I don't squash it like the others."

Omar and Ade each nodded in agreement. Kurt shook off their attitudes towards the creature but seemed slightly annoyed by their ignorance. Sure enough, Grace slowed the barge, and we drifted to a stop. The strider stood frozen in what I imagined to be equal parts curiosity and fear, its emotionless compound eyes unmoving as it inspected us. Kurt demonstrated its calm demeanor by leaning out across the water and caressing its side, barely able to reach its body.

"It has a soft, thin fuzz," he said, continuing his contact. "It mainly eats small reptiles. They don't view us as a threat, so they leave us alone and vice versa. Go ahead, try it."

With Kurt's permission, those of us who could reach it did so and began petting the animal. In its weird way, it was beautiful. I couldn't take my eyes off the intense metallic coloration it displayed. I realized then that maybe there was a side to the Arthropods we weren't seeing. No one was considering something: we couldn't live in harmony with the majority of the species of Arthropods on Earth, but the new experience made me think the situation wasn't as cut and dry as I believed. I needed to ask Arjun if other bugs were as harmless as the strider. Akhil, who had been reluctant, finally caved and leaned over to pet the creature when a spear sprouted from its side, misting those of us closest with fine droplets of its black hemolymph. Then, with a sad, wilting screech, it collapsed slowly into the water. The event filled me with a sense of trickery and betrayal.

"What did you do?" Kurt asked Leni, whose deadpan stare oscillated between the strider's floating carcass and Kurt. "Why would you do that? It was harmless."

"None of the inverts are harmless. I will kill every damn one I see until they kill me," said Leni before ripping out her spear and walking away.

I stood around perplexed and angered at the violence I had just witnessed. Leni had shattered our brief moment of innocence and joy with her hostility and vengeance. Akhil seemed to be taking it harder than the rest of us, exposing his rarely seen softer side. He spent a few extra moments caressing the wake strider. He hadn't struck me as one who had a soft spot for animals.

Despite none of us being in the mood to fish, we knew that the others depended on the food, so we sat silently, catching the fish that would compose our dinner. I was not in any mood to take more lives, so I left Kurt, Omar, and Ade to clean them. Kurt didn't object to my shirking of the duty.

I grabbed Arjun on the way back. "Does Leni have the Shock?"

"It's quite likely. She is emotionally hostile and socially withdrawn. Because of her nightmares, Ciro and I stopped setting up our bivvies near her. She has all the earmarks of the condition, but the wanton violence is a new one."

"Is she trustable? I mean towards humans."

"I don't know. Most of the failed ones back in the pod never handled much responsibility because of their various conditions. The Shock affects everyone differently. But, sadly, I think the biggest threat she poses is to herself."

"Thanks, Arjun. I appreciate your honesty."

"Of course."

I walked back to my little hideout under the truck in an attempt to process what had occurred. I laid down with my back against the dusty plating of the deck and heard a melodic humming behind me. I turned, expecting to see Ariadne, but instead saw Leni. Sitting with her back to me and unaware of my presence, she was carving deep lines into her forearms with her dagger.

CHAPTER 34: ARIADNE

Kurt's lunchtime meal was beautifully prepared and presented from his modest kitchenette in the rear of the supply truck. Initially, I had mixed feelings about eating raw fish, but between my voracious appetite and the attractive display, my stomach needed no further convincing. It took a moment to grow accustomed to the different cold, crunchy texture that varied from its cooked counterpart, but it turned out to be delicious.

Seeing the wake strider killed had nullified my appetite, but my famished body took over once I started eating, scarfing down all that Kurt offered me. He said that being this close to the reservoir was too risky to cook and that sashimi made an excellent raw dish close to Arthropod habitats. I was gaining invaluable knowledge from the experience of the Misfits and grateful for their willingness to share it.

"We're approaching the reservoir!" yelled Grace from the pilot cabin. "There's some activity ahead. Everyone to your stations."

I watched as the Misfits scrambled to ready themselves and their weapons. They sealed the doors, panels, and flaps as I felt the engines slow to a crawl beneath us. The crew made an armed perimeter around the barge, staying close to the trucks and arranging us in the same fashion. Each of us had our weapons at the ready. Mueller did a rapid inspection before addressing us with his booming voice.

"Newbies! There are a few things you need to know about Red Sands. It's a watering hole of sorts for the inverts, but one we have to pass through nonetheless. There will be toadies, striders, and hooks in vast numbers. The hooks don't care much for open water and won't come too close except when we approach the shores." Mueller continued. "It'll take us a few hours to get through this, and we'll turn on the smoke, but I need you on-guard for the duration. If you see any surprises, don't keep them to yourself! Mark my words—things happen fast. Understood?"

"Understood!" yelled everyone unanimously.

Grace let Mueller take the helm and waved for the females to join her. She took us to the back of the boat and unceremoniously dropped her trousers.

"You all better take care of things now because we aren't going to have the time or safety to do it on the open water," she said. "The men will be doing the same, so hurry up."

It was awkward, but I'd regret it if I didn't follow her suggestion. Grace was right about Mueller and the other men, judging by the sounds of water flow emanating from around the barge. I was rapidly learning that Grace knew everything. Sometimes I wondered if it was her, not Mueller, that kept the proverbial ship afloat. We returned to our posts, and Grace vanished into the pilothouse with nary another word. Otto and Zeke bustled about preparing the barge's smoke-based countermeasures. It was good seeing Zeke in his engineering element, obviously relishing it.

Down the length of the barge, I heard Krista throw up again. She had never seemed this nervous in the pod during training, but up until our "final exam," we had never faced real Arthropods. The strain of battle weighs differently on each one of us. It had on

Leni. I had used valerian to help with the anxiety of Release Day, but that wasn't something native to this area. Maybe I could forage for something similar next time we made landfall. I was becoming more and more concerned about her health. Suddenly, I heard the hiss of the smoke canisters begin, bringing my focus back to the present just as a slow-moving, smelly haze covered the barge and camouflaged our passage. Otto said the smoke could make us almost invisible to the "sneaky bastards," but at the cost of our visibility. It seemed like a worthwhile tradeoff, but we had to be that much more diligent of the inverts.

The reservoir was the most extensive body of water I had ever laid eyes on. Before the smoke hid it from view, I saw that its water was dark, beautiful greenish-blue and surrounded by banks of bright orange sand. I desperately wanted to see more of it, but I was grateful for the opaque blanket of protection that the smoke provided. It was going to be a long, taxing day being physically and mentally attentive for signs of threatening movement. Unlike the class time when my mind wandered, here it could easily be the difference between life and death. I recalled tales of ancient societies that put guards to death who failed to maintain their watch.

After only the first few minutes, which slipped by at a glacial pace, I found it surprisingly difficult to stay diligently focused on the mundanity. My mind would predictably begin to daydream, and then after a few moments, I would refocus only to have it wander off again. I was going to be exhausted by the time we reached the end of the reservoir. Aside from an interested strider that had left after encountering the irritating smoke, time was passing by uninterestingly and incrementally.

After about an hour in the irritating smog, we heard the troubling sounds of an unknown creature being attacked and devoured. The disgusting racket occurred just past the limited visibility of the smoke, but my imagination filled in the gory details. Whether animal or Arthropod, it was suffering a horrific death at the jaws of several inverts. I tried in vain to push it out of my mind as the noise grew louder and louder. Then with a sickening sensation, I realized the noises were now originating from the back of the boat—and someone was screaming.

As others made the same realization, we took off toward the back of the boat. The gut-wrenching scene that greeted us was Ade holding on to the rear railing for dear life, screaming for help from Akhil, who was lying on the deck nearby in a fit of stupefied laughter. Stretching Ade between the boat and its mouth was a swimming toadie with its tongue encompassing Ade's left leg. The first responders to the scene were losing a tug of war with the invert. Stretching his body unnaturally long, Ade's parallel position to the water put any doubt of a spring tongues strength to rest. Ade's right hand eventually slipped out of the hands of Omar and was now only being held in place by Mueller and Hemant.

"Don't let me go!" he screamed, tears forming in his eyes. "Please don't let me go."

I could tell their grip was slipping with the spray of the water lubricating Ade's arm. I was desperate to help, but my arms were frozen in fear, rendering my bow useless. I looked back at Akhil, who was now sitting against the tire of the flatbed, snickering at the situation unfolding before him. *What the hell was wrong with him?! Was it the Shock?* I had no idea. His behavior shocked me out of my momentary paralysis, and I turned back to see Ade reaching towards the machete tucked into his belt.

"Good idea, cut the tongue!" I yelled.

Ade grabbed the hilt of his machete with his free hand and started haphazardly swinging at the creature's tongue but couldn't reach it. I could see everyone's strength waning. This couldn't go on forever. I readied my bow to fire on the creature's head and saw Ade's eyes filled with a combination of helplessness and defeat.

Before I could fire, the look on his face changed from fear to resolve. He raised his machete and swung without hesitation, taking off his left leg in several agonizing hits. Immediately he flew across the deck with the inertia of the rebounding force to safety as the toadie disappeared, momentarily satisfied with its morbid snack.

Ade was wincing painfully and growing more pail with each passing second, trying to push his torso up into a seated position while the others prevented him from doing so. Finally, Kurt returned with a syringe and vial of what I assumed was morphine, pulling the cap off the needle with his teeth. As Hemant made a tourniquet, Kurt hurriedly but meticulously measured the dosage and injected Ade, who finally began to calm. Blood covered the decking, causing Mueller to slip in the crimson fluid as he stood. He lunged at Akhil, jerking him up off the ground and slamming him against the side of the buggy almost two meters off the ground, a dagger against his neck.

"What the hell is wrong with you, boyo!?" he asked. "I told you I had no patience for cowards on my boat!"

Akhil continued giggling, almost unaware of the severity of his position. Mueller paused and looked closely at Akhil's eyes, then, taking a deep sniff of his breath, lowered him to the ground and began patting him down. Instantly, Mueller found what he had suspected. In Akhil's chest pocket, he had freshly harvested Arthropod pheromone glands, most potent when refined into Dust, but still an intoxicant when used raw. Mueller was enraged.

"The only thing I hate as much as a coward is a junkie," said Mueller, thrusting his finger into Akhil's chest. "I would kill you where you stand, but you wouldn't even appreciate why I had done it. I'll deal with you tomorrow when you're sober."

He let Akhil collapse in a pathetic, giggling heap, chunking the small, pear-shaped glands into the water. Everyone returned to their positions, except for Kurt and Hemant, who tended to Ade. As

Omar passed Akhil, he gave him a hard, swift kick in the stomach. Akhil spewed blood onto the deck from where he'd bit his tongue.

I offered to help Kurt, who declined before he pushed me out of the way, as he and Hemant moved Ade to the supply truck, which doubled as a triage. I looked around, first at Akhil, who was eyeing me strangely, then at the metal-clad decking drenched with Ade's blood. Then, feeling helpless, I advanced slowly back to my post. We continued through the reservoir north until late afternoon, which I could subtly detect from the sun's hues filtering through the smoke.

Otto came around and warned everyone of the impending shutoff of the countermeasures.

"We've got to disable the smoke so Grace can see to navigate through the ruptured dam," he said. "Everyone needs to be inside or underneath the trucks. And I'd recommend you to cover your ears."

We didn't take our time. The Misfits took most of the onboard space, leaving little room for our group. Turning the supply truck into a mobile operating room further reduced the space. Viewing Leni and Krista as the weaker on board, they gave them the premium space in the vehicles over the others.

"Thank you," I said to Mueller as he shut the door.

"Don't thank me yet," he said. "It's about to get very loud. Don't forget, cover your ears."

I didn't fully appreciate what he meant, but I knew I was about to find out. As our cover drifted away on the currents of wind, the Arthropods took notice. Now I was beginning to understand the warnings. The Misfits, who would generally avoid using their arsenal at the risk of attracting inverts, were about to be surrounded and had no reason to hold back. The tension in the air was thicker than the humidity as the inverts approached. Otto was growing impatient in the gunner position above me, waiting for the command to open fire.

"Wait for it...," I heard Mueller say through the open gun ports.

"Come on, you damn inverts," Otto said, drumming his fingers. "A little closer, a little closer, a little—"

"Fire!" yelled Mueller.

Mueller had been right. The ensuing sound was deafening, even with my ears covered. The repeated pounding of the automatic rifle placements was almost unbearable. Krista was screaming for it to stop, and Mei was mouthing some repeating mantra. The brass casings from the weapons mostly ejected out of the ports. Still, the superheated casings would occasionally drop down onto my exposed skin, burning me. After what seemed like ages, the firing finally ceased.

"Clear for the moment!" yelled Mueller.

Doors began to open, and I finally dropped my hands down from my ears. I could still hear a ringing as I climbed out of the personnel carrier, disoriented. Huck approached me, and after repeating his question a few times, managed to ascertain that I was fine before checking on the others. Leni and Mei climbed out after me, looking about the same way I felt. I looked off to the side and saw the concrete and metal debris from the decimated dam that cluttered the river. Grace had slowed the barge to a crawl and was making her way upriver through the rubble. The carcasses of the dead Arthropods that the Misfits had gunned down littered the river.

"That should be the bulk of 'em for a while," said Otto. "The more we shot, the more they came, so the more we shot. Vicious cycle, really, but makes the grunt work easier, I suppose."

"The ones you didn't kill are more interested in the bodies of the others," I replied.

"That's the twisted beauty of it. You kill enough inverts, and the others lose interest. The easier snack tends to dissuade them. The flipping inverts don't care what meat they eat, just that they eat it."

I shuddered as I observed the remaining Arthropods cannibalizing the mutilated corpses in the river, which were sullying the greenish currents of the river with a dingy shade of gray. I turned away from the disturbing images and saw Krista approaching with her arms crossed, downtrodden.

"I need to tell you something."

"What, Krista? Anything."

"I think I'm pregnant."

CHAPTER 35: HEMANT

We slowly drifted through the collapsed wreckage of the dam without further entanglement in the wake of our skirmish with the inverts. Once Grace had safely navigated us through the minefield of crumbling concrete and rotting iron, we made camp for the night. Sleep came even more reluctantly than it had on previous nights with the expectation of Akhil's execution in the morning. Mueller was livid, and he wasn't one to make idle threats. He clearly warned that he would dispatch anyone who displayed an act of cowardice—Akhil had done that and more. I had no love for Akhil, but I felt that every human loss was another win for the inverts. Eventually, I dozed off, waking up to the cacophonous sounds of breakfast and bright rays of the morning sun shining through my bivvy. I climbed out of my tent and joined the others for coffee and breakfast, watching the earlier risers break down the remainder of our little riverside camp.

"Morning boyos," said Otto, joining Huck and me. "I hope the two of you aren't tired of water 'cuz we still have a long way to float! Now that we're out of the bloomin' reservoir, we'll get to enjoy the sand and sun on the calmer Strider River."

"You make it sound like a vacation," I said. "But I know you're full of it."

Otto laughed heartily.

"It goes all the way to the coast, right," asked Huck.

"That it does," said Otto, still snickering. "Not that we'll be going that way. We take it as far as the decrepit town of Wet Church. From there it's northeast and on to our port Tank Town. Then I'll wave goodbye as your crazy asses sail off to the Saharan Territory."

The Saharan Territory. I had initially expected to make it that far, but the more we traveled, the more I comprehended the full scope of our journey. It was an incredible undertaking for all of us. And it was a journey we had barely begun.

I looked over to see Kurt and Mueller fussing over something. Mueller climbed into the supply truck, undoubtedly checking on Ade's condition. He returned after a few moments and patted Kurt on the shoulder in what appeared to be praise. As Mueller walked past me, I turned to face him.

"Is he awake? Can I see him? I haven't seen him since Kurt kicked me out of the truck last night."

"He is awake, but you need to talk to Kurt first. I appreciate the valor you showed yesterday." said Mueller, then adding, "Unlike your friend."

I finished the remains of my breakfast and hopped onto the barge to catch Kurt. Huck saw what I was doing and joined me.

"Can we see him?" I asked.

"He's resting. We need to limit his interruptions," said Kurt, pausing. "You can have two minutes but no more. I'll send them to you for his condition if anyone else asks. Deal?"

"Deal," Huck and I both answered.

Huck and I ducked under the canvas as we climbed into the truck. Kurt remained outside but kept his head inside to keep an eye on his patient. The floor was still littered with blood-stained rags, though the hemorrhaging had ceased. Ade was lying on the fold-down cot, mostly uncovered so that we could see the mass of bandage on his leg. He was awake and smiled when he saw us.

"Once I put him under, I kicked you out so I could work alone. Nothing personal. I concentrate best by myself," Kurt said. "In addition to anesthesia, I put him on an intravenous antibiotic and cleaned his wound with an antiseptic. Ade, your hack job saved your life but left me a mess to suture. I trimmed and smoothed up everything, reshaping your muscles and nerves, so I believe you will heal nicely with minimal pain. You'll still be subject to phantom sensations. They're common with amputations. Your leg will never be pretty, but the outlook is good. You'll be able to take care of yourself in a few days."

"Thanks, Doc," said Ade.

"You're welcome. I'll leave you guys alone for a few minutes," said Kurt. Then looking at me and Huck added, "Two minutes."

Then he vanished.

"Thanks, Hemant," Ade said. "Everything was a blur yesterday, even during the attack. I'm not even sure I understand what all happened. My mind isn't making a lot of sense right now."

"That's okay, man. Just concentrate on feeling better," I said.

"I'm so glad you're okay, Ade," said Huck. "I don't know that I'd have the strength to do what you did."

"Yeah, you would," said Ade. "When you realize your choices are certain death or possible death, you choose possible. I'm not into being digested alive."

"None of us are," I said, laughing.

"So Mueller's going to kill Akhil?" asked Ade. "I'm pissed, like royally pissed, but I don't want him dead."

"I don't know," I said. "Mueller doesn't seem like the forgiving type.

I heard a knock signaling the end of our time.

"Get some rest, Ade," said Huck. "I'm glad you're okay."

"Thanks, guys," said Ade. "Tell Mei a kiss might help me recover faster."

"I'm pretty sure one of her throwing knives wouldn't, though," I said.

"True," Ade said, grinning.

We ducked under the canvas and headed back to the mob forming around Akhil on the bank. Akhil was standing in the middle of the group, finally demonstrating the emotions that eluded him yesterday. Mueller was pacing back and forth in front of him. He looked up and saw us joining them.

"Good. We can begin," said Mueller, squaring off with Akhil. "Akhil, yesterday you demonstrated two characteristics that, as the leader of the Misfits, I do not tolerate. Granted, I failed to mention my strong distaste for addicts, but I specifically mentioned our zero-tolerance policy for cowardice."

As I stepped up alongside my brother, I looked at Akhil's face as it dampened with tears. He looked terrified, his eyes pleading for clemency.

"You are a danger to the lives of those who depend on you. With that in mind, I have the unfortunate honor of sentencing you to death."

There was a murmur through all the candidates, but only rigidly straight faces among the Misfits. Ariadne immediately stepped forward.

"Boss Mueller, may I appeal to you on Akhil's behalf?" she asked.

I was elated that Ariadne had decided to argue in Akhil's favor.

"I will always bend an ear to those who wish, but our rules are hard and fast, like life on the surface," he said.

"The Arthropods take so many human lives, and I don't want them to have an advantage," she said. "I don't approve of Akhil's actions any more than you all do, but I disapprove of the inverts even more. I wish for Akhil to be left for dead so that he may have a fighting chance at survival."

Mueller twisted the end of his mustache pensively.

"Hmm. Would you leave Akhil with a weapon or defenseless, young Ariadne?" asked Mueller.

"With all of his gear," she said.

"You appeal to my good nature. You are right not to give the inverts any leeway in this war. We will set off immediately, leaving Akhil here with his gear on his own recognizance," said Mueller, pausing. "I have an addition. Kurt, see to it that we leave young Akhil here with the mark of banishment so that others may know of his crimes."

Kurt nodded, and Akhil's shoulders drooped. I walked over to him.

"This is better," I said. "You have a chance to restore your honor."

Akhil met my eyes. He nodded, sniffling. I patted him on the shoulder and went to finish stowing my gear. Minutes later, we were pulling away from the bank, leaving Akhil staring at us forlornly, his arm red and swollen from his new tattoo.

●●●●●●●●●

Over four days, I watched Kurt teach Huck, Ariadne, and Ciro how to bow fish. Their sessions not only provided us with fish but also with entertainment. Huck eventually gave up, losing too many of his limited overpowered bolts in the river, but Ariadne and Ciro had become quite adept in the art. I was sick of river sashimi and lime ceviche. By the end of the fourth day, I was getting excited about the prospect of real food—terrestrial food. Otto told everyone that we were coming to a vast cavern formation filled with prehistoric artwork. Grace needed to stop at the Cave City Pump House to fill up the barge and tanker, which she used to fill up the barge.

Arjun and Ciro were nerding out about seeing these caverns, despite the risk posed by not only the inverts but the natural dangers of a cave. I had some interest in them myself, but only if we could do it safely. I didn't want to do anything to put my brother or our mission in jeopardy. I almost regretted Otto telling us that our campsite would be close to the caverns. Still, admittedly, my brother's intense curiosity for learning and exploration was one of the things I loved so much about him.

I knew I was playing the part of nagging big brother, but I wanted to reiterate being cautious around the formations. So that afternoon, I walked around the barge to his and Ciro's usual hangouts to see if I could have a word with him. As I came around the backside of the flatbed truck, I heard the distinct sounds of Zeke and Krista making out again. I rolled my eyes, preparing to awkwardly interrupt them and ascertain the location of my brother. Instead, I found Arjun and Ciro rocketing apart when I rounded the corner. I don't know how long I stood there with my mouth agape before Arjun finally broke the silence.

"Good afternoon, brother," said Arjun.

I looked at him, then back to Ciro. I had heard of candidates attracted to the same sex back in the pod but had never expected my brother to be. Especially my twin.

"It's perfectly natural. People have done it since the dawn of time by both humans and now-extinct species," Arjun continued, unflustered. "There were several—"

I held up my hand for him to stop.

"I just… I just need a minute, okay?"

I walked back around the corner and ran into Ariadne, who was looking for Ciro. Time to hunt, I supposed. With one look at my face, she realized what had happened.

"You just figured it out, didn't you?" she asked, putting her hand on my arm.

I nodded. "How many people knew about it before I did?"

"Most of the barge," she said. "Sorry. We often have the most trouble seeing what is directly in front of us. I'm here if you ever want to chat, okay?"

"Thanks. Arjun's still my brother, and I love him. I just need a minute to get used to the idea."

"I understand. Let me know if you need anything."

I nodded and continued up the barge, figuring I'd omit the safety lecture. After the shock with Arjun, I had even less of an appetite for aquatic food. With any luck, Ariadne and Ciro would go hunting tonight. That is if Ciro could be torn apart from my brother.

That evening, we made port at a remarkably picturesque natural area, only identifiable as our destination by the pump house. Grace immediately began fueling up, always wanting to be prepared for a quick departure. As I tossed gear off the barge down to Otto, he filled me in on the area. In addition to being an engineer, he also apparently had a penchant for history.

"It's difficult to find books on the subject, but whenever I can get a hold of one of those antiques, I try to read it cover-to-cover. This mind up here is an interesting conglomeration of facts and trivia, you know," said Otto, pointing to his head. "I have what they used to call a photographic memory."

"What did we have for dinner three nights ago, Otto?" asked Mueller, stepping off the barge with a crate.

"Uh…" responded Otto.

"Photographic memory, my ass!" laughed Mueller, walking away.

"He doesn't have a lot of respect for the learned," whispered Otto.

I smiled. Say what you want about Otto; he knew a lot of random crap. Most of which I assumed was at least somewhat factual. He could hold his own with Arjun, so I knew he wasn't an idiot. Once we had finished unloading and setting up base camp, I was thrilled to see Kurt's iron stew pot and tripod make their reappearance. The pot's promise of real food already had me salivating.

"Mueller!" yelled Grace, gesturing him over to the pump house.

Mueller followed her over, as did my attention. I had expected to meet my first pump house engineer, but the look on Grace's face led me to believe that wouldn't happen today. When Grace noticed she had inadvertently hooked everyone's attention, she addressed us all.

"I guess there's no point in keeping secrets. It's a mess in there. Something crawled in and mauled poor Raul, or whatever his name was. The equipment is functional, but we need to clean it thoroughly. The biowaste is caked up and dried everywhere, but the smell is tolerable. I'll fuel us up, and we can have a cleaning party in the morning."

"Sounds good," said Mueller. "Anyone interested in taking a pump house position? It's probably the best view of them all."

No one seemed particularly keen to take him up on his offer after hearing what had just happened to its last attendant. Kurt returned to placing ingredients into his pot. He and Ariadne foraged for local mushrooms and plants in the vicinity of the campsite. As I looked at the faces surrounding the fire, the exhaustion was visibly evident. The Misfits had a hardened resilience, but the day's events had worn out those of us from the pod. Mei hid hers well, but Krista had been struggling, her health only adding to her struggles. Omar had been closed off since the attack on Ade. Leni, who was finally beginning to open up, looked the most tired of us all. Ade, who was somewhat mobile, had joined us at the fire with the help of Kurt and his crutches.

After a quick hunting trip, Ariadne, Ciro, and Mei returned with several snakes. I hadn't ever eaten snakes, but I was open to eating anything that wasn't from the water. After dinner, I concluded that snakes were as bad as fish. They had just as many bones and even more sinew. I never thought I'd prefer varmint. The next morning, we got an unexpected announcement from Mueller.

"Last night, I noticed how tired our new friends are," said Mueller. "I'm officially declaring today a rest day. Otto's been nagging me anyway for time to explore the caves. He's offering a *tour*. So you're on your own for lunch, but I want everyone back here before nightfall."

Several people started to move. Grace coughed, seeking attention.

"Oh, and if you stay here, you must help Grace clean the pump house," Mueller added.

I instantly saw a few more people begin to show interest in Otto's historical cave art tour.

"Gear up," shouted Otto. "The caverns start up that way."

CHAPTER 36: GUILHERME

At 0600, I was standing at the head of the central laborer hall on risers from storage. After removing the cobwebs and shrugging off the rust, they set them up at the natural front of the space. Fabrice had the place wired for sound because my voice wouldn't be able to fill the extensive hall. I looked out among the assembly. A disciplined army it was not, but the turnout was far better than any of us had expected. The residents of Pod Horizonte had turned out en masse to defend their home, their offspring, and their future.

Many of the assembled were citizens, having survived their Release Day and nobly performed their cross-country trek. However, the passage of time had taken its toll. Many of the recruits were overweight, out-of-shape, or simply too old for battle. Some of these citizens may have never completed the Path to Citizenship, which a previous administration had only established forty-five years ago. *How were these people going to invade the Nucleus with its armed and established security force?* Many trainees were also present within the ranks, who we had limited to age fourteen and older. I recognized one candidate, Nikos, from one of my last hearings on the Tribunal Council.

The most exciting additions to the force were unexpected. Many laborers had responded to the call in droves, but the real surprises were from two groups. We had a number of the residents from the well-off echelons of society, possibly there to seek redemption. The more astonishing but welcome recruits were the failed ones. They were considered societal outcasts and deemed worthless, but here they were, willing and able to fight for our cause. I glanced over to stage left, where Aline stood smiling.

"Men, women, adults, and trainees," I began. "Yesterday I called on your help. Your turnout warms my heart. I cannot express how thankful I am that you are willing to help with our cause—the liberation of our pod. We are tired of letting this illness wash over us, taking your children from your arms. I can't imagine what that does to you.

"Today, I want to start by breaking down our first barriers—the mental ones. From this day forward, we will cease using the following terms because of their negative connotations: The terms 'laborers,' 'failed ones,' and 'unabled' will be stricken from use, but not from our history. They will be replaced by the 'skilled,' the 'recouping,' and the 'aided,' respectively. Henceforth we will all be residents and we will confer citizenship upon completing academic and physical training. The raising of children will revert to the parents, with the matriarchs serving a supplemental role. As a member of the pod's leadership, I assure you that we have significant problems, like supply limitations, but those are problems we can overcome together. But only if we are united!

"Today, we will begin your training to invade and retake control of the Nucleus, which will happen in a week's time. By then, the cancer will be starved and ready for removal. Today marks the first day of our pod's future. A future that is truly 'For All!'"

The scores of volunteers began yelling, applauding, and chanting "For All!" "For All!" "For All!" "For All!" I hoped the occupants of the Nucleus could hear that echoing up the central shaft. We were coming for them. We would lose lives, but we would gain life. I looked over at Aline and Fabrice, who was running towards me. I picked up Aline and spun her around in my arms before kissing her.

"What? No spin for me?" Fabrice joked.

"No such luck. Do you think you can train this ragtag army?" I asked.

"I sure hope so."

•••••••••

"You had to say a week, didn't you?" said Fabrice, exasperated. "I've enlisted the help of every cohort training team we have, and they're still nowhere near ready. Some of these people can't think about exercise without getting winded. In others, the spirit is willing, but the flesh is weak. I'm afraid our larger numbers will only translate to a larger death toll. Time has probably eroded the physical and mental stamina of those barricaded in the Nucleus. However, they are still better trained, better armed, and strongly resistant to arrest."

"If anyone can get them ready in the remaining days, you can, Fab," I said. "I wouldn't have asked you if I didn't think you could do it. We cannot successfully run this pod without control of the Nucleus."

"I'm fully aware of that. I'll get your little group in there, and we will take the damn place, but I'm just saying the cost could be catastrophically high."

"Higher than any single recent Release Day?"

"Maybe. People are willing to die for a cause they believe, but they also have short memories. I don't want the residents turning on us once we've retaken the pod, angered at the loss of their loved ones."

"You don't give people enough credit, Fab."

"I'm a realist," said Fabrice, twirling his hair. "I've seen a few changes in power, as have you. The next politician is always saying how they're going to improve things, and then they inevitably follow the same path of their predecessor."

"It's me, Fab. And you know I have Aline to keep me straight."

"Ha! Of that, I have no doubt. Just stay true to yourself, *capisce?* Let's conquer the bad guys and be the good guys. With any luck, your little band of friends will go save the world, and we can return to the surface within our lifetimes."

"That's what I'm trying to do. That's why I'm continuing the mandatory training and planning to implement it for all the residents. If Huck and his friends can accomplish their mission, we'll need every able body from every single pod fighting the Arthropods to extinction if we ever want to reclaim our planet."

"Alright, alright. You've reignited my fire. You're getting good at that," Fabrice said, smiling before walking out the door.

I sat in silence with my glass of throat-igniting hooch, missing the Tier One whisky sitting in my vacated office above. It was tolerable, but I'm sure it also served as a solvent. I leaned my head back against the torn upholstery of the chair and let the strong alcohol do its magic. Aline came in and rubbed my temples from behind, slowly working her way down my neck.

"Venting again?"

"Yeah. He's worried about the loss of life."

"These people know what they are getting into. They'll do whatever you ask of them. They recognize a strong leader with a good heart when they see one."

"I know. I just want to be the leader they see in me."

"If you keep thinking like that, you will be," she said, leaning over the back of the chair to kiss me. "Now, when you get done with your planning, come home, and I'll help you relax."

"That sounds amazing and intriguing. You're going to have me rushing through my work."

"Take your time. I'll be there when you get there," said Aline. "I've been helping Fabrice teach the groups combat first aid, but Trainer Diogo, who's part slave-driver and part asshole, wore my group out this morning. So I gave them the afternoon off to take care of all their bruises. Said it was homework."

We laughed. "I know what I'd do without you, but I don't ever want to do it again. I love you."

"I love you too," she said, kissing me once more before smiling and leaving me to my work.

I tried to focus through the mix of intoxications. I was constructing the invasion of the Nucleus in an elaborate plan that drew on military training and engineering experience. Fortunately, the two had a lot of overlap. As it stood, in a feat of aerial acrobatics, our minimally trained force would be ziplining down across the shaft to the Nucleus, where they would subdue its occupants, non-lethally if possible. Maybe it was selfishness, but I wanted to see all of them in front of the tribunal. There were also several innocents, likely serving as hostages during the encounter, that I didn't want to lose.

The plan was complicated but plausible. I hoped to the universe that it would work successfully. That's why I was checking and rechecking every detail. After a few more hours working, I decided to take Aline's offer and headed back to our apartment, but not before swinging by the training centers. I took the inconvenient route up to the nearest arena to watch the trainees in action. I had no difficulty discerning which trainer was Diogo from my vantage point. He was down in the sand, having recruits come at him, punishing them with a blow every time they missed. His teaching style was hardcore, but it could be what would save their lives. His female counterpart was encouraging the technique of the recruits.

I watched as a disabled recruit struggled to maintain his balance. Surprisingly, he was better able to land a hit on Trainer Diogo than the others. Even Diogo seemed amused and quickly patted him before returning to his defensive posture.

I left the arena feeling slightly more confident than before and went to join Aline in the crusty, cramped apartment that was strangely beginning to feel like home. I was walking across the open plaza of the lower levels when I heard a frantic screaming from above growing louder and louder. The central shaft was too dark in the absence of the Nucleus' lights, making me powerless to help. Then, as quickly as it had begun, the screaming stopped with an echoing juicy thud. Even from a distance, I could see a misshapen form in the dim sodium-orange glow of the plaza. I ran over to examine the body, as did several other bystanders.

We approached the mutilated corpse. The man next to me turned his head, stifling a gag.

"Get Fabrice up here immediately. I don't care what he's doing," I commanded.

The man took off. I made my way over to it, making sure to listen for any others that might be falling. The impact left the person splattered all over the plaza, extending meters. From the height of the Nucleus, they hadn't reached terminal velocity, but they'd been going fast enough. There was little recognizable as human considering the damage, but I could discern something on his clothes. I walked over to examine it and saw it was a note.

"One every hour until power," the note read.

My heart dropped. This was despicable. The twisted leadership knew they were trapped and knew how they were perceived. They had nothing to lose. Fabrice came running up, and I filled him in. He quickly commanded his entourage to collect evidence and clean up the body.

"What are we going to do?" asked Fabrice.

"What choice do we have? We have to invade," I said. "We have to do it tonight!"

"Alright, I'll ready the troops."

"I have to go to Aline and tell her what's happening."

"Send her to the Lower Master Control Station. I'll keep her safe."

"Thanks, Fab," I said, noting the station's name change.

He nodded and sprinted off. Despite the circumstances, I liked hearing the ease with which everyone was already dropping the pod's ingrained derogatory vernacular. I raced home to Aline and found the hatch ajar and no sign of her guard. Where was he? My senses began to tingle. I swallowed the knot forming in my throat and, pulling out my baton, pushed the hatch open slowly. A few things were scattered, but nothing looked too out of place. I saw where Aline had been preparing for us to have a romantic evening that was no longer possible. I looked on the bed and found a small pool of blood and collapsed to my knees. This was the last thing I could handle right now. I balled up the blankets in my fist as I tried to keep my composure. After a minute and a few deep breaths, I stood and saw a note on the back of the door, barely legible from the blood draining down from the ear above it. Seething rage replaced the fear in my bosom.

"Your wife is such a beautiful lady. I almost hated to cut her ear off, but idle threats are worthless. If I don't get what I want, she will be the last to fall. That would be such a shame. Oh, and sorry about your friend Clifton in the plaza. Maybe if you'll cooperate, I'll let you have his job. —DC"

CHAPTER 37: HUCK

I wasn't feeling like roaming a cave, so instead, I opted to help Grace clean the blood-imbrued pump house. Most of the candidates had joined the Misfits on Otto's tour. Despite Mueller's comment about those who remained, it turned out that Grace, Hemant, and I were the only ones cleaning out the pump house. When I looked past the desiccated human fluid, the interior of the pump house was intriguing.

The exterior of the pump house, which was only the pump station interface, was shaped like a trapezoidal prism. Inside the hatch, a ladder led down to the first floor, which was about twelve square meters. The first floor mainly consisted of pipes and knobs, the primary controls for the artesian well and natural gas. The ladder on the room's opposite side led down to the living quarters, the same size as the floor above. Further down was the aquaponic system and kitchen. Then lastly was a non-habitable floor storing the machines, pumps, and tanks, which the attendant could acoustically seal off from the rest of the station.

The attack had left the previous occupants' remains scattered throughout the top two floors of the residence. It took a combination of elbow grease and Otto's home-brewed hooch to clean and sanitize the innumerable surfaces and crevices. It didn't matter how much we cleaned; we kept finding new hidden spatters. Whatever had happened had been messy and violent. I shuddered, thinking of the terrifying ending Raul or whoever faced here. When we had finally finished cleaning, we descended to the third floor to restore the balance of the aquaponic system. The fish were still alive, but their tank needed some light cleaning and the plants, trimming. Due to the mutually beneficial nature of the system, it had maintained most of its homeostasis.

When Grace finally seemed satisfied with our efforts, she nodded in thanks and vanished up the ladder. I followed her up and sat down next to Ade on a log that someone had dragged over as seating.

"How are you doing?" I asked him.

"All things considered, great," he said. "Kurt says I am recovering more rapidly than expected. I'll be out of my bandage in less than two weeks."

"Nice."

"We need to have a conversation."

"Ade, we are having a conversation."

"I mean a serious one, Huck."

"Okay, let me put my serious face on," I said, acting like I was adjusting my face.

Ade laughed. "Seriously though…"

"Of course, man, go ahead," I said.

"I'm going to stay here," said Ade.

"What? Really?"

"Yeah. Kurt doesn't like it at all, but he thinks physically I'll be fine. He's mainly worried about my mobility on the ladders."

"Ade, I just cleaned the previous resident out of the pump house. I don't know how safe the place is even for someone with all their extremities."

"I realize that, but I can stay exclusively inside the pump house until I'm healed. Maybe next time the Misfits swing by, they can bring me a prosthesis."

"I hate to lose you, man. You've been a valuable member of our team."

"I appreciate that," said Ade. "You know I can't go with you. I'd slow you down, not to mention probably not live through another attack."

"I hate to admit it, but you're right. Staying here might be the best thing for you. We have the rest of the day. Maybe we can rig up some things in the pump house to make it more accessible. Sound good?"

"Sounds great, Huck. Thanks for everything. I mean it."

I shook his hand before walking a little way up the trail. Otto had been right. This place was beautiful. If it weren't for our lingering attracting Arthropods, I wouldn't mind staying here a while. I walked a little further up the trail, stabbing an interested blood midge in the process. I sat on a rock, looking down at the mouth of a large cave below me. The stalactites and stalagmites that had taken millions of years to form had an eerie beauty to them. Eventually, I heard voices and saw the returning group of amateur spelunkers. Otto was traipsing down the incline. The rest of the group looked indubitably bored as he regurgitated fact after fact about prehistoric geology and ancient art.

"How was it?" I asked Ariadne and Mei, the first two I saw.

"The caves were amazing," answered Ariadne. "We even saw evidence of a cave grub but didn't see one."

"I'm glad we didn't see one," said Mei. "It was nice to relax away from the stinking inverts, though being put to sleep by Otto wasn't what I imagined."

"I learned a lot about humanity before the Arthropods. It was interesting when you could keep your attention on him," said Ariadne.

I stood up to accompany them back to the camp. "I bet Arjun and Ciro had the time of their lives," I said.

"You know they did! They tried to follow one of those grub trails, but I don't know if they found anything. Hey Arjun, did you guys find anything?" she yelled.

There was no response.

"Arjun! Ciro!" she called.

Otto, who had been continuing his lecture, stopped. "Hey, what are you guys doing? You're interrupting the seeking of valuable knowledge."

Mei rolled her eyes. "We can't see Arjun or Ciro!" she said.

"Now that you mention it, I don't see 'em either," said Otto.

"Exactly." Mei said, then under her breath, "Dimwit."

"Camp is only a few meters further. Let's go back and round up the others. We'll put together a search party," said Otto.

We sped up our pace and got back to camp within minutes. Otto had started planning with Mueller about searching, but Hemant had none of it.

"You lost him?! You led them out into the woods, and you lost him?" he said accusingly to Otto.

"They are trained candidates. I didn't plan to hold their wee little hands," said Otto. "We'll find them, I promise."

Angered, Hemant walked off, stopping at his tent to grab his war hammer.

"What are you doing, boyo?" asked Mueller.

"Going to find my brother and his friend," he replied and disappeared into the trees heading south.

"I'm going with him," I said.

"Not without us," said Ariadne.

I looked and saw nodding from Omar, Mei, and Zeke.

"I'll stay with Leni," said Krista.

"Let's go!" I said, "Mueller, could you guys search north?"

"You're ordering me around now, boyo?" said Mueller.

I gave him an apologetic look.

"I'm messing with you. Go ahead and bring back your friends. Be back before nightfall! If we haven't found them, we'll continue it in the morning when it's safer," he said as we armed ourselves and headed off after Hemant.

Ariadne caught up with me.

"I'll show you where we last saw them, but we need to catch up with Hemant first. He has no idea where we are going," she said.

We walked for over an hour when we found the entrance to a large cave. We still had seen no sign of Hemant, Arjun, or Ciro. Ariadne walked to the mouth of the cave where they had seen the tell-tale signs of the cave grub.

"They were looking just inside the mouth of the cave, right Mei?" asked Ariadne.

Mei nodded.

"I never saw them go into the cave. Omar, you and Zeke were wandering around outside. Did you see anything at all?"

Omar shook his head.

"I never saw them after that," said Zeke. I didn't think about it because Krista and I were—"

"In your little world," finished Omar, raising an eyebrow.

They must have gone into the cave. We have to look for them.

"Didn't you hear what Otto said?" asked Zeke.

"No one heard what Otto said, Zeke," replied Mei.

"He said that the caves here have hidden drop-offs and underground streams, in addition to the fatties."

"We have no idea how old this trail is. For all we know, the damn thing could've died or moved out long ago," I said.

"I don't think they move out, Huck," said Omar. "They're blind. They only breed, eat, die, and then the cycle repeats. So I don't think they get out much."

"He's right," said Ariadne. "The sun is also starting to set."

"We have to look for them inside, just be aware of the dangers, understood?" I said. "If we get separated in there, I want everyone back out within the hour. We have to get back to camp and trust that Arjun and Ciro can take care of themselves overnight."

Everyone nodded, and we walked inside, igniting our recently charged flashlights. The grub trail was easy to follow, leaving giant repeating undulations on the cave floor in the muck. After a while, the cave split off. However, I was reluctant to split the group further, having already lost track of Hemant, so we continued as a group down the tunnel with the more recent trail.

"Umm, it's starting to get mucusy up here, guys," said Mei. "And it smells like barf."

"They regurgitate their food to their young," said Omar. "It means we're getting closer to their lair."

"Wow," said Mei, "Without Arjun, I guess you feel the responsibility to take his place as a professor. I didn't even know you were paying attention in class."

"Shut up, Mei. Pay attention," he said.

Mei left the issue alone and continued following Ariadne, who tracked the cave grub in the increasingly dim cavern. A cool wind started to blow out from inside the cave, making my hairs stand on end. We moved forward cautiously. Suddenly Ariadne slipped. I leaped forward and grabbed her arm and belt as she slid down the side of an abyss.

"I got you. I got you," I said.

"Can you pull me up?" Ariadne cried. "It's too slick. I can't push on anything with my feet."

"Can you guys pull me back?" I asked, lying prostrate on the ground, barely gripping Ariadne.

I felt Mei, Zeke, and Omar's hands pull us back away from the pit's opening. Ariadne leaped to me, giving me a tight embrace.

"Thank you," she said breathlessly. "That could've been it."

"Anytime," I stammered. "Well, try not to do that often, though."

We nervously laughed. The group carefully plodded around the circumference of the hole, and I tried not to think about what could've happened to Arjun and Ciro had they suffered the same fate. After that embrace, the wind wasn't the only thing causing my hair to stand on end. I had never had feelings for anyone else, save for the goofy ones of a little kid. I watched her walk ahead of me in the dim light still buzzing from the contact. Then, suddenly jerking from my distraction, I saw something of pure horror.

"Ariadne, stop," I whispered as forcefully as I could. "Back up towards me slowly."

She looked up from her ground tracking and stifled a scream. A dormant cave grub lay less than a meter ahead of her, its cloudy orange eyes and sharp mandibles protruding from its fat beige face. She began to back away infinitesimally, doing her best not to disturb the loose rock or trip. We panned our lights around for Arjun and Ciro but saw no trace. We finally let out a collective sigh of relief when we were at a much safer distance.

"Jesus Christ, Ariadne," said Omar. "Cutting it a little damn close, don't you think?!"

"Don't attack her," I said. "Any one of us could've done the same thing."

"Shut up. You're just desperate for another hug," Omar said.

My cheeks blushed, as did Ariadne's, though I was unsure from anger or embarrassment.

"Leave him alone, invert turd," she said.

"Guys, we're arguing in an infested bug lair," said Zeke.

The arguing started overlapping, and I had to interrupt.

"Quiet!" I yelled. Everyone froze. "Maybe we should check the other passage."

"Huck, the fatties are blind, not deaf," said Ariadne.

"All Arthropods are deaf. Arjun said so," I said.

"The inverts are deaf but sensitive to vibration, and this cave is a freaking megaphone, Huck," said Mei.

Punctuating her remark, we heard the sound of a low, deep roar.

"Run!" said Zeke. "Watch out for the abyss!"

We heard a thundering behind us and felt the vibration through our soles. We looked up in time to see the corpulent grub slithering after us. We ran faster than any of us ever had before, but the fatty gained despite our speed. We ran so hard that we thought our hearts would explode. Upon reaching the pit, we all jumped over it, the adrenaline helping us clear it like a puddle. I was elated when I saw the fading light of dusk streaming through the cavern's mouth.

"We're not going to make it!" screamed Omar, the furthest behind.

I coaxed every ounce of energy through my body as we all burst forth from the entrance of the cave, splitting off in different directions. I immediately heard an earth-shattering screech and stomach-wrenching tearing sounds. I turned around, struggling to catch my breath, and saw the origin of the disturbance. The fatty had run full force into the sharp mineral deposits forming the tooth-like opening at the mouth of the cave. The inertia had caused it to slice itself to ribbons, covering the ground in its steaming viscous hemolymph as it writhed its last.

"Gross," said Mei, her chest heaving from the exertion.

"I never want to do that again," said Zeke.

"I guess there's no exploring... the other route," I said, realizing the creature had permanently sealed off the entrance. "Surely Arjun and Ciro... weren't in there."

"I hope not," said Ariadne, doubled over.

I collapsed on the ground for a moment's respite before we

headed back. At this rate, it would be dark before we arrived. Just before our departure, Arjun and Ciro topped the next hill over.

"Where the hell have you been?!" yelled Omar, pointing in their faces.

The couple was caught off guard by the anger directed at them.

"Mueller said we could wander as long as we were back by dark," said Ciro. "We told Otto, but I guess he was too busy lecturing. We were looking for more cave grub signs at the entrances of the other caves."

"Otto's always too busy talking," said Mei.

"What in the world?" Ciro said, just noticing the cave grub.

"Wow!" said Arjun, walking closer. "This is a story I can't wait to hear."

"You can hear it on the way back. Mueller's going to have our asses as it is," said Omar.

We returned to camp after pulling Arjun and Ciro reluctantly away from examining the cave grub's corpse. It was dark when we got there, but Mueller was pleased to have us all back.

"Get some rest! We leave at first light," he said.

"Wait!" said Arjun. "Where's my brother?"

CHAPTER 38: ARIADNE

As I hurriedly ate breakfast alongside the others feeling exhausted. No one slept well with Hemant out there alone. I had hoped that I would wake to find him sitting on one of the logs by the campfire, his hammer lying next to him. No such luck. What I did find was a distraught Arjun blathering about how he was at fault as Ciro unsuccessfully attempted to convince him otherwise. I knew Arjun would want to be part of the search party, but I also knew he would be useless. So I packed my bivvy for the search, knowing we wouldn't be departing this morning as Mueller had said.

"I need to talk with you privately," Krista said, approaching me from behind.

"Whoa," I said, jerking around. "You surprised me."

"Sorry. I need to talk about the other day."

"I figured you would. How can I help?"

"I don't want to be pregnant anymore."

I paused. Until that point, the most serious condition anyone had asked me to treat was genital warts. Back in the pod, word had gotten around that I was adept at herbal medicines, and they'd come to me instead of the medics for the more sensitive issues.

"That's an extremely serious decision. Are you sure you want to decide that right now?"

"Ariadne, I've never been so sure of anything in my life. Look around! We are in the middle of nowhere. People are disappearing. We never know when the next invert is going to attack. I can't be a competent warrior with a distended belly. I barely stand a chance of surviving this mission as it is, much less pregnant or toting an infant."

"Krista, do you understand what you are asking me to do?"

"I know. I know you as you know me. You're the only one I'd ask."

"What about Kurt? He's from Munich. They specialize in medicine. I bet he has something much safer than anything I could find."

"I don't want anyone else to know. Anyone! Do you understand?"

"It's dangerous, painful, and not guaranteed."

"I don't care. I have to have this."

I looked behind Krista and noticed Mueller was beginning to assemble two search parties.

"Look, we need to get going. I'll keep a lookout today for those types of herbs. Just promise me you'll consider this more. We'll both have to carry this the rest of our lives."

"Of course. Thank you, Ariadne," she said, tears welling up in her eyes.

We hugged before walking over to the gathering searchers. As if I didn't have enough on my mind, now my best friend was asking for my help to end her pregnancy at significant risk to herself. I knew about some of the abortifacient herbs that people had used throughout history, but finding and correctly identifying them in their native habitat would be quite tricky, not to mention I had no idea of the correct dosages. This was a terrible idea and put me in a very uncomfortable position. I just tried to remember what Krista was going through. I knew she had asked me because of our trust and friendship.

"Ariadne," said Mueller, "You're with Huck's group. Krista, I want you here with Kurt, Leni, Arjun, and Ciro in case Hemant returns."

Mueller knew Krista wasn't well. He had been giving her the side-eye for the last few days but hadn't raised the issue. I appreciated his discreet attempt to keep her out of additional stress and strain. I walked to join Huck's group, which they arranged similar to the day before, but with the addition of Otto.

Aside from the few staying behind with the others, the Misfits would follow a westward path this time, and we would again follow the southern. If any of us got lost, we would make for the river. The plan was to regroup at nightfall tomorrow, whether we had found him or not. I didn't want to think about it, but I knew that meant we'd be setting sail without him. Mueller wasn't mean, but he was pragmatic.

We left camp fully packed, intending to make camp for the night somewhere out in the wilderness, and began the search. After walking a few hours, we arrived at what Mei called "Dead Grub Cave." It was easy to tell when we were getting near by the foul smell wafting on the breeze as the morning sun heated the carcass. We found ourselves face-to-face with two bone arachnids at brunch when we rounded the corner. I immediately prepared to attack, then realized they were more interested in consuming the easy prey than chasing us. We slowly backed away and passed around the cave, giving them a wide berth.

"That's freaking disgusting," said Omar.

"We need to keep moving. Stay on guard," said Otto. If that fatty attracted 'em, it'll be attracting others."

We walked for another hour, swatting down the annoying ever-present blood midges with our weapons.

"I'm sick of these damn bugs!" complained Zeke. "It's like they are attracted to me more than you guys."

"Yeah, they like you more than Krista does," said Mei.

The mention of Krista seemed to eat at Zeke. He dropped back to my position until he and I marched shoulder to shoulder.

"I'm worried about Krista. I know I am her boyfriend, but you know her better than I do. She's not eating right. She seems sick, and her mood has been weird. She says it has nothing to do with me, but I'm worried about her."

"She's got a lot going on. But, I assure you, it's not your fault. I can't talk to you about it, but trust me, we're getting her the help she needs."

"Is there anything I can do for her?" asked Zeke.

"Be supportive. Help her. She needs you now more than ever."

"I can do that. I think I love her." Zeke paused. "God, please don't tell her I said that. I don't want her to know the first person I told was you."

I laughed. "Don't worry, Zeke. I'm sworn to secrecy."

I mimed locking my lips and throwing the key into the woods, where I immediately noticed a familiar plant. I was thankful for my lucky stars. Growing right alongside the elevated path we were taking was a cluster of armadillo's tail, fortunately identifiable by its funny cylindrical growths. I picked as much as I could and stuffed it into my pack, feeling secretive and guilty even though no one in the group noticed or cared. They all assumed that it must have medicinal value if I picked it.

I continued trekking through the undergrowth, dodging blood midges and picking off ticks, a native species of Earth that I had learned to loathe. I still couldn't take my mind off of Krista and her request, but even with the urgency of our search, I felt a calming sensation from the nature surrounding me. Eventually, we found a trail, but not what we were expecting. I had been scouring the ground for evidence of one, possibly injured, person. Instead, the path we found was clear and wide, and numerous footfalls had packed the dirt.

"Could this be a tribe of survivors?" I asked. "It doesn't look like an Arthropod trail. These impressions look like human footprints."

"Survivors, maybe?" answered Otto. "Could be Banished too. Rumor has it that the few Banished that live like to band with survivors."

"I bet Hemant found this trail and followed it, thinking Arjun and Ciro did the same," suggested Mei.

"It's logical," said Otto. "We haven't seen any other sign of him. I was going to suggest we pincer west towards Mueller, but following this trail could be promising. Stay on your guard, though. Both survivors and Banished are unpredictable around others."

We followed the trail for several hours until dusk. The walk through the woods had been hot, sticky, and tiring. We still had yet to see any signs of human life. Our simple lunch had been from our dry stores, so it was looking like I was on the hook for hunting dinner. Finally, we arrived at a small clearing within sight of the trail. A beautiful jungle surrounded the clearing. Colorful flowers and water-filled sinkholes were everywhere.

"I think we should set up camp here," said Otto. "We can see anyone approaching, and maybe we can catch something edible from those sinkholes."

"I don't even care anymore. I'm just glad to be sitting," said Zeke.

"Omar and I'll try to catch something," said Huck.

"I guess that leaves Mei and me to hunt," I said. "Zeke, you and Otto get to cook."

"I'm much better at eating, but I'll give it a whirl," said Otto.

I was glad to see Omar and Huck working side by side. They had gone from despising each other to cordial. Now that he had stopped being so much of a dick, I appreciated Omar. He was keen, innovative, and strong—all attributes we needed on our mission. Mei and I headed into the deeper, darker glen just south of the camp, hoping to find some small game that would cook quickly. We hadn't gone far when we started hearing strange noises. I looked back at Mei, who seemed as curious as I did.

"Should we investigate?" I asked.

"I'm insanely curious, but we shouldn't go without the others," said Mei.

"Let's look over the next ridge. Maybe we can at least see what it is."

"Okay, but then head back, alright?"

We proceeded to the next ridge and peered over. What we saw looked like a small village. It appeared to have a giant sculpture in the middle next to a large fire surrounded by small thatch huts.

"It must be a survivor camp. Let's go get the others," I said.

"You don't have to ask me twice," said Mei.

I turned to get one last glance at the camp and found myself face-to-face with the most disturbing human I had ever seen. I screamed discordantly with Mei, who was experiencing the same at my side. I prayed that the others heard us. The human-like creature leaped over the ridge, yelling, hatchet in hand, as did the two other freaks with him. His gruesome face was missing swathes of skin with rudimentary stitches that seemed to be holding the rest intact. His entire body was dripping with a hot sticky liquid, freezing me in abject horror. They surrounded us, communicating with each other in indiscernible growls and grunts as they paced. Still immobilized by fear, I couldn't convince my arm to reach for my dagger. Each swirling man was armed with a simple weapon, but their animalistic behavior made them wildly unpredictable.

In an instant, one pounced on me and began licking my cheek. I started sobbing and pleading for help, but Mei was enduring a similar experience. I felt the warm tears begin to blur my vision as I turned away from the horrific face above me. I watched as one of them prodded Mei with the blunt end of his spear, testing her muscle mass. Then, I felt the bandage-wrapped hands of the being above me begin to creep up my inner thighs.

"No! Please! No!" I begged. The foul blood and sweat dripped from his face onto mine. I could smell the horrible stench of his breath and body. I closed my eyes, whimpering and praying for it to be over. Before anything could happen, I heard a loud crunch and opened my eyes to find his head had been laid open by Omar's naginata. In addition to the blood, the twisted human's brain matter had spattered my face and chest. I screeched as I flung the corpse off of me and scrambled for the safety of a nearby tree. The one that had been attacking Mei was on the ground, a crossbow bolt sticking out of one of his eye sockets. The third, Zeke was resting one foot on, removing the point of his halberd from its chest with a sickening squish.

Huck rushed to me, grabbing me by the arm. "Are you okay?"

"Don't touch me!" I screamed, kicking myself further into the tree's embrace. "Nobody touch me!"

I knew he was trying to help, but my skin was crawling with the phantom fingers of the uninvited touch. I threw my head in between my legs and sobbed harder than I ever had before. Mei, equally traumatized, came over to sit with me, but we were interrupted by a flood of tribe members as they came over the incline and grabbed us. There were too many to fight. Omar tried, and a tribesman stabbed him in the side with an iron-headed spear. They absconded with our weapons, dragging me kicking and screaming back to their village by my hair.

They unmercifully pulled me past what had appeared to be a sculpture next to the fire. Still, only adding to my horror, I realized it was a live bone arachnid. Wooden pylons and cloth binding completely immobilized it. Its abdomen was cut open, and the tribesmen were pulling organs out of the living, screeching arachnid, consuming them raw as they danced crazily in the flickering light of the fire. Every particle of my body was repulsed and terrified at what we had stumbled upon. The tribesmen threw us into a large barred cage constructed from wooden posts and animal-like sinew. All I could concentrate on was getting somewhere safe; my mind blurred by adrenaline and cortisol. I crawled as quickly as possible into the dark corner, pulling myself into a fetal position.

Huck and Zeke were helplessly trying to tend Omar's wound. They were shouting something at me, but I couldn't hear anything. Even my vision was blurring. I hated everything. I desperately wanted to be back in the safety of my dorm with Krista in the pod. *Why did I have to come out here?* Outside, the chanting grew louder and louder. The bone arachnid was shrieking and convulsing in its death throes as the people of the tribe gnawed and guzzled from its living carapace. *Mercy! Give it Mercy!* I thought, feeling light-headed. This sick, twisted tribe wasn't human. They were worse than the Arthropods. What had they done to each other? All the scars and rents in their flesh. The vile acts didn't stop with the Arthropods. Maybe humanity deserves to be wiped out. At that moment, I wanted nothing more than to die, to fade into oblivion.

I felt something brush my shoulder and ignored it. Then again. I pushed the tear-soaked hair back from my face and looked over. In the bushes behind the cage was Otto. I hadn't noticed he wasn't there with us in all the confusion. He had his dagger out and was gesturing towards the sinew-wrapped bars of the cage. I nodded slowly, realizing his intention. He tossed me the blade. It fell shy of the cage, but I could reach out and grab it. I tried pulling myself together for the simple task, struggling against the hormones racking my body. The din outside the cage reached its crescendo as the event climaxed in the spider's death, resulting in a unified wail of pleasure from the participants. Before I could cut through the first joint, someone opened the cage and dragged me and Mei out. They secured the door behind us, but not before I dropped the dagger on the floor. *Not again!* my mind screamed as my body flailed.

Huck watched in fear, his face contorted in pain. He was shaking the bars so fiercely that I thought his fingers might break. I mouthed "dagger" over and over until he realized what I was saying. The tribespeople removed the spider and attached Mei and me in its place. I didn't know what fate awaited us, but I was beginning to feel a peace come over me. It may have been the disassociation of the Shock, but I was resigned to whatever was coming.

I was almost oblivious as Huck, and the others burst forth from the cage, catching the drugged-out populace off guard. I barely remember being taken down and escorted through the battered, bloody corpses that littered the ground. I saw my bow flashing in the firelight as it hung suspended from Otto's shoulder as they walked or carried us back to camp. I saw where someone tended to Omar with concern. And still, in a mental haze, I was carefully laid inside the sealed cocoon of my bivvy where I could recover in safety.

CHAPTER 39: HEMANT

Ow! I sat up and rubbed my head, feeling as though my brain was pounding against my skull. I scanned the dim surroundings, the light filtering in from above. It appeared to be dawn. *How long have I been here? Where is here, for that matter?* I began to push myself up to a standing posture but felt a sharp stabbing pain radiating from my right leg. I immediately looked down and the pain's source. The leg of my jumpsuit had ripped open, revealing a sizable nasty gash in my upper leg that had crusted over during the night. I felt a rush of gratitude that I hadn't bled out during the night. Making matters worse, my knee was twice its average size and purple. Judging by the contorted look, I had dislocated it.

"Dammit!" I said out loud to no one. "I go to help, and now I'm the freaking liability."

I couldn't just lay here screaming for all the good that would do. At least I had my pack. The more I became aware of my injury, the more the pain was steadily increasing. "Awesome," I said to myself. I slung my pack off of my shoulders, wincing at the additional pain, and pulled out my med-pack. Inside, I grabbed the oral analgesic and dry swallowed it. I sprayed the open wound with topical anesthetic and antiseptic, the pain reliever doing bupkis for the throbbing ache.

I waited a few minutes for the meds to kick while I planned the inevitable escape. If I was going to get out of here myself, I had to set my knee correctly. It would be painful as hell, but I had no choice. I could do it. Our training prepared us for this type of thing. I scooted across the sandy bottom of the small cavern to a double formation of stalagmites, stirring up dust as I did. *That'll do.* I painfully set my foot in between the upward-facing spires, gritting my teeth as I did.

I took a deep breath. That alone had been intense. I tried to psych myself up for the next part. I couldn't hesitate. I needed to set it in one swift movement. I grabbed onto two adjacent rocks slightly above my shoulders for grip. They were damp with the moisture of the cave, which I tried my best to wipe off onto my filthy jumpsuit. *I must stink to high heaven.* I was looking forward to the next opportunity to bathe. Not that bathing had been high on my survival list, though it might come back to bite me if this wound gets infected.

I took a few deep breaths, and then as hard as I could, I yanked with all my might. Then, just as I passed out from the overwhelming pain, I heard the bone pop back into place.

•••••••••

The next time I awoke, I knew where I was and why I was in severe discomfort. I sat up more slowly this time. Judging by the sun, I think it was around noon. I hoped it was the same day. I wondered how long Mueller would wait with the others before they left me for dead. It was in my best interest to get out and make my way back, regardless of the pain. Remaining here meant certain death.

I looked at the hole I had fallen through. It was about my height from the ground and surrounded by the broken sticks that had disguised its opening. It was a tiny cavern but big enough for my dumb ass to fall into and break something. It was eerily reminiscent of the cavern that had saved my life outside of Horizonte. Too bad there was nothing to climb up. I tried to stand, but the cave's smooth dirt and clay walls gave no place for purchase. I eventually resulted in uncomfortably digging my fingers into the soft surface and clawing my way up to standing. My fingernails felt like they would rip off in the process, but it worked. I rubbed my hands to bring back blood flow and provide some comfort as I stood, my weight supported by my good left leg.

I reached up to grab the ledge. It was easy enough to reach. I pulled myself with all my might but couldn't get my body up high enough to get out. I dropped down, accidentally hitting the heel of my hurt leg. I let out a yelp. The agony was so severe that I collapsed to the ground, bringing on further frustration, knowing that now I had to stand again.

"Dammit!" I yelled to no one.

I was starting to kick myself for running off alone as I did. I repeated the process to stand after choking down more of the meds. Upon standing, I looked around, realizing that I couldn't do this. Not without something to increase my height or someone to help me, neither of which I had. I slung the pack off my shoulders and shoved everything I deemed necessary in my nasty jumpsuit's pockets. I threw my bag to the ground, knowing without it I needed to find the others all the more quickly, and stood on it. That was better. I put my war hammer across the outside of the hole to use as a pull-up bar.

From this height, I could almost stick my head out. Though my vision was limited, the coast looked clear. I began to pull my weight up. Without any adrenaline and severe pain, it took every ounce of energy I had to get out to my waist. I froze in that position for a few moments, wondering what to do next. It was an awkward spot. I could fling myself forward onto my face and hope I could grab a root to pull myself up, or I could collapse back into the hole, which would undoubtedly impact my injured leg significantly. I opted for the root.

I leaned forward quickly and face-planted into the dirt, my legs still dangling in the hole. Getting my good leg up wouldn't be an issue, but contorting the hurt one might just kill me. I kicked and flailed with my left leg, trying to get it up to the surface to no avail. I took another deep breath. I tamped my forehead repeatedly into the ground. *Think. Think. Think.* I decided to try shuffling across the floor. I grabbed the next clump up and pulled the vine right out with its roots.

"Dammit!" I yelled. It was becoming my new favorite word.

I whined in a moment of self-pity. I struggled to figure out how to get out of this situation when I heard footsteps coming. I froze out of fear. The footsteps sounded human, but I knew there were countless unfamiliar inverts. If it was the others, why weren't they calling Arjun's, Ciro's, or my name? I heard the steps stop a few meters from my body and craned my head up slowly.

Standing in front of me was a beautiful older woman, draped in a brown cape, with a basket in which were numerous flowers, herbs, and fruits. She looked at me with pity, then sat the basket down. Slowly approaching me, she asked me something in a language I didn't understand. I heard something similar back in the pod spoken by our trainers, but this sounded different somehow. Nevertheless, it sounded calming and soothing. I was in no position to do anything but trust her.

"Can you help me out?" I asked. "Or maybe go get help?" I doubted her weak frame could pull me from my predicament alone.

She seemed to understand what I was asking for and grabbed my arms. With a strength I wasn't prepared for, she extracted me from the hole without difficulty. I was thrilled to be clear of the cavern but winced at the pain it had caused my leg. The woman noticed it and gracefully dropped down in the dirt next to me. She continued to speak, gently inspecting my damaged limb. She pulled something from the basket, then began to chew on it, all the while continuing to rub my leg gently. After a few moments, she removed the cud from her mouth and applied it to my wound. It seemed gross at the time, but it felt good—really good. Next, she tore off part of a sash on her basket and wrapped it around the injured area.

The mysterious woman stood, motioning for me to stay, not that I could run off. Then, she vanished into the woods, leaving her basket. A minute or two later, she returned with a broken y-shaped branch she had quickly crafted into a crutch, and helping me stand, had restored some of my mobility.

"Thank you so much," I said. "What's your name?

She looked at me, confused. I put my hand on my chest. "Hemant."

She immediately understood. "Tais."

"Good to meet you, Tais."

"I need to get back to my friends," I said, gesturing to the northeast.

Again, I got the look of confusion.

"I go. Friends," I said, pointing again.

I wasn't sure of her level of understanding, but she shook her head and pointed northwest before saying something in a negative tone.

"I need to go that way," I repeated, pointing again.

She shook her head more sternly, and her voice began to take on more of a warning. She didn't want me to go that way for some reason. I decided to trust her. If Mueller left me, at least I wouldn't be alone. I let out an exasperated sigh.

"Alright. Let's go." I said, nodding.

She looked pleased, and we began to walk at a snail's pace down a nearly invisible trail. It occurred to me that she must be one of the rumored survivors. They were supposedly the future generations of the people who had not made it to the pods. Somehow, they managed to survive and subsist on the surface despite the invert occupation. It was truly amazing. I was saddened, thinking that Arjun wouldn't meet these people. Knowing him, he would probably understand their language and want to stay and research them. I hoped he and Ciro were okay. Surely they'd been found by the others. Now they just had to find my stupid ass.

Tais led me through some of the most beautiful areas I had seen yet, stopping regularly to check on me. I was in good care. Unlike other places, here I heard more wildlife. I listened to what I guessed were frogs and birds, sounds only described in texts back in the pod. It felt like a fantastical place that they had somehow maintained free of the inverts. After what felt like ages of walking and just when I thought I couldn't go any further, we rounded a bend and were standing among a group of homes built into hillsides. It was serene. At least thirty people were milling about, all dressed in similar brown attire to Tais.

I was beginning to receive a few looks. Mostly of concern and interest, not of fear as I would've suspected. A tall, curly-haired man approached me and spoke to me in the same language as Tais before addressing her. I could discern that they were talking about why I was there. After their brief discussion, he welcomed me as a guest. First, Tais took me to her home, where she and another woman removed all of my clothes. I didn't have time to be embarrassed. The speed at which they had me naked and on a table was astounding. They took a more detailed look at my wound before giving me new herbs and bandages. I took the time to look around Tais' home. It was small, only one room. It had large windows to let in natural light. The furniture appeared handmade from wood and well-crafted. Suspended from the dirt and stick ceiling were numerous drying herbs and hand tools. I was surprisingly relaxed for someone lying naked in front of two strangers of the opposite sex. Eventually, they finished and helped me get dressed in robes similar to theirs.

We left the house together, me still hobbling on my crutch. Everyone in the village had gathered in the meantime around the central fire. They were all touching me and rubbing my arms, though I was never sure why. Many of them would tell me their names, and I'd respond with mine. Finally, they led me to a rock by the fire and brought me dinner, gesturing for me to dig in. It was bizarre. My eating had never been the focal point of an entire tribe, and I was now supremely conscious of my table manners. The wide dish was a sampling of cooked fish, mashed vegetables, and sliced fruit. It looked amazing, and I took no convincing as hungry as I was. Audience or no, I ate like I hadn't eaten in days. And it was delicious. When I had finished, the tribe cheered and clapped, and they brought out similar dishes for everyone else, including more of the same for me.

The curly-haired man, who I presumed was the leader, came over, held my food-covered hands, and spoke to me. He introduced himself as Idal. Judging by his words and gestures, he said I was welcome to stay as long as needed.

"Thank you," I said, playing my hand over my heart so that he understood the significance. "I need to go back to my friends." I pointed to my chest, then towards the river. I picked up a stick and drew some stick figures by the river. He nodded. Then he drew a sunrise.

"Okay. In the morning."

"Morning," he said.

"Yeah," I responded, smiling at the successful communication.

After dinner, there was dancing, clapping, and subtle background music played on stringed instruments. It was beautiful, and in many ways, like a daydream. We had fun into the night, at which point Tais led me to a guest hut. I stripped to my new underclothes and laid down on the simple bed. With my exhaustion getting the better of me, I quickly dozed off. The sound of my door opening and closing woke me. It wasn't surprising, given these people's lack of awareness of privacy due to communal living. When I opened my eyes, standing in front of me was a young, attractive girl, roughly my age. She slipped off her clothing, which was more ornate than the others, and climbed into bed with me wearing only beaded jewelry. I froze. I had never been with a woman. Not to mention, I expected my first time would be with someone I cared about—or at least knew.

She began to caress me softly. I gently held her hand, stopping it. I wanted it like nothing I ever had before. I'd forgotten all about the pain in my leg, which might have been their intention. But this felt weird. I wasn't part of their culture, and I was getting one of their daughters? *Would it be terrible if I turned her down?* My companion sensed my reservations. She gently kissed my fingers and cuddled with me as she blew out the candle.

The next morning I woke up refreshed and rejuvenated. When I woke up, my friend was gone. Making my way to the fire, I was again offered breakfast first, thankfully with a smaller audience. Tais, Idal, and two others were prepared to guide me back to the river. Idal presented me with my pack, which Tais must have retrieved, as well as my freshly cleaned and stitched armor and jumpsuit.

"Thank you," I said, gesturing.

They all bowed. As we made our way out of the idyllic village, I turned to see my evening companion waving to me from the ridge. I smiled as I waved back. I wouldn't be forgetting this place anytime soon.

CHAPTER 40: GUILHERME

I stood in our hastily-constructed command center, struggling to grasp the reality I found myself in. Fabrice rubbed my back reassuringly. I was now leading an invasion into a hostile area that pushed residents down the central shaft in retaliation to their limitations. I was preparing for the attack as fast as possible but had watched tragically as two more fell to their deaths. Everyone was in position, but we still weren't ready—and we were emotional.

"We have to begin," Fabrice said.

I nodded, knowing that among the hostages was my wife, Aline, in the hands of a deplorable asshole who wouldn't hesitate to bring her harm. I couldn't bear losing her again, but I had to focus. I had to take care of the population of an entire city. An old quote came to mind: "Logic clearly dictates that the needs of the many outweigh the needs of the few." It was a wise thought by some historic figure, but logic and emotion were very different things. Moving forward with the attack was the hardest thing I had ever done.

"Let's go," I said, taking a deep breath.

"We'll do everything we can to keep her alive, Memo," said Fabrice.

"I know," I said. "Launch the ziplines."

I looked down on the dark Nucleus and listened to the command relayed around the levels' circumference. The sounds of firing grappling hooks filled the air. I struggled to follow the hooks in the dim light as they followed their desired trajectory across the space to catch on the railing of the Nucleus. Our force was about to attempt nothing like ever before. It was a multi-level invasion to retake control of a pod, something to my knowledge that no one had ever done before.

"Connection," I heard repeating into the distance.

"You ready?" asked Fabrice.

"Send them over," I said without hesitation. "Make sure someone is watching the lines at the Nucleus. Make sure they know not to hurt civilians."

"Go, go, go!" shouted Fabrice to the men, then looking at me, "Trust them. We've trained them well. Your plan is solid. All we need to do is be here for the unexpected."

"Like falling bodies?" I asked rhetorically.

"Yes, like falling bodies," answered Fabrice, guarding his sarcasm.

I watched as the first of the force unclipped from the black web of ropes spanning the space. We deployed a handful of recruits onto each floor of the Nucleus, save for the topmost floor. We would have to breach the bridge from the inside. I had no doubt that's where the regents, Carvalho, and Aline would be.

"We're ready to breach, Major," said one of Fabrice's men.

I paused, weighing the possible consequences.

"Major?" he prompted.

"Breach," I responded.

I heard the sound of our improvised army lobbing sleeping gas into the Nucleus. Fabrice had several non-lethal security measures that the Nucleus had provided for any undesirable scenarios that may have occurred on the lower levels. They never would've suspected that we would use the same measures against them. The Nucleus security would be prepared for the incapacitating gas, but maybe if the civilians were unmasked, they would be unconscious and hopefully out of harm's way.

Following the gas, I heard the thunderous footfalls of the multitudes of our force, stomping across the metal platforms on the various levels to initiate entry into the space occupied by the opposition. Almost immediately, we began to hear the first shots of live ammunition. I felt a blow to my heart with every pop that sounded, knowing it represented another life lost. I prayed none of them would be Aline.

We had armed most of our force with bladed, pointed, or bludgeoning weapons. Weapons that were formidable in the right hands but paled compared to our opponents' fully-automatic projectile weapons. In addition to the few armed with non-lethal projectile weapons, there were a few soldiers armed with their lethal equivalents that we had confiscated from the roaming security patrols trapped outside of the Nucleus.

The siege felt as though it lasted for an eternity. Finally, I began to hear the relieving all-clear calls echoing below. Fabrice patted me on the back. It wasn't over yet, but we had already achieved something. The force fired return zip lines, forming a spider web of rope-based transportation across the shaft, and began to return. Moments later, one of the senior officers arrived at our side.

"How is the invasion proceeding, Commander?" I asked.

"Sir, we have a twenty percent casualty rate. Still have many people injured or unaccounted for. We need the catwalks reactivated for the evacuation. Limited civilian casualties. Most in the suppressing fire from security. The buggers were relentless, but we swarmed them. Their armor wasn't made to resist bladed weapons," he replied, smirking. "We pushed the remaining guards back to the bridge and were bottlenecked."

"Any sign of my wife?" I asked.

"No, sir. Sorry, sir," said the Commander.

"Can we return power to the Nucleus without sending it to the bridge?" I asked Fabrice.

"No, it's an all or nothing deal," he said.

"Get everyone out of the Nucleus that you can, Commander," I said. "Let's get every possible hostage to safety before we try to advance on the bridge."

"Yes, sir," he replied before running off to spread the order.

"That's the right call," said Fabrice after the commander had left.

I simply nodded, thinking that the person I wanted most across safely would likely be the last, if at all.

•••••••••

Our force had taken a brief time to recoup from the assault. We were limited, still holding our position and taking the bridge, but the men and women needed rest and time to assess their injuries. We managed to get a fair number of the civilians and minimally injured across, but the seriously injured would have to remain until the battle was over. As it was, we had sent medics over to deal with them, but more time would cost us more lives. Since the occupants could no longer leave the bridge, they had ceased dropping bodies. I had no doubt the process would continue at a higher rate as soon as they got their bearings. I began to fight the emotional breakdown raising its ugly head, as I had numerous times in the last few hours.

Fabrice and I had some of the soldiers move our command center to the Nucleus, safely two floors below where the assault would take place. Our force had been staging on the floor above, readying to make the advance. With the bottleneck, this had the potential to be a deadly scenario for our side.

The security doors that formed the entrance to the bridge were at the top of a wide ramp on the other side of a security checkpoint, forming the bottleneck. Positioned on the incline was a squadron of the pod's most elite security personnel, forming the last line of defense for the bridge. The First Builders had designed the area to be a defensive fallback, though the idea was for the good guys to be inside, not the other way around. So we would lose a massive number of people, or we needed a clever way of surpassing it.

"I have an idea," I said. "I don't like it, but it's us or them."

"No one comes out of a war with clean hands, Major," said the Commander, who had rejoined us.

"What's your idea?" asked Fabrice.

I told them my plan as they listened intently, asking only the occasional question. When finished, we agreed to accept the burden and made the arrangements.

●●●●●●●●●

To maintain oversight of the perilous plan of attack, Fabrice and I had moved our command up to the topmost level of the Nucleus. We stationed ourselves a reasonable distance back from the confrontation in a relatively safe position. With me was Trainer Diogo and Trainer Lourenço, who had both willingly helped with the plan. A group noisily wheeled a massive metal crate into position as we watched. It had taken a feat of engineering and skill, but we had run electrical conduits across to the Nucleus on ziplines and had rigged power to the primary catwalk. The crate had barely been able to make the trip, as it pushed the size and weight limits of the large freight elevators. The group wheeled the container to the security checkpoint entry, and the commander walked up next to it.

"This is your last opportunity for surrender," he offered. "After this, we will offer no mercy."

"You bastards can go climb into a fatty's ass," the voice said, followed by raucous laughter and foul slurs. I looked over at Fabrice who nodded sullenly, knowing what we had to do.

"We tried," he said.

"Commander," I said, trying to swallow the lump in my throat. "Begin."

The commander motioned for his troops to push the crate into place from the side, completely blocking the entryway to the bridge. Four people came forward and attached giant battery-powered mag clamps onto the bottom ledge of the box.

"Secured, sir."

"Open the gate," said the commander.

The sliding gate on the front of the container was pulled to the side, opening its contents to the bridge's entryway. Without hesitation, the shooting and screaming began. Sounds of terror that would forever haunt our nightmares filled our ears. Just on the other side of the wall, we had released two captured bone arachnids slated for training. Diogo and Lourenço had confirmed my suspicions that the pod's security forces were trained only for civilian entanglements. Being hand-selected, they were not exposed to the everyday rigors of candidacy and had no training against Arthropods. Diogo and Lourenço had also confirmed that Arthropods were vulnerable to projectile weapons but assured me that the wild Arachnids would kill everything in the room before succumbing to the security's defensive barrage.

The men knew their Arthropods. The ensuing sounds of violence emanating from the ramp were unlike the pod's interior had ever seen or heard. Gruesome cries of human desperation filled the level. Sporadic pops of gunfire punctuated the sounds of tearing, ripping, and stabbing of flesh. We knew that a breach would sacrifice a large percentage of our force, but we had spared them with the stomach-turning decision to deploy the creatures. As a result, the vile creatures made short work of the area. What followed was the most haunting sound of all—silence.

"Masks on!" yelled Fabrice.

As everyone donned their masks, a pair of soldiers threw gas grenades through the crate's vents. Diogo and Lourenço had assured me that the gas would also work on the two creatures in the low ventilation area. Once the gas had time to take effect, the commander had his personnel remove the clamps as they retracted the box.

The gas had been unnecessary. The room was lifeless. The floor was littered with the dismembered, mauled, and envenomed corpses of the formerly elite security squadron. I could hear several resisting the urge to retch at the gruesome sight. We had saved lives but at a high moral cost. I justified it to myself, but I would always have trouble living with it.

I looked up the ramp at the powerless camera placed above the door, knowing cowering somewhere behind those giant hatches stood the despicable ousted leadership and my hostage wife. I asked myself how the atrocity that we had just committed was any better than those that had preceded us.

"'There's no honorable way to kill, no gentle way to destroy. There is nothing good in war. Except its ending,'" said Fabrice, walking up behind me. Then after a thoughtful pause, "Abraham Lincoln. He was president of the former United States over half a millennium ago."

"Wise man," I said. "That's what we have to do. We have to end the war. First here. Then… out there."

CHAPTER 41: HUCK

I spent all night staring at the glowing embers popping in the small fire that Otto had prepared. I felt trapped in a confusing spiral of emotions. Part of me was relieved that I was alive, and part of me was furious at myself. I had known all through my training that I would kill Arthropods, but they hadn't mentally prepared me to kill humans, even disgusting ones. They were still humans.

I wanted to bathe.

I wanted to vomit.

I wanted to scream.

I wanted to lash out.

I wanted to break.

I wanted to panic.

I wanted to cry.

Whatever that sick, twisted, vile scourge was, they had still been human—and we had killed them all.

Then there was Ariadne. How could someone so innocent and pure be treated so cruelly? I didn't understand what could make people act like that. I trembled from my core to think what would have happened to her and Mei if we hadn't intervened when we did. I was glad we had saved them and yet racked with guilt over the deaths of the tribe. *Shame or no, I'd do it again if I had to.* When we arrived back at camp after the slaughter, we tended to Omar's grievous wound. Otto lit a fire, risks be damned, and left it to burn all night. Omar was in bad shape, but we couldn't risk moving him at night, much less our traumatized friends. I wondered if either of them would ever be the same. I should never have let them go off alone. I resolved never to do it again.

As dawn brightened the sky, Otto insisted that we return to the shore. I knew it was best for everyone, but I didn't like how it boded for Hemant. Pulling my mind back to the present was the ration bar Otto was waving in front of my face. I took it from him, not that I had any appetite with which to stomach it. Zeke, who had spent the night in his bivvy, was emerging looking as bad as I felt. Otto had spent the night outside keeping a watchful eye on Omar. Eventually, Otto tamped out the fire with his boot, blackening the edges of his soles.

"We have to move, Huck," he said.

I nodded.

"Can you and Zeke gently wake Ariadne and Mei?"

"Sure," I said.

I knew how I felt and how Ariadne had reacted to me last night. I couldn't relate to the fear she had felt, but I knew it could affect her for weeks, maybe even years. So I slowly crouched down next to her bivvy. The tent door was open. I felt the panic rise in my chest. I frantically searched right and left before I saw her sitting down by one of the sinkholes. I felt a wave of relief wash over me. I padded down to the water, where she was resting.

"Ariadne," I said softly. "It's me, Huck."

"Ariadne," I repeated gently.

Her eyes flung open, and she recoiled away from me, saying nothing, her eyes darting back and forth, and I could see the perspiration on her forehead. I was thankful she was weaponless.

"Ariadne," I said in my most calming voice. "It's me, Huck. You're safe, I promise. We need to walk back to the boat. Are you up to that?"

She took a few moments to process what I had said but didn't respond.

"Ariadne, we need to go," I said, holding out my hand openly.

After a lengthy pause, she nodded. Then, refusing my hand, she slowly stood. Zeke, who had awoken Mei from her bivvy, was having a similar experience, though Mei was bouncing back faster than Ariadne. I escorted Ariadne back to the camp, folded her tent, and prepared her pack before offering her the food Otto had provided me. She declined with a shake of her head. As if in a haze, she donned her backpack, and we began our Hemantless march back to the river.

Lately, I had been developing feelings for Ariadne and now found them amplified with concern for her wellbeing. The traumatic experiences we had each endured would impact us both. I fervently hoped we could help each other recover. I prayed through the entire return journey that nothing would attack us, seeing as none of us were in any condition to defend ourselves. The universe seemed aware of my concerns, and we made it back to Mueller and the Misfits late that night, the trip a giant blur. My heart sank when I realized that there was still no sign of Hemant.

Kurt and another Misfit took Omar to the supply truck on the boat for medical care as Otto briefed Mueller on what had passed.

"The Demented?! Here?!" Mueller asked.

Grace pulled Mei and Ariadne aside and spoke to them in a caring manner I had never heard from the harsh captain. Zeke came and sat down beside me, and we both stared out silently across the river as the sun set.

"I never thought I'd kill a person," Zeke finally said, sniffling.

"Me either," I said.

"I know we had to do it," he said. "That doesn't make it any easier, though."

"I keep telling myself that they're alive because of us. Because of what we did."

"We didn't find Hemant," said Zeke. "Was all that for nothing?"

"It feels like it," I said.

"Who were those people?" Zeke asked.

"I heard Otto say they were the Demented. Ring any bells?"

Zeke shook his head.

"I don't remember learning about them in Leonor's class, either."

"What is going to happen to Hemant?"

"I don't know," I said. "I doubt Mueller is going to risk another search tomorrow, especially after what happened."

"Let's try to get some rest," said Zeke. "Maybe we'll be able to think more clearly in the morning."

We each went and set up our tents. As I was readying my bivvy for the night, I saw a shadow next to me and turned around.

"Thank you for everything, Huck," said Ariadne. "I'm still piecing together what happened, but I know you helped me."

"S-sure. If there's anything I can help you with, I'm here," I responded.

She turned and walked away slowly. I stayed there kneeling for a few minutes. I wanted nothing more than to jump up and hug her, but I knew she needed ample time to recover. I was a mix of guilt for my actions and concern for my friends. I crawled into the cramped tent and snuggled into my bag, pulling it over my head. I needed the comfort that only came from tuning out the entire world. I was like that when I finally succumbed to sleep.

That night I dreamed that Ariadne and I were climbing up a never-ending mountain when she stumbled off a cliff's edge. I was holding her arms, keeping her suspended over the violently churning waters below, but she kept slipping out of my grasp. Over and over, a new hand would appear only to again have her slip away.

I awoke with a start, drenched in sweat and hearing chaotic yelling in the camp. I feared the worst and jumped out of my bivvy crossbow at the ready. When I came to my senses, I realized that the shouts were those of joy. *Hemant's back?* Finally, some good news. Everyone was running to the west side of the camp where Hemant was standing on rudimentary crutches with several robed men and women. I ran over to hug him, for which I would have to stand in line.

"Are you okay? What happened?" I asked when I had finally made it to him.

"I'm good! I'm good! I need to get everyone together so I can stop answering that question!" he said, laughing.

I looked at Arjun, standing next to him, a mess of happiness and relief. I didn't think Arjun would ever leave Hemant's side again. I looked at the four strangers who had brought Hemant back and nodded in gratitude. It had already become apparent that there was a language barrier. They cordially smiled back, understanding. Otto was attempting to converse with them, linguistics being among his many obscure abilities. He didn't know their language but could do some rudimentary communication due to its similarity to others he knew.

Shortly after Hemant's arrival, his shy saviors parted from our company, refusing to share breakfast with us, desiring to return to their homes. We led Hemant to the remnants of the night's fire, where Mueller debriefed him among everyone. The details of what had occurred were important to Mueller, but I noticed Grace was itching to get underway, especially having lingered in one location for too long. When Hemant had shared his story, he was all smiles. Admittedly, I wasn't looking forward to bringing him down with the news of what he had missed. Ariadne and the others returned to pack up their belongings.

Otto explained from what little he had gleaned from the others that they were indeed survivors. They lived a simple lifestyle in the area since before the pods—it was astounding! Given that with what Hemant had said about their existence, Ciro surmised that they must have found a naturally-occurring Arthropod-free pocket of the jungle in which they were able to survive. I filed that away to ask Arjun about once he was more composed, but I was afraid it might be a while judging by how he was acting. *This is great. We're all injured or suffering from the Shock.*

Otto explained to Mueller that the survivors had corroborated his theory and that the hostile group we had run into was indeed the Demented.

"Who are the Demented?" I asked as the head of every single Misfit present around the fire swiveled towards me.

"The Demented," began Otto, making sure that Ariadne and Mei were out of earshot, "are the nastiest group of miscreants that exist on the surface. They are a vile, violent, evil spawn of the human race. We think they were originally survivors, maybe Banished, but their minds became more and more twisted with the increasing consumption of their invert food source over the centuries.

"You may have heard that we can ingest the inverts if we cook 'em for long enough. Pah! Not me. Well... maybe in a pinch. If you keep eating the things, they start to mess with your mind. A group like the Demented that's been eating 'em since birth, they get pretty damn deranged.

"You remember the scars? The scars are from when the food gets scarce. The freaks start cutting and eating on each other. The invert thinking worms its way into their brains. They become more like 'em but in human form. Did you ever hear human language from them? No. They are savage animals. I'm not for killing our kind, but they aren't our kind. Not anymore."

"Well, we don't have to worry about that particular group anymore," said Mueller, "Us or Ade, which brings me to my next point. Everyone gather around."

Everyone returned to Mueller save for Kurt, who stared on from the supply truck where he was tending to Omar.

"It saddens me to lose this young man, Ade, who never shied away from the hard work of a Misfit and has proven himself in the face of danger," Mueller said, wrapping his arm around Ade. "By his choice, Ade has honorably decided to take over the Cave City Pump House, where he will live and maintain it as long as he so chooses. After one calendar year from his Release Day, he may elect to return to his home, Pod Horizonte, as a citizen. I, however, have seen enough. I immediately confer on him the title of Misfit."

Everyone cheered and chanted his name. It was a good feeling after negativity had dominated the last few days. I hoped it would be a start to overcoming the emotional roller coaster we had experienced. However, our journey had just begun, and we all needed to prepare for the plethora of challenges we still faced, which apparently now included the Demented.

I collected my gear and saw my crossbow lying next to my bivvy. I was filled with disgust looking at the instrument that had been so destructive. I was the one responsible for those deaths. The blood was on my hands. I shook the feeling off, knowing that the violence was a necessary act. I centered my mind on the friends I had saved. It didn't make the sickening feelings vanish, but it helped. I grabbed the rest of my stuff, saving the bow for last. I quickly threw it over my shoulder and out of my mind. With every step, I could imagine it staining the back of my jumpsuit with the violence that filled its frame.

We loaded up the boat, choosing to eat lunch en route, the discussions and preparations having taken up the entire morning. We were finally ready to move on from this place so overwrought with haunting memories. We pulled away and watched our friend Ade grow smaller and smaller as he receded into the distance.

CHAPTER 42: ARIADNE

Mueller came into focus as I stared at him, piloting the boat down the river. His eyes were fixed on the river as he guided the barge on our northern journey to the ocean. It had been three days since we left Ade at the pump house.

"Ariadne?" said Grace.

"I'm sorry," I said.

"Don't apologize," said Grace. "Are you still having nightmares?"

"They never stop," I said.

I looked around at Mei, Leni, Arjun, and Huck, who were also participating.

We were having our fourth sit-down with Grace. It had started with her comforting Mei and me but had grown into a group share session. During her decade with the Transporters, she had fallen victim to the Shock herself, overcoming some of its harshest symptoms. She encouraged us, guiding each of us back towards normalcy yet knowing we'd never reach it—not entirely.

"Don't avoid reliving the event," she said. "Let it happen. Don't fight it. Each time it does, it lessens its hold over you. Now, let's try physical contact again. Just Mei and Ariadne."

Before we met, she had threatened the crew that if anyone batted an eye at our sessions, she would tie them to a rope behind the boat. Some had laughed, but Grace's face was unwavering. She told us we were free to react however we wanted, but she wanted us to try. I slowly reached out and rested my hand on Mei's knee as she did mine. My anxiety level rose, but I breathed as Grace had taught us. I willed my mind to understand that she meant me no harm. After a few moments, it was over.

"Good job," Grace said. "We'll meet again tomorrow. Not optional. Now, get back to your duties. Mueller may be supportive, but he still doesn't tolerate slacking. Besides, the work's good for you."

I smiled at the others as I rose and returned to my station. Leni was progressing faster than any of us, having dealt with the Shock longer than us. Helping all of us, especially me and Mei, had been more therapeutic than anything Grace had done for her. She was opening up to us, even becoming friendly.

I caught myself wishing that we had known about Akhil's addiction. Maybe Akhil could have been able to get help from Grace, who approved of my herbal remedies like valerian or passiflora but rejected addictive substances like pheromones or Dust. I needed to collect some passiflora since my valerian supply was dwindling, but it wasn't native to the Latin Territory. I needed to find the other plant for Krista as well. I felt the anxiety I fought so hard to be rid of, beginning to return. I promised to help her, but she wasn't the only one dealing with something at the moment.

Huck had been annoyingly tender with me since our encounter with the Demented, treating me like a paper doll. I was getting stronger. Grace had warned us that sucking it up would only harm us in the long run. However, on the wildly unpredictable surface, I felt pressured to return to my previous level of performance as quickly as possible.

I made my way to the supply truck, planning to help Kurt check the medications for heat damage, and was pleased to see Omar up and about. His wound was healing, thanks to Kurt's stitching skills and antibiotics. Omar was happy to walk around without a shirt and show off his battle scar to the few women on the boat. I laughed out loud at the thought of him sunburnt with a bandage tan—*sexy*.

I climbed into the truck through the tied-back canvas with Kurt, and we worked as the sun fell low in the sky. Through the floorboards, I felt the drop in the engine's revolutions as we pulled the boat over to the eastern bank of the river. Since my attack, I could feel the spike in heart rate like a pinprick whenever we set foot on land. I never thought I would feel safer on the water. Besides the omnipresent blood midges, occasional spring tongues, and native pests, our river travel had been gloriously calm. The last time we had crossed paths with a wake strider, even Leni had caressed it a time or two as everyone held their breath. On the other hand, Hemant still adamantly opposed any friendliness with the Arthropods.

Several of the crew were positioned around the barge, trained to watch for approaching toadies. They would have them floating abdomen-up long before they neared the boat. We set up camp as we had the previous nights, balancing the proximity from the water as another measure of protection against the Arthropods. It was a technique the Misfits had learned from their years of surface survival.

"You feel up to hunting? Ciro asked, kicking at a dead branch in the dirt. "Mueller asked me to go with Otto. Everyone is getting tired of fish. I wondered if you felt up to it. Mei said she'd come."

I hesitated for a moment.

"You don't have to go. I just thought I'd ask."

"No, I want to go," I said.

"Great," he said, noticeably perking up.

A few minutes later, we were wandering off into the brush, the small green mountains breaking up the landscape in the distance. The further north we went along the river, the more arid the climate became. Smaller trees and low-lying brush covered the sandy beige ground near the campsite. We scoured the area, finding a few snakes and rabbits. I considered any outing reasonably successful if I made it without a panic attack. To top it off, I had even been able to find the second and last ingredient I needed to help Krista—pearl fruit. As we passed through a clearing on the way back to camp, Otto froze. Fearing an imminent attack, my heart rate skyrocketed as I fumbled to ready my bow.

We dove behind cover as I nocked an arrow to the string, struggling against my trembling hands. "I shouldn't have gone hunting," I muttered. "I wasn't ready." I closed my eyes tightly, trying to breathe as Grace had instructed. Otto whispered for us to stay low. We heard a shuffling, tapping sound emanating from the clearing. I drummed up the courage and peered over the rock protecting us, my breathwork having done little to calm my nerves.

On the other side of the clearing, I saw what had spooked Otto. Two multipedes were scouring a pile of rocks and debris for food. It surprised me that Otto had been afraid of multipedes. Not that I could say much. I could barely hold an arrow in my bow, but while notoriously difficult to kill, multipedes could be outrun and presented minimal cause for alarm.

"Let's go back to camp!" I whispered to Otto.

Otto turned to me, grinning. All traces of fear, gone.

"Not a chance! I've been itching to try this on 'em," Otto said, pulling a small metal canister from his pack. "It's my invert repellant. Well, not mine *per se,* if we're getting technical. Kurt and I made it from the skid marks of our mysterious invert when we noticed the others avoided it—"

"Otto!" Mei said, frustrated.

Battle was not the time for long-winded explanations. Taking the hint, Otto popped the top on the canister and lobbed it between the two multipedes before ducking between Ciro and me. We all peered over the rock as the canister hissed, spewing its contents into the air. The multipedes twitched their feelers for a moment before vanishing into the woods like their spines were on fire.

"That was awesome!" said Otto, raising his arms triumphantly. "It takes us half a day to make one. I need to make Kurt get busy. The bloody things are amazing!"

As I rose to start the journey back, I heard a deafening roar penetrate the vegetation, vibrating the ground.

"What... the hell... was that?" asked Mei.

Otto turned to us, white with sheer terror, and held his quivering finger in front of his lips, crouching down slowly against the rock as we followed suit. I risked glancing over the stone, curiosity getting the better of me. Nothing from my time in the pod remotely prepared me for what I saw. Looming in the distance, a multipede dangling from its narrow maw, was an Arthropod unlike any I had ever studied or seen. I instantaneously understood the horror Otto was feeling as every hair down the length of my body raised on its end.

The creature standing before me was multiple times larger than anything I had ever studied or seen. Spines covered its bulbous matte-black body, on which were several impaled Arthropods, including the second multipede, still twitching with the spasms of its slow demise. In addition, the creature had spiked arm-like appendages that it could use to stab and slice prey positioned in front of its spindly legs. I sank back behind our cover, shivering in the heat.

"What are we going to do?" I mouthed to Otto, knowing we were powerless against the new creature.

"We run," whispered Otto, crossing himself.

I looked over at the others. Mei nodded. I could tell she was afraid but ready to sprint. Ciro was trembling and pale as a sheet. I saw that his jumpsuit leg had darkened with moisture.

"Ciro, look at me," I said quietly.

He slowly turned to face me, scared out of his wits.

"We need to go. Can you run?" I asked.

He nodded as his hand tightened around his compound bow.

"We're ready, Otto," I said.

"Wait!" said Otto.

I sat listening, realizing how quiet the forest had become. Then I heard it. The sounds of the abomination were fading in the distance. It was walking away! I allowed myself the briefest hint of relief. Otto cautiously checked to verify his assumption, then gradually stood.

"Jesus, that was close," said Otto, his voice shaking. "I'm glad that thing went the other way. I didn't think…." Otto paused, regaining his composure. "It didn't occur to me that grenades could attract the same species. That was the scariest damn thing I've ever seen! And I've seen a lot, mind you."

I walked in silence back to camp, the prizes of our hunt slung over my shoulder. After all that had happened, I had little appetite for consuming them. Even Otto, who could perpetually be counted on at dinner, wasn't hungry. To avoid a possible panic, we gathered as few people as possible and briefed them on the encounter.

"What do you think it was?" asked Huck.

"Some sort of ambush bug, I believe," said Arjun, finally acting more like himself. "That would explain why Otto and Kurt never saw it."

"That's bloody terrifying," said Otto. "The damn thing was probably watching us collect its crap."

"Possibly, but unlikely," said Arjun. "If it had seen you, I doubt we'd be having this conversation."

"That's reassuring," said Otto.

"Any ideas how we could kill the thing?" asked Mueller.

"I suspect the only reason that you came across it in the first place was that they are fiercely territorial. When you introduced the scent of another, it came out to claim its habitat," said Arjun. "In the future, you would be wise to draw it back to the mounted weapons. Small arms weapons will be minimally effective. If it's armored on its entire body, we must find a weak point. If you could perhaps find me a specimen…."

"Great, a giant invert we can't kill. That's fantastic," said Omar, now walking on his own.

"I vote we call it a spine back," I said. "Since that's the image I can't seem to shake from my head."

"Doesn't exactly relay the terror, but sure, you lot are welcome to call it a spine back. But, I'm going to call it the Nightmare for what it truly is," said Otto. "Especially since *if* I get any sleep tonight, it'll be plagued with that bloody monstrosity."

"Let's keep this under our hats until we're further down the road," said Mueller. "I don't imagine it poses any more risk tonight. I'll break it to—"

"What the hell?" asked Hemant, looking up at the sky.

In the distance, we watched as thick clouds of Arthropods flew across the sky, migrating northeast to destinations unknown. In the distance, we heard the sounds of their terrestrial counterparts stampeding below them.

"Arjun?" asked Mueller.

Arjun faced him. "This is new."

CHAPTER 43: HEMANT

The monotonous daily work of the barge still needed to be done. Mueller had made accommodations to my workload, giving me tasks that didn't require legwork, but I found myself mindlessly going through the motions. None of those privy to the discussion of the Nightmare had gotten any sleep. I laid awake all night, anxiously anticipating hearing the roar Ariadne described at any moment. I doubted I would be much of a defense against an attack with my bum leg and sleep deprivation. I wasn't even sure if one would come since it seemed as though every invert in the region had flocked somewhere else. The sheer volume rivaled those attracted to our Release Day.

The inverts were up to something, and not even Arjun had any idea what it was. Not having the ability to communicate in real-time with Pod Baghdad puts us at a serious disadvantage. Arjun started to put together several theories of his own. He thought that the inverts must have evolved perfectly over millions, if not billions of years, to colonize the universe. Big thoughts like that gave me the heebie-jeebies. It was one thing for them to be a bunch of big, dumb bugs. The idea that they could organize and be strategic scared the hell out of me. Not to mention the implications for how many more there might be scattered throughout the universe.

Arjun had scoured every resource he and the Misfits had, desperate to find any information about the myriad hypotheses he had generated. He was convinced that the survivors had stumbled upon a simple, repeatable way to live undiscovered, perhaps even unknown to them. So he had been grilling me about everything from the plants to the geography of their camp, hoping to find some granule of knowledge that could give us the advantage.

He also had been frantically searching every resource for any mention of the newly discovered invert but to no avail. It seemed as though we were the first to encounter it and live. It was imperative that the knowledge we had in our possession survived the trip to Kano. Arjun didn't like unsolvable puzzles. He firmly believed that there was a natural explanation for everything. He would die of starvation trying to find answers if I didn't intervene. It wouldn't be the first time intervention was needed. That's part of what I loved about him. We balanced each other. Even though he would be coming with us to the Australian Territory, I know he would've been one of the best additions to the science teams in Baghdad, even though separating from him would have ripped me apart.

After I had greased all the fittings a single person could do in a day, I painstakingly made my way around the barge, looking for a place to sneak in a nap. Instead, I found Arjun and Ciro comparing Kurt's mottled paper compendium of inverts with Arjun's own.

"Hemant! Look at what we've found!" he said beaming. "I think the spine back has been indirectly documented for a while, though no one knew what it was. Arthropods have been found mysteriously dead for decades, usually with pierced exoskeletons. So I think these accounts are evidence of the spine back's dorsal appendages or rostrum."

"Rostrum?" I asked, needing the layman's version.

"Think of it like a beak," said Ciro. "Ambushing Arthropods tend to have a beak-like formation to deliver the killing blow to their prey. We are making some assumptions based on the description from Ariadne and Otto provided. " Ciro paused, his eyes growing damp. "I never saw it. I couldn't move."

I watched as Arjun slid his arm around Ciro's waist, comforting him.

"This creature just keeps getting better and better," I said. "Do you have any idea how to kill it if we run across it?"

"Only ideas," said Arjun. "With many larger Arthropods, the link between the segments can often be the weakest. Remove the head or abdomen from the thorax, and it won't live much longer."

"Exactly how long is 'much longer,' Arjun?"

"That varies with the species and which part," said Arjun. "Cutting off the head will get you the quickest death, but don't assume you're out of harm's way until the movement ceases."

"I'll try to remember that. Thanks," I said, leaving the two alone.

Just when I thought I was tired enough to squeeze in a nap, they gave me more terrifying thoughts to plague my rest. *Thanks, guys.* The quantity of information I had learned since leaving the pod gave me more insight into the issues surrounding the training and preparation of candidates. I had never studied as much as Arjun, but it was apparent that there were many gaps in the knowledge presented to us. *Did they not provide us with the information because of ignorance or intention?* It was truly amazing that anyone survived. We needed to get humanity out of those holes and back onto the surface where we belonged. The success of our mission was paramount. Damn, I was ready to bust into the Hive.

•••••••••

I was getting weary of our journey. Don't get me wrong. I was grateful for our safety, but we'd clean and maintain our equipment all day. By night, we'd camp on the shore before embarking and repeating the process the next day. I wasn't sure how transporters put up with the monotony. Mueller and the Misfits dedicated their lives to couriering goods and messages between the pods. By comparison, I was bored of the lifestyle in less than a month.

I had begun carefully sparring with Omar in the evenings to maintain my skills and physique as well as pass the time. It was challenging not to rely on my leg like I usually would. We evenly matched each other, making it challenging and entertaining. The others would exercise, spar, spectate, play games, socialize, and drink hooch (if Mueller wasn't paying too much attention). Otto always had a story to tell. Arjun, Ciro, and lately, Leni would usually be found reading or studying the wildlife. I had grown quite fond of watching the archers compete, each vying for the status of the best marksman—generally Ariadne.

The days all began to blend. Day after day would pass with little to no attacks from inverts. It was eerie. We hadn't sustained a single injury among the group in days, a fact that even Mueller thought was unusual. He had mentioned he was thankful for the reprieve; however it came. With each passing day, I noticed I was becoming more and more nervous that something was amiss.

We had made port last night on the edge of what the crew called Mountain Lake, another reservoir that Mueller said would dwarf the one we passed through almost two weeks ago. According to him, the lake formed was one of the most beautiful in the Latin Territory, but a high population of inverts haunted its shores. Additionally, the climate grew steadily hotter and drier as we traveled. Mueller said that we would be trading some Arthropod habitats for others.

The inverts had undoubtedly made themselves at home on Earth. I relished the idea that if we were able to knock out the Hive, we might have a chance at reclaiming our planet. That idea is what kept me going through the abysmal daily routine. The following day, I even woke up excited to see the large body of water.

Once we reached the lake, Mueller formed a perimeter like when Ade had lost his leg. We rounded the last bend and saw the first signs of the expansive body of water. The lake was as gorgeous as Mueller had made it out to be. The picturesque mountains giving the lake its name surrounded the beautiful blue water. There were striders everywhere, but at least they were harmless as far as inverts went. Rising from the lake in the sun's morning heat were little wisps of moisture, as though the striders were leaving plumes of dust in their wake.

"If I survive everything that's thrown at us, I want to live somewhere like this after they're gone," I said to myself.

"That wouldn't be a bad choice," said Mueller, approaching me from behind.

I turned to face him as he joined me, looking out over the water.

"Don't let the routine dull you, boyo," he said. "You'll never make it to the Australian Territory if you do. We do the routine to keep us sharp, but if you don't exercise your mind, you won't make it."

"How did you—" I started.

"I've been doing this for a long time," he said. "My advice… learn and apply. You have a wealth of knowledge and skills here. Your friend Ariadne knows plants. Your brother, inverts. Kurt, medicine. You get the picture. Use this time to improve yourself for when you face the inverts at the Hive."

Mueller put his hand on my shoulder and looked me directly in the eyes before walking away. He was right. I had been letting the monotony wear me down. At the very least, I was only maintaining, not growing. I resolved to follow through with the new advice starting tonight when we camped. It was the first night Mueller scheduled multiple guard shifts. I was slated for the third, giving me the evening to study with Ariadne if she was up for it.

We made our way to our site for the evening, only having dealt with a few more toadies, and began to unload. I approached Ariadne cautiously, knowing she was still a bit skittish. Not that I could sneak up on anyone until my injury had healed entirely.

"Hey," I said, struggling with where to begin. "Would you teach me the art of foraging tonight? I learned enough during my survival training to recognize the easy stuff like fruits, but I want to know the less obvious things I can eat."

Ariadne stifled a laugh. "Sure. I'm not laughing at you, I promise. It's just… You can't learn to forage in one evening. But I can teach you to recognize one or two edible things tonight reliably. Will that work?"

"Sure," I said, smiling.

While Kurt prepared our turtle dinner, Ariadne took me to the edge of the camp, barely into the brush. It was substantially more spiny and scratchy than the vegetation from only a few nights' journey south. She showed me a plant with a distinct fan-like leaf.

"This is a cassava plant," she said. "You can recognize it easily by the leaf. It's everywhere, and I'm only seeing more of it the further we go."

"So, do you eat the leaves?" I asked.

"No, the roots," she said.

"Doesn't sound appetizing."

"They aren't really."

"Then why are you showing me these?" I asked.

"For starters, they are more nutritious than anything we had in Horizonte," she said.

"Okay, fine. Now what?"

"We dig them up."

Ariadne started digging, then paused, looked at me, not helping, and pulled me down into the dirt with her. Huck came over to find us flinging the loose, dusty soil on each other.

"I'm glad you guys are having fun while the rest of us are working," he said.

"I'm showing him how to forage for cassava," she said.

"Looks like you're playing in the dirt to me," said Huck.

"I think I am," I said.

Ariadne handed me her little shovel from her pack and showed me how to dig up the roots without damaging them as Huck walked off, annoyed.

"I think I've seen Kurt cook these before. So can I just bite off a hunk like a carrot?" I said, raising it to my face.

"No!" yelled Ariadne.

"Okay…" I said. "Did I miss something?"

"You can't eat it raw," said Ariadne. "They have a poison that you have to cook out. Then you can eat all you want."

"Okay, so on my first outing, you show me a plant that's bland and toxic?" I said, laughing.

"You asked for the less obvious. So here it is," said Ariadne. "You can live on this for a while, though you won't be excited about it."

We walked down to the water so that I could rinse the roots while Ariadne stood watch, bow drawn. We brought the roots to Kurt, who prepared them to accompany dinner. I have to admit, turtle soup and cassava fries were not only good but tasted that much better knowing I had helped source it. Of course, I wasn't the first in line to eat turtle, but Kurt assured me if we ever had the freedom to grill it safely, he would change my mind.

I found Arjun after dinner and bragged about my newfound foraging skills. After stifling their amusement, he and Ciro were supportive, even offering to teach me anything they could. Ciro was becoming like a second brother to me. I felt freer lately knowing that someone who cared so much about Arjun was there to help him while the research completely immersed his mind.

As I prepared my tent for the night, we began to hear a faint buzzing sound, slowly increasing in intensity. Everyone stood, but with the darkness consuming everything, it was hard to pinpoint the origin of the sound. Eventually, the sound became almost deafening, but still, all I could see were the stars. Then, I began to notice clusters of stars disappearing and reappearing across the sky.

"It's a swarm!" yelled someone in the chaos.

Then all hell broke loose. More blood midges than we had ever seen! Lit only by the campfire and starlight, it was almost impossible to see the tiny black parasites until they were on you. I gave up using my hammer, let it fall to the ground, and unsheathed my dagger instead. It was almost impossible to connect with the little suckers, but it was easy enough to dispatch them when you did. The issue was the quantity. There had to be hundreds against the tens of us. As I dropped them to the ground, I could feel the pricks on my back. I suppressed the panic, knowing there would be time to worry about them later. Finally, after an hour of endless battle, I collapsed into the fine dirt, exhausted, my limbs burning from the exertion and loss of blood.

"What the hell is wrong with the inverts!" I yelled, throwing a little tantrum. "Leave us the hell alone! Go back to your own damn planet!"

I don't know what happened. I just broke down and started crying, letting the hemolymph-soaked dagger fall to the ground. I had had enough of the stupid bugs. Despite the corruption in the pod, it seemed like a viable alternative at the moment. I felt the gentle touch of someone removing the midges from my back as they rubbed my shoulder. I had always envisioned myself as Arjun's tough older brother, but at the moment, I was the one who needed comforting.

●●●●●●●●●

As the sun rose, I woke up with a tender back and tired from the lack of sleep. Surely, I wasn't the only one. I struggled out of the bivvy, subject to the ache and soreness from the evening's experience. The corpses of the midges inundated the camp. Mueller was yelling for them to be added to the already burning midge bonfire before they started to attract other inverts. I watched as the odorous, greasy smoke from their burning bodies darkened the morning sky. Otto surrounded the fire with smoke canisters hoping they would further disguise the odor of cooking inverts.

Moving slowly, everyone loaded the barge for the other side of the lake, roughly a day's journey at our current rate. Huck helped me load several of the unwieldy pieces of equipment onboard but had seemed terse with me. I made a note to talk with him later about whatever was bothering him. Maybe the midges had pissed him off too. Once everyone and everything was locked down, we set sail for the other side. The water had even more striders on it than yesterday.

Unconcerned about the wake striders, Grace pushed the barge along as fast as it would travel across the lake. The boat's top speed was not particularly fast, but it was enough to create a nice breeze. As I gripped the worn handrail, I could feel the allure of the area and could almost see myself living here in another life. Everything felt good—the breeze, the smells, the views, the temperature, it was all just—perfect. After the breakdown last night, I felt clear and free. It was something that had been building up inside of me and needed out. I did my daily duties with a bit of pep in my step that I knew Mueller would notice. I'll give it to the guy. He knew what he was doing.

By day's end, I began to see where the shore and the lake returned once again to a river. Mueller had announced earlier that we would be setting up camp once we were back on the river, and I was excited for another lesson from my peers. However, we saw that the striders seemed more focused on us as we approached.

"I know they are nice and all, but why are they staring at us, Arjun?" I asked.

"I don't know. Maybe we stayed in their territory too long."

"I'll be glad when we are out of here. Inverts give me goosebumps, even the *nice* ones."

A trumpeting sound suddenly pierced the air. Panicked, I looked around for its source. In the distance, a strider had begun trumpeting. It was a high-pitched signal immediately joined by the others—every single one. I had to slam my hands over my ears to prevent damage to my eardrums. The sound was so loud that it made my brain hurt. *Was this a weapon? Maybe they weren't as innocent as we thought.* After a moment, the trumpeting subsided, and we all let our hands fall to our sides.

"What in the Sam Hill was that all about?" asked Otto.

"I—" began Arjun.

"Dammit! Not again!" I said, seeing another swarm advancing towards us. "I don't know how many more of the suckers I can take!"

"They aren't midges. They aren't midges!" yelled Arjun. "Don't let them land on you!"

"Arjun, go find cover!" I yelled.

Damn, damn, damn. Something was flying towards us in a swarm that was dredging up my troubling memories from last night, except this time it was worse. It was always worse. Just when I thought there might be a nice invert, they proved me wrong. The only good invert is a dead one. I looked up in horror as I realized what the hundreds of creatures bearing down on us were. It was one of the inverts I did remember from class. It's hard to forget the ones that want to gnaw off your head and lay their eggs inside you.

CHAPTER 44: GUILHERME

It took multiple people working tirelessly to remove the carnage from outside the massive double hatch leading to the bridge. The foreboding doors still stood, just as solid and ominous as they had been, but no longer was anyone barring our access. The bridge wasn't impervious to sound, but I didn't know how aware its occupants were of what had occurred. It was safe to assume that they knew the doors were the last thing standing between them and the resistance.

"We need to communicate with them," I said, turning to Fabrice.

"I've already told you, we can't reconnect their power without returning full control of the pod to them," he said.

"Could we power up the closed-circuit camera feeds directly from out here? The interior feeds have audio that we can reroute," I said. "I mean, a candidate did it for chrissakes."

"Maybe," said Fabrice. "I'll get my guys on it. It may have unintended side effects. The cameras all run through the main communication grid. They might be able to override the communication relays."

"It's a chance I'm willing to take. I don't think they have the people's ear any longer. Just make it happen."

Fabrice nodded and began barking orders. We were getting snappy with each other. It had been ages since any of us had slept, and the situation didn't appear to have an end in sight. Finally, after several more hours, Fabrice had successfully patched in and was ready to go when I was. I took a deep breath. I tried not to dwell on that whatever I said would have direct consequences for my wife. But, being the leader of the coup, I had to see this through. I nodded to Fabrice to power the system.

"Davi Carvalho, I hereby order you and those with you to surrender the bridge immediately and peacefully. We will note your compliance in your tribunal case. Any attempt to disregard this message will result in a full breach with orders to shoot on sight. You have five minutes to respond."

Two minutes ticked by, each second marked by beads of sweat dripping from my brow. I had just issued an ultimatum to the despot holding my wife hostage. I prayed that reason would prevail and he would cooperate. Finally, a crackle originating from the wired speakers on the ground next to me broke the silence. A tube monitor switched from static to a confident ousted Minister Carvalho against dark gray obscurity.

"Major," Carvalho said cockily. "You overstep your bounds. *Tsk. Tsk. Tsk.* I'm afraid you don't realize that I'm the one in control."

His calm demeanor left me disconcerted and doubtful of our success. He was good at the psychological side of warfare, but we had something he didn't—honor. Light overcomes darkness. It didn't matter what he said. We would prevail.

"No, Davi," I said. "Your control is gone. Yours and the regents. Surrender the bridge, or we will take it from you."

"And part with your lovely wife? I don't think so. She's one of several… *tools* at my disposal. The regents and I *will* walk out of here as free men and continue our regime over the pod."

"Regime? Do you hear yourself?" I asked. "You're supposed to be a leader of the people, not a tyrant."

"Memo, you delude yourself," said Carvalho. "It's always been a dictatorship, and you were a part of it. All those improvements to the city you made increased *our* quality of life, not those of the pod. Don't continue this pretense that you weren't aware, that you are the good guy. And where were you on this last Release Day, hmm? Protesting in opposition? No. You were on the bridge with us, reveling in the food and drink as you and your beautiful wife watched the release intently. I have an ultimatum for *you*. Let us walk out freely, and you may resume your place as regent with promotion and your wife again at your side."

"If I refuse?" I asked.

"You can watch as I feed her and the others to the Arthropods outside. *You* have five minutes to respond."

As the monitor and speakers returned to static, I felt my heart stop. I didn't know how he could put her outside, but he would find a way. My head swam with confusion. We had to breach, and soon, but I wasn't sure how we would save my wife and the others in the process.

"He broadcasted that conversation through the entire facility," said Fabrice, having approached me from the side. "There are murmurs questioning your authority."

"Damn that man!" I yelled, pointing at the impenetrable hatch. "I never did anything that wasn't for the good of the pod! And I watched the release for the first time that day—in horror!"

"That's not the people's perception right now," said Fabrice. "You can't start bickering with him. He's distracting them from the real issue. If you start defending yourself, it'll just come across as you downplaying your involvement."

"I have an idea," I said. "Put me on city-wide."

"I don't think that's a good idea right now. You're—" he began.

"Do it, Fabrice!" I interrupted.

He gave some commands to his subordinates and indicated to me when it was ready.

"Residents of Pod Horizonte, while distorted, what Davi Carvalho said is based in fact. I wanted to lead this pod into a new era of democracy, but perhaps I am not the right person to be at the helm. Therefore, after taking the bridge, I submit myself to the people of our pod for judgment before the new Tribunal Council. I nominate Fabrice Toussaint, the head of the skilled, as my successor until the citizens of the pods can vote a new leader into place. Thank you for your trust."

With a nod to a gaped-mouth Fabrice, the production staff cut the feed.

"That was not what I expected," said Fabrice, dumbfounded. "Do you really trust me to lead this entire city?"

"I wouldn't have chosen anyone else, Fab," I said.

The monitors and speakers returned to life.

"You have just issued a death sentence to your wife!" said a livid Carvalho. "I hope you know what you've done! Don't worry, though. I anticipated this! Before you began your insolent broadcast, I initiated the Signal using the power you so graciously provided. Every invert in a one-hundred-kilometer radius is making its way to our location. So they'll be just in time for your precious wife."

I watched as one of the men in the room forced the wall-mounted camera to change perspective, showing me where they had wired power from the communication relay to the bridge's exterior emergency hatch. My pulse dipped as the implications hit me. They were going to push all the hostages out of the bridge, and I would be powerless to stop them.

"No!" I said as Fabrice grabbed my shoulder.

"What a loss. At least everyone in the pod will get to watch Aline's violent death!" hissed Carvalho as the bridge's exterior camera showed on the feed. "I'll release one hostage outside *every minute* until I'm freed! You missed your chance, Memo. She will be the first one out!"

I watched in horror as my wife, dried blood caked on her face, was shoved out of the rusted surface-level hatch.

CHAPTER 45: HUCK

Despite the heat, I stood on the barge shivering, looking at the ominous approaching cloud of chompers. I slung my crossbow onto my back, feeling its useless weight like an anchor. It was a weapon of intense power but considerably limited by its slow reload. I pulled the dagger from my belt and readied myself for the barrage. Unlike the annoying blood midges, split wings were something you *never* want to land on you. They would rip large chunks of flesh from you with each bite and had a reputation for targeting heads. A shudder passed through my body just thinking about it. While attached to their headless victim, their long, thin tail could curl around and deposit its parasitic eggs inside of you. Here I was facing a sky peppered with them.

The buzzing of the approaching cloud became a deafening roar as they neared the barge. I heard a tearing sound coming from behind me and turned to see a rainstorm rapidly approaching from the stern. I could see the line of rain gaining on us as it advanced across the water. *This will be fun.* Then, as the water began pelting us from above, the wave of split wings hit us. I spun and hacked and ducked and stabbed. Chomper heads, abdomens, and viscera began to litter the deck, mixing with the rainwater and making the surface slick. The wave of creatures never lightened up. I couldn't tell if it was rain or hemolymph, but a liquid was starting to cloud my eyes.

Next to me, I saw one of the Misfits struggling with an attached chomper. It was biting his neck and repeatedly stabbing his back with its segmented tail, depositing an egg with each stroke. I ran forward and sliced the thing in half, but as it fell to the deck, so did he, hemorrhaging out of the gaping wound to his carotid artery. I stifled my gag and continued fending off the attackers. I felt one land on my back and had started to swing helplessly at it when Krista sliced it into thirds with her katanas. Her weapons against these creatures were proving far superior to my own.

We both turned when we heard Ariadne screaming and raced to give her aid. A chomper had bitten off the thumb and index finger of her bow hand, and she was losing her blood and focus. I ended the invert and shoved Krista and Ariadne into the nearby personnel carrier for safety, throwing her bow into the back with them.

Again, I felt the familiar touch of one of the loathsome inverts on my back, but this time was rescued by Hemant, feeling the punches from his hammer as it impacted the animal's thorax. I spun to fend off the continuing attacks as Hemant and I, armed only with our daggers, sliced our way through them towards the front of the boat. For the first time, I saw Arjun fighting. He was amazingly adept with his razor net. With each flick of his wrist, he would trap a split wing, cinch the net's barbs down on it, then fling the carcass out into the water to ensnare another. His style was elegant and orchestrated. It was as terrifying as the enemies we faced.

I finally heard cheers and shouts of victory coming from the bow. I finished off the last chompers around me and roared in triumph with the others. Everyone was nasty but alive. I walked around the boat, kicking the carcasses and chitin off into the water but leaving the fallen Misfits. While the candidates hadn't lost anything aside from fingers, the Misfits had suffered a few casualties. I walked past the corpse of one of the fallen Misfits. I turned my head when I saw that only a stump remained where his head had been. Recognizing who it was by his clothing made the event even more troubling. All over his back were the small perforations indicating egg deposits.

"Help me roll him overboard, Huck," said Mueller.

"Overboard, Boss?" I asked.

"Yes. Our dead pose as much of a risk to us as openly cooking," sighed Mueller. "When all this is over, I intend to see to it that there is a month of worldwide mourning."

We respectfully lowered the body of our brother in arms to the water and let him float away with the others, watching them dip under the surface as Todies or whatever else lurked under the surface devoured them.

"With any luck, the damn parasites will eat a few of them from the inside out," said Mueller.

I nodded and left Mueller to have a moment for his comrade. Then, I went directly to the personnel carrier to check on Ariadne. When I opened the hatch, I found it empty and carefully headed to the supply truck, doing my best to avoid slipping down into the goop that slathered the deck. Outside were several people in line for treatment, but I didn't see Ariadne.

"She's inside," said Zeke.

I flipped up the flap on the truck and saw Kurt treating a partially-clothed Ariadne as Krista held her hand.

"Get out!" Krista screamed as Ariadne yelled, "Huck!"

I quickly darted back, turning bright red and feeling guilty. I only wanted to check on her. Around me, the Misfits were patting me on the back as if I had done something noteworthy. I felt ashamed as I walked to the stern, wanting to hide in embarrassment. I fight bravely, save her life, and then show her body off to half of the crew.

"Great Huck, way to end the day," I said to myself.

"Well, it was a great way to end my day," said Omar, coming to a squat next to me.

I turned to him, fuming.

"Relax, man," he said. "I'm kidding."

"Look, man, I don't know—" I started.

"Shut up for a second," Omar said, chuckling. "You like her. Everyone knows you like her. But you need to chill. She's been through a lot in the last few weeks. Hell, we all have. I promise you that if she's interested in you, which I think she is, it'll happen. But you have to let her find herself again, okay?"

I nodded. I was at a loss for words. Omar rose, patted me on the back, and walked off. I was trying to show her I cared, but maybe Omar was right, and I was coming off as annoying. In a moment of self-pity, I felt I wasn't doing a great job at anything lately. Once we were on our own again, I resolved to be a better squadmate and leader. However, I hoped with Ariadne that I could be more than that.

•••••••••

After the onslaught at the lake, we made our way through another demolished dam, which Grace always handled with skill. We continued to make our way upriver for several days before coming to an area where the river widened again. It wasn't quite a lake, but it was further from shore to shore, and quite a bit squirrely, doubling back on itself multiple times. Once we had rounded the first major bend in the river, we set up camp on the beach where the red sand met with the blue water turning it a murky brown.

Low brush surrounded the area, which thankfully allowed for uninterrupted visibility of approaching Arthropods. At the moment, the only thing visible was the ever-present aerials dotting the sky. Large rock formations dotted the beach, upon which some in our company were climbing. If it weren't for possible toadies, I would've given in to the temptation to jump off of one into the cool water below. Hemant had vanished with Arjun to study something, and I was toodling around camp trying to make myself useful. I saw Ariadne, Ciro, and Krista and walked over to join them as Omar cocked one eyebrow at me in a subtle warning. Ariadne was attempting to learn how to fire her bow without her two fingers.

"This is never going to work," she said, frustrated.

"Here, let me help you," said Ciro, closing her hand around the string again. "I think you need to try three fingers below the arrow."

Ariadne fired off another arrow, wildly missing the target. She threw her bow down and started crying.

"I can't do it. And I can't even hold another weapon in my right hand! Maybe I should just take a pump house and grow stupid carrots!"

"I know you can do it," I said. "Your hand just needs to heal first."

I looked at Ciro and Krista, pleading with them to go with my eyes. Finally, Ciro took the hint and started wandering away, but Krista grabbed him by his jumpsuit collar and pulled him back. I shrugged.

"Look," I started. "I'm sorry about the other day. I just wanted to make sure you were okay."

"By flashing me to half the crew?" she asked.

Maybe when Ariadne was at the height of her frustration was a poor time to have this conversation, but I had already committed to it.

"I'm sorry," I said, letting it hang in the air.

I was about to give up and walk away when she said, "It's okay."

I felt a flood of relief. "How is your hand?" I asked.

"It's stitched and scabbing over, but Kurt says it'll be weeks before it's fully healed," she said. "He gave me some antibiotics, and I made my own topical ointment."

"That's a good prognosis then," I said. "How's your off-hand dagger-wielding?"

"It could save my life in a pinch, but it's not great."

"I knew my crossbow had limitations, so I spent a lot of time developing dagger skills," I said. "I could teach you some techniques in our downtime. If you'd like, I mean. Sorry I can't help you with the bow, aside from motivational support."

"I'd appreciate that, Huck, thank you," she said, smiling at me.

Even Krista, who had been downtrodden for days, looked amused.

"After dinner?" I said as we walked back to camp for the meal.

"Sounds good," said Ariadne.

I caught Omar's face out of the corner of my eye. He nodded approvingly.

The after-dinner plans didn't go as expected. That was the thing I was learning about the surface. So little goes according to plan. Mueller had sent a hunting party out into the brush to see what was around. They returned with a few small rodents and lizards and found some animal signs. Mei, being with them, had suggested taking Arjun back to the trail and letting him analyze it, so after our wild-caught dinner, we trekked over to the site. Even to my untrained eyes, it appeared to be the wake of the vast migration we had seen a few days ago. It looked like a large herd of Arthropods had crossed this way heading northeast.

"The recent behaviors demonstrated by the Arthropods don't align with any documented behavior," Arjun stated. "The strider's trumpeting, the migration, and the appearance of the Nightmare, they are all unusual and concerning."

"I don't like it," said Mueller. "We've been in these parts for years. You guys show up, and all hell breaks loose."

"Is it possible they know something about your mission?" asked Kurt.

"That's impossible," said Mueller. "But how would the inverts perceive them as any real threat, especially more of a threat than past teams? No offense, guys."

"None taken," said Arjun. "These Arthropods are more intelligent than I think anyone realizes, though I agree with Mueller. I don't understand how they could understand our intent and the threat we may pose."

"Regardless, this migration is strange," said Kurt.

I looked up at the aerials. One was relatively close to us.

"What do you think they see up there?" I asked. "Can they hear?"

Everyone turned to stare at the network of antenna bugs.

"You know, I've never seen one up close, " said Kurt.

"I think I might be able to help with that," said Ciro, stepping forward, pulling his compound bow down from his shoulder.

"That's quite a shot, boyo," said Otto.

"I'm not worried about making the shot," he replied. "I'm worried about what might come after it."

Ciro pulled back his arrow, took aim, and let it fly. We watched as the aerial gracefully moved sideways to dodge the blow before returning to its original position.

"I didn't expect that," said Ciro. "Any ideas?"

"I think I might have one," said Arjun.

Arjun fetched a small mirror from his pack.

"I have it for silently signaling others, but I think it will do quite nicely," he said.

It took him a minute, but he was able to reflect the sun onto the aerial and into its compound eyes. The invert looked a little drunk but was maintaining its position.

"We're probably sending all sorts of alarm bells over the alien network," said Kurt.

"On it," said Ciro, again raising his bow.

Ciro let the arrow fly, this time hitting its mark. The antenna bug fell from the sky, impacting the ground less than a hundred meters from where we stood. By the time we arrived at its fractured carcass, another had taken its place in the sky.

"No downtime there," I noted.

The aerial was a mess, having plastered the ground in its entrails. It looked like a giant gray and purple fly with a matte patina. Its massive antennas were swept back behind its body, almost triple its length. Its bulbous compound eyes seemed to stare back at us through each node, each one the size of my fist.

"With eyes like that, they can see everything we do and transmit our movements, presumably back to the Hive,'" said Kurt. "But that still doesn't explain why they are viewing us as a threat."

"I don't understand it either," said Mueller, "but I think there is the retaliation for shooting down the damn thing."

We all turned to look in his direction and saw four dust trails approaching us fast. Within minutes, it was clear that there were four multipedes headed straight for us. Everyone in the group stood in a battle stance, ready to receive the threat. I was thankful for an excuse to use my crossbow. Lately, against the smaller inverts, it felt like more of a hindrance than anything helpful. I raised my bow and aimed. Firing at will, I watched the bolt bounce off of the creature's armored exoskeleton. Dammit. *Maybe the thing is useless.* I reloaded as quickly as I could and took another shot, this time at the pede's eye. It was a direct hit. The invert went down face-first into the dirt and skidded to a stop. I heard a few cheers as I ran up to the top of a nearby rock formation where I could reload and fire from safety.

Hemant became a whirling dervish of rage and fury. I watch his war hammer fall with intensity onto the head of one of the pedes, crushing it into oblivion. *Then there were two.* I watched as the Misfits gave a death by a thousand cuts to another of the pedes, but not before it made contact with one of them. I saw it before it happened, but I was powerless to stop it. The creature had isolated one of the women. It swung its body with surprising agility, impaling her throughout her body and flinging her dozens of meters, leaving behind a misty trail of blood. By the time the transporters had finished with it, its chitin spikes and viscera dotted the ground, a visual representation of the anger they felt for their loss. The last pede had surrounded Omar and Kurt. Omar's formidable naginata could do significant damage to the invert in the gaps between its armor, but he was having difficulty building up speed in the confined space with which to deliver a successful blow.

Mueller couldn't reach the head, which was harassing the pair. He made for the last segment, crushing it with his round-headed mace. The invert let out a blood-curdling screech and spun to attack Mueller, giving Omar the room to build the momentum he needed to drive his blade deep into the pede's brain, finishing it off.

"We've got to get back to camp and make sure the inverts didn't attack them," I said.

"Agreed," said Mueller. "Roll out!"

We high-tailed it back to camp. When we arrived, night had fallen. Something had occurred while we were gone, but it didn't seem to involve any Arthropods. No one seemed to be in a talking mood, so we hunkered in for the night, curious but too tired to do anything about it. A sense of anticipation washed over me as I realized that tomorrow would be my final day on the river.

CHAPTER 46: ARIADNE

Last night, while half of the convoy was out investigating the Arthropod trail, I had taken the opportunity in everyone's absence to start preparing the plants I had collected for Krista. I reached into my worn pack, which already showed numerous signs of wear from the journey. As I unclasped the canvas bag and opened it, I smelled the pungent odors of the desiccated plants from inside their burlap pouch. Opening the bag had proven difficult as I learned to cope with my missing digits. I carefully pulled the plants out and laid them on my lap, uncomfortably aware of their capabilities and the risks they presented. I began to tear up, feeling wildly out of my comfort zone. Mei and Leni walked by with an armload of firewood and set it down to sit with me.

"You okay? Should I get Grace?" she asked.

I shook my head. Some stray hairs fell from my haphazard ponytail into my face. "No, it's not that," I said. "It's… well, I can't talk about it." I started crying.

Mei pulled my head gently to her shoulder, her usually sharp personality softening to bring me comfort. She slowly wrapped her arm around me and gently rubbed my upper arm, being ever so careful with her touch. Leni took my hand. We sat there for a few minutes as tears ran down my face. The smells wafting up from my lap were a constant reminder of the obligations I had made to my friend.

Shattering the peaceful moment, Zeke ran up to us. "It's Krista. She needs you, now!"

A feeling of concern replaced my sadness. We took off for the area where we had set up our tents, leaving the herbs behind in the dust. When we arrived at our cluster of tents, Krista was lying on the ground in the fetal position, clutching her stomach and wincing in pain.

"What's wrong?" I asked, knowing Kurt was with the others and her health was on my shoulders.

"I don't know!" she screamed, tears dripping into the dirt. "It feels like someone is punching me in the stomach and the back! Make it stop, Ariadne!"

I racked my brain, wondering what could be causing this. It seemed far too sudden and harsh to be food poisoning. Then it hit me. They were the symptoms of a miscarriage!

"Krista, did you try to eat anything from my bag? Any herbs?" I asked worriedly.

"What? No!" Krista responded, confused.

A natural miscarriage. *What a relief! I was off the hook!* A strong wave of guilt hit me. On the one hand, I was thrilled not to provide the abortion or attempt the dangerous procedure. On the other hand, I felt terrible that I was relieved by my friend's unimaginable pain. I looked at Mei, Leni, and Zeke, realizing that their knowledge of the situation was inevitable.

"Krista," I said, "You're having a miscarriage. It's going to suck, but you should be fine." I squeezed her hand.

Mei's and Zeke's eyes grew wide. Leni wasn't surprised.

"Krista, we need Kurt's help," I said. "Mei?"

"On it," she said, already darting off.

Krista nodded in acceptance and turned her face towards the ground. We all remained with her until the contractions had subsided, Leni singing the entire time softly. Then, I made Zeke leave as Kurt and I helped Krista clean up. The ordeal was one of the most emotional events I had experienced thus far. The loss of the pregnancy was something Krista had been wanting, knowing an infant would be a threat to all of our wellbeing. Of course, that didn't make the painful experience any easier for either of us. The guilt of relief still plagued me, but I knew it was better this way. Even though bivvies were only made for one, Krista and I removed our light armor to reduce bulk and slept together tightly, trading physical comfort for emotional.

•••••••••

Krista was still cramping in the morning and making frequent trips to the woods but was feeling better in all respects. A miscarriage isn't something a person gets over with a good night's sleep, though I was sure the natural process was less risky than the tisane infusion I had planned. At the request of Grace, Mueller told everyone to take a slow morning. Our journey today would be a shorter one, and Grace sensed the need for a break in the air.

I began my usual self-care, which today included bathing. I was tired of my smell and felt bad for Krista having to put up with it all night. Bathing was difficult traveling with a troop of primarily men. You could have safety or privacy but rarely both. Mei, Krista, Leni, and I stole off down to an inlet just over the ridge and bathed, taking turns keeping watch. Other than a spring tongue we saw in the distance, we had no trouble and smelled much better for it. After our light armor and jumpsuits had dried, not taking long in the desert-like heat, we climbed the rocky ridge back to camp.

We ate a lunch of rabbit stew, courtesy of Ciro and Arjun, who had spent the morning out trapping. I had quickly gathered some fragrant herbs myself, pleased not to be hunting for the abortifacient kinds. Ciro said that Arjun was getting so experienced at trapping, he didn't even know why he carried his bow anymore. I didn't care how they caught them, as long as they were. Rabbit had become my favorite meal.

After the cleanup, we loaded up the barge and prepared to make our way on our final stretch of Strider River. Mueller said we would be staying the night in Wet Church, a derelict town now mostly composed of rubble. Near the town, the river took a turn southeast while we would continue northeast over land to the transporter port of Tank Town. Grace said the crumbling dam near the town was still standing and presented much more of an obstacle than the others had. The barge might be a slow way of passage, but its shallow draft made it optimal for navigating the debris-laden post-civilization waters.

I imagined what the area might have looked like the day before the Arthropod Landing. *Were there people in boats fishing before dawn? Were there lovers walking along the beach at sunset?* I wondered what the area would look like a hundred years after the Arthropods were gone. *Would the fishermen and lovers return?* I was optimistic. I could almost see two people holding hands on this beach as they strolled along. I looked at Huck, helping Otto sling a heavy crate onto the boat. He caught my eyes and smiled back, the box catching on the edge and earning him a scolding from Otto. I knew the odds were stacked against us. *Would we be successful? Who would survive?*

Once the boat was underway, everyone continued scrubbing the entrails from the split-wing attack from the decks and bodies of the vehicles. The Misfits would probably be finding chomper guts for weeks. The dried hemolymph had already begun to damage the paint and corrode the materials underneath. As I scrubbed, I learned to depend on my left hand and thumb. You don't realize how valuable a thumb is until you don't have one. I was so frustrated at the lack of fine motor skills that it made a metallic taste in my mouth.

Mid-afternoon, when I had done my duties to Mueller's satisfaction, Huck and Ciro helped me practice drawing my bow, experimenting with finger positionings. I couldn't afford to lose arrows, so there wasn't any actual firing, but the exercises helped develop muscle and coordination with my new finger arrangements. I was anxious to get back to the land to recover the arrows and try firing them again.

Around dusk, we rounded the final bend of our river journey and made our way to the remnants of the long-abandoned town. It finally registered that we would be leaving Grace tomorrow. I had recovered enough to go on without her guidance, but I would miss her personality and understanding as I continued to cope with the Shock. "She stays with the boat," Mueller had said. The boat was Grace's baby, and she didn't leave it for anything. Tomorrow morning, Huck had said we would continue the last phase of our journey to the ocean. *God, the ocean!* I had seen pictures, large lakes and imagined it, but the idea of seeing that much water mesmerized me. Though with how long Mueller said it took to cross it, I'd probably be tired of it by the other side. As we crossed the waterway, I could see a distant construction rising from underneath the water.

I walked over to Mueller, who was observing it as well. "What is that?" I asked.

"That, my dear, is a church of antiquity. Its architecture greets us every time we make a berth here. It serves as a reminder that everything reemerges eventually. It is for that the early transporters named the town."

I took a deep breath and appreciated how far we'd come. Every day was another little win against the Arthropods, another chance to destroy the Hive. I felt more optimistic than ever. *We can do this. We can defeat the inverts.* The barge pulled into a natural inlet and docked. I stepped off the boat and took in the scenery. The breeze smelled of the river and fish as I took in the blue, orange, and green hues. Any signs of civilization had almost entirely returned to the earth, mostly leaving crumbling block walls and the chipped concrete surfaces of foundations and roadbeds. Mueller had said even when it was inhabited, the area had primarily been dwellings.

I wondered what it was like being a family living in a rural village, knowing the impending threat but unable to do anything about it. Billions had died. The UTE and First Builders didn't have the luxury of time, labor, or materials to build enough pod cities for everyone. There must have been billions who knew they would die. They must have felt helpless. *Do you risk the arduous journey to the nearest pod?* The nearest ones being thousands of kilometers away. *Do you sit around, dying from starvation, crime, suicide—or worse, Arthropods?* I could see how in those circumstances, ending life on your terms could look like a viable option. I bet the people of Wet Church continued to live their lives in the face of what was happening. This village seemed like the place where people lived until they didn't.

"Oy! Ariadne!" said Otto. "Care to join us?"

When I returned to reality, I saw that I was the only person not contributing to the work. So I jolted into action and pitched in. The Misfits unloaded the vehicles from their extended static trip upriver in the reverse order they had put them on.

"I keep telling you, the vehicles don't like sitting still," complained Otto to no one.

I watched as the flatbed with the buggies, tank truck, supply truck, cargo hauler, and personnel transport rolled off onto the sandy orange ground, appearing ready and anxious to embark on our terrestrial trip to Tank Town.

"Once we get to Monterrey, Boss, we're going to need more

men," said Kurt. "We've lost quite a few getting these guys here safely." Then turning to us, "Not that I'm complaining. On the contrary, I think your mission is critical. I am glad to have played a part."

Mueller nodded. "I don't disagree. Any of you guys who'd like are welcome to stay with us. You've all demonstrated your merit time and time again."

"Thank you," I said, with the others nodding in agreement.

"As for tonight," Mueller said, changing the subject. "We will sleep inside!"

Everyone cheered. Mueller led everyone to the edge of town, where one building had resisted the test of time. The edifice had a strange curved roof that had somehow stayed in place over the years. Well, at least most of it. The concrete walls were still erect around its entire base. Inside, the building's giant room was partially shaded and significantly cooler than the outdoors. I dropped my gear on the hard floor, disturbing the centuries of dust and revealing the floor's muted colors.

"It was a gymnasium," Zeke said, bending down to investigate the paint. "Maybe a track or a pitch, like we had in the pod. People played games on this, Ariadne. Can you imagine?"

I stood there for a moment, my mind blown at the connection to the past. An idea hit me. "What do you think about playing a game?"

"Really?" Zeke said, pausing for a moment. "That sounds like a fantastic idea!"

We roped everyone in from their evening duties to help clean the floor, getting a raised eyebrow from Mueller. Using whatever implements we could find, we pushed all the dust off the floor and made it somewhat functional. The paint was completely missing in many places, but there was enough to see what we were doing. We played a game Zeke called football that I vaguely remembered learning about in our history classes. Sports were never of much interest to me, but Zeke was fascinated with them. He explained the rules, basically that we couldn't use our hands and kick the round ball into the other side's goal. Due to the region's dry climate, we were able to find functional antique football goals. Grace had run back to the boat for a ball and brought out a spherical float.

Save for Hemant and Krista, who were both still recovering, we took our positions and played, Uninvited versus Misfits. It was a chaotic mess seeing as the only ones who had any knowledge or skill were Zeke, Otto, Omar, and Mei, who was surprisingly good. The dust on the already smooth floor made running humorously treacherous. By the end of the match, if you wanted to call it that, we were all lying on the floor—each of us a dusty, sweaty, hysterical mess. The evening only improved when Kurt, Arjun, and Ciro walked in with local coconuts they had found for us to drink. For those brief moments, we had escaped to a land without fear, concern, or worry. With my stomach pleased, I thought to myself, *That must have been what life in this town had been like before.* I was exhausted, but with relaxed contentment that I hadn't felt in years. I looked to my left to see Huck smiling at me. I blushed, and then I smiled back.

CHAPTER 47: HEMANT

After the football match, Arjun, Ciro, and I walked to the wall where everyone had thrown their packs and tent bags. I was thrilled about sleeping undercover, but the hard floor didn't strike me as the most comfortable. I was thankful my sleeping bag had a built-in pad. The three of us set up our bivvies in the corner of the gymnasium. Arjun and Ciro hadn't played, instead electing to watch the frivolities. When I went to sleep, they were still outside the tents, snuggled up together. I climbed into my bivvy on the unforgiving surface and was thrilled that my knee had mostly returned to normal.

The next morning, everyone seemed a little groggier than usual. Kurt put on extra coffee, which I greatly appreciated. Even Arjun was drinking more tea than normal. I dragged myself outside, where we were each assigned a vehicle to check for travel readiness. Today, we would begin our trip northeast on several old roadbeds that would lead us directly to Tank Town, our final destination of the continent. I'd spent my entire life underground, and in the last month, I had left the pod, traveled across a whole country, and was about to sail across an ocean. It made me light-headed when I thought about it too long. After each vehicle inspection team had sounded off, Mueller called us all into a huddle.

"Listen up," began Mueller. "I've made some adjustments to the seating arrangements based on our losses. It should be pretty similar to what we did last time. Something the inverts are doing is strange. Kurt and Arjun have put their heads together and still can't figure it out." Mueller paused to tug on his wide mustache, a tic I'd noticed he had when he was unsure of something. "Whatever it is, it doesn't bode well for our safety. I want everyone to be extra vigilant. We are stirring a pot, and I want them boiling in it, not us. Understood?"

"Understood," came the choral response.

"Take a piss and give Grace a kiss! We move out in ten," said Mueller.

True to his word, ten minutes later, I felt the low vibration of the natural gas-fueled engines through the chassis. I was thrilled not to have Otto changing gears between my legs. Unfortunately, I still didn't have the luxury of riding with Arjun. Instead, I found myself in the passenger seat of the tank truck as the driver, a tough-looking woman with leathery skin from too much sun exposure, filled the cabin with tobacco smoke. Even with the windows open, I quickly felt the effects of the drug and spent the morning feeling queasy. Fortunately for us, this had been a much less populated region. The lack of moisture had preserved the roadbed over the centuries, meaning faster travel and less motion, something I greatly appreciated with my swimmy head.

As we traveled, I grew more and more accustomed to the fumes filling the cabin. I found myself enjoying the wind and the gradual change to a more verdant landscape. The driver said that the land would become increasingly beautiful as we drove closer to the coast. I had no trouble believing her, having spent many years of her life on the surface under the sun. She was a person of few words, most of what came out of her mouth being thick plumes of smoke.

I rode along, contemplating the journey. I caught myself worrying from time to time about Krista. She had gone from being a bubbly personality to being downtrodden in a matter of weeks. She and Zeke were still spending just as much time together, if not more. It was only my concern as she was a member of our team. I had doubts about her mental and emotional wellbeing. Unstable team members presented a dangerous liability in the field, especially in combat. We needed to be prepared and ready for whatever the inverts would throw at us. That meant all of us.

That afternoon, we came to a stop at a bend in the road where Mueller announced that we'd be camping. While several of the company played Rochambeau for sleeping space in the vehicles, I happily set up my tent on the ground, preferring it to the alternatives like metal or concrete. After a boney dinner of lizards, I aired my concerns with Huck about our team while we sat on a large boulder, watching the sunset over the mountains in the distance. Huck asked Ariadne to join us on the sun-warmed stone.

"I'm worried about Krista," I said. "Is she up for this? I don't want a second Leni on our hands."

"First of all, Leni has improved dramatically," said Ariadne directly. "Krista is working through some things. Can she fight? Yes. Does she still need some time? Also yes. Does that answer your question?"

It really didn't. I knew from experience that someone could crack at an inopportune moment, and I didn't want that moment to be when someone else was at their most vulnerable. I didn't know an alternative short of leaving Krista behind with Grace, but I had missed that opportunity about eight hours ago.

"Sure," was the best response I had.

"Anything else?" asked Ariadne.

"Not really," I said. "Out of curiosity, do you think we'll encounter any resistance between here and the ocean?"

"That's a better question for someone like Arjun or Kurt, but so far, we've had our share of run-ins with the Arthropods and survived. I'm optimistic that we'll kick some ass if we do," said Ariadne, grinning from ear to ear.

I smirked. "Let's hope so. Otherwise, we might have to depend on Huck's slow reloads to save our lives," I said, smacking Huck's leg playfully.

"What the hell, man?" Huck said, laughing. "It took out that pede, didn't it?"

"And how many shots did that take, *hmm?* I asked.

"Only two!" said Huck defensively.

"How long did those two shots—Um, what the hell are those?" I asked, pointing to two dark-winged objects slowly flapping in the sky towards us.

"I don't know, but it's not good. Hey!" Huck yelled, getting everyone's attention. "We have incoming!"

Everyone scrambled, but there was no substantial cover outside the trucks. Huck, Ariadne, and I crouched behind the stone. I had stupidly left my hammer by my tent, which was about thirty meters away. I looked at Huck and Ariadne, who the inverts had also caught without their primary weapons. As the shapes grew closer, Arjun yelled from his hiding spot.

"It's the powder moths! Don't breathe their dust!" he yelled.

I knew it wouldn't be sufficient, but I pulled the slacked fabric of my jumpsuit up over my nose, still smelling the smoke it had absorbed. I made a mental note to ask the developers at Kano if I survived to make a built-in jumpsuit dust mask. I saw where the majority of us had made it into the armored vehicles. Then, as the dusters got closer, I had a jaw-dropping realization.

"They're carrying polies!" I yelled as the first one dropped.

An explosion shook the ground as it detonated. I squirmed in as close to the boulder as possible, feeling the gravel from the explosion pelt me. There was nowhere to run and nowhere to hide. I huddled in with Ariadne and Huck, who had the same disturbing revelation. Ariadne, who still had her pack, pulled a thermal blanket out, and we covered ourselves. I also hoped its reflectivity would camouflage our bodies from the attacking foes. We stayed tightly compacted against that rock for the eternity it took for the air raid to cease. When the explosions had stopped, and the wind had cleared the dust away, we emerged to see the destruction.

In front of us, our tank truck was splayed open like a cracked egg, taking with it the flatbed and the buggies it carried. Otto was standing by one of the downed dusters, a harpoon sticking out of its thorax and kicking it in a fury.

"You damned stupid thing!" he said, crying with several other obscenities. "You killed him!"

I ran up to him. "Otto, what happened? It killed whom?" I asked.

"Kurt!" Otto sobbed. "The damn things killed Kurt!" Finally, Otto collapsed defeatedly into the dirt.

The news hit me like a blow from my hammer. In addition to being our doctor and teacher, he was our friend. Arjun and Ariadne were going to be devastated. I ran past the damaged vehicles and bodies, searching madly for my brother.

"Arjun, Arjun!" I screamed.

"I'm here," I finally heard. I turned to see Arjun climbing out of the personnel carrier with Mei, Zeke, and some of the Misfits.

I threw my arms around him and held him tight, coughing profusely as I did. The cough had me doubled over, thinking only about air. After a few minutes, it eventually subsided.

"Did you breathe the dust?" Arjun asked.

"Some," I answered. Across the clearing, I could hear several others hacking as well.

"You'll be okay, but you might feel rough for a while. A lethal dose is deadly almost immediately."

"That doesn't make me feel better," I said.

Arjun laughed, reminding me that he didn't know about Kurt.

"Arjun," I said, leaning up to hold him by the shoulders, "We lost Kurt. He's dead."

I watched as Arjun focused inward, something I'd seen him do many times, and said, "Okay."

Years with Arjun had taught me that "okay" meant anything but okay. Mueller, who had been standing nearby, nodded to confirm to the others who had heard what I told Arjun, and everyone disbanded to deal with their grief.

The inverts will pay for this.

·········

We had a funeral for Kurt and the others the following day. While no one in our company was devoutly religious, aside from Otto, who conducted the ceremony, the memorial carried with it a desire to dwell on an afterlife. The idea that the Arthropods could take something from us and we could never get it back was distasteful.

"Friends," Otto began. "We're here to honor those of us that we've lost. We commend their souls to eternity dwelling among the stars in peace, where the harms and illnesses of the surface will no longer hinder them. Where sadness and anger are replaced with joy and love. Those we give to the earth served side-by-side with us, as comrades and friends, which our enemies took from us too early. But know ye this: They shall be avenged!"

A cry went up from the group. Otto, who typically had us laughing, humbled us with his commentary about life and death. Even Mueller and Omar were tearing up. Before the ceremony closed, Arjun asked to say a few words, an uncharacteristic trait.

"I grew close to all the Misfits, especially Kurt. He became my close friend and mentor. I was grateful for his companionship and will be at a loss without him."

Arjun received a few sporadic claps. Without knowing him, his directness can come off as insincere or flat. However, if Arjun is willing to stand in front of others and say something, you can bet it's something he's passionate about. Once Arjun had finished, Mueller closed out the funeral with a few words of his own, echoing the sentiments of Arjun and Otto.

"We feel every loss and every loss hurts, but this one hurts the most," began Mueller. "Kurt had been with me longer than any one person in the Misfits. He had become my closest friend, and I will forever carry a breach within my heart. In the Misfits, we say *Mors tua, vita mea.'* Your death, my life. From this day forward, the inverts will have a new understanding of our motto as they feel Kurt's death with every blow dealt by our hands."

"Mors tua, vita mea! Mors tua, vita mea! Mors tua, vita mea!" came the choral cry. Today, everyone was a Misfit.

We grouped the bodies, creating a massive cairn to protect them from the Arthropods and the elements. Mueller said the transporters buried their dead above ground when possible, showing their defiance in death of being driven underground. Afterward, we loaded up the remaining trucks and soberly drove towards the coast, leaving our downed companions' bodies behind but carrying them on in our hearts.

CHAPTER 48: GUILHERME

The predicament I was in left me momentarily dumbfounded, seeing my wife standing on top of the pod, at her most vulnerable to the Arthropods dwelling on the surface. The exterior of the pod offered zero cover. Aside from the bridge's elevated viewport, the city's surface was a nearly flat obtuse cone, dotted sporadically with clusters of dirt and plants that wormed their way into the centuries-old structure. Aline stood there, just outside the bridge's emergency hatch, not cowering but defiant.

"Fabrice, take command," I said. "I'm going to get my wife."

"Like hell you are!" he said. "You've got to see this through. You will be the leader of this pod, and I'm not letting anything happen to you!

Diogo and Lourenço, who had remained nearby, ran up to me.

"Let us get her," said Diogo.

"Go," I said, watching them take off. "Bring her back to me!"

"Are there any volunteers who would go with them?" I pleaded. "I will not order anyone to do this."

Ten of the force quickly pursued them.

"God, what have I done?" I said to myself, doubling over onto the nearest surface, distraught.

"Memo," said Fabrice, resting his hand on my shoulder. "We've got to think about how to breach this hatch."

"It's impossible," I said. "I know how they built the bridge. They designed it to be a fortress."

"We can't give up. There has to be a way!" said Fabrice.

"The only way is through that hatch or the emergency one on top, which is about to be guarded by the inverts," I said.

"Let's go through the hatch then," said Fabrice, who started issuing orders to a number of the skilled in our force.

I looked at the monitor and saw my wife, still bravely erect with her head high. From the camera angle, I could see where the auxiliary hatch next to the city's main gate had opened, and the specks I knew to be Diogo and Lourenço's team were running to save her. I felt my blood run cold when I saw the even tinier dots coming from a distance—the attracted Arthropods. The realization hit me like an impact. The volunteers would reach my wife just in time for everyone to die.

I watched in terror as Fabrice ordered men and women with cutting torches into place and had them start cutting into the massive steel door. It was fruitless, but I knew we had to be doing something. The volunteers were finally arriving at Aline, but the inverts had closed the gap and were visible on the screen. I was going to have to watch her die. I collapsed onto the floor, completely helpless, and began sobbing. I couldn't tear my eyes from the screen.

Diogo had Aline in his arms and turned to face the advancing foes. Armed with only spears and swords, they fought off the harassing bone arachnids and hook beetles, but more kept coming. Infinitely more. I watched as the first volunteer went down. An eight had managed to deflect his weapon, and his fangs sank into his chest before he dropped to the ground, the fangs still dripping their venom. The second one died when he fell, the hook bit off his legs, then his head. The third found himself on the wrong end of an eight's barb. All the volunteers were keeping Aline as far from the attacks as possible. Here, twelve of the most honorable men and women were sacrificing their lives on a suicide mission to save my wife.

In just a few moments, the inverts had whittled the group down to three. I reluctantly decided to watch Aline's death, choosing to spend our last moments together in spirit. I knew full well that it would forever haunt me. Another eight made its advance. I watched as Diogo maneuvered his way around the invert and speared it in its velvety weak spot. The creature twisted away, breaking Diogo's weapon in half as another eight plunged its legs through his chest. Diogo was the hero of the day.

This is it. It's over. I had resigned myself to what I was about to witness, but then something happened. A white haze plumed up from the bridge, clouding the camera so I couldn't see. Maybe it was a last reprieve from Carvalho to let Aline and Lourenço suffer their demise in privacy. I sniffled and hung my head. I was back to being alone. Fabrice said I would be the leader, but even if I made it through the tribunal unscathed, I didn't know how I could manage my life, much less the pod, without the support of Aline. I would pass the yoke onto Fabrice. The pod couldn't have a better leader. He had demonstrated that since the coup began.

My thoughts were interrupted by jeers and laughter. *What the hell could anyone possibly find humorous right now?* I was about to come unhinged when I looked and saw everyone staring at the monitor. The smoke had cleared. I frantically searched for the bodies of Aline and Lourenço to no avail. *Where are they?* Then I realized what had flummoxed the others. Next to the bridge's emergency hatch was Carvalho, alone—surrounded by Arthropods. There was no longer any smoke originating from the bridge. In his hand was the ubiquitous pill of the officers, but before he could deposit it into his mouth, his face distorted into a silent scream as he disappeared in a cloud of Arthropods.

"Stop, Fabrice, stop!" I said, motioning to the monitor. "Something's happened."

I darted to the hatch where the crew was still cutting. As I arrived, we heard the distinct squeak of the handwheel and the resounding clunk of the hatch's bolts returning to their home in the vault-like door. Backing out of the way, we watched the door open slowly, and the regents began to file out with their arms raised in surrender. Aline sprinted out to me, where I lifted her in the air, spinning her around, lost in our own world. I don't know how long we were like that before Fabrice interrupted our reunion.

"They're all here, Major," he said. "All the hostages. The regents unanimously surrender themselves for judgment."

•••••••••

True to my word, I stepped down after the siege of the bridge was complete and, with the regents, turned myself over for trial. Standing Prime Minister Toussaint formed a new Tribunal Council, and while we waited for trial, we were on house arrest and under guard. I couldn't have asked for a better place to be. After Aline had received medical care in the level's medical district, we had been more than happy to disappear together into our apartment. The food was still mediocre, but it was delivered by hand to our door. The lenient incarceration was more like a second honeymoon than a punitive measure. We were only occasionally interrupted when the Tribunal Council summoned me as a witness. Aline had a slightly different appearance now, which she disguised by creatively maneuvering her hair, but it was of no importance to me. On the contrary, having her back filled me with joy.

Fabrice was kind enough to visit often, keeping me updated on the trials, which they had broadcast to the public. All the regents had been found guilty of numerous war crimes leading up to and during the standoff. Grand General Nakamura's crimes had far exceeded the rest, having had decades of testimonies of sexual harassment and assault brought out against him. The people had called for banishment, which the Tribunal Council had awarded on all counts. But, as acting Prime Minister, Fabrice had chosen to commute their sentences, forcing them to spend the remainder of their lives mucking out the farm stalls on the lowest levels. He also stripped them of all their rights, privileges, and honors. To Nakamura, Fabrice had given a choice between banishment or castration. The coward chose to stay.

Finally, the time came for my trial. Aline let go of my hand as I took my place in front of the council. Knowing that the entire city was watching on the closed-circuit feeds increased my anxiety. As I panned the room, I saw several close supporters in the spectator seating, including Fabrice.

"Major Leal," one said. "Let me begin by conveying the gratitude of Pod Horizonte for clearing out the corrupted leadership of the pod."

"Thank you."

"As you were part of the regents, we must judge you alongside them. This panel will determine your guilt or innocence at the conclusion of this trial. Do you understand?"

"I do, your honor."

"What were your duties in the pod?

"My primary duties were to evaluate and improve the pod's recycling and nutritional processes using any available information from Pod Bogota and Pod Pittsburg."

I omitted Pod Bogota's destruction, knowing it was a public feed. The information could incite panic. However, I didn't want to appear to be involved in a cover-up amid my trial. I would publicize the catastrophe when the time was right.

"Did this work benefit some residents more than others?"

"My work equally benefited all."

"Were you aware of the descent of our previously honorable Release Day into the violent spectacle it became?"

"No, Your Honor. I became aware of it when I was required to attend the most recent Release Day."

"And did you participate willingly in any of the ceremonies?"

"I did not, Your Honor."

"Last line of questioning. Did you dispatch an unapproved mission against the Arthropods?

I shifted in my seat. I wasn't sure how the council had discovered the plan. Carvalho may have told the regents. It may have even been Fabrice. I had nothing to hide. Not with the depraved administration ousted from the Nucleus.

"I did, Your Honor."

"What is the purpose of this mission?

"To penetrate the Hive, plant a destructive device, and eradicate the Arthropod leadership and system of reproduction."

The council stifled their laughs.

"Major, we've held our investigation. We've searched your office and obtained testimony from witnesses. These questions were a formality. We have found nothing to incriminate you, in fact, quite the opposite. You held your office with dignity, going above and beyond the call of duty through adversity. Every act of insubordination was in the best interest of our city. Accordingly, we hereby release you from custody, all rights, privileges, and honors restored, and confer on you the rank of Grand General. Dismissed."

I turned dumbfounded at Aline, who had her hands clasped over her mouth in surprise. I made a beeline to her embrace as Fabrice came over and patted me on the back.

"You knew," I said.

"Of course I did. Who do you think recommended you?" said Fabrice. "The only thing we find you guilty of was idealism and optimism. You're a good man, which is why I want to hold an election immediately for Prime Minister. I, of course, will not challenge you."

"Prisoner to the highest-ranking officer in a day," said Aline. "Not bad." Aline smiled. I took her by the neck and kissed her.

"Whew, it's warm in here," Fabrice said, fanning himself.

I embraced him. "I couldn't have done it without you, Fab. If I'm in this, you are too. So, assuming the election goes the way you expect, I'm naming you as Deputy Prime Minister."

Fabrice blushed. "You are too kind. I would graciously accept."

CHAPTER 49: HUCK

I rode silently in the back of the cargo truck, sitting on the pile of hot, sharp scrap metal with Hemant and Zeke. We divided the remainder of our convoy between three vehicles—the personnel carrier, the supply truck, and the cargo hauler. A melancholy mood hung over us after the loss of Kurt and the others. What had felt like our triumphant arrival at the coast was now overshadowed by grief. Mueller had given out seating assignments, putting us in with the cargo. "Sorry, laddies," he had said. "It's just for the last leg." He had elected to give priority seating to the women and Misfits, but I was too exhausted to care.

As we rode along balancing on the metal, I worried that at the rate we were losing team members, there wouldn't be any of us left to complete the mission by the time we arrived at the Hive. I knew its success was a long shot. I could cope with that. What I couldn't handle was losing more of my friends. I looked at Zeke, then at Hemant, jostling with the movements of the truck as it made its way down the bumpy road to Tank Town. I don't know what I'd do if I lost either one of them. I scratched at my back, the heat causing insufferable itching only darkening my mood.

We made good time throughout the day, the clear roads of the region making a quick path to our destination. Every welcome time we stopped for a break, I realized that we had seen no evidence of Arthropod movement or attacks. We had experienced days of relative peace on the river, but this was different. Even after conferring with the others, there was no sign of our enemies. I grabbed Otto and Arjun during our lunch stop.

"It's strange, right?" I asked.

"It is, but I'm not sure what to make of it," said Arjun.

"It's a welcome break, but I don't like it either," said Otto. "I don't trust the ninnies."

"I'm afraid they're up to something. I mean, aside from the aerials, it's as if it's before the Arthropod Landing."

"Well, minus a few billion people, of course," said Otto.

We journeyed for the rest of the afternoon before making camp again for the night. We had hoped to be in Tank Town by nightfall but had to stop early for Krista, who still had some medical side effects. Zeke quickly disappeared to help her while Hemant and I set up his bivvy for him. No one strayed far from the vehicles or their weapons, not after last night.

After another disturbingly calm night, we continued to the coast. According to Mueller, we would be there by lunch, but I was about to lose my breakfast given the road conditions. All morning I had been bumped and jostled. The scrap metal constantly shifted under us, scraping our hands and backsides. My butt armor offered some protection, but it wasn't perfect.

When I felt as though I couldn't stand it any longer, I heard Mueller yell from the cabin, "We're here! ETA in twenty!" I would've preferred five, but the end was in sight. Despite the tragedies, I felt excitement finally start to bloom in my chest.

"We made it!" I shouted. "We made it!"

Hemant and Zeke smiled and began laughing. We were giddy

with happiness and accomplishment. We started patting each other in congratulations when we heard Mueller's voice boom from the cab.

"Stop! Back up! Back up! Back up!" he yelled.

We immediately hushed and listened as best we could over the low rumble of the hauler.

"I can't. The bloody inverts closed off the road!" said the driver.

"Go around!" yelled Mueller.

"They've closed off… everything!"

I heard Mueller scream an obscenity before slamming his fist into the dash.

"It's an ambush! Get us the hell to safety!" he yelled.

I felt the truck moving, but we were thrown around like ragdolls as it did so. Finally, I felt the truck come to a stop and recognized the sound of someone climbing from the cab into the gun turret. Mueller issued the command, and my hands flew to my ears as the convoy's weaponry released an ear-shattering barrage of fire. I could make out shouts between the gunner and Mueller, but I couldn't understand what they were yelling.

I closed my eyes in the safety of the hauler seeking solace until the battle was over. We were under attack. The inverts had strategized, organized, and executed an ambush targeting us and our mission. I didn't know how or why, but somehow they knew what we were doing. Whatever the cause, they felt threatened by us. I was glad, in a way. It was their turn to be scared. *Earth was our planet!* As each round of gunfire exploded from the barrel, the sulfurous odor bolstered my confidence and resolve as I became singularly focused on the mission. At that moment, I felt as though I could jump out and take on the inverts single-handedly.

Suddenly, there was an impact as I felt the hauler lift up on its side. The three of us fell back onto the top of the metal, scraping my hand in the process. Before I could ask, we felt a second impact, then a third as the vehicle started to tip. The fourth and final impact tipped the hauler, and we all fell against the side, the heavy metal piled against us.

"I'm trapped!" I said.

"Me too," said Zeke.

"I'm… out!" said Hemant. "I got you."

Hemant looked at the mound of metal covering Zeke and came for me first. He grabbed an oxidized piece of steel and, using tremendous force, flipped it off of me. I rubbed my calf that had absorbed most of the impact.

"You okay?" he asked.

"Nothing's broken. Let's get Zeke."

We went to Zeke, who had a large aluminum beam and several pipes across his stomach. We easily removed the light metal, but the beam would take serious effort.

"Are you injured?" I asked.

"I don't think so. It's resting on something else. I'm just trapped," said Zeke.

Then I heard it—the recognizable popping of exploding polies.

"Dammit! We're sitting ducks! We've got to get him out of here!" I yelled.

Hemant and I strained, but we couldn't get it off of him.

"Leave me! Get out of here!" Zeke yelled.

"I'm not leaving you, man!" Hemant said.

Just then, the hatch opened, and Mueller climbed in and saw our predicament. Without a word, he jumped in, and the three of us were able to lift the beam off of Zeke. We jumped out of the truck and saw we were in a large open field with scattered trees. Arthropods surrounded the convoy.

As I took in what I saw, I realized it was much more than a simple ambush. Surrounding the entire multiple-hectare field was a three-meter wall of invert corpses. It dawned on me that the inverts built the whole wall from the migration we had seen. Some commanding force had instructed them to come here, unknowingly to their deaths for a barricade. *Humanity had no idea what it was dealing with!* This strategy was far more cunning than anyone perceived was within the Arthropods' capabilities.

Mueller grabbed my arm, jerking me out of the way as the hook that had flipped our vehicle came down right where I had been standing. Zeke drove his halberd into its side. We ran from the vehicles to the cover of some trees, dodging the inverts' bodies brought down by the gunfire. I looked back at the other vehicles that the eights and hooks had toppled and saw the others emerging, fighting, and running to join us. As they ran across the field, I noticed the impact crater from the polie I had heard earlier in front of the personnel carrier and saw where other polies were milling around the area.

Another wave of inverts appeared from the clusters of trees and began to advance. We were without our mounted weapons and vastly outnumbered. I watched in horror as a hook ran forward, taking a polie in its beak and slung it across the field and into the cargo hauler. It exploded violently, sending shrapnel all over the area. The shockwave threw the convoy members close to the detonation to the ground. They stood and continued running to the safety of an invert-free clump of trees. Once everyone had reached the trees, we assessed the situation.

"What do we do?!" screamed Leni.

"We fight!" Mueller said. "There's no escape. They've trapped us in a slaughter zone. Our only choice is to fight our way out and hope they killed enough of each other to give us a chance."

I looked back at the opposing tree line, realizing Mueller was right. We were trapped and outnumbered. I took Ariadne's hand and squeezed it. The odds were stacked against us, but I had no intention of dying.

"We can do this! We can take them!" I yelled.

Everyone yelled in agreement as we ran towards the front lines of our foes. I ran into the thick of them and crouched behind a rock for cover. I aimed at a polie crawling between several hooks, and its detonation rewarded me with a shower of hemolymph. Next, I turned my fire on a pede harassing some Misfits. I missed the eye but distracted it enough that Hemant could bring his war hammer down on its carapace. I aimed at the eight's abdominal soft patch but missed, bringing its attention to my location.

The eight sprinted for me, covering ground faster than Zeke could. Krista ran forward and, in a scissoring motion, sliced off half of its legs. The creature fell to the ground, where Omar finished it off by thrusting his naginata into its head before he ran to help Ariadne. She was firing arrow after arrow, strafing the hooks. I looked up and saw a swarm of chompers headed straight for her. I slung my crossbow onto my back and unsheathed my dagger as I ran towards her. I took out several inverts mid-flight and got the last one as it had just touched down on Ariadne.

I jumped over an oozing eight abdomen and went to help Arjun. With the fluid movements of his deadly net, he was protecting the others from the attacking swarms of split wings. I swung my blade around, finding it far more useful against the chompers than my crossbow. Ciro was behind Arjun, firing his high-poundage arrows directly into the heads of the nearby Arthropods. A pede crawled up behind him, and before I could yell for his attention, it swung its lengthy body towards him, flipping him up into the air before landing hard on his back. At least he had missed the spikes!

"Ciro!" yelled Arjun, losing his focus.

I watched as a hook headed straight for him. I slung my bow down and rapidly fired a bolt into its side. It crashed into the ground with an impact that broke its beak. I ran to the pair to check on them. Arjun was cradling Ciro's head.

"He's unconscious," cried Arjun. "I have to get him to safety."

"Go, I'll cover you!" I yelled, pointing to a bushy tree nearby.

Arjun nodded and dragged Ciro away. Mei noticed our plight and ran over to help me. I fired off arrows as slow as I dared, knowing I was exhausting my quivers. Mei was throwing her knives and scoring direct hits into the brains of our attackers, but she was running out as well.

"Leni, we need help!" I yelled.

Leni ran over to us, spinning her spear as she arrived into the abdomen of an eight. We pushed forward. Mei and I were mainly fighting with daggers, letting Leni drive back the larger creatures. A pede was about to sweep its spines across the three of us when Otto brought down an enormous double-handed sword, slicing it asunder.

"What the hell is that?" I asked.

"This? This is my lady, Ophelia!" answered Otto. "She doesn't put up with anything, just like my ex-wife." Otto laughed and swung again, cleaving the head off of a hook. I looked out across the field at the carnage we had reaped. Mueller and Omar were beating the entrails out of a stubborn multipede as more of them advanced from behind. The desperation of our situation hit me. We had fought for what seemed like hours, but the battle raged on. We were holding our ground but not making progress. They just kept coming. I spun around and saw legions more coming out from the trees.

"Hey," I said to those around me.

We stopped fighting long enough to appreciate the hopelessness of our situation. We couldn't give up, but there was no way we could survive. I got a bad taste in my mouth when I realized I *would* die today. I looked at Ariadne and quickly kissed her cheek. I was about to reenter the battle when I noticed Arjun cradling Ciro under the tree, surrounded by inverts that weren't attacking.

"Look!" I yelled. We all looked and noticed the unusual behavior.

"Let's go!" yelled Mueller.

We ran to the tree, stabbing and slicing the inverts in our way, before sliding under the tree. Otto was the last to join us, his small frame sluggish with his giant Arthurian sword.

"What is this place?" I asked Arjun.

"I don't know," he said.

"I do," said Ariadne. "It's neem! It has a chemical that messes with our native insects' physiology. The Arthropods must share a similar aversion. If we stand under these, maybe we can fight them off!"

"Alright!" yelled Omar.

As I readied my weapons, I heard a deafening roar. There was no doubt of its source when I saw the blood drain from Ariadne's face.

CHAPTER 50: ARIADNE

When I heard the all-too-familiar roar of the spine back, I struggled to keep my heavy breathing from transitioning to hyperventilating. My hands were trembling from exertion and fear. I knew exactly what it was before its thin crimson legs stepped over the invert's carcass barrier. I heard the gasps from the others who weren't with us the day we stumbled upon it. I'd say the difference this time was the Nightmare knew we were here, but I wasn't so sure that it hadn't last time.

How long have they been toying with us? The fact was the inverts came to Earth intending to make a new home for themselves. We assumed that the intelligence was limited to a few mystery-shrouded minds in their Hive, but the coordinated measures they had taken against us now make me think otherwise.

Here we were, cowering under our discovery—a bug-repelling tree. This finding would be outstanding if we survived to tell anyone about it. According to Mueller, the transporters' vessel was only kilometers away, but now I doubted if it was. Even if we survived, if the Arthropods were this intelligent, I imagined that they had already destroyed our boat, ending this mission before it began. I tried to build my optimism, but the giant holy terror in front of me was squelching it. It was now entirely enveloped in the battle arena they had created.

As it began to drizzle, the creature came to a stop about a hundred meters away and once more bellowed its obnoxious sound. From the proximity, the sound nearly ruptured our eardrums. For creatures that didn't hear, they were insanely loud. Our distance weapons' quivers were exhausted, our mounted weapons destroyed, many of the Misfits were dead, and a single small tree protected us. I wanted to collapse into the mud forming from all the rain, blood, and hemolymph.

Without warning, the Nightmare sped towards us like a bullet train of old. We fled in every direction from our savior tree, Hemant with Ciro flung over his shoulder like a bag of produce. My adrenaline surged as my flight response took complete control of my mind. Then, I heard an intense crack behind me and turned to see the tree on its side and shattered. *Jesus, we can't get a break!* The creature was so large that the neem posed little to no threat.

We had run from safety into the arms of the smaller Arthropods, but they weren't attacking. *Dammit, the Nightmare was toying with us!* It grabbed several nearby multipedes with its pedipalps and impaled them on its spiked back. The multipedes, still living, formed long flailing implements of death and destruction. I struggled to retain my composure, refusing to abandon my friends. One of the remaining Misfits surrendered to his panic and fled to the creature barricade as fast as his feet would carry him. Two bone arachnids spun towards him like saw blades, and in the blink of an eye, he was shredded and scattered over the terrain. I turned my head and retched. That was all I could handle.

I looked back at the Nightmare, wiping my mouth, thinking maybe an arrow to its brain might bring it down. I ran from one corpse to the next, grabbing any arrows I could find. When I had enough to fill my quivers partially, I wiped the hemolymph off onto my armor and nocked an arrow. The creature had advanced toward Mueller and some of the Misfits, who were fruitlessly throwing spears and firing arrows into its bulbous abdomen with no effect. I took my time, aiming right between its antennae and let loose. The arrow plunged into its intended target and had little impact like the arrows in its body.

"Dammit!" I yelled. "How do we kill this thing?"

"Its head is its weakest point!" responded Arjun.

"Leni, can you throw your spear between its eyes?" I yelled.

"I'll try!" she said.

Leni took off running for the beast, but as she released the spear, she tripped in the mud, and the spear passed harmlessly below its body. She quickly searched the ground for another spear to try again. The creature completed its advance towards Mueller and the others, engaging them. It was slamming its rostrum repeatedly down into the ground in an attempt to stab one of the zigzagging Misfits. It finally succeeded and slammed its spear-like mouth into a Misfit who had fallen on his stomach. The force of the rostrum drove her deep into the ground, breaking the woman in half and partially burying her, her angled torso slumping as she died.

I quickly nocked another arrow and fired it into its compound eye. The creature roared in pain but didn't slow. *If I can't kill it, I'm going to hurt it!* I fired one arrow after another into its right eye, sending it into a fury. I watched in horror as one of the flailing multipedes on its back connected with Mueller and another Misfit. Mueller was lucky. He was thrown about twenty meters before skidding to a stop and standing. The other transporter was impaled throughout his body and waved through the air before being slung into the distance.

Leni again threw her spear, this time connecting just left of the head in the creature's thorax but doing only minor damage. Sensing

Leni as a threat, the beast directed its wrath towards her. She pulled a nearby spear from the carcass of a hook and readied herself, attempting to time her throw perfectly as it closed the distance. Just when she was about to launch the spear, the invert dramatically increased its speed, and in one motion, slammed its rostrum down through the stomach of a shocked Leni.

"No!" I screamed. "No!" I fell to my knees, breaking down crying as my vision blurred.

Leni, the candidate who had begun our journey as a negative, reserved, and troubled sufferer of the Shock, had become a close friend as she recovered. She was a fierce warrior and a loyal companion. Now the creature had further lived up to its name. I watched as she struggled to breathe, hearing her gurgling from meters away, the beast still pinning her to the ground. I wanted desperately to run to her and be with her as she died but knew that would also spell my demise. I felt my heart shattering, but in a final act of defiance, she raised her spear and, with her last breath, thrust it deep into its rostrum, severing it from its head. Then her body relaxed. The Nightmare reared back, roaring louder and with fury. It was seriously injured, and it was pissed. I ran forward, continuing to fire arrows at its head.

"Ariadne, behind!" I heard Huck yell.

I swung around to see that the blow to the creature had resumed the attacks from the smaller Arthropods. I quickly fired an arrow at a pill bug, detonating it and taking out several other inverts. A bone arachnid had snuck up behind me, and as I whirled around to face it, its leg sliced out, barely missing me but shattering my bow. As panic rushed through my body, I drew my dagger, feeling impotent against the dripping fangs in front of me. I watched the eight slump to the ground as Huck ran up to me. He'd shot it from behind. He grabbed my hand, and we headed back to the fallen neem tree.

Taking advantage of the Nightmare's weakened state, Krista

ran forward and hacked off one of its legs with her katanas. The creature bellowed and started jabbing its pedipalps in every direction. The spike-tipped blades nearly sliced Krista in half as she retreated. The beast charged towards me, almost connecting as I slid underneath its girth before rolling out the side to safety. Even with the inflicted damage, the Nightmare posed just as much threat. And we were losing people fast. I heard a scream and turned to see yet another Misfit succumbing to the creature. The Nightmare had stabbed its pedipalps through his body, then scissored them apart, flinging his remnants in different directions and spattering us with more viscera.

I dry heaved, having nothing left in my stomach to vomit out. I wanted desperately to curl up under a tree and wait for the despicable battle to end. Instead, I heard the movement of inverts all around me and continued with Huck towards the downed tree. I saw Ciro's compound bow upon our arrival and picked it up. Maybe if I fired enough arrows into its eyes, it would retreat. Since I had no better strategy, I began filling its left eye with arrows as Omar and Mei threw everything they had at its front. As I loaded one of my last arrows into the bow, I heard Arjun yell.

"Wait!" he said.

I watched as Arjun gently laid Ciro against the trunk of the tree and ran over to me, picking up a dagger on his way. He snapped the blade from the hilt using the exoskeletal plates of a dead multipede, then took the arrow from me. He had Hemant drive the arrow through its metal shaft using his hammer, positioning the thin blade perpendicular to the arrow's length. He returned the arrow to the bow, wrapping his hand around my injured one.

"The neck is its weakest point," he said.

I saw where the head connected to the thorax was the thinnest portion of its entire body, roughly the width of a dagger blade. I took careful aim, taking into account the different setup, then fired.

An eternity took place between when the arrow left and when it impacted the beast's neck, but impact it did—partially severing its head. The creature wobbled around drunkenly before collapsing to the ground. Without hesitation, Omar drove his naginata through the remainder of the neck, cleaving the head from its body.

Frenzied by its death, the smaller inverts began to disappear over the barricades. Since the Arthropods were intelligent, judging by their reaction to the Nightmare's death, they felt fear as well.

"We did it!" Hemant yelled. "I can't believe it."

"Something's happening!" yelled Omar.

We looked towards the creature. Its abdomen was rippling and shaking.

"Arjun?" Mueller asked.

"Not sure," he said. "But I would back up."

Omar and Mei heeded his warning as we watched the movements become more and more pronounced. Finally, when they couldn't have been more vigorous, the creature's abdomen exploded as thousands of tiny Nightmare nymphs ran off into the trees.

"Oh, hell no!" said Hemant. "I'm never coming back to the Latin Territory. I don't care how pretty that lake was!"

"I'm right there with you, man," said Zeke.

"Let's have a moment for our dead, then get to the port," said Mueller. "The inverts were scared off, but I assure you they'll be back."

We tended to Ciro, who had regained consciousness. He was okay but bruised and scraped as we all were. We all bowed our heads in respect as Otto said a brief eulogy for our fallen, his giant sword, Ophelia, plunged into the ground next to him. The rain continued steadily, adding to the somber mood. I sobbed when he mentioned Leni, and I felt Huck's arm slide over my shoulder gently. When the moment was over, we reluctantly left our fallen where they lay, fearing the return of the inverts. We grabbed the essential supplies and critical communiques destined for the pods of the east from the damaged vehicles and climbed over the disgusting wall entrapping us. Then, we exhaustedly began walking the few remaining kilometers to the port at Mueller's behest.

We made our way through the rubble of the old port town, nervously advancing around the blind corners. Mueller and Otto were familiar with the way, but the inverts had scattered after the Nightmare's fall. So we had to be on our guard. Our group had dramatically dwindled. All that remained of the Misfits were Mueller, Otto, and the distant Grace.

"Will you guys be okay without the others?" I asked.

"Transporting is a dangerous business," said Mueller. "We never get over our fallen. Sadly, we're used to losing people, just not so many at once. Otto and I will be okay. Don't you worry about us. We'll head to Monterrey, get outfitted with new gear, and maybe steal a few guys from their ranks. We'll rebuild. I know you guys will make their deaths count."

"Yes, we will," I said.

"Agreed," echoed Huck and Hemant.

We continued down what was left of the main street of the port, seeing the fragments of the storage tanks to our right, the town's namesake, and disintegrating shipping containers to our left. The gigantic port had initially served the territory's large population but now sat largely unused, save for the transporters. The pleasant smell of seawater hit me as the rain let off, a mixture of fishiness and saltiness, drawing me to the coast. I took a deep, cleansing breath and again marveled at our progress. I looked at Arjun and Ciro and Krista and Zeke, who were strolling in front. Our cute couples. I liked Zeke. His calm demeanor and deep love had helped her through the issues she had dealt with on the trip. I thought about how Huck had acted on the battlefield; his concern for my well-being seemed greater than his own.

There was suddenly a blood-curdling scream from Krista,

surprising me. Our jaunt through the port had disturbed a hiding bone arachnid. The eight was perched on the remnants of a dilapidated vehicle directly ahead of Krista, paralyzing her in fear.

Zeke was screaming, "Krista, your katanas!"

With Krista helpless, Zeke and Arjun sprinted to her aid. The spider flung its mass onto the pair, rapidly stabbing its fangs into each of their torsos.

"No!" Hemant screamed.

Hemant, fueled by adrenaline, darted up with unexpected speed for his size and obliterated the head of the eight with one forceful blow of his war hammer.

"No, no, God, no!" he screamed, dropping himself and his hammer next to his brother and Ciro, who was weeping.

Huck had crouched next to Zeke and Krista, and each of them held Zeke's hand.

"It's all my fault. It's my fault," sobbed Krista. "I killed him!"

I stood around the heart-breaking scene, unable to do anything to help. A bone arachnid's venom is always injected and always lethal. There was nothing I could do but feel my heart shatter in my chest.

"Huck, the vial," Zeke whispered, blood bubbling out of his mouth. "Give it to… Arjun."

Huck pulled out a small purple vial from his pocket.

"Huck, what is that? Will it save them?" Krista asked.

"I don't… I don't know," Huck said. "I think it's for venom."

"Give it to them!" Krista said.

"I only have enough for one!" Huck answered.

Krista pleaded with her eyes.

"Give it… to Arjun, Huck." Zeke said, pushing the vial away with his remaining strength.

Huck nodded as Krista screamed, cradling Zeke's head in her lap.

"Sit him up!" Huck told Ciro.

Huck poured the vial's contents into Arjun's throat, who hacked but held it down. Krista's scream intensified as he started slipping away. After a few painful contractions, he was gone. Krista looked destroyed, and Huck didn't seem much better. Arjun's color began to return to his face. Whatever the antivenin had, it was helping. Arjun's shoulder would need a long recovery, but he was going to pull through. As I bandaged his injection site, I couldn't keep my eyes off of Krista, still cradling Zeke. Mueller, Otto, Hemant, and Omar fashioned stretchers and carried a weakened Arjun and lifeless Zeke to the port.

CHAPTER 51: HEMANT

I had been through a whirlwind of emotions in the last few days. Sheer terror, rampant death, and increasing concern for my brother had plagued me constantly. His run-in with the eight had just about killed me. It'd be a while before I felt right again. I needed this ocean time. Hell, we all did. The port lay just ahead of us, and, thank the universe, there were no places for any more flipping inverts to hide. Nothing ahead of us but clear, blue water. We carried Arjun's and Zeke's stretchers to the edge of the docks. Ahead of us lay a massive antiquated platform that seemed to float on the water.

"That's where the boat will dock," Mueller said, pointing.

"How long will we have to wait?" asked Huck.

"The boat waits just out to sea where it's safer. See that red light to your right?"

Huck nodded.

"Below that is the port's pump house, which signals the boat to come in. That's where we're going to meet up with Kofi and signal the boat."

I made my way to the pump house, my hand never leaving

Arjun's good shoulder. The path was easy, not having much growth blocking our path. This was one of the most extensive areas I had encountered outside the pods that nature hadn't completely consumed. Everywhere I looked was covered in concrete and metal, leaving tiny spaces for plants to reclaim. The sun blasted down on us, but the breeze coming off the water kept us cool. I closed my eyes, feeling the salty mist tingle my face. Once we arrived at the large metal protrusion, Mueller yelled for Kofi. After a few yells, the hatch opened, and Kofi emerged. Kofi was a bald, squat man of Saharan descent. He hugged Mueller and addressed us.

"Who are these fine people? Where are my other friends?" he asked, his piercings jingling as he moved his head.

"They didn't make it," said Mueller, hanging his head. "We were ambushed by the inverts a few kilometers back. They pinned us in, Kofi."

"Oh, my. Ambushed, you say?" Kofi stroked his braided beard, a twin to Mueller's quirks. "I've been saying for years that they're up to something."

"I know," said Mueller. "Now, I'm inclined to agree."

"No vehicles either?"

Mueller shook his head.

"If you're not here to load the boat, why are you here?"

"That brings me to the introductions. These guys call themselves the Uninvited. This is Huck, their leader, Hemant, Ariadne, Omar, Krista, Arjun, Ciro, and Mei. You know Otto."

"Of course, I remember Otto. And it's a pleasure to make your acquaintances. Mueller keeps me down in this god-awful hole, so I don't get to spend much time with other humans. My closest friends are my fish. Well, until I eat them. A man's got to live," he said, smiling and patting his rounded stomach.

"They've been through a lot. Lost many good people. Some today. They're on a mission to the Hive. They need to get to Freeport."

"To the Hive?!" Kofi asked. "You keep interesting company, my friend. I'll turn on the signal. They'll be here in less than an hour if they haven't drunk too much to notice. You and your friends are welcome here as long as you like. I don't have much in the way of food, but you can catch wild fish here without difficulty."

"Thank you, Kofi," said Mueller.

"We appreciate your generosity," I added.

Kofi nodded. "Mueller, you and Otto are welcome to my buggy when it's time for you to leave. Please tell the guys at Monterrey I would like a new one, perhaps with wider seats."

We took him up on his hospitality. After setting up camp in a small grassy area nearby, we built a cairn for Zeke, each paying our respects throughout the afternoon in our own way. Arjun was feeling noticeably better, but I was still waiting on him hand and foot. Our morning departure would begin his convalescence at sea.

"I don't know how, but the Arthropods know what we are up to," said Arjun. "At least that we represent a significant threat to their existence and domination of the planet."

"I agree," I said. "I'm still concerned about what they will have waiting for us across the ocean."

"There's something else that's been bothering me," said Ciro. "They didn't eat the Arthropods they used as the wall."

"I'm not sure I follow, Ciro," I said.

"We witnessed multiple species demonstrating self-control and self-sacrifice for the good of the Arthropods as a whole. It's not entirely uncommon in our own animal kingdom. There are theories about Queens, but I'm not so sure. Their hierarchy seems more complex and advanced. At the very least, we have no idea what we are dealing with."

"Wow," I said. "And we are trying to walk into that."

"Exactly," said Arjun. "We have to learn as much as possible before we get there if we want this mission to have any odds of success. I want to start with that tree."

Arjun pulled a piece of the neem from his pocket. "I think we can work with the scientists at Kano to concentrate this into a defensive weapon. I suspect this is something the survivors have used. How else could they have lived unharmed on the surface for so long."

"You were asking me all those questions about their village. Now that you mention it, I seem to remember those trees around its perimeter. I didn't think anything about it, I mean, they looked like all the trees, but I think they were there."

"I suspected as much. The downside about living in pod cities is that we can't be out in the field studying their behavior. Most candidates are just trying to make it safely to the next pod. We have an opportunity here to observe behaviors in multiple territories. We need to share all of our observations whenever possible."

"Always the scientist," Ciro said, shaking his head. "Nearly dies and is worried more about not sharing his knowledge than survival."

"Not true. I wouldn't wish my death to put any emotional strain on you or my brother," said Arjun.

"I'll take it," said Ciro, laughing. "That's why I like you, Arjun.

•••••••••

The transporter's boat had come in last night, just like Kofi had said it would. However, the ocean vessel was less of a boat than I expected. It appeared more like a small cylinder floating upright out among the waves when it arrived at dusk. Mueller saw my confusion and laughed.

"It's an underwater boat, son," he said. "The bulk of the vessel remains submerged."

I wasn't thrilled about being so far out on open water, to begin with, and now I was going to be under it. *It's for Arjun and humanity,* I reminded myself. Once the crew had come ashore and joined us for dinner, Mueller explained to the crew about us. Their leader, Captain Lolade, seemed friendly but cool in a manner fitting for a mariner. The crew helped us load the supplies and communiques and settle into our berths, which were even tinier than the dorms at Pod Horizonte, but we were safe. Then, taking advantage of our last night on land, we opted to sleep in our tents.

I stayed awake, staring at the starry sky, thinking about the trip until I could no longer keep my eyes open. Captain Lolade assured us that the inverts wouldn't bother us on the ocean. Arjun reinforced what she had said, adding that non-aquatic inverts disliked freshwater, and all inverts loathed saltwater—at least as far as we knew. If my short time on the surface had taught me anything, it was that we had no idea what their capabilities were. Early scientists theorized that the inverts had taken the shortest possible routes across the oceans as they spread. We had already seen some bugs carry others, so I knew they were capable of many skills. I would never feel truly safe, not until they were all gone. Maybe not even then, considering the surprise attack on Arjun and Zeke today.

The following morning, I went to drink my coffee, staring out at the ocean. When I arrived at the dock, I saw Krista already awake. So I went and grabbed a second cup and brought it to her.

"Damn you. Damn all of you," she said, looking at me with eyes colder than those of an eight.

"I'm sorry about Zeke, Krista. He was my friend too."

"Don't you say his name ever again. In fact, don't ever talk to me again."

She turned her icy gaze to the ocean, and I set the cup down next to her. It was still there an hour later when we went to say our goodbyes to Kofi and thanked him for his hospitality. Mueller and

Otto joined us on the dock. I even teared up as I hugged them for the last time.

"Come back to us," said Mueller. "I wanted to let you know that I won't be reforming the Misfits. Otto and I will continue to be transporters, but I want to pass the name off to you guys. You've earned it. Seeing the trouble you're going to stir up, I can't think of a better name to suit you than Memo's Misfits."

"Thank you," I said. "We couldn't have made it this far without your help."

"Oh, they'll be back alright," said Otto. "After they kick some invert arse!"

"Sure you don't want to come with us, Otto?" Huck asked, scratching his lower back yet again. I made a mental note to remember to ask Ariadne to check on him.

"No, thank you! My place is here. Someone needs to protect Mueller as he gets older."

The deep barrel laugh that elicited from Mueller made us all burst out laughing.

"I'll miss you guys," said Ariadne.

After we had all said our goodbyes and stowed away our gear, I stood with Huck and Ariadne, looking out over the ocean.

"I was just thinking we might never see this place again," Huck said.

"We have the entire world ahead of us," said Ariadne.

"And we have each other," I said.

CHAPTER 52: ALINE

Three days after my husband had been in front of a tribunal determining his fate, he was sworn in as Prime Minister of Pod Horizonte. The thunderous applause of its residents filled the ample space of the central forum. During the ceremony, Fabrice was also sworn in as Deputy Prime Minister. Following the swearing-in, Memo was officially promoted to grand general by his newly established deputy, and Fabrice read the nominations for the vacant regent positions. I watched with anticipation as he stood to address the audience.

"My fellow residents. We are free!" he said, pausing as the room filled with cheers. "Today, we've taken the first step in establishing a new democratic government. We do this in honor of all of us who have endured, fought, and died. For my first official act, I hereby abolish Release Day. Even with its initially honorable intentions, leaving the pod should be a choice presented to each candidate. In the absence of its population control, I am launching what I believe to be a fair contraceptive and lottery campaign for reproductive rights.

"True to my word, I have assigned Deputy Minister Toussaint

to create a system to reunite our parents with the unknown children they have submitted for candidacy. I also established an act to allow parents to raise and house their children throughout their training and education. The matriarchs will continue their job as caretakers of the children, the aided, and the recouping, but at the guardians' request or by individual choice.

"For the first time in our recent history, we have created a city that is truly, 'For All.'"

"For All, For All, For All…" the crowd chanted, filling the pod with the echoes of the excited citizens. He publicized Pod Bogota's destruction and its implications for our existence but left out key details, limiting the potential panic. Additionally, he shared the details of the mission he had dispatched to the Hive, which had become public during the trial. The speech ended with roaring cheers for Fabrice, Guilherme, and the deceased, whose sacrifice made the day possible. My heart soared as he and Fabrice walked off the stage to where I was standing.

"I think that went over well," he said.

"I think so too," I said, smiling and listening to the crowd.

"When does the lottery begin?" I asked.

"Immediately, I suppose, Fab and I haven't ironed out every detail yet. Why?"

"Because I'm pregnant."

I watched as my husband picked his mouth up off the floor and closed the space between us to embrace me tightly. I could see the joy and excitement in his eyes. Despite all the years we had been married, we had never been able to conceive, so our feelings of happiness were profound.

"This is the happiest day of my life! I love you! I'll never let you go again!" he said, beaming.

"Yay!" Fabrice screamed, clapping. "So exciting! I call godfather!"

I looked at Fabrice and nodded. "I wouldn't ask anyone else."

●●●●●●●●●

In a broadcast official ceremony the next day, the Signal was removed from the bridge and destroyed by Trainer Marcia's war hammer. In addition, Guilherme expanded education to include the underappreciated older vocational skills, such as broadcasting and mechanics, which we had seen were grossly undervalued by the previous administration, assigning them to only the outcasts of the city's society.

That evening, I had prepared dinner in our pod for Memo and Fabrice with food that Memo would describe as 'questionable nutritional value,' not that he'd ever say it regarding my cooking. Recently, he talked to Fabrice about the possibility of sending out foraging teams under guard to incorporate fresher nutrition into the collective diet—an idea that would've been unheard of in the past. I heard the knock at the door and let them in. Instead of excited banter as they typically did, they were both unusually serious.

"What's wrong?" I asked my husband.

"We've been going through Carvalho's office," he said. "Incidentally, I would've sentenced him to banishment had he survived just based on the evidence I've found so far."

"We knew he was an asshole," I said. "But he's gone. So let's move past him, together." I took his hand.

"It's not that simple. We found a letter," said Memo.

"A letter?" I asked.

"Well, a carbon-copy receipt for one," said Memo. "It's addressed to Prime Minister Zabu."

"From Pod Kano," added Fabrice. "Just show her."

Memo handed me a wrinkled-up old piece of yellow paper.

The letter was typical logistical and governmental mumbo

jumbo, but the letter closed with a postscript saying, "Should they succeed, regard your newest visitors as a threat to our way of life. And Ndulue, please don't do anything foolish with your new toy."

Memo looked me in the eyes. "The receipt says it went with the last group of transporters that came through here. The same transporters I sent Huck and his team with."

"What are you saying?" I asked.

"He's saying that the corruption extends to other pods," said Fabrice.

"And Huck and his friends are carrying their death sentence to Pod Kano," said Memo.

ACKNOWLEDGEMENTS

I would be remiss to thank anyone but my family first. My wife and daughters spent countless days watching me work away at the expense of my free time through the course of this project. They have been amazingly supportive as I planned, wrote, revised, queried, designed, and published *Release Day*.

This book also wouldn't be possible without the editing help and feedback I received from Jessica, my lovely wife, and Camille Pruett.

A huge thanks also goes out to all of my beta readers: Missy Wood, Emily Wan, Deshea Surratt, Joshua Elder, Tim Justice, Ross Kyzar, and José Manuel Díaz Pérez. Their commentary was invaluable.

I'd also would like to thank Scott Leger, who unbeknownst to him, helped send me down this road with an off-hand recommendation to watch some Brandon Sanderson videos on YouTube.

Lastly, thank you to everyone who put up with me talking virtually non-stop about the writing process for months on end.

AUTHOR'S NOTE

I've always wanted to write a book. I spent decades waiting for the perfect idea to come along. Then I heard a quote from Brandon Sanderson that a good writer could make a great story from any idea, and I decided to simply sit down and write. I took a dream-inspired idea of hostile alien bugs and underground dystopian cities and combined the two.

As I wrote *Release Day,* the experience was almost like watching a movie (a technique I later learned was called discovery writing). I felt more like a spectator than an author as I watched the development of enjoyable characters (my favorite is Otto) and despicable enemies as they dealt with real-world and not-so-real-world problems. Writing has been such a rewarding and fantastic experience.

Lastly, as an English to Speakers of Other Languages (ESOL) teacher, it was also important to me to tell this story of survival with diverse voices from an inclusive perspective. The characters are meant to be representative of varying ethnicities, genders, sexualities, and abilities.

RYAN MATTHEWS

The Release Day Saga is the debut series of Ryan Matthews, an English as a Second Language (ESL) teacher and graphic designer. In addition to writing and teaching, he enjoys spending time with his family, taking insect and mushroom pictures on hikes, and plowing through his extensive reading list. He also dabbles in foreign languages, open-world video games, and the French horn. Ryan holds a Bachelor's Degree in Art and a Master's Degree in Education. He lives in Tennessee with his wife, daughters, and the family pets, Luna and Coda.

  @ryanmatthews501
ryanmatthewsauthor.com

NEWSLETTER

For the latest updates, events, and behind-the-scenes information, visit Ryan's website and subscribe to his newsletter.

RATE & REVIEW

If you wish to support authors like Ryan, please leave reviews on sites like Amazon and Goodreads for all of your favorite books.